Édition de Luxe

La Dame de Monsoreau

IN TWO VOLUMES
VOL. II.

BY ALEXANDRE DUMAS

WITH ILLUSTRATIONS

BOSTON

ESTES AND LAURIAT

1893

LA DAME DE MONSOREAU.

VOLUME II.

CONTENTS.

LIST OF ILLUSTRATIONS.

Vol. II.

LA DAME DE MONSOREAU.

──────•──────

CHAPTER I.

THE RUE DE LA FERRONNERIE.

CHICOT had good legs, and would have made good use of
them to join the man who had just beaten Gorenflot, if
something peculiar in the aspect of this man, and particularly in that of his companion, had not made him
understand that there might be danger in seeking an
acquaintance which they seemed so anxious to avoid. In
fact, the two fugitives were visibly eager to lose themselves
in the crowd, and turned only at the street corners to see
that they were not followed.

Chicot thought that the best way not to seem to follow
them was to precede them. Both were going to the Rue
Saint-Honoré, through the Rue de la Mounan and the Rue
Tirechappe ; at the last corner he passed them, and, running
on ahead, hid himself at the end of the Rue des Bourdonnais.
The two men went up the Rue Saint-Honoré, in the shadow
of the houses, with their hats slouched over their eyes,
and their cloaks drawn up over their faces, walking with a
quick and martial tread towards the Rue de la Ferronnerie.
Chicot continued to precede them. At the corner of the
Rue de la Ferronnerie the two men stopped again to throw
a rapid glance around them.

During that time, Chicot had continued in advance, and had reached the middle of the street.

In the middle of the street, before a house so old that it seemed crumbling to pieces, was a litter, to which were attached two strong horses. Chicot looked about, saw the driver asleep, and a woman, apparently uneasy, looking through the blind. It flashed through his mind that the litter might be waiting for the two men; he turned around it, and protected by its shadow combined with that of the house, he slipped under a stone bench which served as a stall to the vegetable sellers who, twice a week, held a market in the Rue de la Ferronnerie.

Scarcely was he hidden when he saw the two men appear at the horses' heads, where they stopped again, uneasy. One of them woke up the coachman whose sleep was very sound, and as he found some difficulty in rousing him, let fall a " *Cap de diou!* " strongly accented, while the other, still more impatient, pricked the driver with his dagger.

" Oh, oh," said Chicot, "I was not mistaken. They are compatriots, and I am no longer surprised that they pounded Gorenflot when he spoke contemptuously of the Gascons."

The young lady, recognizing the two men, leaned out of the window, and Chicot was enabled to see her plainly. She was about twenty or twenty-two, very beautiful and very pale. Had the light been strong, one might have been able to see by the dark rings under her eyes and the languid attitude of her whole body that she was suffering from an illness the secret of which was made plain by the enlargement of her waist.

But of all this, Chicot could only see that she was young, pale, and fair.

The two men approached the litter, and found themselves between her and the bench beneath which Chicot was concealed. The taller of the two, taking in both of his the little white hand extended to him through the window, rested both arms on the ledge.

"Well, my love, my little heart, my pet," he said, "how are you?"

The lady shook her head with a sad smile, and showed a bottle of smelling-salts.

"Still fainting-spells, *ventre saint-gris!* How provoked I would be to see you ill, dear love, if I were not the cause of your sweet malady."

"Why the devil did you bring Madame to Paris?" asked the other man, rather rudely. "On my word, it is a curse that you must always have some petticoat pinned to your doublet."

"Ah, my dear Agrippa," said the first speaker, who seemed to be the lover or husband of the lady, "it is so great a grief to part from those we love," and he gave her a loving glance.

"*Cordioux!* upon my soul, it drives me mad to hear you speak," replied the sour companion. "Did you come to Paris to make love. It seems to me that Béarn is large enough for your sentimental promenades without continuing them in Babylon, where you have come near being killed at least twenty times this evening. Go home, if you wish to make love, behind the curtains of a litter, but here, *mordioux!* confine yourself to your political intrigues, my master."

At this word *master*, Chicot would have liked to raise his head, but he could scarcely risk the movement without being seen.

"Let him scold, my love, and don't trouble yourself about what he says. I think he would be ill himself if he could not scold."

"But at least, *ventre saint-gris!* as you say yourself, get into the litter and say your sweet things to Madame; you will run less risk of being recognized than by standing in the street."

"You are right, Agrippa," said the amorous Gascon. "And you see, my love, that his advice is not so bad as it seems. There, make room for me, my sweet one, and permit me to sit beside you, as I cannot be at your feet."

"Not only do I permit it, sire, but I wish it most earnestly," replied the young lady.

"Sire!" murmured Chicot who, carried away by impulse, raised his head and struck it against the stone bench. "Sire! What is she saying there?"

But in the mean while the happy lover took advantage of the permission, and the creaking of the litter announced an increase of its burden. This creaking was followed by the sound of a long and tender kiss.

"*Mordioux!*" cried the companion, who had remained outside, "man is in truth a very stupid animal."

"I'll be hanged if I can understand any of this," murmured Chicot, "but I shall wait; my patience is sure to be rewarded."

"Oh, how happy I am," continued the one who was called sire, and who did not appear in the least concerned at the remonstrances of his friend, to which he was no doubt accustomed. "*Ventre saint-gris!* this is a good day; here are my good Parisians, who hate me with their whole soul and who would kill me if they could, doing their very best to smooth my way to the throne, and I have in my arms the woman I love. Where are we D'Aubigné? When I am king, I will erect on this very spot a statue to the genius of the Béarnais."

"Of the Béarn—" began Chicot, but he stopped, having given his head a second bump.

"We are in the Rue de la Ferronnerie, sire, and it does not smell nice," said D'Aubigné, who was still in a bad humor and found fault with things when men paid no attention to him.

"It seems to me," said Henri, for our readers have doubtless recognized the King of Navarre, — "it seems to me that I see before me the whole course of my life; that I see myself king; that I am on the throne, strong and powerful, but perhaps not so much loved as I am at this hour; and that my gaze peers into the future, to the very hour of my death. Oh, my darling, tell me again that you love me, for my very heart melts at the sound of your voice." And the Béarnais, yielding to the feeling of sadness which sometimes invaded him, sighed deeply, and let his head fall on the shoulder of his mistress.

"Oh, *mon Dieu!*" cried the lady, frightened, "are you fainting, sire?"

"Good! that alone was wanting," said D'Aubigné; "fine soldier, fine general, fine king who faints away!"

"No, sweet one, have no fear," said Henri; "if I faint near you, it will be with happiness."

"In truth, sire, I know not why you sign Henri de Navarre; you should sign Ronsard or Clément Marot. *Cordioux!* how is it you get on so badly with Madame Margot when you are both so inclined to poetry?"

"Ah, D'Aubigné! have pity; do not speak of my wife. *Ventre saint-gris!* you know the proverb; if we were to meet her?"

"Though she is in Navarre?" asked D'Aubigné.

"*Ventre saint-gris!* am I not too in Navarre? Am I not at least supposed to be there? Come, Agrippa, you have made me shiver; get in and let us go home."

"Faith, no," said D'Aubigné, "I shall walk behind; I should annoy you, and, what is worse, you would annoy me."

"Then close the door and do as you please, surly bear," said Henri; then turning to the coachman, "Lavarenne, you know where!" he said.

The litter went slowly off, followed by D'Aubigné, who, though he scolded the friend, had wished to watch over the king.

This departure delivered Chicot from a terrible apprehension; because after the conversation he had had with Henri, D'Aubigné was not the kind of man to spare the life of the imprudent one who had chanced to hear it.

"Let me see," said Chicot, crawling out from underneath his bench, "must Valois know what has just taken place?"

Chicot straightened out his long legs, which had become stiff in their cramped position.

"And why should he know it?" resumed the Gascon, continuing his soliloquy. "Two men and a woman who hide themselves. That would be cowardly; no, I will not tell. I am informed, and that is the important point; for is it not I who reign?" and Chicot capered about joyfully.

"Lovers are very nice," he pursued, "but D'Aubigné is right; that dear Henri de Navarre loves too often for a king *in partibus*. A year ago he came back to Paris for Madame de Sauve; now he is accompanied by that charming little creature who has fainting-spells. Who the devil can she be? La Fosseuse, in all probability. And now that I think of it, if Henri de Navarre is a serious pretender, if he truly aspires to the throne, he must think a little of destroying his enemies Le Balafré, the Cardinal de Lorraine, and that dear Duc de Mayenne. Well, I love the Béarnais, and I am sure that sooner or later he will play some ugly trick on that horrible Lorraine butcher. I have decided not to say a single word of what I have seen and heard."

At this moment a band of drunken Leaguers passed, crying, "*Vive la messe!* Death to the Huguenots! Death to the heretics!" but the litter had turned the corner of the cemetery of the Holy Innocents and passed into the depths of the Rue Saint-Denis.

"Come, let us recapitulate," said Chicot. "I have seen the Cardinal de Guise, the Duc de Mayenne, the King Henri de Valois, the King of Navarre. One single prince is wanting to complete my collection; that is the Duc d'Anjou.

Come, where is my François III. ? *Ventre de biche!* I am dying to see that worthy monarch," and Chicot turned in the direction of Saint-Germain-l'Auxerrois.

Chicot was not the only person in search of the Duc d'Anjou, and uneasy at his absence; the Guises too were looking for him on all sides, but they were not more fortunate than Chicot. M. d'Anjou was not the man to risk himself imprudently, and we shall see later what precautions had kept him from his friends.

Once, Chicot thought he had found him in the Rue de Béthisy; a large group had gathered before the door of a wine-shop, and Chicot recognized M. de Monsoreau and Le Balafré among the number.

"Good!" he said. "Here are the sucking fish; the shark cannot be far."

Chicot was mistaken; M. de Monsoreau and Le Balafré were busy pouring out numerous potations to an orator whose eloquence they thus encouraged. This orator was Gorenflot, in a state of complete intoxication, relating his journey to Lyons, and his duel in an inn with a dreadful Huguenot. M. de Guise listened intently to this tale, in which he fancied there was some coincidence with the silence of Nicolas David. Besides, the Rue Béthisy was filled with people; several gentlemen Leaguers had tied their horses to a sort of ring, frequently found in the cities at that period. Chicot stopped on the outside of the group and listened. Gorenflot, storming, bursting, always tumbling from his living pulpit, and as often replaced on Panurge, uttered only jerky sentences; but as he could still speak, he was the object of an examination by MM. de Guise and Monsoreau, who drew from him fragments of confession and information.

Such a confession frightened the Gascon far more than the presence of the King of Navarre in Paris. He foresaw the moment when Gorenflot would utter his name, — that name which would throw a fatal light on the mystery. He lost no time. In one moment he had cut the bridles of some of the horses fastened there, and distributing two or three violent blows, sent them through the crowd, which broke and dispersed before them.

Gorenflot feared for Panurge; the gentlemen were afraid for their horses, their valises, and many for themselves. The crowd opened and scattered. The cry "Fire!" was heard, repeated by a dozen voices. Chicot shot like an arrow through the different groups, approached Gorenflot with flaming eyes, which began the work of sobering him, caught Panurge by the bridle, and instead of following the crowd, turned his back on it. This double movement left between Gorenflot and the Duc de Guise, a considerable space, which was soon filled by a rush of new-comers.

Chicot then dragged the monk to a kind of *cul-de-sac* formed by the apse of Saint-Germain-l'Auxerrois, and placed him and Panurge against the wall, as a *bas-relief*.

"Ah, drunkard!" he said to him, "ah, pagan! ah, traitor! ah, renegade! will you always prefer a bottle of wine to your friend?"

"Ah, Monsieur Chicot!" stammered the monk.

"What! I feed you, wretch; I give you drink; I fill your pockets and your stomach, and you betray me?"

"Ah, Chicot," said the monk, with tenderness.

"You tell my secrets, rascal!"

"Dear friend."

"Hush! You are but a sycophant, and you deserve chastisement."

The monk, short, vigorous, enormous, powerful as a bull, but overcome by repentance and wine, trembled in Chicot's hands who shook him like a balloon filled with air. Panurge alone protested against the violence to his friend by kicks, which Chicot answered with blows.

"Chastisement to me!" murmured the monk, "a chastisement to your friend, dear Monsieur Chicot!"

"Yes, yes, chastisement," said Chicot; "and you will receive it," and the Gascon's stick passed from the donkey to Gorenflot's broad, fleshy shoulders.

"Oh, if I were fasting!" said Gorenflot, angrily.

"You would beat me, ungrateful one, — me, your friend?"

"You my friend, Monsieur Chicot, and you treat me thus!"

"He who loves well, chastises well."

"Take my life at once, while you are about it!" cried Gorenflot.

"I ought to."

"Oh, if I were but fasting!" said the monk, with a groan.

"You have already said so," and Chicot redoubled his proofs of affection towards the poor monk, who began to bellow loudly.

"Come, after the ox, here is the calf," said the Gascon. "Now, hold on to Panurge, and go and sleep at the Corne d'Abondance."

"I can no longer see my way," cried the monk, from whose eyes large tears were falling.

"Ah," said Chicot, "if you could weep the wine you have drunk, you would be sober. But no, I shall have to guide you." So Chicot took the ass by the bridle, while the monk, holding on with both hands, exerted himself to preserve his centre of gravity. They passed over the Pont aux Meuniers, the Rue Saint-Barthélemy, the Petit-Pont, and went up the Rue Saint-Jacques, the monk still weeping, and Chicot still pulling.

Two of Bonhomet's assistants, in obedience to Chicot's orders, helped the monk to alight, and conducted him to the little room with which our readers are already acquainted.

"It is done," said the host, returning.

"Is he in bed?" asked Chicot.

"Snoring."

"Very good! But as he will wake up some day or other, remember that I do not wish him to know how he came here, or one word of explanation. Indeed, it will be better that he should not know that he has been out since the famous night when he made such a scandal in the convent, and that he should believe all the rest to be a dream."

"Very well, Monsieur Chicot; but what has happened to the poor monk?"

"A great misfortune. It seems that at Lyons he picked a quarrel with an agent of M. de Mayenne, and killed him."

"Oh, *mon Dieu!*" cried the host.

"So M. de Mayenne has sworn, it seems, to have him broken on the wheel, alive or dead," replied Chicot.

"Have no uneasiness," said Bonhomet; "under no pretext will he leave here."

"Very good; and now," continued the Gascon, reassured about Gorenflot, "I must find the Duc d'Anjou." So he started off in search of his Majesty François III.

CHAPTER II.

THE PRINCE AND HIS FRIEND.

As we have seen, Chicot vainly sought the Duc d'Anjou through the streets of Paris on the evening of the League.

We may remember that the duke had invited the prince to go out. This invitation had disturbed the suspicious prince. François had reflected; and after reflection; he surpassed the serpent in prudence. However, as his interests demanded that he should see with his own eyes what was taking place that evening, he decided to accept the invitation, but resolved, at the same time, not to leave his palace unless he were duly attended. As every man who fears, gets his favorite weapon, the duke went in search of his sword, which was Bussy d'Amboise.

To decide upon this step, the duke must have been very much frightened. Since his deception in regard to M. de Monsoreau, Bussy sulked; and François acknowledged to himself that if he were in Bussy's place, and had taken his courage as well as his place, he would have showed more than contempt for the prince who had betrayed him in so cruel a manner.

Bussy, like all sensitive natures, felt sorrow more vividly than pleasure. It is rare that a man, intrepid in danger, cold and calm in the face of fire and sword, does not give way to grief more readily than a coward. Those from whom a woman can draw tears most quickly are the men most feared by other men.

Bussy was asleep in his sorrow, so to speak. He had seen Diane received at court, recognized as Comtesse de

Monsoreau, admitted by Queen Louise among her ladies-in-waiting; he had seen a thousand curious glances directed to that unrivalled beauty which he had, so to speak, discovered and rescued from the grave where it was buried. During the whole evening he had fastened his ardent gaze on the young woman, who did not raise her heavy eyelids, in spite of all the brilliancy of this fête. Bussy, unjust like every man truly in love, forgetting the past, and destroying in his own mind all those phantoms of happiness inspired by the past, — Bussy did not consider how great Diane's suffering must be to induce her to forego the happiness of gazing at the one sympathetic face amid the crowd of indifferent or simply curious ones.

"Oh," said Bussy to himself, as he waited in vain for a glance, "women have cleverness and audacity only to deceive a tutor, a husband, or a mother. They are awkward and cowardly when they have a simple debt of gratitude to pay. They fear so much to seem to love, they attach such exaggerated importance to their slightest favor, that they do not mind breaking the heart of him who loves them, when such is their humor. Diane could tell me frankly, 'I thank you, M. de Bussy, for what you have done for me, but I do not love you.' The blow would kill or cure me. But no, she prefers to let me love her hopelessly; but she has gained nothing by it. I no longer love her; I despise her."

And he left the royal circle with rage in his heart. At this moment his was no longer the noble face on which all men gazed with terror and all women with love; his brow was clouded, his eye crafty, and his smile deceitful. Bussy, as he glanced at his image in a large mirror, found it an unbearable sight.

"I am mad," he said. "What! I shall torment myself about a person who scorns me, and make myself odious to a hundred who like me? But why does she scorn me, or

rather, for whom ?   Is it for that long, livid skeleton who
stands beside her and watches her incessantly, and who also
feigns not to see me ?   And to think that if I wished it,
in a quarter of an hour I could have him mute and cold
beneath my knee, with ten inches of my sword in his body ;
to think that, if I only wished, I might stain that white
dress with the blood of him who has sewed those flowers
on it ; to think that, if I am not loved, I might at least be
hated and feared !   Oh, her hatred, her hatred, rather than
her indifference !   Yes ; but to act thus would be mean
and commonplace, — would be doing what a Quélus or a
Maugiron would do if they knew how to love.   Better
resemble that hero of Plutarch whom I so greatly admired,
— that young Antiochus, dying of love, and never confessing it, never uttering a complaint.   Yes, I will be silent, —
I who have fought with all the best men of the time ; who
have seen Crillon (the brave Crillon himself) disarmed
before me, and held him at my discretion.   I will subdue
my sorrow and stifle it in my soul, as Hercules did with
the giant Anteus, without letting his foot touch his mother
Hope.   No, nothing is impossible to me who, like Crillon,
have been called ' the brave.'   I shall do all that the heroes
have done."

With these words he relaxed the clinched hand with
which he tore his breast, wiped the sweat from his brow,
and walked slowly to the door.   His fist was about to strike
the tapestry ; but he summoned all his patience and gentleness and went out with smiling lips and a placid brow, but
with a volcano in his heart.

It is true that on the way he encountered the Duc d'Anjou,
and turned aside his head, because he felt that even all his
fortitude could not make him smile, or even bow, to the
prince who called him his friend and had so odiously
betrayed him.

As he passed, the prince called Bussy's name ; but Bussy

did not even turn around. He went home, placed his sword
on the table, drew his dagger from its sheath, unfastened
his cloak and doublet himself, and sat down in a large armchair, leaning his head against the scutcheon which ornamented its back. His attendants saw that he was absorbed;
they thought he wanted to rest, and withdrew. Bussy was
not sleeping, he was dreaming. He spent several hours in
this way, without noticing that at the other end of the room
was a man who, also seated, was watching him attentively
without speaking or making a gesture, probably waiting for
a suitable occasion to enter into communication by word or
sign. At length a cold shiver shook Bussy's shoulders and
his eyes wandered. The observer did not stir.

The count's teeth soon began to chatter; his arms stiffened; his head, becoming too heavy, slipped along the back
of the chair, and fell on his shoulder. At this moment the
man who was observing him rose from his chair, and heav-
ing a sigh, approached him.

"Monsieur le Comte," he said, "you have fever."

The count raised his face, flushed by the fever's heat.

"Ah, it is you, Rémy!" he said.

"Yes, count; I was waiting here for you."

"Here!—and why?"

"Because one does not remain long in the place where
one suffers."

"Thank you, my friend," said Bussy, taking the young
man's hand. Rémy held in his own that terrible hand
which had become weaker than a child's, and pressed it to
his heart with affection and respect.

"Now," he said, "the question, Monsieur le Comte, is to
know whether you wish to remain in this condition. Do
you wish the fever to increase until it overcomes you? Then
remain as you are. Do you wish to subdue it? Then get into
bed and have some one to read to you from a beautiful
book from which you may draw example and strength."

The count had nothing to do but to obey; so he did.
All his friends who came to visit him found him in bed.
During the whole of the next day Rémy never left his bedside. He exercised the double function of physician for
the body and for the soul; he had cooling drinks for the
one, and soft words for the other. But the next day, which
was that of M. de Guise's visit to the Louvre, Bussy looked
around him. Rémy was not there.

"He is tired," thought he; "it is very natural, poor lad,
and he wants to enjoy the air, the sun, and the springtime.
And then Gertrude no doubt expected him. Gertrude is
but a servant, but she loves him. A servant who loves is
better than a queen who does not love."

The day passed and Rémy did not return. Just because he was absent, Bussy wanted him, and felt terribly
impatient.

"Oh," he murmured once or twice, "I still believed in
friendship and gratitude, but henceforth I shall believe in
nothing at all."

Towards evening when the streets were beginning to fill
with people and noise, when the absence of light no longer
permitted him to distinguish the objects in the room,
Bussy heard loud voices in the ante-chamber, and a servant rushed in, saying, —

"It is Monseigneur the Duc d'Anjou."

"Let him enter," said Bussy, frowning at the thought
that his master was concerned about him, — this master
whose very politeness he scorned.

The duke entered. Bussy's room was without lights:
heavy hearts are fond of darkness, which they people with
phantoms.

"It is too dark here," said the duke; "it must make you
sad." Bussy remained silent; disgust closed his mouth.

"Are you seriously ill, that you do not answer me?" continued the duke.

"I am really very ill, monseigneur," murmured Bussy.

"Is that the reason why you have not appeared for two days?" said the duke.

"Yes, monseigneur," replied Bussy.

The prince, piqued by these short answers, walked two or three times around the room to look at the sculptures, which stood out in the shadow.

"You seem to have fine lodgings, Bussy," said the duke.

Bussy did not answer.

"Gentlemen," said François to his attendants, "remain in the next room. I believe my poor Bussy is really ill. Now, why have you not sent for Miron. The king's physician is not too good for Bussy."

Bussy's servant shook his head, and the duke observed the movement.

"Come, Bussy, are you in trouble?" he said, almost obsequiously.

"I do not know," replied the count.

The duke approached like those lovers who, the more they are rebuffed, the more gracious they become.

"Come, speak to me," he said.

"And what shall I say to you, monseigneur?"

"You are angry with me," he said in a low voice.

"I, angry? For what? Besides, it is of no use to be angry with princes; what good would that do?"

The duke was silent.

"But let us waste no time in preliminaries," said Bussy. "Come to the point, monseigneur."

The duke looked at Bussy.

"You need me, do you not?" said the latter, with incredible harshness.

"Ah, M. de Bussy!"

"Eh, you need me, I repeat. Do you suppose I think you come here through friendship? No, *pardieu!* for you love no one."

"Oh, Bussy, can you say such things to me?"

"Come, speak, monseigneur; what do you want? When one belongs to a prince, and when this prince dissimulates to the point of calling one his friend, — well! one must be grateful for the dissimulation and be ready to sacrifice everything, — even life. Speak."

The duke flushed; but as he was in the shadow, no one saw the flush.

"I wanted nothing," he said, "and you were mistaken in believing that my visit had an interested motive. I desire only, seeing that it is a fine evening, and that all Paris is excited to-night over the signing of the League, that you should accompany me a little about the streets."

Bussy looked at the duke.

"Have you not D'Aurilly?" he asked.

"A lute-player!"

"Ah, monseigneur, you are not giving him all his other qualities. I thought he fulfilled other functions near you, and besides D'Aurilly, you have with you ten or twelve gentlemen whose swords I hear striking against the wood-work of my ante-chamber."

The *portière* was raised gently.

"Who is this?" asked the duke, haughtily, "and who enters unannounced in the room where I am?"

"I, Rémy," replied Le Haudoin, without any embarrassment.

"Who is Rémy?" asked the duke.

"Rémy is the physician, monseigneur," replied the young man.

"Rémy," said Bussy, "is more than the physician, — he is the friend."

"Ah!" said the duke, feeling the blow.

"You have heard what Monseigneur desires?" asked Bussy, preparing to leave his bed.

"That you accompany him; but — "

"But what?" asked the duke.

"But you will not accompany him, monseigneur," replied Le Haudoin.

"Why so?" cried François.

"Because it is too cold, monseigneur."

"Too cold?" said the duke, surprised that any one should dare resist him.

"Yes, too cold. Therefore, I who answer for M. de Bussy's health to his friends, and particularly to myself, —I must forbid his going out."

Bussy was none the less ready to jump out of bed when Rémy's hand found his and pressed it significantly.

"Very good;" said the duke, "since the risk would be so great, he shall remain," and his Highness, very much piqued, walked towards the door. Bussy did not move.

The duke returned towards the bed.

"So you have decided, — you will not risk it?"

"You see, monseigneur, that the doctor forbids me."

"You should see Miron; he is a great doctor."

"Monseigneur, I prefer a friendly doctor to a learned one," said Bussy.

"In that case, adieu."

"Adieu, monseigneur."

The duke left with great noise. Hardly was he gone when Rémy, who had watched his departure, hastened to his patient.

"Now, monseigneur," he said, "get up at once, if you please."

"Why shall I get up?"

"To go out with me. It is too warm in this room."

"But you have just told the duke that it was too cold outside!"

"Since his departure the temperature has changed."

"So that—?" said Bussy, rising with curiosity.

"So that I am convinced that the air at this moment would do you good," replied Le Haudoin.

" I do not understand," said Bussy.

" Do you understand the drugs I give you ? Yet you swallow them. Come, get up; a walk with M. d'Anjou was dangerous, but with the physician it will be beneficial. I tell you so. Have you no more confidence in me ? Then you must dismiss me."

" Well, then, since you wish it," said Bussy.

" You must."

Bussy rose, pale and trembling.

" An interesting pallor," said Rémy; " the handsome invalid."

" But where are we going ? "

" In a neighborhood the air of which I analyzed to-day."

" And that air ? "

" Is excellent for your malady, monseigneur."

Bussy dressed himself.

" My hat and sword," he said.

He put on the one, and fastened the other, and both went out together.

CHAPTER III.

ETYMOLOGY OF THE RUE DE LA JUSSIENNE.

RÉMY took his patient by the arm, turned to the left, took the Rue Coquillière and followed it down to the rampart.

"It is strange!" said Bussy; "you are leading me near the marsh of the Grange-Batelière, and call it healthy."

"Oh, monsieur," said Rémy, "a little patience; we shall turn around the Rue Pagevin, leaving the Rue Breneuse on the right, and we shall enter the Rue Montmartre. You shall see what a beautiful street the Rue Montmartre is."

"Do you think I do not know it?"

"Well, so much the better if you know it; I shall not have to lose time by pointing out its beauties, and shall lead you at once to a pretty little street. Come, you will see."

In fact, after having passed the Porte Montmartre, and gone about two hundred yards in the street, Rémy suddenly turned to the right.

"Are you doing it on purpose?" cried Bussy. "We are going back to our starting-point!"

"This," said Rémy, "is the Rue de la Gypecienne, or de l'Egyptienne, if you prefer, — a street which the people are already beginning to call 'de la Gyssienne,' and which, before long, will be called 'de la Jussienne,' because that is softer, and as you go towards the south, the tendency of language is to multiply the vowels; you ought to know that, monseigneur, you who have been in Poland. Do not those rascals still use four consonants together, so that

when they speak they seem to be cracking pebbles, and
swear as they do so ? "

"That is very true ; but as I do not suppose you brought
me here to discuss philology, come, tell me, where are we
going ? "

"Do you see that little church ? " asked Rémy, without
replying directly to Bussy. "Eh, monseigneur, is it not
well situated, with its façade on the street, and its apse on
the garden of the community ? I would wager that you had
never noticed it before."

"In fact," said Bussy, "I did not know it."

And Bussy was not the only nobleman who had never
entered that church of Sainte-Marie-l'Egyptienne, frequented
almost exclusively by the people, and also known under the
name of Chapelle Quoqhéron.

"Well," said Rémy, "now that you know the name of
that church, monseigneur, and that you have gazed long
enough at the exterior, let us enter and see the stained
glass windows of the nave ; they are most curious."

Bussy looked at Le Haudoin and saw such a pleased
smile on his face that he understood at once that the
young doctor must have some other reason for wishing him
to enter besides showing him windows which it was too
dark to see. There were, however, other things to look at ;
for the interior of the church was lighted up for service.
There were some of those naïve paintings of the sixteenth
century, such as Italy preserves, thanks to its fine climate ;
whereas with us, dampness on the one hand and vandalism
on the other, have effaced from our walls those traditions
of another age, and those proofs of a faith that no longer
exists. In fact, the artist had painted in fresco, and by order
of the king, the life of Saint Mary the Egyptian. Now,
among the most interesting scenes of this life, the artist,
simple-minded and a great lover of truth, — historical, if
not anatomical, — had placed, in the most conspicuous spot

in the chapel, that critical moment when Saint Mary, having no money to pay the boatman, offers herself in payment for the passage.

It is only just to say that, in spite of the veneration of the faithful for Saint Mary the Egyptian converted, many good women of the neighborhood thought that the painter might have placed the scene in some other spot, or else treated it with less truth to nature; and the reason they gave, or rather did not give, was that certain details in the fresco attracted too often the eyes of the young shop clerks, whom the drapers, their patrons, brought to church on Sundays and fête days.

Bussy looked at Rémy, who seemed to have become a shop clerk for the present, and was giving his whole attention to the picture.

"Do you pretend to awaken in my mind Anacreontic ideas, with your chapel of Sainte-Marie-l'Egyptienne?" asked Bussy. If so, you are mistaken; you should bring here monks and students."

"God forbid!" said Le Haudoin. "*Omnis cogitatio libidinosa cerebrum inficit.*"

"Well, then?"

"Well, one cannot become blind to enter here."

"Come, you had some other object in bringing me here, besides making me look at the knees of Saint Mary the Egyptian."

"Why, no."

"Then I have seen them. Let us go."

"Patience, the service is just ending. If we left now, we would disturb the faithful."

And Le Haudoin gently held Bussy by the arm.

"Ah, every one is going now," said Rémy. "Let us do the same, if you please."

Bussy walked towards the door, visibly indifferent and absent-minded.

"Well," said Le Haudoin, "here you are going out without taking holy water. What the devil are you thinking about ? "

Bussy, obedient as a child, directed his steps towards the column near which was the holy water font. Le Haudoin took advantage of this movement to make a sign to a woman, who immediately approached the same column. So at the moment when the count extended his hand towards the shell-shaped font, held up by two black marble Egyptians, a hand somewhat large and red, but still the hand of a woman, was extended towards his own, and dampened his fingers with the water. Bussy could not help lifting his eyes from the red hand to the face. But he recoiled and turned pale ; he had just recognized in the owner of this hand, Gertrude, half-hidden beneath a black veil.

He stood there with his arm extended, and never thought of making the sign of the cross, while Gertrude bowed and passed on ; but behind Gertrude, whose robust elbows made way for her, came a woman, carefully wrapped in a silk mantle, — a woman whose elegant and youthful figure, charming foot, and slender waist recalled to Bussy's mind the fact that there was only one woman in the world so charming.

Rémy said nothing ; he only looked at him. Bussy now understood why the young man had brought him to the Rue Sainte-Marie-l'Egyptienne and made him enter the church.

Bussy followed this woman ; Le Haudoin followed Bussy.

This procession of four people following each other at equal distances would have been very amusing if the pallor and sadness of two of them had not betrayed cruel sufferings.

Gertrude, who walked on before, turned the corner of the Rue Montmartre, walked a few steps, then suddenly entered an alley on which opened a door. Bussy hesitated.

"Well, Monsieur le Comte," said Rémy, "shall I walk on your heels ? "

Bussy walked on.

Gertrude, who still led the way, drew a key from her pocket, and made way for her mistress, who entered without turning her head.

Le Haudoin spoke a few words to the maid, and stood aside to let Bussy pass; then he and Gertrude entered together, closed the door, and the alley was once more deserted.

It was half past seven in the evening, in the early part of May; the first leaves were beginning to open in the balmy air that heralded the approach of spring. Bussy looked around, and found himself in a little garden about fifty feet square, surrounded by very high walls covered with moss and vines, whose tendrils often detached bits of stone and plaster, and perfumed the night air with the fresh and vigorous odor of their leaves.

Wall-flowers grew out of the cracks in the old church wall, and joyously showed their buds, red as pure copper.

Finally, the first lilacs, which had bloomed that very morning, sent out their sweet perfumes ; and the young man, who, one hour before, had been so weak, so lonely, and so abandoned, asked himself if all this perfume, this warmth, this life did not come from the mere presence of the woman he loved so tenderly.

On a little wooden bench, placed near the church and shaded by jessamines and clematis, sat Diane, with her head bowed down, and her hands listlessly tearing to pieces a flower whose petals fell on the sand.

At this moment a nightingale, hidden in a neighboring chestnut-tree, began its long and melancholy song, enlivened from time to time with joyous notes.

Bussy was alone in the garden with Madame de Monsoreau, for Rémy and Gertrude stood at a distance. He approached ; Diane raised her head.

"Monsieur le Comte," she said in a timid voice, "all

subterfuge would be unworthy of us; if you found me just now in the Rue Sainte-Marie-l'Egyptienne it is not chance that led you thither."

"No, madame," said Bussy. "Le Haudoin took me out without my knowing where I was going, and I assure you that I was ignorant — "

"You have mistaken the meaning of my words, monsieur," said Diane, with sadness. "Yes, I know that Monsieur Rémy brought you to this church, and perhaps by force."

"Madame," said Bussy, "it was not by force, and I did not know whom I was to see."

"These are harsh words, Monsieur le Comte," murmured Diane, shaking her head and raising her tearful eyes to Bussy. "Do you wish me to understand that had you known Rémy's secret, you would not have accompanied him?"

"Oh, madame!"

"It is natural and just, monsieur. You did me a great service, and I have not yet thanked you for your courtesy. Pardon me, and receive my thanks."

"Madame — " Bussy stopped; he was so bewildered that he could command neither his thoughts nor his words.

"But I wish to prove to you," continued Diane, becoming more animated, "that I am neither an ungrateful woman nor have I a forgetful heart. It was I who begged Monsieur Rémy to procure for me the honor of this interview; it was I who indicated the place of meeting. Forgive me if I have displeased you."

Bussy placed his hand over his heart.

"Oh, madame," he said, "you do not think that!"

Ideas were beginning to return to this poor brokenhearted man; it seemed to him that this gentle evening breeze, which brought him such sweet perfumes and tender words, at the same time removed the cloud which was before his eyes.

"I know," said Diane, who was the more composed, because she had long been preparing this interview, — "I know all the trouble you had in fulfilling my commission; I know all your delicacy; I know you, and appreciate you, be assured. Think what I must have suffered at the thought that you would misunderstand the sentiments of my heart."

"Madame," said Bussy, "for three days I have been ill."

"Yes, I know," said Diane, with a blush which betrayed all the interest she took in this illness; "and I suffered more than you, because Monsieur Rémy — he no doubt deceived me — made me believe — "

"That your forgetfulness caused my suffering? It is true."

"Then I was right to do as I did," replied Madame de Monsoreau; "to see you, to thank you for your kindness, and to swear to you an eternal gratitude. Now, believe that I speak from the bottom of my heart."

Bussy shook his head sadly, and did not reply.

"Do you doubt my words?" continued Diane.

"Madame," replied Bussy, "those who feel friendship show it as best they can. You knew I was at the palace on the night of your presentation; you knew I was close to you; you must have felt the weight of my glance, yet not once did you raise your eyes; not by a word, sign, or gesture did you let me know that you were aware of my presence. Now, perhaps I was wrong, and you did not recognize me; you had seen me only twice, madame."

Diane answered by a glance so sadly reproachful that Bussy was moved.

"Forgive me, madame, forgive me!" he said; "you are not a woman like all others, and yet you act like them. This marriage?"

"Do you not know how I was forced to it?"

"Yes; but it was easy to break it."

" On the contrary, impossible."

" Did nothing tell you that a devoted friend watched near you ? "

Diane looked down.

" It was specially that which made me fear."

"And you sacrificed me to these considerations ? Oh, think what my life will be, now that you belong to another ! "

" Monsieur," said the countess with dignity, "a woman cannot change her name without great detriment to her honor when there live two men, the one bearing the name she has given up, the other the name she has taken."

" So you keep the name of Monsoreau from choice ? " he asked.

" Do you think so ? " murmured Diane. " So much the better." And her eyes filled with tears. Bussy, who saw her head drop on her bosom, walked up and down before her in a state of agitation.

" Well," he said, "I have once more become what I was before, — a stranger to you, madame."

" Alas ! " said Diane.

" Your silence speaks plainly enough."

" I can only speak by my silence."

" Your silence, madame, is the sequel of your greeting at the Louvre. At the Louvre you did not see me ; here you do not speak to me."

" At the Louvre I was in the presence of M. de Monsoreau. M. de Monsoreau looked at me ; he was jealous."

" Jealous ! Well, what does he want, *mon Dieu !* What happiness can he envy when every one envies his happiness ? "

" I tell you he is jealous, monsieur. For the past two or three days he has seen some one wandering around our new abode."

"You have, then, left the little house of the Rue Saint-Antoine?"

"What!" cried Diane, thoughtlessly, "this man was not you?"

"Madame, since the public announcement of your marriage, since your presentation, since that evening at the Louvre when you did not even look at me, I have been in bed ill, dying with fever. You see that your husband could not be jealous of me, since it was not I he saw wandering around your house."

"If it be true, as you say, Monsieur le Comte, that you had some desire to see me again, thank this stranger; for, knowing M. de Monsoreau as I know him, this man made me tremble for your safety, and I wished to see you and say to you, 'Do not expose yourself so, monsieur; and do not make me more unhappy than I am.'"

"Reassure yourself, madame; I repeat it was not I."

"Now let me finish what I have to say to you. For fear of this man,—whom I do not know, but whom M. de Monsoreau does perhaps,—he demands that I should leave Paris; so that," added Diane, extending her hand to the count, "you may look upon this as our last meeting, monsieur. To-morrow we start for Méridor."

"You are going, madame?" cried Bussy.

"There is no other way to reassure M. de Monsoreau. This is the only way for me to have peace. Besides, I myself hate Paris, the world, the court, and the Louvre. I am happy at the thought of retiring to the home of my childhood. It seems to me that in walking through those same paths some of my former happiness will drop on my head, like the dew from heaven. My father accompanies me, and I shall find there M. and Madame de Saint-Luc, who regret my absence. Farewell, M. de Bussy!"

Bussy hid his face in his hands. "Ah," he murmured, "all is over for me!"

"What are you saying there?" asked Diane, rising.

"Madame, I say that this man exiles you; that he takes from me the only hope that was left me, — that of breathing the same air as yourself; of seeing you sometimes at your window; of touching your dress as you pass; of adoring a living being, and not a shadow. I say that this man is my mortal enemy; and should it cost me my life, I will destroy him with my own hands."

"Oh, Monsieur le Comte!"

"The wretch!" cried Bussy. "What! it is not enough for him that you are his wife, — you, the purest and most beautiful of creatures; but he must be jealous, jealous! The ridiculous and devouring monster would absorb the whole world."

"Oh, calm yourself, count. *Mon Dieu!* he may be excusable."

"Excusable! Do you defend him, madame?"

"Oh, if you knew!" said Diane, covering her face with both her hands, as though she feared Bussy might see her blushes in spite of the darkness.

"If I knew?" repeated Bussy. "Eh, madame, I know one thing, — he that is your husband is wrong to think of the rest of the world."

"But," said Diane, in a broken, passionate voice, "if you were wrong, Monsieur le Comte, and if he were not."

And the young woman, touching with her· cold hand Bussy's burning ones, rose and fled as light as a shadow through the dark alleys of the little garden, seized Gertrude's arm, and disappeared with her before Bussy, overwhelmed, mad and radiant with delight, had time to stretch out his arms to hold her.

He uttered a cry and tottered. Rémy reached him just in time to catch him in his arms and make him sit on the bench which Diane had just left.

CHAPTER IV.

HOW D'EPERNON'S DOUBLET WAS TORN, AND HOW SCHOMBERG WAS STAINED BLUE.

WHILE Maître la Hurière accumulated signatures, while Chicot consigned Gorenflot to the Corne d'Abondance, while Bussy returned to life in the little garden filled with perfume, songs and love, — Henri, annoyed at all he had seen in the city, irritated by what he had heard in the churches, and furious against his brother whom he had seen in the Rue Saint-Honoré accompanied by M. de Guise, M. de Mayenne, and a train of gentlemen apparently commanded by M. de Monsoreau, — Henri, we say, had returned to the Louvre in company with Maugiron and Quélus.

The king, according to his habit, had gone out with his four friends; but at a short distance from the Louvre, Schomberg and D'Epernon, annoyed by the king's ill-humor, and counting on meeting with some adventures in this crowd, took advantage of the first crush to disappear at the corner of the Rue de l'Astruce; and while the king and his two friends continued their walk along the quay, they were carried down the Rue d'Orleans.

They had not gone a hundred yards before each one had found what he sought. D'Epernon passed his cane between the legs of a *bourgeois* who was running, and who consequently tumbled down; and Schomberg had pulled the cap off the head of a woman whom he thought old and ugly, and who turned out to be young and pretty.

But both had badly chosen their day for attacking those good Parisians, usually so patient; everywhere was to be felt that fever of revolt whose wings sometimes touched the walls of the capital. The *bourgeois* rose from the ground and cried out, "Down with the heretic!" As he was zealous, the others believed him, and rushed upon D'Epernon. The young woman had cried, "Down with the favorite!" which was much worse; and her husband, who was a dyer, sent his apprentices after Schomberg. Schomberg was brave; so he made a stand, spoke out boldly, and placed his hand on his sword. D'Epernon was prudent, and fled.

Henri had not troubled himself about his two favorites, knowing they were able to get out of scrapes, — the one with his legs, the other with his arms. He therefore continued his walk, and when he had finished it, returned to the Louvre, as we have seen.

He had entered his room, and was seated in his armchair, trembling with impatience, and seeking a good subject on which to vent his anger.

Maugiron was playing with Narcissus, the king's large greyhound; Quélus, with his cheeks resting on his hands, was lounging on cushions and looking at Henri.

"There they go!" said the king. "Their plot is working. Sometimes serpents, sometimes tigers; when they do not spring, they crawl."

"Eh, sire," said Quélus, "are there not always plots in a kingdom? How in the devil would you occupy the brothers and cousins of kings if they did not plot?"

"Really, Quélus, your maxims are absurd; and with your puffed cheeks you remind me of Gilles of the fair of Saint-Laurent."

Quélus whirled on his cushions and irreverently turned his back on the king.

"Come, Maugiron," resumed Henri, "am I right or wrong? *Mordieu!* and must I be soothed with twaddles and nonsense, as if I were an ordinary king, or a linen-draper who fears to lose his pet cat?"

"Well, sire," said Maugiron, who was always and in all things of the same opinion as Quélus, "if you are not an ordinary king, prove it by showing yourself a great king. How the devil! here is Narcissus who is a good dog, but when you pull his ears he growls, and if you step on his tail he bites."

"Good!" said Henri, "here is the other one who likens me to my dog."

"Not at all, sire," said Maugiron; "you see, on the contrary, that I set Narcissus far above you, since he knows how to defend himself while your Majesty does not."

And he too turned his back on Henri.

"Well, here I am alone," said the king. "Very well, continue, my good friends, for whom they accuse me of despoiling the kingdom; abandon me, insult me, kill me. Upon my word, I am surrounded by tormentors! Ah, Chicot, my poor Chicot, where are you?"

"Well," said Quélus, "here he is calling for Chicot, now."

"That is very simple," replied Maugiron, and the insolent fellow began to mutter between his teeth a certain Latin axiom which might be translated, "Birds of a feather flock together."

Henri frowned, and a look of terrible anger flashed from his large black eyes; this time it was a right royal look that the king gave his indiscreet favorites. But no doubt exhausted by this sudden spark of anger, Henri fell back in his chair and rubbed the ears of one of the little dogs in his basket.

At this moment a rapid footstep was heard in the antechamber, and D'Epernon appeared without hat or cloak, and with his doublet all torn. Quélus and Maugiron turned round; and Narcissus ran barking at the new-comer as if he only recognized the king's courtiers by their clothes.

"Good God!" cried Henri, "what has happened to you?"

"Look at me, sire, and see how your Majesty's friends are treated."

"And who treated you so?"

"*Mordieu!* your subjects, or rather those of M. le Duc d'Anjou, for they were crying, ' *Vive la Ligue! vive la Messe! Vive Guise! Vive François!* ' In fact, they cheered for every one except for the king."

"Well, what had you done to the people to be treated in this manner?"

"I? nothing. What can one man do to the people? I was recognized for one of your Majesty's friends, and that sufficed."

"But Schomberg?"

"What about Schomberg?"

"He did not come to your assistance? He did not defend you?"

" *Corbœuf!* Schomberg had enough to do taking care of himself!"

"How so?"

"I left him in the hands of a dyer, whose wife's hat he had pulled off, and who with the aid of five or six apprentices was making him have a rather hard time of it."

"*Par la mordieu!* where did you leave my poor Schomberg?" cried Henri, rising. "I shall go to his assistance myself. They may be able to say that my friends abandon me," added the king, looking at Maugiron and Quélus, "but no one shall ever say that I abandon my friends."

"Thank you, sire," said a voice behind Henri, "thanks! but here I am. *Gott verdamme mich!* I extricated myself without assistance, but not without difficulty."

"Oh, it is Schomberg's voice," cried the three favorites, "but where the devil is he?"

"*Parbleu!* you see where I am," cried the same voice, and from the darker portion of the room, they saw coming towards them, not a man, but a shadow.

"Schomberg!" cried the king, "where do you come from, and why are you of that color?"

In fact Schomberg, from head to foot and without excepting any portion of his person or his garments, was of a most beautiful shade of royal blue.

"*Der Teufel!*" he cried, "the wretches! I am not surprised that all the people ran after me."

"But what is the matter?" asked Henri. "If you were yellow that might be explained by fright, — but blue!"

"The matter is that they dipped me in a vat, the rascals! I thought they were only dipping me in water, and it was indigo."

"Oh, *mordieu!*" said Quélus, bursting out laughing, "they are punished for their sin. Indigo is very expensive, and you must have carried off about twenty crowns of dye."

"I advise you to joke; I wish you had been in my place."

"And you did not rip open any of them?" asked Maugiron.

"All I know is that I left my dagger somewhere sheathed in flesh; but all was over in a second. I was taken, picked up, dipped in the vat, and nearly drowned."

"And how did you get away from them?"

"I had the courage to perform an act of cowardice, sire."

"And what did you do?"

"I cried ' *Vive la Ligue!* '"

"So did I," said D'Epernon, "only they made me add, '*Vive le Duc d'Anjou!* '"

"I had to do the same," said Schomberg, biting his fingers with rage. "But that is not yet all."

"What!" said the king, "did they make you cry out something else, my poor Schomberg?"

"No, they made me cry nothing else, thank God! that was enough; but just as I was crying, '*Vive le Duc d'Anjou*' — "

" Well ? "

" Guess who passed ? "

" How can I guess ? "

" Bussy, — his cursed Bussy, — who heard me."

" The fact is, he must have been at a loss what to make of it," said Quélus.

" *Parbleu !* it was not difficult to understand. I had a dagger at my throat, and I was in a vat."

" What ! " said Maugiron, " he did not come to your assistance ? Nevertheless, he owed it to you as a gentleman."

" He seemed to be thinking of very different things ; he only needed wings to fly away ; he hardly seemed to touch the ground."

" And then," said Maugiron, " he may not have recognized you."

" A very poor reason."

" Were you already dyed blue ? "

" Ah, that is true ! " said Schomberg.

" In that case he would be excusable," replied Henri, " because really, my poor Schomberg, I myself do not recognize you."

" Never mind," replied the young man, who was not German for nothing, " we shall meet some day when I shall not be in a vat."

" Oh, as for me," said D'Epernon, " it is not the servant against whom I bear a grudge, but the master. It is not Bussy that I wish to punish ; it is Monseigneur the Duc d'Anjou."

" Yes, yes ! " cried Schomberg, " Monseigneur d'Anjou, who wishes to kill us with ridicule while waiting to kill us with a dagger."

" The Duc d'Anjou, whose praises were being sung in the streets. You heard them, sire," said Maugiron and Quélus together.

" The fact is, that the duke seems to be master of Paris

and not the king; try to go out and see if you will be
treated with more respect than we were," said D'Epernon.

"Ah, my brother, my brother!" murmured Henri, in a
menacing tone.

"Ah, sire, you will repeat more than once what you have
just said; but you will do nothing against him," said
Schomberg. "Yet I declare it is clear to me that this
brother is at the head of some plot."

"Eh, *mordieu!* that is exactly what I was saying to
these gentlemen when you came in just now, D'Epernon;
but they replied by shrugging their shoulders and turning
their backs."

"Sire," said Maugiron, "we shrugged our shoulders and
we turned our backs, not because you said there was a
plot, but because we saw you were in no mood to sup-
press it."

"And now," continued Quélus, "we turn to you to say,
'Save us, sire, or rather, save yourself; for if we fall, you
perish. To-morrow, M. le Duc de Guise will come to the
Louvre and ask you to appoint a chief for the League;
to-morrow you will appoint the Duc d'Anjou, as you promised to do. And once chief of the League'—that is to say,
at the head of one hundred thousand men excited by this
night's orgies, — the Duc d'Anjou will do with you whatever he wishes."

"Ah, ah," said Henri, "if I take a decisive step, will
you be disposed to support me?"

"Yes, sire," replied the young men with one voice.

"Provided your Majesty will give me time to put on
another cap, another cloak, and another doublet," said
D'Epernon.

"Go into my room, D'Epernon, and my valet will give
you all that; we are of the same size."

"And provided you will give me time to take a
bath."

"Go into my bath-room, Schomberg, and my bather will
attend to you."

"Sire," said Schomberg, "may we hope that the insult
will be avenged?"

Henri extended his hand to command silence, and looking down, seemed buried in thought; after a short pause he
said, —

"Quélus, ask if M. d'Anjou has returned to the
Louvre."

Quélus went out. D'Epernon and Schomberg awaited
with the others Quélus' return, so much was their zeal
revived by the imminence of the danger. It is not during
a storm, but in the calm, that sailors become mutinous.

"Sire," asked Maugiron, "has your Majesty decided on a
course of action?"

"You will see," replied the king.

Quélus returned.

"M. le Duc has not yet come in," he said.

"Very well," said the king. "D'Epernon go and change
your clothes; Schomberg, go and change your color. Quélus and Maugiron, go down and watch for my brother's
return."

"And when he returns?"

"Have all the doors shut; now go."

"Bravo, sire!" said Quélus.

"I shall be back in ten minutes, sire," said D'Epernon.

"I cannot say when I shall be back; that depends on the
quality of the dye," said Schomberg.

"Come as soon as possible," replied the king.

"But will your Majesty remain alone?" asked Maugiron.

"No, Maugiron, I remain with God, whose protection I
shall ask for our enterprise."

"Pray Him well, sire," said Quélus, "because I am
beginning to think that He has made an agreement with
the devil to damn us all in this world and the next."

"Amen!" said Maugiron.

The two young men who were to watch went out through one door; the two who were to change their costumes went out through the other, and the king, left alone, knelt down on his *prie-Dieu*.

CHAPTER V.

CHICOT IS MORE THAN EVER KING OF FRANCE.

THE bells tolled midnight. The doors of the Louvre were usually closed at midnight; but Henri had wisely calculated that the Duc d'Anjou would not fail to sleep at the Louvre that night, to afford less ground for the suspicions to which the tumult of Paris might have given rise in the king's mind. He had therefore given orders that the gates should remain open until one o'clock.

At a quarter after twelve Quélus came up.

"Sire, the duke has returned," he said.

"What is Maugiron doing ? "

"Watching that he does not go out again."

"There is no danger."

"Then — " said Quélus, making a movement to indicate that there was nothing left but to act.

"Then — let him go to bed quietly," said the king. "Who is with him ? "

"M. de Monsoreau and his usual gentlemen."

"And M. de Bussy ? "

"M. de Bussy is not there."

"Good!" said the king, greatly relieved to find his brother deprived of his best sword.

"What are the king's commands ? " asked Quélus.

"Send word to D'Epernon and Schomberg to hasten, and let M. de Monsoreau know that I wish to speak to him."

Quélus bowed, and executed the commission with a promptness due to the combination of hatred and the desire of vengeance united in a single heart.

Five minutes later, D'Epernon and Schomberg returned, the one newly dressed, the other having bathed, only the wrinkles of his face were still of a bluish tinge, which, according to the bather, would disappear only after several steam baths.

Behind the two favorites came M. de Monsoreau.

"The captain of the guards has just told me that your Majesty did me the honor to summon me," said the master of the hounds, with a deep bow.

"Yes, monsieur," said Henri. "As I walked out this evening, I saw the stars so bright and the moon so fair that the idea came to me that we might have a splendid chase to-morrow, with such beautiful weather. It is only twelve o'clock, Monsieur le Comte. Set out at once for Vincennes ; harbor a stag for me, and to-morrow we shall hunt it."

"But, sire," said Monsoreau, "I thought your Majesty was to see Monseigneur d'Anjou and M. de Guise, to appoint a chief for the League."

"Well, monsieur, what of that ? " asked the king, in a haughty tone, which admitted of no reply.

"After that, sire, there might not be time."

"There is always time, monsieur, when one knows how to employ it; this is why I say to you, 'You have time to set out to-night, provided you set out at once.' You have time to track a stag to-night and have everything in readiness for to-morrow at ten o'clock. Therefore, go at once ! Quélus, Schomberg, accompany M. de Monsoreau, and have the gate of the Louvre opened for him, and have it closed again, by order of the king."

The master of the hounds withdrew in astonishment.

"Is this a whim of the king's ? " he asked the two young men, as they passed through the ante-chamber.

"Yes," laconically replied the latter.

M. de Monsoreau saw he could learn nothing from them, and was silent.

"Oh, oh!" he murmured to himself, as he glanced towards the Duc d'Anjou's apartments, "this does not seem very promising for his Royal Highness."

But there was no way of sending a word of warning to the prince. Quélus and Schomberg stood, one on his right, and the other on his left. For one moment he imagined that the two favorites had special orders, and held him prisoner; and it was only when he stood outside of the Louvre, and heard the gate close behind him, that he understood that his suspicions were unfounded.

At the end of ten minutes, Schomberg and Quélus had returned to the king.

"Now," said Henri, " silence, and follow me, all four."

"Where are we going, sire?" asked the ever-prudent D'Epernon.

"Those who come, will see," replied the king.

"Come!" said the four young men, with one voice.

The favorites saw to their swords, fastened their cloaks, and followed the king, who, with a lantern in his hand, conducted them through the secret corridor we already know, and through which the queen-mother and King Charles IX. had passed more than once, to visit Queen Margot, whose apartments were now occupied by the Duc d'Anjou.

A valet was watching in this corridor; but before he had time to run back and give warning to his master, Henri had seized him, commanded him to be silent, and handed him to his favorites, who pushed him into a closet, the door of which they locked.

It was therefore the king himself who turned the knob of Monseigneur the Duc d'Anjou's bedroom.

François had just gone to bed, filled with the dreams of ambition to which the events of the evening had given birth in his mind; he had heard his name exalted, and the king's name abused. Accompanied by the Duc de Guise, he had seen the people of Paris make way for him and his gentlemen, while the king's favorites were hooted, insulted, and abused. Never since the beginning of that long career, so full of treacherous dealings and timid plots, had he been so advanced in popularity and therefore in hope.

He had just laid on the table a letter from M. de Guise, brought by M. de Monsoreau, and in which Le Balafré enjoined upon him not to fail to be present at the king's levee, the next morning.

The Duc d'Anjou had no need of such a recommendation, as he had every intention of being present at his own triumph. His surprise was great when he saw the door of the secret passage open, and his terror reached its height when he recognized the king on the threshold. Henri signed to his companions to remain outside, and advanced towards the bed, grave, frowning, but silent.

"Sire," stammered the duke, "the honor that your Majesty confers on me, is so unlooked for —"

"That it frightens you, does it not?" asked the king. "I understand that. But, no, no! remain, brother; do not rise."

"But sire, permit me —" said the duke, trembling, and drawing towards him the Duc de Guise's letter, which he had just finished reading.

"You were reading?" asked the king.

"Yes, sire."

"Something interesting, no doubt, since it kept you awake at this late hour."

"Oh, sire, nothing of great importance," replied the duke, with a frigid smile; "only the evening mail."

"Yes," said Henri, "I understand that, — evening mail, Venus' mail. But no, I am mistaken; seals of that dimension are not used on notes sent by Iris or Mercury."

The duke hid the letter altogether.

"That dear François is discreet," said the king, with a laugh, which greatly frightened his brother. However, the latter made an effort, and tried to recover some assurance.

"Does your Majesty wish to speak to me in private?" asked the duke, who noticed from some movement on the part of the four young men at the door, that they were listening with pleasure to the beginning of this scene.

"What I have to say to you, monsieur," said the king, laying particular stress on this title, which was the one granted by etiquette to the sons of France, "you will allow me to say to-day before witnesses. Now, gentlemen," he continued, turning to the four young men, "listen; the king permits it."

The duke raised his head.

"Sire," he said, with that glance full of hatred and venom which man has borrowed from the snake, "before insulting a man of my rank, you should have refused me the hospitality of the Louvre; in the Hôtel d'Anjou, I should at least have been able to answer you."

"In truth," said Henri, with terrible irony, "you forget that wherever you may be, you are my subject, and that every house is mine. Thank God, I am the king!—the king of the soil!"

"Sire," cried François, "I am at the Louvre, at my mother's."

"And your mother is in my house," replied Henri. "Come, let us be brief, monsieur; give me this paper."

"Reflect, sire," said the duke.

"About what?"

"That you are making a request unworthy of a gentleman, but in return, worthy of an officer of your police."

The king became livid.

"That letter, monsieur," he said.

"A woman's letter! Reflect, sire," said François.

"There are women's letters which are good to see, and

very dangerous if not seen, particularly those written by our mother."

"Brother!" said François.

"That letter, monsieur," cried the king, stamping his foot; "that letter, or I shall have it taken from you by four Swiss."

The duke bounded out of bed, holding the letter in his hand, and with the evident intention of reaching the chimney to throw it into the fire.

"You would do that to your brother?" he asked.

Henri guessed his intention, and placed himself between him and the chimney.

"Not to my brother," he said, "but to my deadliest enemy. Not to my brother, but to the Duc d'Anjou, who has spent the whole evening running through the streets of Paris behind M. de Guise; to my brother, who is trying to conceal from me the letter written by one or the other of his accomplices, the Lorraine princes."

"This time," said the duke, "your police is at fault."

"I tell you that I saw on the seal the three famous merlets of Lorraine which pretend to swallow the *fleur-de-lis* of France. Give it, *mordieu!* give it, or — "

Henri took one step towards the duke, and placed his hand on his shoulder.

François had no sooner felt the weight of the royal hand, and seen the threatening attitude of the favorites who were beginning to draw their swords, than, falling on his knees near the bed, he cried, —

"Help! help! my brother wants to kill me."

These words, uttered in an accent of profound terror, prompted by conviction, made a great impression upon the king, and mitigated his rage. He thought that François could, in fact, fear assassination, and that this murder would have been fratricide. The idea flashed quickly through his mind, that in his family, accursed like all those which are the last of a race, brothers always assassinated their brothers as by tradition.

"No," he said, "you are wrong, brother, and the king wishes you no harm of the kind you seem to dread; you have struggled, and should acknowledge yourself beaten. You know that the king is the master, or if you did not, you know it now. Well, say it, not only to yourself, but aloud."

"Oh, I say it, brother, and I proclaim it," cried the duke.

"Very well; now this letter. The king orders you to give up that letter."

The Duc d'Anjou dropped the paper. The king picked it up, and without reading it, folded it and placed it in his pouch.

"Is this all, sire?" asked the duke, with his sinister glance.

"No, monsieur," said Henri. "As a punishment for this rebellion, which, fortunately, was not attended with any evil results, you must remain in your room until all my doubts about you are completely cleared. You are here, and the apartment is comfortable, and not too much like a prison, therefore remain. You will have good company on the other side of the door, at least; for to-night these four gentlemen will keep guard. To-morrow they will be replaced by a picket of Swiss."

"But my own friends! Shall I not be able to see them?"

"Whom do you call your friends?"

"M. de Monsoreau, for instance, M. de Ribeirac, M. d'Antraguet, M. de Bussy."

"Oh, I advise you to speak of the latter!"

"Has he had the misfortune to displease your Majesty?"

"Yes," said the king.

"When?"

"Always, and particularly to-night."

"To-night? What has he done to-night?"

"He had me insulted in the streets of Paris."

"You, sire?"

"Yes, — or my friends, which amounts to the same."

"Bussy had some one insulted in the streets of Paris to-night? You have been deceived, sire."

"I know what I am saying."

"Sire," cried the duke, triumphantly, "M. de Bussy has not left his *hôtel* for two days. He is at home in bed, ill, and burning with fever."

The king turned towards Schomberg.

"If he were burning with fever," said the young man, "it was not in his own home, but in the Rue Coquillière."

"Who told you that Bussy was in the Rue Coquillière?" asked the Duc d'Anjou.

"I saw him."

"You saw Bussy out?"

"Bussy; fresh, joyous, and seeming to be the happiest man on earth, accompanied by his usual attendant, Rémy, that squire, doctor, or whatever he may be."

"Then I can understand nothing," said the duke, in a stupor. "I saw M. de Bussy during the evening. He was buried under blankets. He must have deceived me."

"Very well," said the king. "M. de Bussy will be punished like the rest and with the rest, when matters are explained."

The duke, who thought he might divert the king's anger from himself on to Bussy, made no further attempt to defend his follower.

"If M. de Bussy has done this," he said; "if after refusing to go out with me he went out alone, he must have had some intentions which he could not acknowledge to me, whose devotion to your Majesty he knows so well."

"You hear what my brother pretends," said the king; "he says he did not authorize M. de Bussy."

"So much the better," said Schomberg.

"Why so much the better?"

"Because your Majesty may then let us do as we wish."

"Very well, very well; we shall see later," said Henri. "Gentlemen, I recommend my brother to your care; as you will have the honor of guarding him, treat him with all the respect due to a prince of the blood, — that is to say, the first in the kingdom after me."

"Oh, sire," said Quélus, with a glance which made the duke shiver, "rest assured that we know all that we owe to his Highness."

"Very well, adieu, gentlemen," said Henri.

"Sire," cried the duke, more frightened by the absence of the king than he had been by his presence, "am I seriously a prisoner; my friends will not be able to visit me? I shall not be able to go out?"

The thought of the next day flashed through his mind, — of that next day when his presence was so necessary near M. de Guise.

"Sire," said the duke, who saw that the king was about to yield, "let me at least appear near your Majesty; my place is near your Majesty. I am a prisoner there as well as anywhere else, and better watched there than elsewhere. Sire, grant me the favor of remaining near your Majesty."

The king, on the point of granting the duke's request, which he did not find objectionable, was about to say "Yes," when his attention was diverted from his brother to the door, where a very long and agile body was making with its neck, arms, head, — in fact, with every movable portion of itself, — the most emphatically negative signs.

It was Chicot who was saying "No."

"No," said Henri to his brother; "you are very comfortable here, and it suits me that you should remain."

"Sire!" stammered the duke.

"When such is the king's good pleasure, it seems to me that should suffice, monsieur," added Henri, with a haughty air which completely crushed the duke.

"When I said I was the real King of France!" murmured Chicot.

CHAPTER VI.

HOW CHICOT PAID A VISIT TO BUSSY, AND WHAT FOLLOWED.

ON the day following this night, Bussy was quietly breakfasting at about nine o'clock in the morning, with Rémy, who, in his capacity of a physician, ordered nourishing food; they were talking over the events of the preceding day, and Rémy was trying to remember the inscriptions on the frescoes of Sainte-Marie-l'Egyptienne.

"Tell me, Rémy," suddenly asked Bussy, " did you not fancy you recognized the gentleman who was being dipped in a vat at the corner of the Rue Coquillière ? "

"Yes, Monsieur le Comte, and I have been trying ever since to recall his name."

"Then you did not recognize him ? "

" He was already very blue."

"I should have gone to his assistance," said Bussy. "It is a duty one gentleman owes to another; but in truth, Rémy, I was too busy with my own affairs."

" But if we did not recognize him," said Le Haudoin. "He surely recognized us, because we were of our natural color; and it seems to me he glared at us furiously, and shook his fist at us as he uttered some threat."

"Are you sure of that, Rémy ? "

"I can answer for the looks; but I am less sure about the fist and the threats," said Le Haudoin, who knew Bussy's fiery temper.

" Then we must find out who this gentleman is, Rémy; I cannot allow such an insult to pass."

"Wait, wait!" cried Le Haudoin, as if he had come out of cold water or jumped into hot water. " Oh, *mon Dieu!* I have it! I know him!"

"How?"

"I heard him swear."

"*Mordieu!* I should think so. Any one would have sworn under those circumstances."

"Yes, but he swore in German."

"Pshaw!"

"Hê said, '*Gott verdamme!'*"

"Then it was Schomberg."

"Himself, Monsieur le Comte, himself!"

"Then, my dear Rémy, prepare your ointments."

"Why so?"

"Because before long you will have to mend his skin or mine."

"You will not be mad enough to have yourself killed when you are in such good health, and so happy?" asked Rémy, with a knowing wink. "Saint Mary the Egyptian has already resurrected you once, and she might weary of performing a miracle which Christ himself tried only twice."

"On the contrary, Rémy," said the count, "you cannot imagine how pleasant it is to risk one's life when one is happy. I assure you that I never fought with a good heart when I had lost a large sum at cards, when I had surprised my mistress betraying me, or when I had something on my mind; but, on the contrary, whenever my purse is full, my heart light, and my conscience clear, I go boldly on to the field: I am sure of my hand, I read through my antagonist, and crush him with my superiority. I am in the position of a man who plays cards and feels his adversary's gold pushed into his hand. Then is the time I am brilliant. I shall fight admirably to-day, Rémy," said the young man holding out his hand to the doctor, "for, thanks to you, I am very happy."

"Stop a moment!" said Le Haudoin; "you will please forego that pleasure. A fair lady of my acquaintance has recommended you to me, and made me swear to keep you safe and sound under pretext that you already owe her your life and that one cannot dispose of that which one owes."

"Good Rémy!" said Bussy, losing himself in that mist of thought which allows the man in love to see and hear all that is said and done as on the stage we see objects through a gauze veil which conceals their angles and glaring colors, — a delightful condition which is almost a dream; for while the soul follows its sweet and faithful thought, the senses are diverted by the words or gestures of a friend.

"You call me, 'good Rémy' because I took you to see Madame de Monsoreau; but will you still call me so when you will be separated from her? — and unfortunately the day approaches, if it has not already dawned."

"What is that?" cried Bussy, with energy. "Let us not jest on that subject, Maître le Haudoin."

"Eh, monsieur, I am not jesting. Do you not know that if she departs for Anjou, I too shall have the sorrow of being separated from Mademoiselle Gertrude? — ah!"

Bussy could not help smiling at Rémy's pretended despair.

"Do you love her very much?" he asked.

"I should think so! And she, — if you knew how she beats me!"

"And you let her?"

"For the love of science; I have been forced to invent a salve which causes all black-and-blue spots to disappear at once."

"In that case, you should send a few pots to Schomberg."

"Let us speak no more of Schomberg. It is understood that we shall leave him to get clean as best he can."

"Yes, and let us return to Madame de Monsoreau, or rather to Diane de Méridor, because you know — "

"Oh, *mon Dieu*! yes, I know."

"Rémy, when do we start?"

"Ah, this is what I expected! As late as possible, Monsieur le Comte."

"Why so?"

"First, because we have here M. le Duc d'Anjou, who seems to have managed his affairs in such a way last night that he will evidently have need of us."

"Well, what next?"

"Then because M. de Monsoreau, by a special blessing, suspects nothing, at least so far as you are concerned; and that he would suspect something if he saw you disappear from Paris at the same moment as his wife who is not his wife."

"Well, what if he should suspect?"

"Oh, it matters greatly to me, my dear count. I undertake to mend all the sword-cuts you receive in duels, because, as you are an unequalled swordsman, you never receive any very serious ones; but I refuse the dagger thrusts given by jealous husbands in ambushes. In such cases, they are animals who strike hard; look at that poor Saint-Mégrin, who was so cruelly put to death by our friend M. de Guise."

"Well, my friend, suppose it is my fate to be killed by M. de Monsoreau?"

"Well?"

"Well, he will kill me."

"And then a week, a month, or a year afterwards, Madame de Monsoreau will marry her husband, — a fact which will cause great torment to your poor soul that will look on from above, or below, without being able to oppose it, as it will have no body."

"You are right, Rémy, I wish to live."

"Very good! But it is not sufficient to be alive; believe me, you must follow my advice and be charming for Monsoreau. He is at present horribly jealous of M. le Duc d'Anjou, who, while you were in bed, ill with fever, was wandering beneath the lady's windows like an enamoured Spaniard, and was recognized, thanks to his D'Aurilly. Make all sorts of advances to this husband, and do not even pretend to ask him what has become of his wife (that is useless, since you already know), and he will spread the report everywhere that you are the only gentleman possessing Scipio's virtues, — sobriety and chastity."

"I think you are right," said Bussy. "Now that I am no longer jealous of the bear, I will tame him, and that will be supremely comical. Ah, Rémy, you may now ask me what you will; all is easy for me, — I am happy."

At this moment some one knocked at the door and the two friends were silent.

"Who is there?" asked Bussy.

"Monseigneur," said the page, "there is a gentleman below who wishes to speak to you."

"To speak to me so early? Who is it?"

"A tall gentleman, dressed in green velvet with rose-colored stockings. He has a rather comical face, but the appearance of an honest man."

"Eh," thought Bussy aloud, "can it be Schomberg?"

"He said a tall gentleman."

"That is true. Or Monsoreau?"

"He said 'the appearance of an honest man.'"

"You are right," said Bussy, "it can be neither the one nor the other; ask him in."

The visitor soon appeared on the threshold.

"Ah, *mon Dieu!*" cried Bussy, quickly rising on catching sight of the new-comer, while Rémy discreetly retired into an adjoining closet, "Monsieur Chicot!"

"In person, Monsieur le Comte," replied the Gascon.

Bussy's eyes were fixed upon him with an astonishment which said as plainly as words, —

"Monsieur, what have you come for?"

Without being questioned any further, Chicot replied in a very serious tone, —

"Monsieur, I have come to propose a little bargain to you."

"Speak, monsieur," replied Bussy, with surprise.

"What will you promise me if I render you a great service?"

"That depends on the service," replied Bussy, rather scornfully.

The Gascon pretended not to observe this scornful air.

"Monsieur," he said, sitting down and crossing his long legs, "I observe you have not invited me to sit down."

Bussy reddened.

"This is to be added to my reward for the service I shall render you," he continued.

Bussy made no reply.

"Monsieur," said Chicot, not in the least disconcerted, "do you know the League?"

"I have heard a great deal about it," replied Bussy, who now began to pay some attention to the words of the Gascon.

"Well, monsieur," said Chicot, "you must know that it is an association of honest Christians, formed for the purpose of religiously massacring their neighbors the Huguenots. Do you belong to the League, monsieur? I do."

"But, monsieur —"

"You have only to say yes or no."

"Permit me to be surprised," said Bussy.

"I had the honor of asking you if you belonged to the League; did you hear me?"

"Monsieur Chicot," said Bussy, "as I do not like questions which I do not understand, I beg you to change the conversation, and I will wait a few minutes for the sake of courtesy before repeating to you that, not liking questions, I naturally do not like questioners."

"Very well, 'courtesy is courteous,' as M. de Monsoreau says when he is in a good humor."

At this name of Monsoreau, which the Gascon had uttered without apparent intention, Bussy listened again.

"Eh," he murmured to himself, "does he suspect something, and has he sent Chicot to spy on me?" then aloud, "Come, Monsieur Chicot, to the point; you know that we have only a few minutes."

"*Optime!*" said Chicot. "Well, in a few moments we can say a great deal; I shall therefore say that I might have dispensed with questioning you, because if you are not of the Holy League, you will soon be, since M. d'Anjou is a member."

"M. d'Anjou? Who told you so?"

"Himself, speaking to my person, according to the formula used by the fraternity of lawyers; for example, by that good and dear M. Nicolas David, the light of the *forum parisiense*, — a light which was extinguished, though no one knows who blew it out. Now understand that if M. le Duc d'Anjou belongs to the League, you cannot help belonging to it also, — you who are his right arm. The League knows better than to accept a maimed chief."

"Well, Monsieur Chicot, what next?" asked Bussy, in a far more courteous tone than he had yet used.

"What next?" asked Chicot. "Well, if you belong to it or if they think you are likely to belong, what has happened to his Royal Highness will certainly happen to you."

"What has happened to his Royal Highness?" cried Bussy.

"Monsieur," said Chicot, rising and imitating the attitude taken by Bussy a moment before, — "monsieur, I do not like questions; and if you will permit me to say so at once, I do not like questioners. I have therefore a great mind to let them do to you what has already been done to your master."

"Monsieur Chicot," said Bussy, with a smile containing

all the excuses that a gentleman can make, "speak, I pray you. Where is M. le Duc?"

"He is in prison."

"Where?"

"In his room. Four of my good friends guard him, — M. de Schomberg, who was dyed blue last night, as you know, since you passed by at the moment of the operation; M. d'Epernon, who is yellow from the fright he had; M. de Quélus, who is red with anger; and M. de Maugiron, who is white with *ennui*. It is beautiful to see, to say nothing of M. le Duc, who is beginning to turn green with terror, so that we privileged ones of the Louvre, we shall soon have a perfect rainbow to delight our eyes."

"Therefore, monsieur," said Bussy, "you think there is some danger for my liberty?"

"Danger; stop a moment, monsieur. I suppose they are — they may be — they should be on the way to arrest you."

Bussy started.

"Do you like the Bastille, M. de Bussy? It is a place very suitable for meditations; and M. Laurent Testu, the governor, gives very good fare to his prisoners."

"I would be sent to the Bastille?" cried Bussy.

"Faith! I must have in my pocket something like an order to take you there. Would you like to see it?"

And Chicot drew from the pocket of his hose, wide enough to contain three legs of the size of his own, an order from the king, drawn up in due form, to apprehend, wherever he might be, M. Louis de Clermont, lord of Bussy d'Amboise.

"Written very nicely by M. de Quélus," said Chicot.

"Then, monsieur," cried Bussy, touched by Chicot's action, "you are really rendering me a service?"

"Well, I think so," said the Gascon. "Do you agree with me, monsieur?"

"Monsieur," said Bussy, "I beg you to treat me like a man of honor. Is it to injure me on some other occasion that you save me to-day? — for you love the king, and the king does not love me."

"Monsieur le Comte," said Chicot, rising to bow, "I save you to save you; now you may think what you will of my action."

"But how can I explain such kindness?"

"Do you forget that I asked for a reward?"

"True."

"Well?"

"Ah, monsieur, most willingly!"

"You will do what I shall ask of you some day?"

"On my honor, if it be possible."

"Well, that satisfies me," said Chicot, rising. "Now mount your horse and disappear; I shall carry this order to those for whom it is meant."

"You were not to arrest me yourself?"

"For whom do you take me? I am a gentleman, monsieur."

"But I abandon my master."

"Have no remorse; he has already abandoned you."

"You are a gallant man, Monsieur Chicot," said Bussy to the Gascon.

"*Parbleu!* I know it," replied the latter.

Bussy called Le Haudoin, who, to do him justice, was listening behind the door.

"Rémy!" he cried; "Rémy, Rémy, our horses!"

"They are saddled, monseigneur," calmly replied Rémy.

"Monsieur," said Chicot, "that young man has a great deal of intelligence."

"*Parbleu!* I know it," said Rémy; and they saluted each other as Guillaume Gorin and Gauthier Gargouille might have done fifty years later.

Bussy took a few handfuls of crowns, which he crammed

into his pockets and those of Rémy. After which, bowing to Chicot, and thanking him again, he prepared to go down.

"Pardon me, monsieur," said Chicot, "but permit me to be present at your departure." And he followed Bussy and Le Haudoin to a little stable-yard where a page held two saddled horses.

"Where are we going?" asked Rémy, carelessly picking up the reins.

"But —" said Bussy, hesitating, or seeming to hesitate.

"What do you say to Normandy, monsieur?" asked Chicot, who was looking on, and examining the horses with a critical eye.

"No," replied Bussy; "it is too near."

"What do you think of Flanders?" continued Chicot.

"Too far."

"I think," said Rémy, "that you should decide for Anjou, which is at a reasonable distance, — eh, monsieur?"

"Yes, let it be Anjou," said Bussy, with a blush.

"Monsieur," said Chicot, "since you have made your choice, and are about to start —"

"At this very moment."

"I have the honor of saluting you; remember me in your prayers." And the worthy gentleman walked off, grave and majestic, scraping the corners of the houses with his immense sword.

"It is destiny, monsieur," said Rémy.

"Come quickly," cried Bussy, "and we may perhaps overtake her."

"Ah, monsieur," said Le Haudoin, "if you aid chance you take away all its merit." And they set off.

CHAPTER VII.

WE may safely say that Chicot, notwithstanding his apparent coldness, was returning to the Louvre in a perfectly joyful state of mind. He enjoyed the threefold satisfaction of having rendered a service to a brave man like Bussy, of having been engaged in an intrigue, and of having rendered possible for the king the political stroke which circumstances required.   Indeed, what with Bussy's head, and particularly his heart, and the spirit of organization of MM. de Guise, a stormy day was likely to rise on the good city of Paris.

All that the king had feared, all that Chicot had foreseen, came to pass, as might have been expected.

M. de Guise, after having received in the morning the principal Leaguers, who had come from all sides to bring him the registers covered with signatures which we have seen in the squares, at the doors of the principal inns, and even on the altars of the churches; M. de Guise, after having promised a chief to the League, and made them all swear to recognize the chief whom the king would appoint; after having conferred with the cardinal and M. de Mayenne, — went out to visit M. le Duc d'Anjou, whom he had lost sight of the night before at about ten o'clock.

Chicot had anticipated this visit, so on leaving Bussy he went at once to lounge in the neighborhood of the Hôtel d'Alençon, situated at the corner of the Rue Hautefeuille and the Rue Saint-André.

He had been there about a quarter of an hour when he saw the one he expected come down the Rue de la Huchette. Chicot hid himself at the corner of the Rue du Cimetière, and the Duc de Guise entered the *hôtel* without having perceived him.

The duke found the prince's valet rather uneasy about his master's absence, but he suspected what had taken place, — that the duke had slept at the Louvre. The duke asked if in the prince's absence he might not speak to D'Aurilly. The valet replied that D'Aurilly was in his master's room, and that he was at the duke's orders.

Guise accordingly went in.

D'Aurilly, the lute-player and confidant of the prince, was acquainted with all the Duc d'Anjou's secrets, and therefore better informed than any one as to his master's whereabouts.

D'Aurilly was quite as concerned as the valet, and from time to time he left his lute, on which his fingers wandered idly, to go to the window and look to see if the duke were not coming.

He had sent three times to the Louvre, and each time the answer had been that monseigneur, having returned very late, was still sleeping. M. de Guise asked D'Aurilly about the Duc d'Anjou. D'Aurilly had been separated from his master at the corner of the Rue de l'Arbre-Sec, by a group which came to increase the crowd already assembled before the hostelry of the Belle Étoile; so that he had returned to the Hôtel d'Alençon without knowing anything of the duke's intention to spend the night at the Louvre.

The lute-player then told the prince of the three messengers he had sent to the Louvre, and repeated the identical answer brought by each of the three.

"It seems most unlikely that he should be asleep at eleven o'clock," said the duke; "the king himself is usually up at that hour. You should go to the Louvre, D'Aurilly."

" I have thought of it, monseigneur," said D'Aurilly, " but I feared this pretended sleep might be only a tale invented to satisfy my messenger, while the duke is amusing himself somewhere in the city ; now, if this is the case, Monseigneur might be annoyed at my seeking him."

" D'Aurilly," said the duke, " believe me, Monseigneur is too sensible a man to be amusing himself on a day like this. Go to the Louvre without fear, and there you will find him."

" I shall therefore go since you wish it, monsieur ; but what shall I say to him ? "

" Say that the convocation at the Louvre was for two o'clock, and that we were to confer together before meeting at the king's. You understand, D'Aurilly," said the duke, with a rather disrespectful display of temper, " that the time when the king is about to appoint a chief for the League is no time for sleep."

" Very well, monseigneur ; I shall tell his Highness to come here."

" Where I await him impatiently. Though the convocation is not until two o'clock, a great many are already assembled at the Louvre, and there is not a moment to lose. I, during that time, shall send for M. de Bussy."

" It is understood, monseigneur ; but in case I do not find his Highness, what am I to do ? "

" If you do not find his Highness, D'Aurilly, do not affect to look for him ; it will suffice to tell him later on with what zeal I tried to see him. At all events, I shall be at the Louvre at a quarter before two."

D'Aurilly bowed to the duke and left.

Chicot saw him go out, and guessed the reason why. If M. le Duc de Guise should hear of M. d'Anjou's arrest, matters would become very complicated.

Chicot saw that D'Aurilly went up the Rue de la Huchette to take the Pont Saint-Michel ; he, on the contrary, ran down the Rue Saint-André-des-Arts with all the speed of his long legs, and passed the Seine at the lower Nesle when D'Aurilly had hardly come in sight of the great Châtelet.

We shall therefore follow D'Aurilly, who conducts us to the very scene of the important events of that day.

He walked down the quay, thronged with *bourgeois* who all had a triumphal expression, and reached the Louvre, which seemed to him most quiet and innocent.

D'Aurilly knew the world and the court; he talked first with the officer at the door, who is always an important personage in the eyes of those in quest of news and scandals.

The officer was all amiability; the king had waked up in the very best of humors. From the officer, D'Aurilly passed on to the *concierge*, who was engaged in the inspection of an army of servants trying on new costumes and giving them halberds of a new design. He smiled on the lute-player and replied to his remarks on the weather, all of which gave D'Aurilly the very best opinion of the political atmosphere.

D'Aurilly consequently passed on, went up the grand staircase which led to the duke's apartments, bowing right and left to the courtiers already assembled in the passages. At the door he found Chicot, sitting on a stool playing chess, and apparently absorbed in the deepest meditation: D'Aurilly tried to pass, but Chicot with his long legs blocked up the doorway. He was forced to touch him on the shoulder.

"Ah, is it you? Pardon me, M. d'Aurilly."

"What are you doing, M. Chicot?"

"Playing chess, as you see."

"All alone?"

"Yes, I am studying a move. Do you play chess, monsieur?"

"Very little."

"Yes, I know, you are a musician, and music is such a

difficult art that those who cultivate it must give up to it all their time and intelligence."

"It seems that the move is an important one," said D'Aurilly, laughing.

"Yes, my king worries me. You must know, M. d'Aurilly, that at chess, the king is a very insignificant personage who has no will of his own, who can only go one step at a time, forward, backwards, right or left, while he is surrounded by very active enemies, — by knights who jump three squares at a time, and by a crowd of pawns who surround him, pursue him, and harass him, — so that if he is ill advised, he is a ruined king in no time; now, M. d'Aurilly, my king is at present in a most perilous position."

"But, Monsieur Chicot, how does it happen that you are playing chess at the door of his Royal Highness's room?"

"I am waiting for M. de Quélus, who is in there."

"Where?" asked D'Aurilly.

"Why, there, with his Royal Highness."

"M. de Quélus with his Royal Highness?" asked D'Aurilly, with surprise.

During this dialogue, Chicot had made room for the lute-player to pass, but in such a way that M. de Guise's messenger was now placed between him and the door. Yet D'Aurilly hesitated to open this door.

"What is M. de Quélus doing with the duke?" he asked. "I did not know them to be such friends."

"Hush!" said Chicot, in a most mysterious way; and still holding his chess-board in both hands, he described a circle, which enabled his mouth to reach D'Aurilly's ear while his feet did not move. "He has come to ask the duke's pardon for a little quarrel they had yesterday."

"Really?" asked D'Aurilly.

"The king insisted upon it. You know on what excellent terms the brothers are at present. The king would not suffer an impertinence from Quélus to pass unpunished, and ordered him to apologize."

"Truly?"

"Ah, M. d'Aurilly, I think we are entering the golden age. The Louvre will become Arcadia, and the two brothers *Arcades ambo*. Ah, pardon me! I always forget that you are a musician."

D'Aurilly smiled and passed into the ante-chamber. As he did so, he opened the door wide enough for Chicot to be able to exchange a significant glance with Quélus, who was probably forewarned.

Chicot pursued his combinations, scolding his monarch not more harshly than a real king would have deserved, but rather too severely for an innocent piece of ivory.

D'Aurilly, as he entered the ante-chamber, was courteously saluted by Quélus, in whose hands a superb ebony cup and ball, inlaid with ivory, was performing rapid evolutions.

"Bravo, M. de Quélus," said D'Aurilly, seeing the young man perform a difficult feat. "Bravo!"

"Ah, my dear M. d'Aurilly," said Quélus, "when shall I play cup and ball as you play the lute?"

"When you will have studied your plaything as many days as I have spent years studying my instrument," said D'Aurilly, a little piqued. "But where is Monseigneur? Were you not with him?"

"I have an audience with him, my dear D'Aurilly; but Schomberg has precedence."

"Ah, M. de Schomberg too!" said the musician, with increased surprised.

"Oh, *mon Dieu!* yes. The king arranged all that; he is there in the dinning-room. Go in M. d'Aurilly, and kindly remind the prince that we are waiting."

D'Aurilly opened the second door and perceived Schomberg sitting, or rather lying, on a kind of couch.

Schomberg, in this position, was amusing himself by shooting through a ring suspended from the ceiling little balls of perfumed earth, an ample provision of which he had in his pouch, while a favorite dog brought back those balls which were not broken against the wall.

"What!" said D'Aurilly," such an occupation as this? "Ah, M. de Schomberg!"

"Ah, *guten Morgen!* M. d'Aurilly," said Schomberg, suddenly interrupting his game. "You· see I am amusing myself while waiting for an audience."

"But where is Monseigneur?" asked D'Aurilly.

"Hush! Monseigneur is now busy, forgiving D'Epernon and Maugiron. But will you not enter,—you the privileged one?"

"It might, perhaps, be indiscreet."

"Not in the least; on the contrary, you will find him in the next room. Go in, M. d'Aurilly, go in," and he pushed D'Aurilly through the door.

The astonished musician now perceived D'Epernon standing before a mirror, stiffening his moustache with gum, while Maugiron, seated near the window, was busy cutting out images, by the side of which the bas-reliefs on the temple of Venus Aphrodite and the paintings of the bath of Tiberus, at Capræ, would have seemed holy.

The duke, without his sword, sat in his armchair between these two men, who looked at him only to watch his movements, and spoke only disagreeable words.

Seeing D'Aurilly, he rushed to meet him.

"Take care, monseigneur," said Maugiron, "you are stepping on my images!"

"*Mon Dieu!*" cried D'Aurilly, "what do I see? He insults my master."

"Ah, M. d'Aurilly," said D'Epernon, continuing to arrange his moustache, "how are you? Very well, I hope, but you seem a little flushed."

"Pray be so kind as to bring me your little dagger," said Maugiron.

"Gentlemen, gentlemen," said D'Aurilly, "have you forgotten where you are?"

"Not at all, my dear Orpheus," said D'Epernon; "this is why I ask for your dagger. You see that M. le Duc has none."

"D'Aurilly," cried the duke, in a tone full of grief and rage, "do you not understand that I am a prisoner?"

"Of whom?"

"Of my brother. Could you not know that, on seeing my jailers?"

D'Aurilly uttered a cry of surprise.

"Oh, if I had only suspected it!" he said.

"You would have brought your lute to amuse his Highness," said a mocking voice; "but I thought of it, dear M. d'Aurilly. I sent for it, and here it is," and Chicot really handed the lute to the unfortunate musician. Behind Chicot, Quélus and Schomberg were yawning frightfully.

"How is your game of chess, Chicot?" asked D'Epernon.

"Ah, yes, true!" said Quélus.

"Gentlemen, I think I can save my king, but it will not be without difficulty. Come, M. d'Aurilly, give me your dagger in return for the lute, — a fair exchange."

The amazed musician obeyed, and seated himself at his master's feet.

"Here is one rat in the trap," said Quélus; "let us pass on to the others."

At these words, which gave D'Aurilly the explanation of the preceding scenes, Quélus returned to his position in the ante-chamber, but he begged Schomberg to give him his blow-gun in exchange for the cup and ball.

"That is only fair," said Chicot, "we must vary our pleasures. For a change, I shall go and sign the League."

And he closed the door, leaving the poor lute-player in company with his Highness.

CHAPTER VIII.

HOW THE MASTER OF THE HOUNDS FOLLOWED THE WRONG SCENT.

THE hour of the great reception had arrived, or rather was near at hand; since noon the Louvre had already received the principal chiefs, the interested parties, and even the lookers-on.

Paris was nearly as tumultuous as the day before, but with this difference, — that the Swiss, who had had no part in the fête of the previous evening, were now the principal actors. Paris had sent towards the Louvre its deputations of Leaguers, corporations of workmen, aldermen, militia, and ever increasing masses of spectators, who, on those days when the whole population was busy with something, came to look on as active and interested as if Paris had had two populations, as if in this great city, a little image of the world, each individual was divided into two parts, the one acting, and the other looking on.

The Louvre was therefore surrounded by a mass of populace; but we need not tremble for the Louvre.

It was not yet the time when the murmur of the people, changed into thunder, rocked down with the breath of its cannon the walls of the master's castle. The Swiss, those ancestors of the 10th of August and the 27th of July, smiled on the masses of Parisians, though these masses were armed, and the Parisians smiled on the Swiss. The time had not yet come when the vestibule of the kings was the scene of bloodshed.

Let us not believe that the drama was less interesting for being less gloomy; on the contrary, it was one of the most curious scenes ever presented in the old Louvre.

The king was in the great hall, seated on his throne, surrounded by his officers, his friends, his servants, and his family, waiting for all the corporations to file past him, and go to the places assigned to them in the courtyard, leaving their chiefs in the palace.

He could thus, at a single glance, count his enemies, prompted from time to time by Chicot, hidden behind the royal chair, warned by a sign from the queen-mother, or by some movement on the part of the minor Leaguers, who were more impatient than their chiefs, because they were less advanced in the secret. M. de Monsoreau entered abruptly.

"Look, Henriquet," said Chicot.

"What do you want me to see?"

"Look at your master of the hounds, *pardieu!* he is well worthy of it. He is pale and muddy enough to deserve a good look."

"Yes," said the king, "it is indeed he."

Henri made a sign to M. de Monsoreau, who approached.

"How is it that you are at the Louvre, monsieur?" asked Henri. "I believed you to be at Vincennes."

"I had everything in readiness there at seven o'clock this morning; but when noon came, and I had no news, I feared that some misfortune might have happened to your Majesty, and I hurried back."

"Really?"

"Sire," said the count, "if I have failed in my duty, attribute it to an excess of zeal."

"Yes, monsieur," said Henri, "and be assured that I fully appreciate it."

"Now," continued the count, with hesitation, "if your Majesty demands that I should return to Vincennes, as I am quite reassured—"

"No, no, remain. This chase was a mere whim that
passed through our head, and went as it came. Remain;
I shall have need of all those who are devoted to me, and
you have just placed yourself among those on whose devotion I can rely."

Monsoreau bowed.

"Where does your Majesty wish me to stand?" he asked.

"Will you give him to me for half an hour?" whispered
Chicot to the king.

"What for?"

"To torment him a little. What do you care? You owe
me some compensation for forcing me to be present at this
tiresome ceremony."

"Well, take him."

"I had the honor of asking your Majesty where I am to
stand," said the master of the hounds a second time.

"I thought I had answered; wherever you like. Behind
my chair, for instance; there is where I generally place my
friends."

"Come here," said Chicot, giving M. de Monsoreau a
portion of the space he had reserved for himself; "come
and get the scent of these fellows. Here is game that can
be tracked without a hound. *Ventre de biche!* Monsieur le
Comte, what scent! Here are the shoemakers who pass,
or rather, who have passed; and here are the tanners, —
mort de ma vie! if you lose the scent of these I will discharge you from your place!"

M. de Monsoreau pretended to listen, or rather listened
without hearing. He was very much preoccupied, and
looked around with an anxiety which did not escape the
king, particularly when Chicot drew his attention to it.

"Well," he whispered to the king, "do you know what
your master of the hounds is now hunting?"

"No."

"Your brother D'Anjou!"

"At all events, he is not in sight," replied Henri, laughing.

"No. Do you wish him to remain in ignorance of his whereabouts?"

"I should not be sorry to see him follow the wrong track."

"Wait, wait! I am told that the wolf has the same scent as the fox; he will make the mistake. Only ask him where the countess is."

"Why?"

"Ask, and you will see."

"Monsieur le Comte," said Henri, "what have you done with Madame de Monsoreau? I do not perceive her among the ladies."

The count shuddered, as if a serpent had bitten his foot. Chicot scratched his nose and winked at the king.

"Sire," replied the master of the hounds, "the countess is not well, and the air of Paris does not agree with her. She set out last night with her father, the Baron de Méridor, after having taken leave of the queen."

"And towards what part of France did she travel?" asked the king, delighted to have an opportunity of turning his head away while the tanners were passing.

"Towards her home in Anjou, sire."

"The fact is," said Chicot, gravely, "that the air of Paris is not good for women in her situation, — *gravidis uxoribus Lutetia inclemens.* I advise you to imitate the count's example, and to send the queen away when she will be —"

Monsoreau turned pale, and glared furiously at Chicot, who, leaning his elbow on the royal chair, and his chin on his hand, seemed to be looking very attentively at the passementerie makers as they passed.

"Who tells you, impertinent, that Madame de Monsoreau is *enceinte?*" murmured Monsoreau.

"Is she not?" said Chicot. "It would be more impertinent to suppose that, I think."

"She is not, monsieur."

"Well, well," said Chicot, "have you heard, Henri? It seems that your master of the hounds has committed the same mistake as you, — he has forgotten to bring together the chemises of Notre-Dame."

Monsoreau clinched his fists and swallowed his rage, after having shot at Chicot a glance of malicious hatred, to which Chicot replied by pulling his hat over his eyes, and shaking the long, slender plume which ornamented it.

The count saw that the moment was ill chosen, and shook his head as if to drive away the clouds from his brow. Chicot also changed his expression and assumed the most gracious smile.

"Poor countess," he said, "she is in danger of perishing of *ennui* on the way."

"I told the king," replied Monsoreau, "that she was travelling with her father."

"I do not deny that a father is very respectable, but not amusing. And if she had only that worthy baron to amuse her on the way — But luckily —"

"What?" quickly asked the count.

"Why, what?" replied Chicot.

"What do you mean by 'luckily'?"

"Ah, ah, you were making an ellipsis, Monsieur le Comte."

The count shrugged his shoulders.

"I beg your pardon, the interrogative form of which you made use is called an 'ellipsis.' Ask Henri, who is a philologist."

"Yes," said Henri; "but what was the meaning of your adverb?"

"Which adverb?"

"'Luckily.'"

"'Luckily' signifies 'luckily.' Luckily, I said (and in this I admire the goodness of God), there exist at this hour on the road some of our friends, and even very entertaining ones, who, if they met the countess, would surely amuse her; and," carelessly added Chicot, "as they are travelling along the same road, they will probably meet. Oh, I see them now! Do you not, Henri,—you who are a man of imagination? There they go, along a beautiful shady lane, on prancing horses, saying a thousand sweet things which greatly delight the dear lady!"

This was a second dagger, sharper than the first, planted in M. de Monsoreau's breast; but he could not show his rage. The king was there, and Chicot had in him a momentary ally; therefore, with an affability which testified to the efforts he had made to curb his temper, he said, —

"What, you have friends travelling towards Anjou?"

"You might even say *we* have, Monsieur le Comte, because these friends are more yours than mine."

"You astonish me, Monsieur Chicot," said the count. "I know no one, who—"

"That is right, be mysterious."

"I swear to you."

"Oh, you know they are there, Monsieur le Comte, and they are even such very dear friends that I saw you looking around for them from mere force of habit, though you know perfectly well that they are on the way to Anjou."

"I!" said the count. "You saw me?"

"Yes, you, the master of the hounds, the palest of all present, past, and future, from Nimrod to M. d'Autefort, your predecessor."

"Monsieur Chicot!"

"The palest, I repeat, — *veritas veritatem.* This is a barbarism, because there is only one truth; for if there were two, one, at least, would not be true, — but you are not a philologist, my dear M. Esau."

"No, monsieur, I am not; therefore I shall beg you to return at once to those friends of whom you spoke, and be kind enough to name them for me, if your superabundant imagination will allow you to do so."

"Ah, you always repeat the same thing. Seek monsieur, *morbleu!* seek. It is your business to hunt animals, — witness that unfortunate deer whom you disturbed this morning, and who surely did not expect that from you. If some one were to prevent you from sleeping, would you like that?"

Monsoreau's eyes wandered about in terror.

"What?" he cried, seeing an empty seat near the king.

"Come now!" said Chicot.

"M. le Duc d'Anjou!" cried the master of the hounds.

"Tally-ho, tally-ho!" cried the Gascon, "the game is started."

"He left to-day!" exclaimed the count.

"He left to-day, but it is possible he may have left last night. You are not a philologist, monsieur, but ask the king, who is one. When did your brother disappear, Henriquet?"

"Last night," replied the king.

"The duke gone!" murmured Monsoreau, pale and trembling. "Ah, *mon Dieu! mon Dieu!* what are you telling me, sire?"

"I do not say that my brother is gone," said the king; "I only say that he disappeared last night, and that his best friends do not know where he is."

"Oh," angrily cried the count, "if I believed that —"

"Well, well, what would you do? Besides, where would be the harm if he made a few soft speeches to Madame de Monsoreau. Our friend François is the gay member of the family; he was a beau in the reign of Charles IX., and he is now, under our king Henri III., who has other things to do besides making love. The devil! there should be at least one prince at court who represents the French mind."

" The duke gone ! " repeated Monsoreau.   " Are you quite sure, monsieur ? "

" And you ? " asked Chicot.

The master of the hounds looked once more towards the place usually occupied by the king's brother, and which continued unoccupied.

" I am lost ! " he murmured, with such a marked intention of escaping, that Chicot held him.

" Be quiet, *morbleu !* You do nothing but move, and that nauseates the king. *Mort de ma vie !* I should like to be in your wife's place, to see every day a prince with a double nose, and to hear M. d'Aurilly, who plays the lute like the late lamented Orpheus. What luck your wife has ! "

Monsoreau shivered with anger.

" Gently, monsieur," said Chicot; " hide your joy. Here is the business beginning. It is indecent to show one's passions. Listen to the king's speech."

The master of the hounds was forced to keep his place, because the hall had become gradually filled; he therefore remained motionless.

The whole assembly was present. M. de Guise had just entered, and bent his knee before the king, but not without an anxious glance at the Duc d'Anjou's vacant seat.

The king rose, the heralds commanded silence.

CHAPTER IX.

HOW THE KING APPOINTED A CHIEF FOR THE LEAGUE
WHO WAS NEITHER THE DUC D'ANJOU NOR THE DUC
DE GUISE.

"GENTLEMEN," said the king, amid a profound silence,
after assuring himself that D'Epernon, Schomberg, Maugiron, and Quélus had taken their places behind him,
leaving their prisoner in the charge of ten Swiss guards, "a
king, placed as he is between heaven and earth, hears equally
well the voices from above and the voices from below, —
that is to say, the commands of God and the commands of the
people. I understand that this association of all the powers for the defence of the Catholic religion is a guarantee
for my subjects; therefore I approve of the counsels given
by my cousin Guise. I then declare the Holy League
duly authorized and instituted; and as it is necessary that
this great body should have a good and powerful head, that
this chief who is called upon to maintain the Church
should be one of the most zealous sons of the Church,
— zealous from the very nature of his duties, — I choose a
Christian prince for the head of the League, and declare
that he shall henceforth be called — "

Henri purposely paused for an instant. The buzzing of
a fly could have been heard amid the general stillness.
Henri repeated, —

"He shall henceforth be called Henri de Valois, King
of France and Poland."

As he uttered these words, the king raised his voice
with a sort of affectation, to mark his triumph, and to

stimulate the enthusiasm of his friends, ready to burst forth, as well as to crush the Leaguers, whose half-suppressed murmurs betrayed their discontent, surprise, and fear.

As for the Duc de Guise, he was absolutely prostrated; large drops of perspiration gathered on his brow. He exchanged a glance with each of his two brothers, the Duc de Mayenne and the cardinal, who stood on either side of him. Monsoreau, more surprised than ever at the Duc d'Anjou's absence, was becoming reassured as he recalled the king's words. In fact, the duke might have disappeared without going away. The cardinal left the group with which he was standing and stole up to his brother.

"François," he whispered to him, "I fear we are no longer in safety here. Let us hasten to take leave because the people are strange, and the king whom they abhorred will become their idol for a few days."

"Very well," said Mayenne, "let us go. Wait here for our brother while I prepare our retreat."

During that time, the king had signed the first act prepared on the table, and drawn up in advance by M. de Morvilliers, who, with the exception of the queen-mother, was the only person in the secret; then passing the pen to M. de Guise, he said, in that mocking tone which he knew so well how to assume, —

"Sign, my cousin;" then pointing with his finger to the place, "there, there, below me. Now pass it to Monsieur le Cardinal, and to M. le Duc de Mayenne."

But the Duc de Mayenne had already reached the foot of the steps, and the cardinal was in the other room. The king noticed their absence.

"Then pass it to the master of the hounds," he said.

The duke signed, handed the pen to Monsoreau, and made a motion to go.

"Wait," said the king.

And while Quélus took the pen from the hands of M. de Monsoreau, — and not only all the noblemen present, but all the chiefs of corporations assembled for this great event, signed their names on loose sheets which were to complete the registers used the day before, — the king was saying to the Duc de Guise, —

"Was it not your advice, my cousin, to guard our capital with a good army, composed of all the forces of the League ? The army is formed, and properly formed, since the natural general of the Parisians is the king."

"Certainly, sire," replied the duke, without well knowing what he said.

"But I do not forget," continued the king, "that I have another army to command, and that the command of this army belongs to the greatest general of the kingdom. While I command the League, you, my cousin, must go and command the army."

"And when do I set out ? "

"At once," replied the king.

"Henri, Henri !" said Chicot, who, in obedience to the laws of etiquette, could not run after the king and stop him in the midst of his speech, as he had a great mind to do. But as the king had not heard him, or if he had, not understood him, he advanced respectfully, holding in his hand an enormous pen, and made his way to the king.

"Will you hush, double idiot !" he whispered ; but it was too late. The king had already announced his nomination to the Duc de Guise, and handed him his commission signed in advance, and this in spite of all the Gascon's signs and grimaces.

The Duc de Guise took his brevet and left. The cardinal was waiting for him at the door of the room, and the Duc de Mayenne was waiting for both at the palace gates.

They got into the saddle at once, and ten minutes had not elapsed before they had all three left Paris. The rest

of the assembly gradually withdrew. Some cried " *Vive
le roi!* others cried " *Vive la Ligue!* "

" I have at least solved a great problem," said Henri,
laughing.

" Ah, yes, you are a fine mathematician," said Chicot.

" No doubt," said the king. " By making these rascals
utter two different cries, I succeed in making them cry the
same thing."

" *Sta benè!* " said the queen-mother, pressing her son's
hand.

" You believe that," said the Gascon. " She is furious;
her beloved Guises are nearly crushed by the blow."

" Oh, sire, sire," cried the favorites, crowding around the
king, " what a sublime imagination you have ! "

" They think money will rain on them like manna from
heaven," whispered Chicot to the king.

Henri was escorted in triumph to his apartment, and
amid the throng of courtiers, Chicot played the part of
the slave of antiquity, as he pursued his master with his
lamentations. This persistence on his part in recalling to
the demi-god the fact that he was after all but a man,
struck the king so forcibly that he dismissed every one
and remained alone with Chicot.

"Now," said Henri, turning towards the Gascon, "do
you know that you are never pleased, Maître Chicot, and
that becomes a bore. The devil! I do not ask for complais-
ance, but for common-sense."

"You are right, Henri," said Chicot, "that is what you
need the most."

" At least admit that it was cleverly done."

" That is exactly what I cannot admit."

" Ah, you are jealous. M. le Roi de France ! "

" I ?   Heaven forbid !   I would make a better choice of
subjects."

" *Corbleu!* "

"Oh, what ferocious pride!"

"Come, am I, or not, king of the League?"

"Why, you are, unquestionably. But —"

"But what?"

"But you are no longer King of France."

"And who is King of France?"

"Everybody except you, Henri; to begin with, your brother."

"My brother! Of whom are you speaking?"

"Of M. d'Anjou, *parbleu!*"

"Who is my prisoner."

"Yes, but prisoner though he is, he is anointed, and you are not."

"By whom was he anointed?"

"By the Cardinal de Guise. Really, Henri, I advise you to speak of your police. A king is crowned here in Paris at the Abbey of Sainte-Genevieve, before thirty-three persons and you do not even know it."

"And you know it, perhaps?"

"Certainly, I do."

"And how can you know what I do not?"

"Because M. de Morvilliers manages your police, and I attend to my own."

The king frowned.

"As kings of France, we already have, besides Henri de Valois, François d'Anjou; and then," said Chicot, pretending to search in his mind, "we also have the Duc de Guise."

"The Duc de Guise?"

"The Duc de Guise, Henri le Balafré, Henri de Guise. I repeat: we have also the Duc de Guise."

"A fine king, whom I exile, and send to the army."

"Well, were you not exiled to Poland? Is it not nearer from La Charité to the Louvre, than from Cracow to Paris? Ah, yes, you send him to the army, and this is the clever-

ness of the stroke : you send him to the army, and you put
thirty thousand men under his orders, — *ventre de biche!* and
what an army! A real army, — not like your army of the
League ; no, no, an army of *bourgeois* is good enough for Henri
de Valois, king of the favorites. Henri de Guise must have
an army of soldiers ; and what soldiers! Tried veterans,
loving the smell of powder, and capable of destroying
twenty armies of the League ; so that if, being king in fact,
Henri de Guise should one day wish to become king in
name, he will only have to turn towards the capital, and
say, 'Forward! Let us swallow Paris, Henri de Valois, and
the Louvre at one mouthful!' and the rogues would do it.
I know them."

"You forget one thing in your argument, illustrious
politician," said Henri.

"Ah, that may be, if you mean a fourth king."

"No," said Henri, with supreme disdain, "you forget
that to reign in France when a Valois wears the crown, it
is necessary to look back a little, and to count one's
ancestors. That M. d'Anjou should have such an idea, I
understand. He may lay claim to it; his ancestors are
mine, and the rights would be equal as between us; there
is only a question of primogeniture. But M. de Guise —
Come now, Master Chicot, go and study heraldry, and tell
me if the lilies of France are not better than the merlets of
Lorraine."

"Ah," said Chicot, "that is where you make a mistake."

"Where is the mistake ?"

"Why, M. de Guise is of far better nobility than you
believe."

"Better than mine, perhaps," said Henri, with a smile.

"There is no 'perhaps,' my little Henriquet."

"You are mad, Monsieur Chicot; I say absolutely mad.
Go and learn how to read, my friend."

"Well, Henri, you who already know, and who have no

need to go back to school like me, read this a little." And Chicot drew from his bosom the parchment on which Nicolas David had written the genealogy that we know, — the same which had come back from Avignon, approved by the Pope, and which made Henri de Guise descend from Charlemagne.

Henri turned pale after he had glanced at the parchment, and recognized near the legate's signature, the seal of Saint Peter.

"What do you say to that?" asked Chicot. "The lilies are left a little behind, eh? *Ventre de biche!* the merlets seem ready to fly as high as Cæsar's eagles. Take care, my son!"

"But by what means did you obtain possession of this genealogy?"

"Do I think of such things? It came to me of its own accord."

"But where was it before it came to you?"

"Beneath the bolster of a lawyer."

"And what was the name of this lawyer?"

"Maître Nicolas David."

"Where was he?"

"At Lyons."

"And who went to Lyons to take it from beneath that lawyer's bolster?"

"One of my good friends."

"What does he do?"

"He preaches."

"So he is a monk?"

"Exactly."

"And his name is — "

"Gorenflot."

"What!" cried Henri, "that abominable Leaguer who made an incendiary speech at Sainte-Genevieve's, and who insulted me last night in the streets of Paris?"

" Do you remember the story of Brutus, who pretended to be mad ? "

" Then your friend is a deep politician."

" Have you heard of M. Machiavelli, secretary of the Republic of Florence ? Your grandmother was his pupil."

" Then he took this document from the lawyer ? "

" Yes, by main force."

" From Nicolas David, that assassin ? "

" From Nicolas David, that assassin."

" Is your monk brave ? "

" As brave as Bayard."

" And having done this, he has not yet come to me for his reward ? "

" He has humbly withdrawn to his convent, and asks but the thing, — that it may be forgotten that he ever left it."

" Then he is modest ? "

" As Saint Crepin."

" Chicot, upon my word as a gentleman, your friend shall have the first vacant abbey," said the king.

" Thank you for him, Henri. *Ma foi !* " said Chicot to himself, " here he is between Mayenne and Valois, — between a rope and a reward. Will he be hanged ? Will he be abbot ? He who can tell me must be clever. At all events, if he is still asleep, he must have curious dreams."

CHAPTER X.

ETEOCLES AND POLYNICES.

THIS day of the League ended as noisily and brilliantly as
it had begun. The king's friends rejoiced; the preachers of
the League were preparing to canonize Brother Henri, and
spoke, as had been done for Saint Mauritius, of the warlike
deeds of the Valois who had so distinguished himself in
his youth.

The favorites said, "The lion has at last waked up;" the
Leaguers, "The fox smelt the trap." And as the character
of the French nation is chiefly made up of pride, and as
Frenchmen do not like chiefs of inferior intelligence, the
conspirators themselves rejoiced in having been outwitted
by their king. It is true that the principal ones had placed
themselves beyond reach. The three Lorraine princes had
galloped away from Paris, and their principal agent, M. de
Monsoreau, was about to leave the Louvre and make preparations for departure, in the hope of overtaking the
Duc d'Anjou; but just as he passed the threshold, Chicot
approached him.

The Leaguers had all left the palace, and the Gascon no
longer feared anything for his king.

"Whither are you going in such haste, monsieur?" he
asked.

"To his Highness," laconically replied the count.

"To his Highness?"

"Yes, I am anxious about Monseigneur. We do not live
in a time when princes may set out on a journey without a
good escort."

"Oh, that one is so brave that he is foolhardy," said Chicot.

The master of the hounds looked at the Gascon.

"At all events, if you are anxious about him," said the latter, "I am even more so."

"About whom?"

"His Highness."

"Why?"

"Do you not know what is said?"

"Do they not say he is gone?" asked the count.

"They say he is dead," whispered the Gascon.

"Pshaw!" said Monsoreau, in a tone of surprise which was not free from a certain joy, "you said he was travelling."

"Well, I had been persuaded of the fact, — I am so credulous that I believe all the tales I hear; but now, you see, I have every reason to believe that if he is travelling, it is to the next world, poor prince."

"What gives you these funereal ideas?"

"He entered the Louvre yesterday, did he not?"

"No doubt, since I entered with him."

"Well, no one has seen him come out."

"From the Louvre?"

"No."

"But D'Aurilly?"

"Disappeared."

"But his attendants?"

"Disappeared, disappeared, disappeared."

"Is this a jest, Monsieur Chicot?" asked the master of the hounds.

"Ask."

"Whom?"

"The king."

"His Majesty may not be questioned."

"Pshaw! if you do it the right way."

"Come," said the count, "I cannot remain thus in doubt."

And leaving Chicot, or rather going before him, he went towards the king's room. His Majesty had just left it.

"Where is the king?" asked the master of the hounds, "I must report to him about some orders he gave me."

"With M. le Duc d'Anjou," replied the one to whom he spoke.

"With M. le Duc d'Anjou," said the count to Chicot; "then the prince is not dead."

"Oh," said the Gascon, "I fear his case is not much better."

After this, M. de Monsoreau became thoroughly bewildered; it was certain that M. d'Anjou had never left the Louvre. Certain reports which reached him convinced him of the fact. Now, as he was ignorant of the real causes of the duke's absence, this absence, at such a moment, greatly surprised him.

The king was in fact in M. d'Anjou's room; but as the master of the hounds, notwithstanding the greatness of his desire, could not go there too, he was forced to stand in the corridor and wait for news.

We have already said that in order to be present at the ceremony, the four favorites had left some Swiss guards in their stead; but no sooner was it over than they hastened back, notwithstanding the great *ennui* caused by this occupation, so great was their desire to be disagreeable to the prince, and announce to him the triumph obtained by the king. Schomberg and D'Epernon were in the drawing-room, Quélus and Maugiron in the room with his Highness. François, on his part, was weary of his confinement as well as anxious, and it must be said that the conversation of these gentlemen was not of a nature to amuse him.

"You see," said Quélus from one end of the room to Maugiron at the other, as if the duke were not present, —

"you see, Maugiron, it is only within the last hour that I have been able to appreciate our friend Valois; he is really a great politician."

"Explain yourself," said Maugiron, sprawling on a lounge.

"The king spoke aloud of the conspiracy, therefore he no longer fears it; so long as he did, he kept it quiet."

"That is logic," replied Maugiron.

"If he no longer fears it, he will punish it. You know Valois; he surely shines with a great number of qualities, but his resplendent person is rather obscure when it comes to clemency."

"Agreed."

"Now, if he punish the said conspiracy, there will be a trial; if there be one, we shall enjoy a second performance like the affair of Amboise, and that without moving."

"A fine sight, *morbleu !* "

"Yes, and in which all our places will be marked in advance unless — "

"Unless what ? "

"Unless — which is very possible — they should put aside all judicial formalities on account of the position of the accused, and settle the matter quietly."

"That is my opinion," said Maugiron. "Family affairs are usually settled in this way; and this last conspiracy is a real family affair."

D'Aurilly exchanged an anxious glance with the prince.

"Faith !" said Maugiron, "I know one thing: in the king's place, I would not spare the high heads. Really, these gentlemen are twice as guilty as others when they plot; they think that everything is permissible. I would shorten one or two and drown the small fry. The Seine is deep before Nesle; and, upon my word, in the king's place, I would not resist the temptation."

"In that case," said Quélus, "I do not think it would be safe to revive the famous invention of the sacks."

"What was that?" asked Maugiron.

"A royal fancy, which dates from the year 1350 or there-
abouts: they tied a man in a sack in company with three
or four cats and threw the whole thing into the water.
Cats cannot bear water, and the minute they felt it they
attacked the man; then took place things which, unfortunately, no one was able to see."

"Really," said Maugiron, "you are a mine of information,
Quélus, and your conversation is most interesting."

"This invention could not be applied to the chiefs,
because they always have the right to demand decapitation
on a public square or assassination in some corner. But as
you said, for the small fry, and by small fry I mean the
favorites, squires, butlers, lute-players — "

"Gentlemen!" stammered D'Aurilly, pale with terror.

"Do not answer, D'Aurilly," said François; "this cannot
apply to me or my followers. Princes of the blood are not
a subject for jesting in France."

"No, they are treated more seriously," said Quélus; "they
are beheaded. Louis XI. did not hesitate, witness M. de
Nemours."

The favorites had reached this point of their dialogue
when a noise was heard; the door opened and the king
appeared on the threshold. François rose.

"Sire," he cried, "I appeal to your judgment against the
unworthy treatment I suffer at the hands of your followers."

But Henri seemed to have neither seen nor heard his
brother.

"Good-morning, Quélus," he said, kissing his favorite
on both cheeks. "Good-morning, my child, your very
sight gladdens my soul; and you, my poor Maugiron, how
are you?"

"Bored to death!" said Maugiron. "When I consented to
guard your brother, sire, I thought he would be more
amusing. Fie! the tiresome prince; can he be the son of
your father and mother?"

"Sire, you hear him," said François. "Is it your royal wish that your brother should be insulted?"

"Silence, monsieur," said Henri, without even turning round. "I do not like to hear prisoners complain."

"Prisoner as much as you please, but this prisoner is none the less your —"

"The title which you invoke is fatal to you. A guilty brother is doubly guilty."

"But if he were not?"

"He is."

"Of what crime?"

"Of having incurred my displeasure."

"Sire," said François, humiliated, "do we need witnesses for our family quarrels?"

"You are right, monsieur. Leave me, my friends; I wish to be alone with my brother."

"Sire," whispered Quélus, "it is not prudent for your Majesty to remain with two enemies."

"I shall take away D'Aurilly," whispered Maugiron, on the other side.

The two gentlemen led away D'Aurilly, who was burning with curiosity and at the same time dying with uneasiness.

"We are now alone," said the king.

"I was impatiently awaiting this moment, sire."

"So was I! Ah, you wished to have my crown, worthy Eteocles; you used the League as a means to attain this end. You had yourself quietly anointed in a corner of Paris to show yourself some day to the Parisians, all shining with holy oil."

"Alas!" said François, who felt the king's anger gradually rising, "your Majesty does not allow me to speak."

"What for?" asked Henri, — "to let you lie, or tell me things that I know as well as you do. But no, you would lie, brother; because if you confessed those things that you have done, you would be confessing that you deserve death. You would deserve it. I shall therefore spare you this shame."

"Brother," said François, "is it your intention to over-whelm me with insults?"

"Well, if what I say may be considered an insult, then it is I who speak falsely. Come, speak, I shall listen; let us know that you are not disloyal, and what is worse, a blunderer."

"I do not know what your Majesty means. You speak in riddles."

"Then I will explain my words," cried Henri, in a voice filled with menaces, which rang in François' ears. "You have plotted against me as you formerly plotted against my brother, Charles IX., only what you formerly did with the aid of the King of Navarre, you do now with that of the Duc de Guise. Yours is a fine project, which I admire, and which would have given you a high place in the history of usurpers. It is true that formerly you crawled like a snake, and now you wish to bite like a lion. After perfidy, open force; after the poison, the sword."

"Poison! What do you mean, monsieur?" cried François, pale with anger, and like the Eteocles to whom Henri had compared him, seeking a place where the flash from his eyes could strike his brother, "What poison?"

"The poison with which you assassinated our brother, Charles IX.; the poison which you destined for Henri de Navarre, your associate. That fatal poison is known; our mother has so often made use of it. That may be why you gave it up for me; that is why you wished to play the part of a general in taking the command of the League. But look me in the face, François," continued Henri, taking one step nearer his brother, "and be convinced that a man of my stamp will never be killed by a man like you."

François staggered beneath this terrible attack, but without any consideration of pity for his prisoner Henri resumed, —

"The sword! the sword! I should like to see you in

this room alone with me, and holding a sword. I have already circumvented you in cunning, François, for I too took unfair means to reach the throne of France; but these means were necessary to outwit one million of Poles. If you wish to be wily, be so in this manner; if you wish to imitate me do so, but do not belittle me. Those are royal intrigues, those are stratagems worthy of a general. I therefore repeat it, in stratagem you have been outwitted, and in a loyal combat you would be killed; therefore no longer attempt to struggle either in one way or the other. Henceforth I shall act as king, as master, as despot; I shall watch you in your oscillations, pursue you in the darkness, and at the slightest doubt, at the slightest hesitation, I shall lay my hand on you and throw you to the axe of my executioner. This is what I had to tell you about family affairs, why I wished to speak with you alone, and why I shall order my friends to leave you alone to-night that you may reflect in solitude on my words. If night really brings good counsel, it must most particularly do so to prisoners."

"Therefore," murmured the duke, "for a mere whim, for a suspicion that looks like nightmare, I have fallen into disgrace with your Majesty."

"Better still, François; you have fallen beneath my justice."

"But at least, sire, fix a term to my captivity, that I may know what to expect."

"When you will hear your sentence read, you will know."

"But my mother, — shall I not see my mother?"

"Why so? There are in the world only three copies of the famous hunting-book which my poor brother Charles devoured, — that is the word for it; and of the others, one is in Florence and the other in London. Besides, I am not a Nimrod like my poor brother. Adieu, François."

The prince dropped on his chair.

" Gentlemen," said the king, opening the door, "M. le
Duc d'Anjou has asked my permission to reflect to-night on
the answer he is to give me in the morning. You will
therefore leave him alone in his room, except for occasional
visits of precaution. You may perhaps find your prisoner
a little excited by the conversation we have just had
together. Remember that in conspiring against me M. le
Duc d'Anjou has renounced his title of brother; consequently you see before you only a captive who needs no
ceremonies. If he should give you any trouble, warn me.
I have the Bastille near at hand, and in the Bastille
M. Laurent Testu, the best man in the world for calming
rebellious moods."

" Sire, sire ! " murmured François, making a last effort,
" remember that I am your — "

" You were also the brother of Charles IX., I believe,"
said Henri.

" Let me at least have my attendants, my friends."

" I advise you to complain ! Am I not depriving myself
of mine for your sake ? " and Henri closed the door in the
face of his brother, who staggered to an armchair, on which
he sank.

CHAPTER XI.

HOW ONE DOES NOT ALWAYS LOSE TIME IN SEACHING IN EMPTY CUPBOARDS.

THE scene which the Duc d'Anjou had just had with the king, led him to consider his position as desperate. The favorites had not left him in ignorance of all the events which had taken place at the Louvre; they had showed him the defeat of MM. de Guise and Henri's triumph greater than they really were. He had heard the voice of the people crying a thing which seemed at first utterly incomprehensible to him, — *vive le roi!* and *vive la Ligue!* He had felt abandoned by the principal chiefs, who also found it necessary to save themselves.

Abandoned by his family, which had been reduced by poisonings and assassinations, divided by rancor and discords, he sighed as he looked back on this past which the king's words had recalled to him, and he thought that in his struggle against Charles IX. he had for confidants, or rather for dupes, those two devoted swords, those two flaming swords called Coconnas and La Mole.

The regret of certain lost advantanges is the remorse of many souls. For the first time in his life, when he felt lonely and isolated, M. d'Anjou felt a sort of remorse for having sacrificed La Mole and Coconnas. In those days his sister Marguerite loved him and consoled him. How had he rewarded her? There was his mother, Queen Catherine; but she had never loved him, She had only used him as a tool, as he made use of others, and François did himself justice.

Once in the hands of his mother, he felt that he was no more his own master than the ship in mid-ocean when a storm is raging.

He remembered that even recently he had had at his side a sword well worth all the others; and Bussy, the brave Bussy, returned to his memory.

Ah, this time François' feelings resembled remorse because he had offended him to please Monsoreau; he had wished to please Monsoreau because the count knew his secret, and all at once this dangerous secret reached the ears of the king so that Monsoreau was no longer to be feared. He had therefore uselessly quarrelled with Bussy, which, according to a great politician, was worse than a crime, — it was a fault.

Now, what an advantage it would have been for the prince to know that Bussy, grateful and consequently faithful, was watching over him, — Bussy, the invincible, the loyal hearted, the favorite of all; Bussy watching over him meant probable liberty and sure vengeance.

But as we have said, Bussy, wounded to the heart, sulked, and had retired to his tent, so that the prince remained with fifty feet of wall on the one side, and four favorites guarding the corridor on the other, without counting the courts filled with Swiss and soldiers.

From time to time, he returned to the window and measured the distance to the ground; but such a height would have made the bravest man hesitate, and M. d'Anjou was far from being proof against vertigo.

Besides this, every hour one of the prince's guardians, either Schomberg or Maugiron, D'Epernon or Quélus, entered, and without concerning himself about the duke's presence, sometimes without even saluting him, went the rounds, opening the doors and windows, inspecting the drawers and chests, looking under the beds and tables, even ascertaining that the curtains were in their places and that the sheets were not cut into strips.

From time to time, they leaned out and looked down; and the height of forty-five feet reassured them.

"Faith!" said Maugiron, as he returned from his inspection, "I give it up; I beg leave to remain in this room, where our friends can see us during the day, and not to wake up every four hours to pay a visit to M. le Duc d'Anjou."

"Of course," said D'Epernon, "we behave like children. It is easy to see that all our lives we have been officers and never soldiers; we really do not know how to obey an order."

"How so?" asked Quélus.

"Why, what does the king wish, that we should guard the duke but not look at him?"

"All the more," said Maugiron, "that he is good to guard but not good to look at."

"Very good," said Schomberg; "but we must not think of relaxing our discipline, because the devil is wily."

"True," said D'Epernon, "but it is not sufficient to be wily to pass over the bodies of four men like us."

And D'Epernon drew himself up as he twirled his moustache.

"He is right," said Quélus.

"Well," said Schomberg, "do you believe M. le Duc d'Anjou to be such a fool as to try to escape precisely through our gallery? If he wishes to escape, he will make a hole in the wall."

"With what? He has no weapons."

"He has the windows," timidly said Schomberg, who remembered that he himself had measured the distance.

"Ah, the windows! Upon my word, that is charming!" cried D'Epernon. "Bravo, Schomberg! The windows! that means that you would jump down forty-five feet?"

"I confess that forty-five feet — "

"Well, he who is lame, heavy, cowardly as — "

"You," said Schomberg.

"My dear fellow," said D'Epernon, "you know that I am only afraid of phantoms; that is a question of nerves."

"That is because all those he has killed in duel appeared to him one night," gravely said Quélus.

"Let us not laugh," said Maugiron. "I have heard of a number of miraculous escapes, — with sheets, for instance."

"Ah, as for that, Maugiron's remark is most sensible," said D'Epernon. "I saw at Bordeaux a prisoner who had escaped with the sheets."

"You see!" said Schomberg.

"Yes," resumed D'Epernon, "but his back was broken and his head open; his sheet had happened to be thirty feet too short. He had been obliged to jump, so the evasion was complete, — his body had escaped from prison, and his soul had escaped from his body."

"Well, besides, if he should escape," said Quélus, "that will give us an opportunity to hunt him. We shall pursue him, track him; and as we do so, we shall try to break something of his, quite accidentally."

"Well, *mordieu!* we shall resume our true characters," cried Maugiron, "we are hunters, not jailers."

This decision seemed final, and they talked of something else, though they concluded that from hour to hour they would continue to visit the Duc d'Anjou.

The favorites were perfectly right in their supposition that the Duc d'Anjou would never attempt to make his escape by force, while, on the other hand, he would never attempt anything difficult or perilous. Not that the worthy prince lacked imagination; and we must say that his imagination was given up to a furious work, as he paced the distance from his bed to the famous closet occupied during three nights by La Mole when Marguerite had sheltered him on the night of Saint-Bartholomew.

From time to time the prince's pale face was seen near the window overlooking the ditch of the Louvre. Beyond the ditch was an open space about fifteen feet broad, and then rolled the Seine, gleaming in the darkness and smooth as a mirror. On the other side, a giant rose, immovable in the shadow; it was the Tour de Nesle.

The Duc d'Anjou, with the true interest of the prisoner, had observed the sunset in all its phases; he had followed the decline of light and the increase of darkness. He had contemplated the beautiful sight of old Paris, whose roofs were, within the space of one hour, gilded by the last rays of the sun, and silvered by the first beams of the moon; then he was gradually seized with a great terror at seeing immense clouds roll over the sky, heralding a storm for that night. Among other weaknesses, the Duc d'Anjou was afraid of thunder, and he would have given a great deal to have his guardians in the room with him, even if they did insult him. Yet he could not call them; that would have showed his weakness too plainly.

He tried to throw himself on his bed, but found it impossible to sleep; he tried to read, but the letters danced before his eyes like black devils; he drank, but the wine had a bitter taste; he touched with his fingers D'Aurilly's lute, suspended to the wall, but he felt that the vibrations of the chords affected his nerves in such a way that he was tempted to weep.

Then he began to swear like a trooper, and break everything he could lay his hands on.

This was a little family failing to which the inhabitants of the Louvre were accustomed. The favorites opened the door to see the meaning of the noise; then having ascertained that the prince was only amusing himself, they had closed the door, which had increased the prisoner's anger.

He had just broken a chair, when an unmistakable

sound, a crashing noise near the window was heard, and at the same moment he felt a rather sharp blow on his thigh. His first idea was that he had been wounded by a musket-shot, fired by one of the king's emissaries.

"Ah, traitor! ah, coward!" cried the prisoner, "you are having me shot, as you promised. Ah, I am dead!" and he fell on the carpet. But as he fell, his hand came in contact with a hard, uneven object, much larger than a bullet.

"Oh, a stone!" he said. "It must be a falconet, but I heard no explosion;" at the same time he extended his leg, and though he felt a pain, there was nothing broken. He picked up the stone, and examined the window-pane. The missile had been thrown with such force that it had made a hole without shivering the glass. It was wrapped up in a piece of paper.

Then the duke's ideas began to change. Might not this stone come from a friend as well as an enemy?

A cold perspiration gathered on his brow; hope, as well as terror, has its anguish.

The duke went to the light. Around the stone was a piece of paper, carefully tied with silk. The paper had naturally softened the shock of the hard substance, which would otherwise have caused the prince even greater pain.

Breaking the silk, unrolling the paper, and reading it was the affair of a second; he was completely revived.

"A letter!" he murmured, glancing around, and he read:

Are you weary of confinement? Do you like fresh air and liberty? Enter the closet where the Queen of Navarre hid your poor friend M. de la Mole, open the cupboard, and if you raise the lower shelf, you will find a double bottom; in this double bottom there is a rope ladder. Fasten it yourself to your balcony, and two strong arms will hold it from below. A horse, swift as thought, will carry you to a place of safety.

A FRIEND.

"A friend!" cried the prince, "a friend! Oh, I did not know I had a friend. Who is this friend who thinks of me?"

And the duke reflected for a moment. Not knowing on whom to place his suspicions, he ran to the window, but he saw no one.

"Can it be a snare?" murmured the prince, in whom fear was always the first feeling aroused. "But first," he added, "I must ascertain if the cupboard has a double bottom, and if there is a ladder"

The duke, without changing the position of the light, resolved to trust to the testimony of his hands, went towards the closet, the door of which he had so often opened with a beating heart when he expected to find there the Queen of Navarre, radiant with that beauty which François appreciated more than was befitting in a brother.

This time the duke's heart was beating violently. He groped his way to the cupboard, explored all the shelves, and having reached the lower one, after having weighed on the front and back, he pressed on one of the sides, and felt the board give way. He immediately put his hand in the cavity and felt the contact of the silk ladder.

Like a robber carrying off prey, the duke fled to his room with his treasure. Ten o'clock struck, and the duke immediately remembered that the inspection of his jailers took place every hour; he therefore hid the ladder beneath the cushion of a chair, and sat on it. It was so artistically woven that it held perfectly in the narrow space where the prince had placed it. In fact, five minutes had not elapsed before Maugiron appeared in his dressing-gown, holding a drawn sword under his left arm and a candle-stick in his right hand. As he entered the duke's room, he continued conversing with his friends outside.

"The bear is furious," said a voice. "He was breaking everything a moment ago; take care he does not eat you up, Maugiron."

"Insolent!" murmured the duke.

"I believe your Highness did me the honor to speak to me," said Maugiron, with his most impertinent manner.

The duke was about to retort, when he reflected that a quarrel would bring about a loss of time, and might perhaps make him lose his chance of escape. He swallowed his anger, and turned his chair around so as to present his back to the young man.

Maugiron, following the established custom, approached the bed to examine the sheets, and the windows to ascertain the presence of the curtains. He saw a broken pane, but he thought the duke himself had smashed it in his anger.

"Oh, Maugiron," cried Schomberg, "are you eaten up that you do not utter a sound? In that case breathe just a sigh, that I may know I should avenge you."

The duke was impatiently cracking his fingers.

"Not at all," said Maugiron; "on the contrary, my bear is very gentle and quite tame."

The duke smiled to himself in the shadow. As for Maugiron, without even saluting the prince, which was the least he might do for one of such lofty birth, he went out, and as he did so locked the door. The prince let him do it, and when the key had ceased to turn, —

"Gentlemen," he murmured, "take care! a bear is a very cunning animal."

CHAPTER XII.

VENTRE SAINT-GRIS!

LEFT alone, the Duc d'Anjou, knowing that he had at least an hour before him, drew out his ladder, unrolled it, and examined every knot most carefully.

"The ladder is good," he said; "and so far as that goes, it is not offered to me as a means to break my bones."

Then he unrolled it all, and counted thirty-eight rounds, fifteen inches apart.

"Well, the length is sufficient," he thought; "there is nothing to fear on that score." He paused for a moment.

"Ah, I know now!" he said. "Those cursed favorites have sent me this ladder. I shall tie it to the balcony, and while I go down they will come and cut the strings. That is the snare."

Then he thought again.

"No, this is not possible. They are not foolish enough to believe that I will go down without barricading the door; and that being done, they will calculate that I would have time to escape before they break it open. I shall do that," he said, as he looked around; "I shall certainly do that if I make up my mind to flee. Yet how can I believe in the innocence of this ladder found in my sister Marguerite's closet? Who in the world, besides the Queen of Navarre, can know of the existence of this ladder? Come," he repeated, "who is the friend? The note is signed, 'A friend.' Who is this friend who knows so well the contents of the wardrobes in my apartment or that of my sister?"

The duke had hardly concluded this argument, which seemed final, and was reading over the note to recognize

if possible the handwriting, when a sudden idea flashed
through his mind.

"Bussy!" he cried. Bussy, whom so many women
loved; who seemed a hero to the Queen of Navarre to
such a point that in her Memoirs she confesses of having
screamed with terror every time he fought a duel; Bussy,
discreet, versed in the science of the closets, and in all
probability the only one of his friends on whom he could
rely, — was it not Bussy who had sent the note ? Here the
duke's perplexity increased. Everything combined to make
him believe that the note came from Bussy. The duke did
not know all Bussy's reasons for being angry with him, as
he was ignorant of his love for Diane de Méridor. It is true
that he suspected it a little. As he himself had loved
Diane, he could understand how difficult it was for Bussy
to see that beautiful young woman without loving her;
but this slight suspicion vanished before the probabilities.
Bussy's loyalty would not have allowed him to remain idle
while his master was chained up; he had been attracted by
the adventurous spirit of this expedition. He had wished
to revenge himself on the duke by restoring him to freedom. He had no more doubts; it was Bussy who had
written and who was waiting for him.

The prince again approached the window. He saw
through the mist that rose from the river three oblong
shadows which must be the horses, and two sorts of posts
standing on the bank; these must be two men. Two men,
that was right, — Bussy and his faithful Le Haudoin.

"The temptation is strong," said the duke; "and if it is
a snare, it is too clever for me to suspect it."

François then looked through the keyhole and saw his
four guardians. Two were asleep, and the other two had
inherited Chicot's chessboard and were playing a game.
He extinguished his light. Then he opened his window
and leaned out from his balcony. The abyss, as he meas-

ured it with his glance, seemed more terrible in the darkness. He drew back, but air and space have such an irresistible attraction for a prisoner that François fancied he was being stifled when he re-entered his room. This feeling was so strong that something like disgust of life and indifference to death flashed through his mind.

The prince was astonished, and imagined that courage had returned to him; so, taking advantage of this moment of exaltation, he seized the ladder and fastened it to the balcony by the iron hooks which were on one end; then he returned to the door, which he barricaded the best way he could, persuaded that to upset the obstacles he had placed they would be forced to lose ten minutes, — that is to say, more time than he would need to reach the end of his ladder. After this he went back to the window.

He tried to see the men and horses, but nothing was in sight.

"I would like that even better," he murmured. "To flee alone is better than to flee with one's best friend, — particularly with an unknown friend."

At this moment the darkness was complete, and the first sounds of the approaching storm could now be heard; a great cloud, fringed with silver, extended like a recumbent elephant from one side to the other of the river, its body leaning against the palace, its trunk extending indefinitely beyond the Tour de Nesle.

A flash of lightning illumined for one instant the immense cloud, and the prince fancied he saw in the ditch below those whom he sought on the bank. A horse neighed: there was no more doubt; he was expected. The duke shook the ladder to see that it was firmly fastened; then he stepped over the balcony and placed his foot on the first rung. Nothing could render the terrible anguish of the prisoner placed between a fragile silk cord and the deadly threats of his brother.

But scarcely had he placed his foot on the first wooden
rung when it seemed that the ladder, instead of shaking as
he might have expected, stiffened, and the second rung
found itself under his foot without performing that movement of rotation which would have been very natural in
this case.

Was it a friend or an enemy who held the bottom of
the ladder? Would he be received below with open arms or
with weapons? François was seized with an irresistible
terror; he still held the balcony with his left hand and
made a motion to return. One might have thought that the
unseen person who awaited the prince at the foot of the
wall could guess all that was taking place in his heart,
because at that moment a little undulation, very gentle and
even, a sort of solicitation of the cord, came up to his foot.

"They are holding the ladder from below," he said; "they
do not wish me to fall. Come, a little courage," and he
continued his descent. The two sides of the ladder were as
stiff as poles. François observed that they carefully
pulled the ladder from the wall to facilitate his descent.

He therefore dropped down like an arrow, sacrificing in
his rapid descent the lining of his cloak. All at once,
instead of touching the ground, which he instinctively felt
to be near his feet, he was caught in the arms of a man
who whispered into his ear these three words, —

"You are saved."

He was then carried to the edge of the ditch, and pushed
up a narrow path; he finally reached the top of the bank.
On the bank was a second man, who seized him by the
collar and drew him up; then, assisting his companion in
the same manner, he ran, bent like an old man, to the river
brink. The horses were where François had first spied
them. The prince understood that he could no longer
hesitate; he was at the mercy of his saviors.

He ran to one of the three horses and jumped on it,

while his companions did the same. The same voice that had already been heard whispered again, "Quick!" and they set off at a gallop.

"All goes well," thought the prince to himself; "let us hope that the end of the adventure will not differ from the beginning."

"Thank you, thank you, my brave Bussy," murmured the prince to his right hand neighbor, wrapped to his eyes in a large brown cloak.

"Ride on!" replied the latter, from the depths of his cloak; and the three horses and their riders passed on like phantoms. In this manner they reached the great moat of the Bastille, which they crossed on a bridge, improvised the day before by the Leaguers, who, not wishing to cut off communications with their friends, had found this means of facilitating all intercourse. The three horsemen rode on towards Charenton. The prince's horse seemed to have wings.

All at once the man on the right jumped the ditch and rode into the forest of Vincennes saying to the prince:

"Come!"

The man on the left did the same, but without speaking. Since the moment of departure, not a word had he uttered. He had not even any need to urge his horse; the noble animal cleared the ditch at one bound, and as he neighed, several other horses replied.

The duke wished to check his horse, as he feared some ambuscade, but it was too late. The animal was started at such a pace that he no longer felt the bit. However, his two companions slackened their speed, and he did the same, finding himself in an open space in which were eight or ten men whose weapons glittered in the moon.

"Oh, oh," said François, "what does this mean, monsieur?"

"*Ventre saint-gris!*" cried the one to whom the question was put, "this means that we are safe."

"You Henri!" cried the Duc d'Anjou, in amazement.
"You my liberator?"

"Eh," said the Béarnais, "does that surprise you? Are
we not allies?" Then glancing around in search of
his second companion, "Agrippa, where the devil are
you?"

"Here I am," said D'Aubigné, who had not yet opened
his lips; "but how you treat your horses, — as if you had
so many."

"Come, come," said the King of Navarre, "do not scold.
Provided we have two on which we may travel twelve
leagues, it is all I need."

"But where are you taking me, cousin?" asked François,
uneasily.

"Wherever you like," said Henri, "but let us go quickly.
D'Aubigné is right, the King of France has better stables
than I; and he is rich enough to kill twenty horses if he
takes it into his head to pursue us."

"Am I really free to go where I wish?" asked
François.

"Certainly, and I await your orders," said Henri.

"Very well, then, to Angers."

"You wish to go to Angers? Very well; you are at
home there."

"But you, cousin?"

"I shall leave you within sight of Angers and hasten on
to Navarre, where my good Margot expects me; she must
be very lonesome without me."

"But did no one know you were here?" asked the duke.

"I came to sell three of my wife's diamonds."

"Ah, very well!"

"And also to know if the League would really ruin me."

"You see it will not."

"Yes, thanks to you."

"How, thanks to me?"

HENRY IV.

" Oh, yes, no doubt, if instead of refusing to be chief of
the League when you heard it was directed against me,
you had accepted and joined my enemies, I was lost. So
when I heard that the king had punished your refusal with
imprisonment, I swore to free you ; and I did."

" Always so simple," said the Duc d'Anjou to himself,
" really, it is a sin to deceive him."

" Go, my cousin," said the Béarnais, with a smile, "go to
Anjou. Ah, M. de Guise, you think you have it all your
way, but I send you a rather troublesome companion : take
care ! "

And fresh horses being brought, both jumped into the
saddle accompanied by Agrippa d'Aubigné, who followed
them growling.

CHAPTER XIII.

THE FRIENDS.

WHILE Paris was in a ferment, Madame de Monsoreau, accompanied by her father and two of those servants who, in those days, could be recruited like auxiliary troops for an expedition, was journeying towards the Château de Méridor by stages of ten leagues a day.

She too was beginning to enjoy that liberty so precious to those who have suffered. The azure of the sky, compared to that sky always suspended like a pall over the black towers of the Bastille, the green foliage, the beautiful roads winding like undulating ribbons in the depths of the woods, — all this seemed fresh and young, rich and new, as if she had really left the grave in which her father believed she lay buried.

The old baron had grown twenty years younger. Any one seeing him erect in his saddle, spurring old Jarnac, might have mistaken the noble lord for an old husband, lovingly watching over his bride.

We shall not undertake to describe this long journey, free from all incidents save the rising and setting of the sun.

Diane would sometimes impatiently rise from her bed when the moon shone through the windows of her room in some wayside inn, wake up the baron and the attendants and ride on a few leagues to hasten the end of this interminable journey.

At other times she would let Jarnac pass on, remaining on the top of a hill to see if any one followed; but she saw only the valley, deserted save for a few scattered flocks, or the solitary steeple of some village church. Then her father would look at her and say, —

"Fear nothing, Diane."

"What should I fear?"

"Were you not looking to see if M. de Monsoreau was following us?"

"Ah, true! Yes, I was thinking of that," said the young woman, with another look behind. Thus going from fear to hope and from hope to deception, Diane, about the end of the eighth day, reached the Château de Méridor, and was received at the draw-bridge by Madame de Saint-Luc and her husband, who had remained there during the absence of the baron.

Then began for these four people an existence such as has been dreamed by every man who has read Virgil and Theocritus. The baron and Saint-Luc hunted from morning till night. The hounds rushed up and down the hills in pursuit of a fox or a hare, and when this furious cavalcade thundered through the woods, Diane and Jeanne, seated side by side on the moss in some wooded nook, were startled for a moment, and soon resumed their tender and mysterious conversation.

"Tell me," said Jeanne, — "tell me all that happened in your grave, — for you were really dead to us. See, the hawthorn is shedding on us its last snowy blossoms, and the elders send us their sweet perfume. The soft sunlight falls between the great branches of the oaks. Not a breath of air, not a living being in the park, for the deer and foxes fled away at the sound of the hounds. Tell me, little sister, tell me."

"What shall I tell you?"

"Are you happy? Oh, those beautiful eyes, encircled by blue shadows, the pallor of your cheeks, your lips that vainly attempt to smile, — Diane, you must have a great deal to tell me."

"No, nothing."

"You are, then, happy — with M. de Monsoreau ? "

Diane shuddered.

"You see!" said Jeanne, with a tender reproach.

"With M. de Monsoreau!" repeated Diane. "Why did you utter that name? Why do you evoke that phantom amid our woods, our flowers, our happiness?"

"Well, I know now why your beautiful eyes are encircled with blue, and why they are so often raised towards heaven; but I do not yet know why your mouth tries to smile."

Diane sadly shook her head.

"You told me, I think," continued Jeanne, placing her plump white arm around Diane's neck, "that M. de Bussy had showed much interest in you."

Diane blushed so violently that even her delicate, shell-like ear seemed suddenly aflame.

"M. de Bussy is a charming man," said Jeanne, and she sang, —

> "Un beau chercheur de noise,
> C'est le Seigneur d'Amboise."

Diane rested her head on her friend's shoulder and murmured in a voice sweeter than the song of the birds:

> "Tendre et fidèle aussi,
> C'est le brave —"

"Bussy! — say it," said Jeanne, warmly kissing her friend.

"Enough nonsense," suddenly said Diane; "M. de Bussy no longer thinks of Diane de Méridor."

"That is possible," said Jeanne, "but I believe Diane de Monsoreau likes him."

"Do not say that."

"Why? Does it displease you?"

Diane did not reply to the question.

"I tell you that M. de Bussy does not think of me; and

he is right. Oh, I have been a coward," murmured the
young woman.

" What are you saying ? "

" Oh, nothing, nothing ! "

" Come, Diane, do not begin to weep and accuse yourself.
You, a coward, — you, my heroine ? No, you were forced."

" I thought so. I saw dangers, precipices, before me.
Now, Jeanne, these dangers seem mere fancies; these
precipices, a child could have crossed them. I was a
coward, I tell you. Oh, why did I not have time to
reflect ! "

" You speak in riddles."

" No, it is not yet that," cried Diane, rising in agitation.
" No, it is not my fault; he did not wish it; I recall the
situation, which seemed terrible to me; I hesitated, I
doubted. My father offered me his support, and I was
frightened. He, — *he* offered me his protection, but not in a
way to convince me. The Duc d'Anjou was against him.
You will say that the Duc d'Anjou was in league with Monsoreau. If I wanted something, — if I loved some one, —
neither prince nor master could resist me. You see, Jeanne,
if ever I loved — "

And Diane, a prey to excitement, leaned against an oak,
as if her soul had exhausted her body, which no longer had
the strength to stand alone.

" Calm yourself, dearest, and reason."

" I tell you that we have been cowards."

" We ? Oh, Diane, of whom are you speaking ? This *we*
is eloquent, my dearest Diane — "

" I mean my father and me. I hope you did not understand anything else. My father is a gentleman, and could
appeal to the king. I am proud, and do not fear a man
when I hate him. But here is the secret of this cowardice.
I understood that *he* did not love me."

" You are deceiving yourself," cried Jeanne. " If you

believed that, in your present state, you would go and reproach him yourself; but you do not believe that, and you know the contrary, you hypocrite," she added, with a tender caress.

"You may well believe in love," said Diane, as she resumed her place beside her friend, — "you, whom M. de Saint-Luc married in spite of the king; you, whom he carried away from Paris ; you, who repay him for proscription and exile with your caresses."

"And he thinks himself richly paid."

"But I (reflect a little, and do not be egotistical) — I, whom that fiery young man pretended to love, I who have fascinated the invincible Bussy, that man who knows no obstacles, well, I was publicly married. I appeared before the whole court, and he did not even look at me. I trusted myself to him in the cloister of La Gypecienne. We were alone ; he had Gertrude and Rémy, his two accomplices, and myself, — an even more willing one. Oh, when I think of it ! He could have carried me off through the church, under his cloak ! At this moment I saw him ill and suffering on account of me. I saw his languishing eyes, and his lips pale and parched with fever. If he had asked me to die to restore the light to his eyes, and the freshness to his lips, I would have died. Well, I went away, and he did not even attempt to hold me by a corner of my veil. Wait, wait ! Oh, you do not know how much I suffer ! He knew that I was leaving Paris to return to Méridor. He knew that M. de Monsoreau, — well, I blush to say it, — that M. de Monsoreau was not my husband. He knew that I was coming alone ; and all along the way, dear Jeanne, I kept turning, thinking every moment that I heard the gallop of his horse behind us. It was only the echo of the road. I tell you he is not thinking of me, and that I am not worth a journey to Anjou, when there are at court so many beautiful women, whose smiles

are worth a hundred avowals of the provincial buried at
Méridor. Do you understand now ? Are you convinced
that I am right ? Am I not forgotten and despised ? "

She had not finished these words when the branches of
the oak cracked violently; a cloud of dust and plaster came
down from the old wall, and a man bounding from the
ivy and wild berries fell at Diane's feet, who uttered a
terrible cry. Jeanne drew back as she saw and recognized
this man.

"You see I am here," murmured Bussy, kneeling and
respectfully kissing the hem of Diane's dress which he held
in his trembling hands. Diane also recognized the count's
voice and smile, and overcome by this unexpected happiness she opened her arms and fell unconscious on the
breast of him whom she had just accused of indifference.

CHAPTER XIV.

THE LOVERS.

SWOONS of joy are neither long nor dangerous. Some have been dangerous, but the examples are very rare. Diane was not long in opening her eyes and finding herself in Bussy's arms, for he had not wished to allow Madame de Saint-Luc the privilege of receiving Diane's first glance.

"Oh, count, it was horrible to surprise us so," she murmured.

Bussy expected other words, and, who knows (men are so exacting), — who knows if he did not expect something more than words, he who had so often witnessed returns to life after swoons ?

Not only did Diane stop there, but she even gently withdrew from the arms of him who held her captive, and returned to her friend, who had discreetly walked a few steps away, then curious like all women of that charming spectacle offered by a reconciliation, she had softly returned, not to take part in the conversation, but to be near enough not to lose anything.

"Well, madame," said Bussy, "is this the way you receive me ? "

"No," said Diane ; "really, Monsieur de Bussy, what you have done is tender and affectionate, but —"

"Oh, no 'but' " sighed Bussy, as he resumed his place at Diane's feet.

"No, no, not so on your knees, Monsieur de Bussy ! "

"Oh, let me pray to you thus for an instant," said the count, clasping his hands, "I have so longed for this place."

"Yes, but to come and take it, you have climbed over the wall. That is not only improper for a man of your rank, but very imprudent on the part of one who cares for my honor."

"How so?"

"If any one had seen you!"

"Who could have seen me?"

"Our hunters, who passed behind the wall not fifteen minutes ago."

"Oh, rest assured, madame, that I take too many precautions for that!"

"Precautions! Oh, really," said Jeanne, "that is most romantic! Tell us about it, Monsieur de Bussy."

"To begin with, if I did not overtake you on the way, it was not my fault. You travelled by one road and I by another; you came through Rambouillet and I through Chartres. Then listen and judge if your poor Bussy be not in love. I did not dare join you, and yet I could have done it. I felt that Jarnac was not in love, and that the worthy animal would not return in such haste to Méridor; neither did your father have any reason to hurry, since he had you with him. But I did not wish to see you in the presence of your father and the servants, for my greatest wish is not to compromise you. I travelled slowly, devouring the handle of my whip, which was my greatest nourishment during those days."

"Poor fellow!" said Jeanne. "See how thin he is!"

"You finally arrived," continued Bussy. "I had taken lodgings in the suburbs of the city, and concealed behind the window, I saw you pass."

"Oh, *mon Dieu!*" said Diane, "are you in Angers under your own name?"

"For whom do you take me?" replied Bussy, with a smile. "No, I am a travelling merchant. See my cinnamon-colored doublet. That is a very popular color with drapers and goldsmiths. And then I have a certain anxious and uneasy look which is common to botanists. In short, I have not been noticed."

"Bussy, the handsome Bussy, has been two days in a provincial town, and has not yet been noticed! No one would ever believe that at court."

"Continue, count," said Diane, with a blush. "How do you come here from the town ?"

"I have two horses of choice stock. I ride out of the town on one, stopping to look at all the signs ; and no sooner am I out of sight than my horse takes a gallop which brings me three and a half leagues in twenty minutes. Once in the woods of Méridor, I ride until I find the park wall, which is very long, as the park is large. Yesterday I explored this wall for four hours, climbing here and there, in the hope of catching a glimpse of you. I had almost despaired of success, when, towards evening, I saw you, just as you were returning to the house. The baron's two great dogs capered around you, and Madame de Saint-Luc was holding up in the air a partridge which they tried to catch. You then disappeared; I jumped the wall and ran here. I saw that the grass had been crushed, and concluded that you had adopted this spot, which is charming during the heat of the day. To be able to find my way back, I broke off some branches; then sighing, which hurts me dreadfully —"

"From want of habit," interrupted Jeanne, with a smile.

"I do not deny it, madame. Well, then, sighing, I resumed the way to the city. I was very tired; I had, moreover, torn my cinnamon-colored doublet as I climbed the trees ; and yet, in spite of the holes in my clothes and my weariness, my heart was filled with joy. I had seen you."

"This is an admirable story," said Jeanne, " and you have overcome many obstacles; that is fine and heroic, but in your place, I would have preserved my doublet, and above all, taken care of my white hands. Look at yours, all scratched by the briers."

"Yes, but I would not have seen the one I came to see."

"On the contrary, I would have seen Diane de Méridor and even Madame de Saint-Luc much better than you did."

"What would you have done?" hastily asked Bussy.

"I would have gone straight to the Château de Méridor. M. le Baron would have pressed me in his arms, Madame de Monsoreau would have placed me beside her at table, M. de Saint-Luc would have welcomed me with joy, and Madame de Saint-Luc would have jested with me. It was the simplest thing in the world; it is true that lovers never think of easy methods."

Bussy shook his head, with a smile and a glance at Diane.

"Oh, no," he said, "your plan would have been suitable for any one else, but not for me."

Diane blushed like a child, and the same smile and glance were reflected in her eyes and on her lips.

"Good!" said Jeanne, "it seems I understand nothing about good manners."

"No," said Bussy, shaking his head, "no, I could not go to the *château*. Madame is married, and the baron owes to his daughter's husband, whoever he may be, a strict vigilance."

"Well," said Jeanne, "this is a lesson for me. Thank you, Monsieur de Bussy, I deserved it; that will teach me how to interfere with the affairs of madmen."

"Of madmen?" repeated Diane.

"Of madmen or lovers," replied Madame de Saint-Luc, "therefore —" she kissed Diane on the forehead, bowed to Bussy, and ran away. Diane tried to stop her, but Bussy seized both her hands so she had to let her friend go. Diane and Bussy remained alone.

The young woman watched Madame de Saint-Luc as she walked away, then she sat down with a blush. Bussy lay down at her feet and said, —

"Was I not right, madame, and do you not approve me?"

"I do not wish to feign," replied Diane, "and besides, you know the truth. Yes, I approve, but here my indulgence must stop. In wishing for you, in calling you as I did just now, I was mad, I was guilty."

"What are you saying, Diane?"

"Alas! count, I speak the truth. I have the right to make M. de Monsoreau unhappy, for he has driven me to this extremity; but I have this right in abstaining from making another happy. I can refuse him my presence, my smiles, my love; but if I give these favors to another, I would be robbing the one who is, after all, my master."

Bussy patiently listened to this moral lecture, which was greatly softened, it is true, by Diane's grace and gentleness.

"Is it now my turn to speak?" he asked.

"Speak," replied Diane.

"Frankly?"

"Yes."

"Well, of all that you have just said, madame, you do not find one word in your heart."

"What do you mean?"

"Listen to me patiently, as I listened to you. You have overwhelmed me with sophisms."

Diane made a movement.

"The commonplaces of morality do not apply here," continued Bussy. "In exchange for sophisms, madame, I shall give you truth. You say this man is your master, but did you choose him? No; fatality imposed him on you, and you submitted. Now, do you mean to suffer all your life the consequences of this odious constraint? Then I must deliver you."

Diane opened her mouth to speak, but Bussy stopped her with a gesture.

"Oh, I know what you will say," continued the young man. "You will say that if I challenge M. de Monsoreau and kill him, that you will never see me again. Well, I may die of grief at this separation, but you will live free and happy; you may give happiness to some gallant man who, in his joy, will sometimes bless my name and say, 'Thanks, Bussy, thanks for having delivered us from that terrible Monsoreau.' And you yourself, Diane, who will not dare to thank me while I live, you will thank me when I am dead."

Diane seized the count's hand and pressed it tenderly.

"You have not yet implored," she said, "and you already threaten."

"Threaten you? Oh, God hears me, and he knows my intentions. I love you so ardently, Diane, that I do not act as another man would. I know that you love me. Do not deny it and class yourself with those vulgar hearts whose words are in contradiction to their actions. I know it, because you have confessed it. Then a love like mine radiates like the sun and vivifies all the hearts that it touches. I will not beg you, nor consume myself with despair. No, here at your feet I shall tell you, with my right hand on my heart, — on that heart which has never lied, either from interest or from fear, — Diane, I love you for my whole life! I swear before Heaven that I shall die for you, that I shall die loving you! If you say to me, 'Go; do not rob another of his happiness!' I will rise from this place where I am so happy, and bow to you as I say to myself, 'This woman does not love me; she never will love me.' Then I shall go, and you will never see me again. But as my devotion to you is even greater than my love, as my desire to see you happy will survive the certainty that I cannot be happy myself, as I did not rob another of his happiness, I will have the right to take his life if I sacrifice my own. This is what I shall do, madame, to

save you from eternal slavery and deprive you of a pretext
for rendering miserable any brave man who may love you."

Bussy was greatly moved as he uttered these words.
Diane read in his brilliant and loyal glance all the vigor
of his resolution. She understood that he would do as he
said, that his words would turn into actions; and like the
April snow which melts in the sun, her resistance melted
away beneath the fire of his glance.

"Well," she said, "I thank you for the violence you do
me. It is still a delicacy on your part to take from me
even the remorse of having yielded to you. Now, will you
really love me even unto death as you say? Shall I not
be the toy of your fancy, and shall I not have some day the
odious regret of not having listened to M. de Monsoreau's
love? But no, I have no conditions to make; I am conquered, I surrender; I am yours, Bussy, in love at least.
Remain, then, friend; and now that my life is yours, watch
over us."

As she said these words, Diane placed one of her white
and slender hands on Bussy's shoulder and offered him the
other, which he pressed lovingly to his lips. Diane thrilled
beneath that kiss.

Jeanne's light footsteps were now heard approaching,
accompanied by a little warning cough. She brought back
a bunch of new flowers, and perhaps the first butterfly that
had dared risk itself in the open air, — a red-and-black one.

The clasped hands parted instinctively. Jeanne noticed
the movement.

"Pardon my disturbing you, my good friends," she said,
"but we must go in, under penalty of being sent for. Monsieur le Comte, please return to your excellent horse, which
travels four leagues in half an hour, and let us return as
slowly as possible, because we shall have much to say to
each other. Well, Monsieur de Bussy, this is what you
lose by your stubbornness, — the dinner, which is excel-

lent, particularly for a man who has just had a long ride and climbed walls, then a hundred other amusements, to say nothing of the tender glances you might have exchanged. Come, Diane, let us go in."

And Jeanne took her friend's arm and made a slight effort to drag her away. Bussy looked at the two friends with a smile. Diane, who was still turned towards him, extended her hand. He approached.

" Well," he asked, " have you nothing more to say ? "

" Till to-morrow," replied Diane. " Is it not agreed ? "

" Only to-morrow ? "

" To-morrow and always."

Bussy could not restrain a little cry of joy. He bent over Diane's hand; then, throwing a last farewell to the two women, he went, or rather fled, away.

He felt the need of an effort of will to consent to separate from the one whom he had so long despaired of seeing. Diane followed him with her eyes until he had disappeared, and listened until the sound of his footsteps had died away.

"And now," said Jeanne, when Bussy had entirely disappeared, " let us have a little talk."

"Oh, yes !" said the young woman, starting as if her friend's voice had awakened her from a dream. "I am listening."

" Well, you see, to-morrow I shall go hunting with Saint-Luc and your father."

" What ! will you leave me alone in the *château* ? "

" Listen, dear friend," said Jeanne, " I, too, have my principles of morality ; and there are certain things to which I cannot consent."

" Oh, Jeanne," cried Madame de Monsoreau, turning pale, " can you speak so harshly to me, your friend ? "

" This is not a question of friends ; I cannot continue so."

"I thought you loved me, Jeanne, and now you are breaking my heart," said the young woman, with tears in her eyes. "You say you will not continue what?"

"Continue to prevent two poor lovers from loving each other to their heart's content," murmured Jeanne in her friend's ear.

Diane seized in her arms the laughing young woman and covered her face with kisses. While she held her, the joyous sound of hunting-horns was heard.

"Come, they are calling us," said Jeanne. "Poor Saint-Luc is becoming impatient. Do not be harder on him than I wish to be on the lover in the cinnamon doublet."

CHAPTER XV.

HOW BUSSY WAS OFFERED THREE HUNDRED PISTOLES FOR HIS HORSE, AND GAVE HIM FOR NOTHING.

THE next day Bussy left Angers before the earliest waking *bourgeois* had had his breakfast. He did not ride, he flew along the road. Diane had gone on the terrace, whence she could see the white road winding in among the green prairies. She saw a black speck advance like a meteor, and immediately went down, not to give Bussy time to wait. The sun had hardly reached the summit of the great oaks; the grass was glistening with dew; far away in the mountains could be heard Saint-Luc's hunting-horn, which Jeanne urged him to sound to remind her friend of the service she was rendering her in leaving her alone.

There was such deep, heartfelt joy in Diane's heart; she felt so intoxicated with her youth, her beauty, and her love, that it seemed sometimes as if her soul had wings which raised her body nearer to God. But the distance was a long one from the house to the thicket, and she was soon wearied of running through the thick grass. She was forced several times to stop to breathe, and reached the place of meeting just as Bussy appeared above the wall.

He saw her run; she uttered a little cry of joy. He came to her with open arms, and she rushed to meet him with both hands pressing her heart. They met with a long, tender embrace.

What had they to say? That they loved each other. What had they to think about? They saw each other. What had they to wish for? They were seated side by side and hand in hand.

The day passed like an hour.

When Diane first awakened from that soft torpor which is the sleep of the happy soul, Bussy pressed her to his heart and said, —

"Diane, it seems to me that my life has begun only to-day, that only now do I begin to see on the road which leads to eternity. You are the light that reveals so much happiness to me. I knew nothing of this world nor of the condition of men, so I can only repeat what I said yesterday, that having begun to live by you, it is with you that I shall die."

"And I," she replied, — "I who one day threw myself without regret into the arms of death, I tremble to-day at not being able to live long enough to enjoy all the treasures of your love. But why do you not come to the *château*, Louis? My father would be happy to see you; M. de Saint-Luc is your friend, and he is discreet. Think of being able to see each other one hour longer."

"Alas! Diane, if I go to the castle for one hour, I shall go always; if I go, the whole province will know of it, and the report will reach the ears of that ogre, your husband, who will hasten hither. You have forbidden me to deliver you from him."

"Why should you?" she asked, with that expression which we never find but in the voice of the woman we love.

"Well, for our safety, for the safety of our love, we must hide our secret from all. Madame de Saint-Luc already knows it; Saint-Luc will know it too."

"Oh, why?"

"Would you conceal anything from me now?" asked Bussy.

"No, that is true."

"I wrote this morning to Saint-Luc to ask him to meet me to-morrow at Angers. He will come, and I shall have his word as a gentleman never to breathe a word of this adventure. This is all the more important, dear Diane, as they are doubtless seeking me everywhere. Things looked serious when I left Paris."

"You are right; and then my father is a scrupulous man, and though he loves me, he might be capable of denouncing me to M. de Monsoreau."

"Let us hide well; and if God should hand us over to our enemies, we may at least say it was impossible to act otherwise."

"God is good, Louis; do not distrust him at a time like this."

"I do not distrust God, but I fear some demon jealous of our happiness."

"Bid me good-by then, and do not ride so fast; your horse frightens me."

"Fear nothing, he already knows the way. He is the safest, gentlest horse that I have ever ridden. When I turn towards the city, buried in my pleasant thoughts, he takes me there without my even touching the bridle."

The two lovers exchanged many other tender speeches, interrupted by kisses. Finally the hunting-horn rang out the call which had been agreed upon with Jeanne, and Bussy left.

As he approached the city, dreaming of this happy day, and proud of being free from the honors and favors of a prince which are always gilded chains, he observed that the hour approached for the closing of the gates. The horse, which had browsed all day on the grass and foliage, continued to do the same on the way home, and night was falling.

Bussy was preparing to ride on to make up for lost time, when he heard behind him the gallop of several horses. For a man who hides, and above all, for a lover, everything seems threatening. Happy lovers have this in common

with thieves. Bussy was wondering if it would be better
to gallop ahead or throw himself to one side to allow the
horsemen to pass on, but they rode so swiftly that they
were soon near him.

There were two.

Bussy, thinking it would be cowardly to avoid two men
when one is worth four, drew to one side, and perceived one
of the horsemen, whose spurs were buried in the flanks of
his steed, which was stimulated besides by the blows of his
companion.

"Come, here is the city," said the man, with a most pro-
nounced Gascon accent; "three hundred more blows with
the whip and spur! courage and vigor!"

"The animal can no longer breath; he shivers and
totters," replied the one who rode before, "I would give a
hundred horses to be in my city."

"It is some belated Angevin," said Bussy to himself,
"yet — how stupid do people become when they fear!—I
thought I recognized this voice. But that man's horse is
falling —"

At this moment the horsemen were near Bussy.

"Ah, take care, monsieur," he cried. "Leave your horse;
he is about to fall."

The horse did, in fact, fall heavily on one side, moved
one leg convulsively, and all at once his labored breathing
ceased, his eyes grew dim, and he died.

"Monsieur," cried the dismounted horseman to Bussy,
"three hundred pistoles for your horse."

"Ah, *mon Dieu!*" cried Bussy, as he approached.

"Do you hear me, monsieur? I am in a hurry —"

"Ah, monseigneur, take it for nothing," said Bussy,
trembling with indescribable emotion, for he had just recognized the Duc d'Anjou. At the same moment the prince's
companion was heard cocking his pistol.

"Stop!" cried the Duc d'Anjou to this pitiless defender;
"the devil take me! M. d'Aubigné, it is Bussy."

"Yes, prince, it is I; but why the devil are you killing horses on this road and at this hour?"

"Ah, it is M. de Bussy," said D'Aubigné, " then, monseigneur, you no longer need me. Permit me to return to him who sent me."

"Not without receiving my very sincere thanks and the promise of my firm friendship," said the prince.

"I accept both, monseigneur, and will recall your words to you some day."

"M. d'Aubigné — monseigneur — what is all this?" asked Bussy.

"Did you not know?" asked the prince, with an expression of discontent and suspicion which did not escape Bussy. "As you are here, did you not expect me?"

"The devil!" said Bussy to himself as he reflected how very curious his mysterious presence in Anjou would seem to the suspicious mind of the prince. "Let us not compromise ourselves. — I did better than expect you," he said; "and if you wish to enter the city before the closing of the gates, jump into the saddle, monseigneur."

He offered his horse to the prince, who was busy removing some important papers from the saddle of the dead animal.

"Farewell, monseigneur," said D'Aubigné as he turned his horse's head, "M. de Bussy, your servant."

And he rode away.

Bussy jumped lightly on the horse behind his master, and directed his horse towards the city, asking himself if this prince dressed in black were not some evil spirit sent to disturb his happiness. They entered Angers just as the trumpets of the aldermanship sounded.

"What shall we do now, monseigneur?"

"To the castle! Let them raise my banner, and recognize me, and I wish all the nobility of the province to be summoned."

"Nothing is easier," said Bussy, who made up his mind to gain time by being submissive, and who was, moreover, too surprised to be anything but passive.

"Hey! trumpets!" he cried to the heralds who were returning after their first flourish. The latter looked at him and did not pay much attention because they saw two warm, dusty men with no retinue.

"Ho! ho!" said Bussy advancing towards them. "Is not the master known in his own house? Send for the alderman on duty."

His haughty tone imposed on the heralds; one of them approached.

"Great heavens!" he cried in terror after a good look at the duke, "is not this our lord and master?"

The duke was easily recognized on account of the deformity of his nose, divided in two according to the words of Chicot's song.

"Monseigneur the duke," he added, seizing the arm of the second herald, who started in surprise.

"You now know quite as much as I do," said Bussy, "so get up your wind, that the whole city may know within fifteen minutes that the duke has arrived. We shall go slowly on to the *château*. By the time we reach there, everything will be in readiness to receive us."

At the first sound of the trumpets a group collected; at the second, the women and children ran about crying, —

"Monseigneur is in the city! *Noël* to Monseigneur!"

The aldermen, the governor, the principal gentlemen, rushed to the palace, followed by a crowd which increased at every minute. As Bussy had foreseen, the authorities of the city had preceded the duke to the palace to give him a fitting reception. When he reached the quay, he could scarcely get through the crowd; but Bussy found one of the heralds, who used his trumpet to open a passage for the prince as far as the steps of the Hôtel de Ville. Bussy formed the rear guard.

"Gentlemen and faithful subjects," said the prince, "I have come to throw myself into my good city of Angers. In Paris, the most terrible dangers have threatened my life ; I had even lost my liberty. I succeeded in escaping, thanks to my good friends !"

Bussy bit his lip as he felt the ironical meaning of these words.

"And since I am in your city, I feel that my peace and life are assured."

The astonished magistrates gave a feeble cry of, "Long live our lord!" while the people, hoping for the usual gratuities, shouted lustily, "*Noël !*"

"Let us sup," said the prince. "I have taken nothing since the morning."

The duke was immediately surrounded by all the train of retinue he kept at Angers as Duc d'Anjou, though the principal officers alone knew their master. Then came all the gentlemen and ladies of the city. The reception lasted until midnight.

The city was illuminated, musket-shots were heard in the streets and squares, the cathedral bell rang, and the wind carried to Méridor the sound of the noisy joy of the good Angevins.

CHAPTER XVI.

THE DIPLOMACY OF THE DUC D'ANJOU.

WHEN the firing of the muskets had ceased in the streets, the bells ceased to ring, and the ante-chambers emptied themselves; when the Duc d'Anjou and Bussy were at last alone, —

" Let us talk," said the duke.

François, with his usual quickness, had understood that Bussy had made more advances than usual. With his knowledge of the court, he concluded that Bussy was in an embarrassing position, and that with a little skill he might take advantage of him. But Bussy had had time to recover himself and was ready for the prince.

" Let us talk, monseigneur," he replied.

" The last time we met," said the prince, " you were very ill, my poor Bussy."

" Very true, monseigneur," replied the young man, " and I was only saved by a miracle ! "

" That day," continued the duke, " you had with you a certain doctor very anxious to save you, for he snapped most vigorously at all who approached you."

" That is still true, for Le Haudoin loves me dearly."

" He kept you rigorously in bed, did he not ? "

" At which I was in a great rage, as your Highness must have seen."

" But if you were so enraged," said the duke, " you might have sent the faculty to the devil, and come with me, as I begged you."

"Well!" said Bussy, turning and twisting his apothecary's hat.

"But," continued the duke, "as it was a grave affair, you were afraid of compromising yourself."

"What!" said Bussy, planting his hat on his head. "I think you said I was afraid of compromising myself."

"I did," replied the Duc d'Anjou.

"Well, then it is a lie, monseigneur," he cried, — "a lie to yourself, because you do not believe one word of what you say. There are twenty scars on my body which prove that I have sometimes compromised myself, but that I have never been afraid; and upon my word, I know a good many people who could not say as much, and above all, prove as much."

"You always have unanswerable arguments, M. de Bussy," replied the duke, very pale and agitated. "When you are accused, you cry louder than the accuser, and persuade yourself that you are right."

"I am not always right, monseigneur, and I know it; but I also know when I am in the wrong."

"And when are you in the wrong? — pray tell me."

"When I serve ungrateful people."

"In truth, monsieur, I think you are forgetting yourself," said the prince, rising with that dignity he could assume at times.

"Well, I forget myself, monseigneur," said Bussy. "Once in your life do the same, and forget yourself, or forget me." Bussy stepped towards the door, but the prince was quicker, and barred the way.

"Will you deny, monsieur, that after refusing to go out with me, you went out a few minutes later?"

"I deny nothing, monseigneur," said Bussy, "unless it be what you would like to force me to confess."

"Then tell me why you obstinately remained in your house."

"Because I had business."

"At home?"

"At home or elsewhere."

"I thought that when a gentleman was in the service of a prince, his principal business was that of the prince."

"And who does your business usually, if not I, monseigneur?"

"I do not say the contrary," said François, "and I usually find you faithful and devoted. I shall even say more: I excuse your ill-temper."

"Ah, you are very kind."

"Yes, because you had some reason to be angry with me."

"You acknowledge that, monseigneur?"

"Yes. I had promised you the disgrace of M. de Monsoreau. It seems you detest him cordially."

"I? Not at all. I find his face ugly, and I wanted him away, not to have that face before my eyes. You, on the contrary, like that face; there is no accounting for tastes."

"Well, as this was your only excuse to sulk like a cross, spoiled child, I shall say that you were doubly wrong not to wish to come out with me and then go out afterwards to commit follies."

"I committed useless follies, and just now you reproached me — Come, monseigneur, be consistent; what follies have I committed?"

"No doubt you hate M. d'Epernon and M. de Schomberg, and I understand that. I, too, hate them mortally; but you should have been satisfied with hating, and bided your time."

"Oh, oh," said Bussy, "what next, monseigneur?"

"Kill them, *morbleu!* kill them both! kill them all four, and I shall be more than grateful; but do not exasperate them, particularly when you are safely away, because then their exasperation falls on me."

" Come, what have I done to this worthy Gascon ? "

" You mean D'Epernon ? "

" Yes."

" Why, you had him stoned."

" I ? "

" So that his doublet was in shreds, his cloak in rags, and he returned to the Louvre in his hose."

"Good!" said Bussy, "so much for one; now let us pass on to the German. What have I done to M. de Schomberg ? "

" Will you deny that you had him dyed blue ?   When I saw him, three hours after his accident, he was still azure colored; and you call that a good joke.   Come now ! "

And the prince began to laugh in spite of himself, while Bussy, recalling Schomberg's appearance in the vat, broke into peals of laughter.

" Well," he said, " so I have the credit of having played them these tricks ? "

" *Pardieu!*   It is I, perhaps ? "

" And you have the courage to reproach a man who has such ideas !   As I said just now, monseigneur, you are an ungrateful man."

" Very good.   Now, if you really went out for that, I forgive you."

" Really ? "

" Yes, upon my word ; but you are not yet at the end of my complaints."

" Go on."

" Let us talk about myself."

" I am listening."

" What did you do to save me from my difficulties ? "

" You see for yourself what I did," said Bussy.

" No, I do not see."

" Well, I started for Anjou."

" That is, you ran away."

" Yes, because by saving myself I saved you."

"But instead of going so far, could you not remain near Paris ? I think you might have been more useful to me at Montmartre than at Angers."

" Ah, here we differ, monseigneur; I preferred coming to Anjou."

" You will acknowledge that your whim is a very poor reason."

"No, because the object of this whim was to gather your partisans."

" Ah, this is different. Now, what have you done ? "

" I shall explain to-morrow, monseigneur, because I must now leave you."

" And why must you go ? "

"I have an appointment with a most important personage."

" Ah, in that case go, Bussy, but be prudent."

"Prudent ? Why ? Are we not the strongest here ? "

"No matter; you must risk nothing. Have you already done much ? "

" How could I, when I have only been here two days ? "

" But you keep yourself concealed, I hope ? "

" I should think so, *morbleu!* Look at my costume. Am I in the habit of wearing cinnamon-colored doublets ? Yet it is for your sake that I assumed this horrible garb."

" And where are you lodging ? "

" Ah, here is the time for you to appreciate my devotion, — in a tumble-down old house near the rampart, with an outlet on the river. But how did you get out of the Louvre ? How did I happen to meet you on the high-road in company with M. d'Aubigné ? "

"Because I have friends," said the prince.

"You have friends ? " said Bussy. "Come now ! "

"Yes, friends whom you do not know."

" Ah, indeed ! and who are these friends ? "

" The King of Navarre and M. d'Aubigné, whom you saw."

"The King of Navarre, — ah, very true! Did you not plot together?"

"I have never plotted, M. de Bussy."

"No? Ask poor La Mole and Coconnas."

"La Mole," said the prince, gloomily, "had committed another crime besides‚ the one for which he is supposed to have died."

"Well, let us leave La Mole and return to you, particularly as we shall have some trouble in agreeing on that point. How the devil did you leave the Louvre?"

"Through the window."

"Ah, indeed! Through which one?"

"The one in my bedroom."

"So you knew about the rope ladder?"

"What rope ladder?"

"The one in the closet."

"Ah, it seems you knew it too," said the prince, turning pale.

"Well," said Bussy, "your Highness knows that I have sometimes had the good fortune of entering that room."

"In my sister Margot's time? And you came in through the window?"

"Why, you came out that way. I am only surprised that you should have found the ladder."

"I did not find it."

"Well, who, then?"

"No one; I was told about it."

"Who told you?"

"The King of Navarre."

"Ah, ah, the King of Navarre knows the ladder! I would not have thought so. However, you are now safe and sound, and we shall put Anjou in flames and Angoumois and Béarn will catch the light; that will make a nice little fire."

"But did you not speak of an appointment?" asked the duke.

"Ah, yes, *morbleu!* but this interesting conversation made me forget it. Adieu, monseigneur."

"Do you take your horse?"

"Well, if it will be of use to you, monseigneur, you may keep it; I have another."

"Then I accept. We shall settle our accounts later."

"Yes, monseigneur, and I pray to Heaven that I may not remain your debtor."

"Why so?"

"Because I do not like the one who settles those matters for you."

"Bussy!"

"Ah, true, monseigneur, we had agreed not to speak of that."

The prince, who felt how much he needed Bussy, held out his hand to him.

Bussy gave him his own, shaking his head, and they parted.

CHAPTER XVII.

M. DE SAINT-LUC'S DIPLOMACY.

BUSSY returned home in the pitch dark, but instead of finding Saint-Luc, as he expected, he found only a letter announcing the visit of his friend for the next day. In fact Saint-Luc left Méridor at about six o'clock in the morning, and followed by one attendant, took the road to Angers.

He had reached the foot of the ramparts at the opening of the gates, and without noticing the agitation of the people, he had reached Bussy's house.

The two friends embraced warmly.

" My dear Saint-Luc," said Bussy, " accept the hospitality of my poor hut; I am only camping at Angers."

" Yes," said Saint-Luc, " after the fashion of conquerors, on the field of battle."

" What do you mean, my dear friend ? "

" That my wife has no secrets for me, as I have none for her, my dear Bussy, and she has told me all. We have everything in common. Receive my congratulations, my master in all things; and since you have sent for me, allow me to offer you a piece of advice."

" Speak."

" Rid yourself at once of that abominable Monsoreau. No one at court knows of your relations with his wife; now is the moment, only you must not let it escape. When you marry the widow later on, no one will say that you made her a widow in order to marry her."

"There is only one objection to this fine project, which had also occurred to me."

"You see: well, what is it?"

"I have sworn to Diane to respect the life of her husband, so long as he does not attack me of course."

"You were wrong."

"I?"

"You were very wrong."

"Why so?"

"Because you should never take such oaths. The devil! if you do not hasten and take the initiative, Monsoreau will discover you; and as he is anything but chivalrous, he will kill you."

"I shall bow to the will of God," said Bussy, with a smile. "But besides the fact that I would break my oath to Diane if I killed her husband —"

"Her husband! — you know he is not."

"Yes, but he bears the title, nevertheless. Besides breaking my promise, every one would blame me; and that man who is now a monster in the eyes of all, would appear an angel that I had laid in his grave."

"Therefore, I do not advise you to kill him yourself."

"Assassins! Ah, Saint-Luc, you are giving me poor advice."

"Come now, who spoke of assassins?"

"Well, what else are you thinking about?"

"Nothing, my friend; only an idea which came to me, and which is not sufficiently ripe to be communicated. I do not love Monsoreau any more than you do, though I have not the same reasons for hating him; let us therefore leave the husband and speak of the wife."

Bussy smiled.

"You are a splendid companion, Saint-Luc," he said, "and you may count on my friendship. Now, you know my friendship consists of three things, — my purse, my sword, and my life."

"Thank you," said Saint-Luc, "I accept, but with the privilege of returning the devotion."

"Now, what did you want to tell me about Diane?"

"I wanted to ask you if you had not the intention of coming sometimes to Méridor."

"My dear friend, I thank you for insisting, but you know my scruples."

"I know everything. At Méridor you run the risk of meeting Monsoreau, though he is two hundred miles away; you run the risk of having to take his hand, and it is hard to take the hand of a man you would like to throttle; finally, you might have to see him kiss Diane, and it is very hard to see another man kiss the woman we love."

"Ah," cried Bussy, with rage, "how well you understand why I do not go to Méridor! Now, my dear friend —"

"Do you dismiss me?" asked Saint-Luc, mistaking Bussy's intention.

"Not at all; on the contrary," replied the latter, "I beg you to remain, as it is now my turn to question."

"Speak."

"Did you not hear the sound of bells and musketry last night?"

"Yes, and we even wondered what could be the matter."

"Did you not notice some change this morning as you passed through the city?"

"Something like a great agitation?"

"Yes."

"I was about to ask you the cause of it."

"It is caused by the arrival of the Duc d'Anjou."

Saint-Luc jumped up as if he had just heard of the presence of the devil.

"The duke at Angers? He was said to be imprisoned at the Louvre."

"It is exactly because he was a prisoner at the Louvre

that he is now at Angers. He succeeded in escaping through the window and has taken refuge here."

"Well?" asked Saint-Luc.

"Well, my dear friend," said Bussy, "here is an excellent opportunity to revenge yourself for the king's little persecutions. The prince already has a party; he will have troops, and we shall stir up something like a nice little civil war."

"Oh, oh!" said Saint-Luc.

"And I counted on you to fight beside me."

"Against the king?" asked Saint-Luc, with sudden coldness.

"I do not exactly say against the king," said Bussy. "I say, against all who will oppose us."

"My dear Bussy," said Saint-Luc, "I came to Anjou to breathe the country air, and not to fight against his Majesty."

"But let me at least present you to Monseigneur."

"It is useless; I do not like Angers, and shall soon leave here; it is a dark and gloomy city. The stones are as soft as cheese, and the cheese as hard as stone."

"My dear Saint-Luc, you would do me a great favor in consenting to this; the duke asked me what I was doing here, and not being able to tell him, because he too loved Diane and failed with her, I made him believe that I was drawing to his cause all the gentlemen of the province. I even added that I had an appointment with one this morning."

"Well, say that you have seen the gentleman, who wishes six months for reflection."

"I think, my dear Saint-Luc, that your logic is as stubborn as my own."

"Listen; I care but for one thing in this world, — my wife; you only care for your mistress: let us make an agreement. Under all circumstances you will defend Madame de Saint-

Luc as I pledge myself to defend Diane. We shall make a treaty for love, but not for politics. This is the only manner in which we can agree."

"I see I must yield to you, Saint-Luc, because at this moment you have the advantage. I need you."

"Not at all. It is I, on the contrary, who claim your protection."

"How so?"

"Suppose the Angevins, — because that is the name the rebels will take, — suppose they besiege and sack Méridor?"

"Ah, the devil! you are right," said Bussy; "and you do not wish the inhabitants to suffer the consequences of a capitulation."

The two friends began to laugh, and as the firing of cannon was heard in the city, and Bussy's valet came to say that the prince had already called for him three times, they again pledged themselves to their agreement, and parted delighted with each other.

Bussy ran to the ducal palace, where the nobility thronged in large numbers. The Duc d'Anjou's arrival had soon spread throughout the provinces, and the towns and villages around Angers had all risen at this news.

The count hastened to arrange an official reception, a banquet and speeches; he thought that while the duke would be receiving, feasting, and above all, making speeches, he would have time to see Diane, even if only for a moment. Then when he had given the duke occupation for several hours, he went home, jumped on his second horse, and galloped in the direction of Méridor.

The duke, left to himself, made very fine speeches, and produced a great effect by speaking of the League, touching discreetly on those points relating to his alliance with the Guises, and presenting himself in the light of a prince persecuted by the king on account of the excess of confidence which the Parisians had showed him.

During the answers the Duc d'Anjou passed all the gentlemen in review, carefully noting those who had already
arrived, and even more carefully those who were absent.

When Bussy returned, it was four o'clock in the afternoon; he jumped off his horse and presented himself before
the duke, covered with dust.

"Ah, my brave Bussy, it seems you have been working."

"As you see, monseigneur."

"Are you warm?"

"I have galloped very fast."

"Take care not to make yourself ill."

"There is no danger."

"Where have you been?"

"In the neighborhood. Is your Highness pleased? Has
there been a large gathering of nobles?"

"Yes, I am rather pleased; but I missed some one."

"Who?"

"Your *protégé*."

"My *protégé*?"

"Yes, the Baron de Méridor."

"Ah!" said Bussy, coloring.

"And yet I must not neglect him, though he neglects
me. The baron has influence in the province."

"You think so?"

"I am sure; he was the correspondent of the League at
Angers. He had been chosen by MM. de Guise, and those
gentlemen usually know how to make a selection. He
must come, Bussy."

"But if he should not come?"

"If he does not come, I shall make the advances and go
to Méridor."

"In person?"

"Why not?"

Bussy could not keep back the jealous fire that flashed
from his eyes.

"After all, why should you not? You are a prince, and a prince may do anything."

"Then you think he is still angry with me?"

"I don't know. How should I know?"

"Have you not seen him?"

"No."

"As you have had business with all the great men of the province, I thought — "

"I should not have failed to go to him if he himself had not some cause to complain of me."

"About what?"

"I was not sufficiently lucky in the promises I made him to be in any hurry to present myself before him."

"Has he not what he wished?"

"How so?"

"He wished his daughter to marry the count, and she has married him."

"Well, monseigneur, let us say no more about it," replied Bussy, and he turned his back on the prince.

François' words had furnished him with much food for thought. What could be the prince's real ideas with regard to the Baron de Méridor? Were they really those he had expressed? Did he look upon the old baron merely as a powerful and influential support to his cause, or were his political plans merely an excuse to approach Diane?

Bussy examined the prince's position just as it was; he saw him embroiled with his brother, exiled from the Louvre, and the head of a provincial insurrection. He weighed in the same scales the prince's material interests and his love fancies, and found that the former greatly outweighed the others.

Bussy was ready to forgive the duke all his other grievances in favor of that.

He spent the night feasting with his Royal Highness and the Angevin gentlemen, and in paying his respects to the

Angevin ladies.   Then, as musicians had been summoned, he taught them the newest dances.

It is needless to say that he excited the admiration of the ladies and the despair of the husbands; and as some of the latter looked at him in a way he did not like, he twirled his moustache, and asked three or four of them if they would not like to take a walk in the moonlight.   But as his reputation had preceded him to Angers, his offers were declined.

CHAPTER XVIII.

IN WHICH BUSSY FINDS A FRIEND.

AT the gate of the ducal palace, Bussy found a frank, loyal, and merry face, which he thought two hundred miles away.

"Ah," he said, with a feeling of genuine joy, "is it you, Rémy?"

"Eh, *mon Dieu!* yes, monseigneur."

"I was about to write to you to come and join me."

"Really?"

"Upon my word."

"In that case, all is for the best. I was afraid you might scold me."

"Why?"

"Because I came without permission. But I heard that the Duc d'Anjou had escaped from the Louvre, and gone to his province; I remembered that you were in the neighborhood of Angers; I concluded there would be civil war, and a liberal exchange of blows, together with a good many holes in skins. Now, as I love my neighbor as I love myself, and even more, I hastened hither."

"You did right, Rémy. On my honor, I missed you."

"How is Gertrude, monseigneur?"

The gentleman smiled.

"I promise you I shall ask Diane the next time I see her," he said.

"And I, in return, shall inquire about Madame de Monsoreau, the next time I see her."

"You are a charming companion. How did you find me?"

"*Parbleu!* that was very difficult. I inquired the way to the ducal palace, and waited for you at the gate, after having taken my horse to the stable, where I recognized yours."

"Yes, the prince had killed his horse, so I lent him Roland; and as he had no other, he kept it."

"I recognize you there. You are the prince, and the prince is the servant."

"Do not place me so high, Rémy; you will see Monseigneur's lodgings," and as he spoke, he introduced Rémy into the little house on the rampart. "You see the palace; now settle yourself where you will, and how you will."

"That will not be difficult, and you know I do not need much room; besides, if necessary, I can sleep standing. I am tired enough for that."

The two friends, for Bussy treated Rémy more as a friend than as a servant, now separated; and Bussy, doubly happy at being between Diane and Rémy, slept until morning.

It is true that, to be able to sleep more peacefully, the duke had given orders that all firing should cease; as for the bells, they had ceased of themselves, thanks to the sores on the ringers' hands.

Bussy rose early and ran to the castle, leaving orders that Rémy should come and join him. He was anxious to be present at the duke's awakening, to read his thoughts if possible, in the very significant yawns of the sleeper.

The duke awoke, but like his brother Henri, he seemed to wear a mask to sleep in. Bussy learned nothing in this way; but he came prepared with a catalogue of things, each more important than the last.

First, a walk round the walls to examine the fortifications, a review of the inhabitants and their arms, a visit to the arsenal, a careful examination of the taxes of the province for the purpose of obtaining supplementary resources, finally, correspondence.

But Bussy was well aware that he could not count too much on the last named article; the Duc d'Anjou wrote but little. Even at that time he observed the saying, that all writing remains. He was therefore prepared against all the evil thoughts that might come to the duke, but he was unable to discover anything.

"Ah, ah," said the duke, "you, already!"

"Faith! monseigneur, I have been unable to sleep, so much did your interests weigh on my mind. What shall we do this morning? What do you say to a hunt?—Good!" said Bussy, to himself, "here is an occupation I had not yet thought about."

"What!" said the duke, "you pretend you have been thinking all night about my interests, and as a result of your meditation you come and propose a hunt; come now!"

"True," said Bussy; "besides, we have no hounds."

"And no master of the hounds," said François.

"Ah, really, I would find a hunt without him all the more agreeable."

"Well, I am not like you; I miss him."

The duke said that in a singular tone, which Bussy observed.

"That worthy man, your friend, did not deliver you either, it seems."

The duke smiled.

"Good!" said Bussy, "I know that smile; it is the bad one. Let Monsoreau look to himself."

"You hate him, then?" asked the duke.

"Monsoreau?"

"Yes."

"Why should I hate him?"

"Because he is my friend."

"On the contrary, I pity him."

"What do you mean?"

"That the higher you raise him, the greater will be his fall."

"Ah, I see you are in a good humor."

"I?"

"Yes, you always say such things to me when you are in a good humor; no matter, I maintain what I said, that Monsoreau would have been very useful to us here."

"Why so?"

"Because he has property in the neighborhood."

"He?"

"He or his wife."

Bussy bit his lip; the duke was bringing the conversation back to the same point which had given him so much trouble the day before.

"Ah, you think so?" he said.

"No doubt. Méridor is three leagues from Angers; you know it, you who brought the old baron to me."

Bussy understood that he must not lose his position.

"Why, I brought him because he clung to my cloak; and unless I had left one half in his hands, as Saint Martin did, I was compelled to take him. Besides, my protection was not of much use to him."

"Listen," said the duke; "I have an idea."

"The devil!" said Bussy, who always feared the prince's ideas.

"Yes. Monsoreau won the first game, but would you like to win the second?"

"What do you mean, prince?"

"It is very simple. You know me, Bussy?"

"I have that misfortune."

"Do you think I am a man who will suffer an affront with impunity?"

"That depends."

The duke's smile contained even more evil intentions than the first one, while he bit his lip and nodded his head.

"Explain yourself, monseigneur."

"Well, the master of the hounds robbed me of a young girl I loved and made her his wife; I, in turn, will rob him of his wife and make her my mistress."

Bussy tried to smile, but in spite of his efforts, he only succeeded in making a grimace.

"Rob M. de Monsoreau of his wife?" he stammered.

"Why, nothing seems easier to me," said the duke. "The wife is on her estates, and you told me that she hated her husband. I can therefore conclude without too much vanity that she will give me the preference over Monsoreau, particularly if I promise — what I shall promise."

"And what will you promise, monseigneur?"

"To rid her of her husband."

Bussy was on the point of crying, "Ah, why did you not do so at once?" but he had the courage to contain himself.

"Would you do this fine action?" he asked.

"You will see. In the mean time, I shall pay my respects at Méridor."

"You will dare?"

"Why not?"

"You will present yourself before the old baron whom you abandoned after having promised me —"

"I have an excellent excuse to offer."

"Where the devil will you find it?"

"Eh, no doubt I shall say, 'I did not break off this marriage because Monsoreau, who knew that you were one of the principal agents of the League of which I was the chief, threatened to denounce us both to the king.'"

"Ah, ah, did your Highness invent that one?"

"Not altogether, I must admit," replied the duke.

"Then I understand," said Bussy.

"You understand?" asked the duke, deceived by this answer.

"Yes."

"I shall make him believe that in sanctioning his daughter's marriage I saved his own life, which was threatened."

"That is superb," said Bussy.

"Is it not? But look out of the window, Bussy."

"What for?"

"How is the weather?"

"Well, I am forced to acknowledge that it is fine."

"Then order the horses and let us go and see Méridor."

"At once, monseigneur," and Bussy, pretending to go out, walked to the door and came back. "Pardon me, monseigneur," he said, "but how many horses must I order?"

"Four or five, if you will."

"Then, if you leave it to me, I shall order one hundred."

"Why a hundred?" cried the prince, surprised.

"To have about twenty-five on whom I can depend in case of attack."

The duke started. "In case of attack?" he repeated.

"Yes, I have heard that there are a great many forests around here," said Bussy, "and there would be nothing surprising if we were to fall in an ambuscade."

"Ah, ah," said the duke, "you think so?"

"Your Highness knows that real courage does not exclude prudence."

The duke became pensive.

"I shall order one hundred and fifty," said Bussy; and he advanced the second time towards the door.

"Wait a moment," said the prince.

"What is the matter, monseigneur?"

"Do you really think I am in safety in Angers, Bussy?"

"The city is not very strong, but if it were well defended —"

"Yes, but it may not be well defended; and brave as you are, you can only be in one place at a time."

"Most probably."

"If I am not in safety in the city, and I am not, since Bussy has doubts —"

"I did not say I had any doubts, monseigneur."

"Well, if I am not in safety, I must attend to that at once. I shall visit the castle and intrench myself."

"You are right, monseigneur; good intrenchments are by far the best."

Bussy stammered; he was not accustomed to fear, and words of prudence came with difficulty from his lips.

"And here is another idea —"

"The morning is fruitful, monseigneur."

"I shall have the Méridors come here."

"Monseigneur, your ideas this morning are remarkable for their strength and vigor. Get up and visit the castle."

The prince called his attendants. Bussy took advantage of this moment to go out. He went in search of Rémy, and found him in the ante-chamber. He took him into the duke's study, wrote a short note, gathered a bunch of roses in a hot-house, rolled the note around the stems, went to the stable, saddled Roland, invited Rémy to mount. and putting the bouquet into his hand, led him out of the city to the entrance of a sort of little path.

"Now," he said, "let Roland go. At the end of the path you will find the forest, in the forest a park, and around this park a wall; and at the part of the wall where Roland will stop you will throw this bouquet."

"The one who is expected will not come," said the note, "because the one who was not expected has come, more threatening than ever, because he still loves. Take with your lips and your heart all that is invisible to the eyes in this paper."

Bussy let go the bridle, and Roland started off at a gallop

in the direction of Méridor. Bussy returned to the palace and found the prince already dressed. As for Rémy, he executed his commission in half an hour. Carried off like the wind, Rémy, trusting to his master's words, rode over prairies, fields, brooks, and hills, until he reached a crumbling stone wall, where the horse stopped.

Having reached this point, Rémy stood up in his stirrups, and having securely fastened the note to the flowers, he gave a loud "hem!" and flung the bouquet over the wall. A little cry from the other side told him it had reached its destination.

Rémy had nothing more to do, as he had not been told to bring any answer, so he turned his horse's head towards the city, much to Roland's dissatisfaction, who evinced a lively discontent at being deprived of his accustomed repast on the acorns; but Rémy made energetic use of the whip and spurs, and Roland resumed his natural gait.

Forty minutes later he found his way to his new stable, as he had just found it in the woods, and took his place before the manger filled with hay and oats. Bussy was inspecting the castle with the prince. Rémy joined him just as he was examining a subterranean passage leading to the postern.

"Well," he said to his messenger, "what have you seen, what have you heard, what have you done?"

"A wall, a cry, seven leagues," replied Rémy, with the laconism of those sons of Sparta who allowed foxes to devour their bodies for the greater glory of the laws of Lycurgus.

CHAPTER XIX.

A FLOCK OF ANGEVINS.

Bussy contrived to occupy the Duc d'Anjou so well with his warlike preparations, that for the next two days he found neither the time to go to Méridor nor the opportunity to send for the baron.   However, from time to time the duke returned to his ideas of visiting; but Bussy always had a thousand things to suggest, — inspection of the muskets of the guards, equipment of the horses, placing the cannons, etc., as if they intended to conquer one quarter of the earth.

Rémy, seeing all this, began to make lint, to sharpen his instruments, and prepare his salves, as if he was to cure half of the human race.

The duke then shrank before these enormous preparations.

It is needless to say that from time to time Bussy, under pretext of inspecting the exterior fortifications, would jump on Roland, and in forty minutes he had reached a certain wall, over which he climbed all the more easily that at every visit a few more stones crumbled down.

As for Roland, there was no need to give him any directions; Bussy had but to close his eyes and leave him to himself.

"I have already gained two days," said Bussy, "and I shall be very unlucky if, before two more days are passed, some other good fortune does not come to me."

Towards the evening of the third day, as a large convoy of provisions was being brought into the city, — the produce

of a requisition levied by the duke on his good Angevins,
— while M. d'Anjou was gaining popularity by tasting the
black bread and eating the salted herrings and fresh cod-
fish of the soldiers, a great noise was heard at one of the
gates of the city. The duke inquired whence came this
noise, but no one could tell him.

There was a goodly interchange of blows being witnessed
by a large number of citizens. A man, mounted on a
white horse covered with foam, had presented himself at
the Paris gate.

Now, Bussy, in consequence of his system of intimidation, had had himself appointed captain-general of Anjou,
grand master of all the places, and had established the
most severe discipline, notably in Angers. No one could
leave the city without a password; no one could enter
without a password, a letter, or some other sign.

The only object of all this discipline was to prevent
the duke from sending any one to Diane without his
knowledge, or to prevent Diane's entering Angers. This
will perhaps seem a little exaggerated, but fifty years
later, Buckingham committed many other follies for Anne
of Austria.

The man and the white horse therefore arrived at a
furious gallop, and rushed headlong against the post of
sentinels. But the post had received orders. The orders
had been given to the sentinel, who had shouldered his
musket; the horseman seemed to pay little attention to
this, but the sentinel cried, —

"To arms!"

The post had appeared, and explanations had ensued.

"I am Antraguet," said the horseman, "and I wish to
speak to the Duc d'Anjou."

"We do not know Antraguet," replied the man in command, "but your desire to speak to the duke will soon be
satisfied, because we shall arrest you and conduct you
before his Highness."

"Arrest me!" replied the horseman. "What a nice idea to arrest me, Charles de Balzac d'Entragues, Baron de Cuneo, and Comte de Graville!"

"Yet it shall be done," replied the *bourgeois*, who had twenty men behind him, and saw only one in front.

"Wait a second, my good friends," said Antraguet. "You do not know Parisians, eh? Well, I shall give you a sample of what they can do."

"Let us arrest him! Let us take him to Monseigneur!" cried the furious militiamen.

"Gently, my little lambs of Anjou," said Antraguet; "it is I who shall have this pleasure."

"What is he saying?" asked the *bourgeois*.

"He says that his horse has only travelled ten leagues, so he will pass over the whole of you, if you do not stand aside. Stand aside, I say, or *ventre bœuf* —"

And as the Angevin *bourgeois* did not seem to understand the Parisian oath, Antraguet drew his sword, and had soon disposed of the nearest halberds directed against him. In less than ten minutes, fifteen or twenty halberds were changed into so many broomsticks.

The furious *bourgeois* rushed on the new-comer, who warded off their sticks with his sword, laughing all the while.

"Ah, what a fine *entrée!*" he said, as he roared with laughter. "Oh, these good citizens of Angers! *Morbleu!* how we can amuse ourselves here! The prince was right to leave Paris, and I was right to come and join him."

And Antraguet not only continued to tarry, but when his aggressors came too near, he would disable them with a stroke of his good Spanish blade. The citizens did their best, often striking each other, but returning to the attack; like the soldiers of Cadmus, they seemed to spring up from the ground.

Antraguet felt himself grow weary.

"Come," he said, as he saw the ranks grow thicker, "this will do. You are brave as lions, that is agreed, and I shall testify to that; but you see that you only have the handles of your halberds, and you do not know how to load your muskets. I had resolved to enter the city, but I did not know it was defended by an army of Cæsars. I abandon the attempt to conquer you. Good-night, I am going away. Only tell the duke I came on purpose to see him."

However, the captain had succeeded in lighting the match of his musket; but just as he was raising it to his shoulder, Antraguet struck him with his flexible cane such a furious blow on the knuckles, that he dropped his musket and began hopping, now on one foot, now on the other.

"To death! to death!" cried the bruised and furious militiamen. "He must not fly! he must not escape!"

"Ah," said Antraguet, "you would not let me enter a moment ago, and now you will not let me go. Take care! I shall change my tactics, and instead of using the flat of the sword, I will use the point; instead of cutting the halberds I will cut the wrists. Now, my little lambs of Angers, will you let me go?"

"No; to death! to death! He is weakening! let us knock him down!"

"Very well, then, you are in earnest?"

"Yes, yes!"

"Well, take care of your fingers; I shall cut hands."

He had scarcely finished speaking, and was preparing to carry his threat into execution, when a second horseman appeared on the scene and rushed like lightning into the *mêlée*, which was gradually turning into a real combat.

"Antraguet!" cried the new-comer, "what the devil are you doing among these *bourgeois?*"

"Livarot!" cried Antraguet turning round. "Ah, *mor-*

dieu! you are welcome. Montjoie et Saint-Denis, to the rescue!"

"I was sure I would overtake you; four hours ago I had news of you, and since then I have been following. But where are you? Why are you being massacred?"

"These are our friends of Anjou, who will neither let me go in nor out."

"Gentlemen," said Livarot, raising his hat, "would it please you to stand to the right or to the left as we pass in?"

"They insult us!" cried the *bourgeois.* "To death! to death!"

"Ah, so this is the way they are at Angers?" cried Livarot, putting his hat on his head and drawing his sword.

"Yes, you see," said Antraguet; "unfortunately they are numerous."

"Pshaw! we three will soon put an end to them."

"Yes, if we were three, but we are only two."

"Here is Ribeirac."

"He too?"

"Do you hear him?"

"I see him. Hey, Ribeirac! here! here!"

In fact Ribeirac, in no less of a hurry than his two friends, made the same kind of entrance into the city.

"Why, they are fighting," said Ribeirac; "what luck! Hey, Livarot, Antraguet!"

"Let us charge them," replied Antraguet.

The *bourgeois* looked with amazement at the new reinforcement which had joined the two friends, who had now passed from the condition of the assailed to that of assailants. But apart from the fact that the invitation of their commander made them prudent, they saw the horsemen form in line and present such a warlike front that the stoutest hearts quaked.

"It is their advance guard!" cried the *bourgeois*, wishing to have some pretext to flee. "Alarm! alarm!"

"Fire!" cried the others, "fire!"

"The enemy, the enemy!" cried the remainder.

"We are fathers of families, and we belong to our wives and children; save yourselves!" roared the captain. And in consequence of all these cries, which tended to the same object, a frightful tumult arose in the street, and blows fell on those of the bystanders who prevented the flight. It was at this moment that the sound of the fray reached the square where the prince was busy tasting the bread and fish of his soldiers.

Bussy and the prince made inquiries, and were told that three men, or rather three devils from Paris, were making all this noise.

"Three men?" asked the prince. "Go and see what that means, Bussy."

"Three men?" said Bussy, "come, monseigneur."

Both started. Bussy went first, and the prince came behind, prudently escorted by about twenty horsemen. They arrived just as the *bourgeois* were beginning to execute the above-mentioned manœuvre, to the great detriment of the shoulders and skulls of the bystanders. Bussy rose in his stirrups, and his eagle eye recognized Livarot's long face in the *mêlée*.

"*Mort de ma vie!*" he cried to the prince in a thundering voice, "come, monseigneur. They are our friends from Paris who are besieging us."

"No," cried Livarot, whose voice rang out above the roar of the battle, "it is our friends of Anjou who are killing us."

"Down with your arms, knaves!" cried the duke, "down with your arms! These are friends."

"Friends!" cried the bruised and torn *bourgeois*, "then they should have had the password. For the past hour we have been treating them like pagans, and they have been treating us like Turks." And they continued to retreat.

Livarot, Antraguet and Ribeirac now advanced in triumph in the open space, and hastened to kiss the duke's hand, after which they threw themselves into Bussy's arms.

"It seems," philosophically said the captain, "that we mistook a flock of Angevins for a flock of vultures."

"Monseigneur," whispered Bussy to the duke, "will you please count your militiamen?"

"Why so?"

"Count them at a rough guess."

"They are about one hundred and fifty."

"Yes, at least."

"Well, what are you driving at?"

"That you have not very famous soldiers, since three men defeated them."

"True," said the duke. "What next?"

"Why, go out of the city with such fellows?"

"Yes, but I can go out with the three men who whipped the others."

"Oh, I had not thought of that," murmured Bussy. "Trust a coward to be logical."

CHAPTER XX.

ROLAND.

THANKS to the reinforcement which had arrived, M. le Duc d'Anjou was able to explore all the surrounding country. Accompanied by his friends, his suite had a warlike aspect of which the inhabitants of Angers were justly proud, though the comparison between these well-mounted and well-equipped gentlemen and the torn garments and rusty weapons of the militiamen was not precisely to the advantage of the latter.

They explored, first the ramparts, then the gardens adjoining these ramparts, then the country beyond the gardens; and it was not without a feeling of pride that the duke rode through those woods which had at first so greatly frightened him.

The Angevin gentlemen came with money, and they found at the court of Anjou far more liberty than at the court of Henri III.; they could not fail, therefore, to lead a merry life. Three days had not elapsed before Antraguet, Ribeirac, and Livarot had become intimate with many of the nobles, particularly those who most admired Parisian fashions and customs. It is needless to add that these worthy nobles had young and pretty wives. It was therefore not for his own particular pleasure that the Duc d'Anjou rode so frequently through the streets of Angers. No; these rides contributed to the pleasure of the Parisian gentlemen who had come to join him, of the Angevin nobles, and particularly of the Angevin ladies.

God must have greatly rejoiced at them, for the cause of the League was the cause of God. Then the king must unquestionably have been furious. Finally, the ladies were made supremely happy.

The great trinity of the period was therefore represented. God, the king, and the ladies. The general joy reached its height when twenty riding horses, thirty carriage horses and forty mules, together with litters, carriages, and wagons, all the property of the duke, arrived at Angers.

All this came from Tours for the modest sum of fifty thousand crowns, which the duke applied to these purchases.

It must be said that the horses were saddled, but the saddles were not yet paid for; the coffers had magnificent locks which locked with a key, but the coffers were empty. This last fact was greatly to the prince's credit, because he might have filled them by exactions. However, it was not in his nature to take openly; he preferred other means.

Nevertheless, the entrance of the *cortége* produced a magnificent effect in Angers. The horses were put in the stables, the wagons placed under the sheds. The coffers were carried in by the prince's most intimate friends, — he must trust in safe hands the sums they did not contain.

The palace gates were closed in the face of a rather considerable crowd. Thanks to this precautionary measure, the people were convinced that the prince had just brought about two millions into the city, whereas, on the contrary, he intended to get that amount from the inhabitants.

The duke's reputation for wealth was established from that day on; and after the sight on which they had feasted their eyes, the whole province was convinced that he was rich enough to make war against the whole of Europe if need be. This faith led the *bourgeois* to accept most patiently the taxes which the duke, following the advice of his friends, levied on the Angevins.

Besides, the Angevins almost anticipated all the duke's desires. We never regret the money we give or lend to the rich. The King of Navarre, with his reputation of poverty, would not have obtained one fourth of what the Duc d'Anjou obtained with his reputation of wealth.

But let us return to the duke.

That worthy prince lived like a patriarch on the fat of the land, and we all know that Anjou is a good province. The roads were covered with horsemen, coming from all sides to offer their adhesion or their services. M. d'Anjou, on his side, was always going about in search of some treasure. Bussy had succeeded in preventing any of these expeditions from going to the castle inhabited by Diane.

Bussy reserved that treasure for himself alone, and plundered after his own fashion that little corner of the province, which, after having properly defended itself, had made an unconditional surrender.

Now, while M. d'Anjou was reconnoitring and Bussy was plundering, M. de Monsoreau, mounted on his hunting-horse, reached the gate of Angers. It might have been four o'clock in the afternoon; to reach there by four o'clock, M. de Monsoreau had ridden thirty-five miles that day. His spurs were red, and his horse, white with foam, was half dead. The time had passed for objecting to any one's entering the gates; the Angevins were now so proud and disdainful that a battalion of Swiss commanded by Crillon himself would have been allowed to enter.

M. de Monsoreau, who was not Crillon, entered, saying: "To the palace of Monseigneur the Duc d'Anjou."

He did not listen to the answer which the guards shouted after him. His horse was able to stand on his legs only thanks to a miracle of equilibrium due to the rapidity of his gait. The poor animal went on unconsciously, and would probably fall down when he stopped. He stopped before the palace, but both horse and rider remained standing.

"Monsieur le Duc!" cried the master of the hounds.

"Monseigneur is out reconnoitring," replied the sentinel.

"Where?" asked M. de Monsoreau.

"Yonder," replied the functionary, pointing to one of the points of the compass.

"The devil!" said Monsoreau. "I had something very important to say to the duke; what shall I do?"

"First, put your horse in a stable," replied the sentinel, "because if you do not lean him against a wall, he will fall."

"The advice is good," said Monsoreau, "where are the stables, my good man?"

"There."

At this moment a man approached the master of the hounds and asked for his name. M. de Monsoreau gave it, and the major-domo bowed respectfully; the gentleman's name was well known in the province.

"Monsieur," he said, "please enter and take some rest. Monseigneur only went out ten minutes ago, and will not return until eight o'clock to-night."

"Eight o'clock to-night!" replied Monsoreau, biting his moustache, "that would be too much waste of time. I am the bearer of a piece of news which I must tell him at once. Can you not give me a horse and guide?"

"There are ten horses, monsieur," said the major-domo. "As to a guide, that is different, as Monseigneur did not say where he was going; besides, I could not take any one from the castle walls. That is one of his Highness's recommendations."

"Ah, ah," said the master of the hounds, "are we not in safety here?"

"Oh, monsieur, one is always in safety in the midst of such men as MM. de Bussy, Livarot, Ribeirac, and Antraguet, without counting our invincible prince, Monseigneur the Duc d'Anjou; but you understand —"

"Yes, I understand that when they are away, there is less safety."

"Exactly, monsieur."

"Then I shall take a fresh horse and try to join his Highness."

"I am quite sure, monsieur, that you will succeed in overtaking Monseigneur."

"Did they not gallop away?"

"No, monsieur, quite the contrary."

"Very well, then, show me the horse I may take."

"Go into the stable, monsieur, and choose for yourself: all belong to Monseigneur."

"Very well."

Monsoreau entered. Ten or twelve beautiful fresh horses were enjoying a plentiful meal of the freshest hay of Anjou.

"There they are," said the major-domo.

Monsoreau glanced along the line of quadrupeds with the eye of a connoisseur.

"I shall take that bay horse," he said; "have it saddled."

"Roland."

"Is that his name?"

"Yes; he is Monseigneur's favorite horse. He rides him every day; he was given to him by M. de Bussy, and you would surely not find him in the stable if his Highness were not trying the new horses that have just come from Tours."

"Ah, it seems I am not a bad judge."

A groom approached.

"Saddle Roland," said the major-domo.

As to the count's horse, he had entered the stable of his own accord and lain down in the straw without even waiting to be unsaddled.

Roland was ready in a few minutes.

M. de Monsoreau vaulted lightly into the saddle and inquired a second time the direction in which the duke's party had ridden away.

"They passed out of this gate and rode up that street,"
said the major-domo, pointing in the same direction as the
sentinel had done.

"Faith!" said Monsoreau, letting the reins hang loosely
as he saw the horse go that way of his own accord, "it
seems that Roland follows the scent."

"Oh, do not be uneasy," said the major-domo. "I have
heard M. de Bussy and his physician, Monsieur Rémy say
that he is the most intelligent animal in existence. So
soon as he scents his companions, he will join them. See
his beautiful legs; a deer might envy them."

Monsoreau looked down. "Magnificent!" he said.

In fact the horse had started off, and went slowly out of
the city; before reaching the gate, he even took a turn
which shortened the way.

While he gave this proof of intelligence, the horse shook
his head as if to rid himself of the bit which pressed against
his mouth; he seemed to say that all attempt to guide him
was useless, and as he approached the city gates, he quick-
ened his pace.

"Really," murmured Monsoreau, "I was not deceived.
Since you know the way so well, go, Roland, go," and he
dropped the reins on the horse's neck. The horse having
reached the outer road, hesitated for a moment whether to
turn to the right or to the left. He turned to the left. A
peasant passed at that moment.

"Eh, my friend, have you seen a troop of horsemen?"
asked Monsoreau.

"Yes, monsieur," replied the man, "I met them down
there," and he pointed in the direction taken by Roland,
who now went off at a swinging trot, which meant three or
four leagues an hour.

The horse followed the boulevard for some time longer,
then turning suddenly to the right, took a path which cut
right across the country.

Monsoreau hesitated for an instant to know if he should not stop Roland, but the horse seemed to know so well what he was about that he let him continue. As the animal went on, he gradually changed his trot into a gallop, and in less than a quarter of an hour had lost sight of the city. As the rider advanced, he seemed to recognize the localities.

"Well," he said, as he entered the forest, "one would say we are going to Méridor; I wonder if his Highness has come this way?" Monsoreau's brow became clouded as this idea passed through his mind for the first time. "Oh, oh," he murmured, "I who was going to see the prince and put off seeing my wife until to-morrow, shall I have the pleasure of seeing them both together?" A terrible smile flitted across his lips.

The horse galloped along, keeping to the right with a tenacity which showed a most thorough knowledge of the way.

"On my soul," thought Monsoreau, "I can no longer be very far from the park of Méridor!"

At this moment the horse began to neigh, and another horse replied from the neighboring thicket.

"Ah, ah," said the master of the hounds, "it seems that Roland has found his companions!"

The horse galloped on, and passed like a flash through the tall trees. Monsoreau suddenly caught sight of a wall and of a horse tied near the wall. The horse neighed a second time, and Monsoreau realized that he must have neighed first.

"There is some one here!" he said, growing pale.

CHAPTER XXI.

WHAT M. LE COMTE DE MONSOREAU HAD COME TO ANNOUNCE.

M. DE MONSOREAU went from one surprise to another; the wall of Méridor rising before him, the horse he found there caressing the one on which he came, as if they were intimate companions, — all this was sufficient to rouse the suspicions of any one. As he approached, and we may be sure he did so quickly, he noticed the dilapidation of the wall. There was a real ladder which threatened to become a breach; the feet seemed to have hollowed out steps in the stones, and the newly uprooted brambles hung by their withered stems.

The count took in the whole scene at a glance, then from the whole he passed to the details. The horse deserved the first place. The indiscreet animal wore a silver embroidered saddle-cloth; in one of the corners was a double FF entwined round a double AA.

There was no doubt that this horse came from the prince's stables, since these were the initials of François d'Anjou. At this sight the count's suspicions were changed into certainties.

The duke had come this way; he came often; for besides the horse waiting there, another knew the way. Monsoreau concluded that since chance had put him on that track he must follow it to the end. This belonged to his attributes as master of the hounds and as a jealous husband.

But so long as he remained on the other side of the wall, it was evident that he would see nothing. He therefore tied

his horse near the other, and bravely began the ascent. This
was an easy task; there were places for the hands and
feet, and even the overhanging branches of an oak had been
carefully cut away. So many efforts were crowned with
entire success. M. de Monsoreau had no sooner reached
his point of observation than he perceived at the foot of a
tree a blue mantle and a black velvet cloak. The mantle
belonged unquestionably to a woman and the black cloak to
a man. Besides, there was no need to look any further;
the man and woman were walking arm in arm, about fifty
feet away. Their backs were turned to the wall, and they
were half concealed by the foliage.

Unfortunately for M. de Monsoreau, the wall was not
accustomed to his violent mode of ascent, and a large stone
rolled from the crest and fell to the earth with a dull
sound.

At this sound the individuals whose faces were concealed
by the foliage turned and saw him, because the cry of a
woman was heard, followed by a rustling of the branches
as the lovers ran away like startled deer. At this cry
Monsoreau felt cold drops of perspiration gather on his
brow. He had recognized Diane's voice. Incapable of
resisting the movement of fury that seized him, he jumped
from the wall, and drawing his sword, began to follow the
fugitives through the bushes. But they had disappeared,
and nothing broke the stillness of the park, — not a shadow
in the alleys, not a trace, not a sound, only the song of the
birds, who, accustomed to the presence of the lovers, had
not been frightened by them.

What could he do in the presence of this solitude? What
would he decide? The park was large, and one might meet
those one did not seek.

M. de Monsoreau concluded that the discovery he had
made sufficed for the present; besides, he felt too violently
agitated to act with all the prudence necessary in dealing

with a rival as powerful as François. Not one moment did he doubt that the prince was his rival. Then, if perchance it were not he, he had a mission to fulfil near the prince. Besides, when he found himself in the duke's presence, he would soon know whether he were innocent or guilty. Then a sublime idea came to him. That idea consisted in getting at once over the wall and taking away with him the horse of the intruder surprised in the park. This vengeful project doubled his strength; he ran to the wall and reached it, breathless and covered with perspiration. Then, with the help of the branches, he scrambled to the top and dropped down on the other side; but there were no more horses. His idea was so good that it had also occurred to his enemy, who had taken advantage of it.

M. de Monsoreau was furious, and shook his fist at the impudent man who was no doubt laughing at him in the thick shadow of the woods; but as his will was not easily conquered, he re-acted against the fates who seemed to be bent on overwhelming him. He found his way at once, and in spite of the approaching night, summoned his strength and returned to Angers by a cross-road which he had known from his earliest childhood. Two hours and a half later he reached the city gates, dying with thirst, heat, and fatigue; but the exaltation of his mind gave strength to his body, and he was still the same man, at once violent and wilful.

He was, moreover, sustained by one idea. He would question the sentinels; by going from gate to gate, he would know what man had come in with two horses; he would empty his purse, make any promises, but would get a description of that man. Then, whoever he might be, sooner or later, this man should pay his debt. He examined the sentinel, but the soldier had just taken the post, and knew nothing. He entered the guard-house and inquired. A militiaman had seen a riderless horse return about two hours before, and the animal had taken the road to the palace. He thought some accident had happened to the rider, and that the intelligent horse had found his way back to the stable.

Monsoreau struck his head. The fates had decided that he should know nothing. He then went towards the ducal palace. There was great animation, great noise, and mirth. The windows shone like suns, the kitchens sent forth enticing odors of game and cloves, capable of making the stomach forget its proximity to the heart. But the gates were closed, and here was another difficulty, — he must have them opened. Monsoreau called the *concierge* and gave his name, but the man would not recognize him.

" You were straight, and now you are bent," he said.

" It is from fatigue."

" You were pale, and you are now red."

" It is from heat."

" You were on horseback, and you return without a horse."

" My horse took fright, shied, and threw me. Did you not see him return ? "

" Yes, so I did," said the *concierge*.

" At all events, call the major-domo."

The *concierge*, delighted at this opportunity of discharging his responsibility on another, sent for Monsieur Rémy.

Monsieur Rémy came and recognized Monsoreau.

" Ah, *mon Dieu!* whence do you come in such a state ? " he asked.

Monsoreau repeated the same story he had already told the *concierge*.

" In fact," said the major-domo, " we were very uneasy when we saw your horse return without a rider; particularly Monseigneur, whom I had notified of your arrival."

" Ah, Monseigneur seemed uneasy ? " asked Monsoreau.

" Extremely so."

WHAT MONSOREAU HAD COME TO ANNOUNCE.   177

"What did he say?"

"That you should be sent to him at once on your return."

"Very well; I shall only take time to visit the stable and see that nothing happens to his Highness's horse."

Monsoreau went to the stable, where he found the intelligent animal in the same stall whence he had taken him and eating with a good appetite. Then without even taking time to change his costume, because he thought the importance of the news he brought would excuse him from the formalities of etiquette, he went to the dining-hall. His Highness and all the gentlemen of his suite were sitting round a table magnificently served and lighted. They were attacking pheasant pies, boars' heads, and other delicacies, accompanied by the dark-colored wine from Cahors, or the topaz-colored wine of Anjou, which goes to your head before it has ceased sparkling in the glass.

"The court is full," said Antraguet, as rosy as a maiden, and drunk as a trooper, — "full as Monseigneur's cellar."

"Not at all, not at all," said Ribeirac; "we have no master of the hounds. It is really shameful that we should eat the duke's dinner, and not get it for ourselves."

"I vote for any master of the hounds," said Livarot, "no matter who, — even M. de Monsoreau."

The duke smiled. He alone knew of the count's arrival. Livarot had scarcely finished his sentence, and the prince his smile, when the door opened, and M. de Monsoreau appeared.

As he caught sight of him, the duke uttered an exclamation, which sounded all the more noisy because it broke the general silence.

"Well, here he is," he said. "You see we are favored by heaven, since he is sent to us just when we wish for him."

Monsoreau, rather embarrassed by the prince's assurance, which was not customary in such cases, bowed rather awkwardly, and averted his head as though the glare of the lights hurt his eyes.

"Seat yourself and sup with us," said the duke, pointing to a place opposite his own.

"Monseigneur," replied Monsoreau, "I am thirsty, hungry, and weary; but I shall neither eat, drink, nor rest until I have delivered a message of the utmost importance which I have for your Highness."

"You come from Paris, do you not?"

"Yes, in great haste."

"Well, speak," said the duke.

Monsoreau advanced with smiling lips, but with hatred in his heart and whispered to him, —

"Monseigneur, the Queen-mother is travelling hither by rapid stages; she comes to visit your Highness."

The duke, on whom all eyes were fixed, showed his sudden joy.

"It is well; thank you," he said. "M. de Monsoreau, I find you to-day, as ever, a faithful servant. Let us continue our supper, gentlemen." And he moved up to the table.

The feast continued. The master of the hounds was no sooner in a comfortable seat, and before a well-served table, than he lost all appetite.

The mind gained the ascendency over matter.

His mind, carried away by sad thoughts, returned to the park of Méridor, travelling over the same road already followed by that same weary body. He saw once more the neighing steed, the crumbling wall, the fleeting shadows of the two lovers; he heard once more Diane's scream, — that scream which had echoed in the very depths of his heart. Then, indifferent to noise, lights, and even to the meal, forgetting in whose presence he was, he buried himself in his own thoughts; his brow gradually became clouded and he uttered a groan which drew the attention of the astonished guests.

"You are dead with fatigue, count," said the prince, "you really ought to go to bed."

"Yes," said Livarot, "the advice is good; and if you do not follow it, you run great risk of dropping asleep in your plate."

"Pardon me, monseigneur," said Monsoreau, raising his head. "I am tired out."

"Drink," said Antraguet; "there is nothing so restful."

"And then," said Monsoreau, "when we drink, we forget."

"Pshaw!" said Livarot, "there is nothing to do; see, gentlemen, his glass is still full."

"Your health, count," said Ribeirac, raising his glass.

Monsoreau was obliged to answer the gentleman and emptied the glass at one gulp.

"He can still drink very well; see, monseigneur," said Antraguet.

"Yes," replied the prince, who tried to read the count's heart. "Yes, very well."

"You must give us a fine hunt," said Ribeirac; "you know the country, count."

"You have estates and forests here," said Livarot.

"And even a wife," added Autraguet.

"Yes," replied the count, mechanically. "Yes, estates and forests and Madame de Monsoreau."

"Give us a boar hunt, count," said the prince.

"I shall try, monseigneur."

"Eh, *pardieu!*" said one of the Angevin gentlemen, "you will try. What a fine answer! The woods are full of boars. If I hunted, I would like to raise ten."

Monsoreau turned pale in spite of himself.

"Ah, yes, to-morrow," cried the gentlemen together.

"Will you hunt to-morrow, Monsoreau?" asked the duke.

"I am always at your Highness's orders," replied Monsoreau; "but as Monseigneur observed but a few seconds
ago, I am very weary to hunt to-morrow. Then I must
explore the neighborhood and see the condition of the
woods."

"You must let him see his wife. The devil!" said the
duke, in a good humoured way, which convinced the poor
husband that he was the rival.

"Agreed, agreed," cried the young men, gaily. "We
give M. de Monsoreau twenty-four hours to do all he can in
his woods."

"Yes, gentlemen, give me that time," said the count,
"and you may be certain that I shall employ it well."

"Now, count," said the prince, "I allow you to go to
bed. Conduct M. de Monsoreau to his room."

M. de Monsoreau bowed and went out, being relieved of
a great weight. Persons in affliction are even fonder of
solitude than happy lovers.

CHAPTER XXII.

HOW KING HENRI III. HEARD OF THE FLIGHT OF HIS
BELOVED BROTHER, THE DUC D'ANJOU, AND WHAT FOL-
LOWED.

WHEN the master of the hounds had retired from the room,
the repast continued more gay, joyous, and unrestrained
than ever. Monsoreau's gloomy face had kept the young
men in check because, under the pretext, and even the
reality of fatigue, they had guessed that continual preoccu-
pation of gloomy subjects which put on the count's brow
that mortal sadness which formed the characteristic of his
expression.

When he was gone, the prince, who always seemed awkward in his presence, resumed his tranquil expression.

"Come, Livarot," he said, "when the master of the
hounds entered you had just begun to tell us about your
escape from Paris. Continue." And Livarot continued.

But as our title of historian gives us a better opportunity
of knowing what had taken place, we shall substitute our
story for that of the young man. It may, perhaps, lose in
character, but it will gain in length, since we know what
took place at the Louvre.

Towards the middle of the night Henri III. was roused
by an unusual noise in the palace, where everything was
usually so still after the king had retired. There were
oaths, blows on the wall, rapid footsteps, and in the midst
of all these sounds these words, repeated like an echo, —

"What will the king say? What will the king say?"

Henri sat up in bed and looked at Chicot, who, after having supped with his Majesty, had gone to sleep in the large armchair with his legs wound round his sword. The noise increased; Henri jumped out of bed covered with pomatum, and cried, —

"Chicot! Chicot!"

Chicot opened one eye. He was a prudent man, who appreciated sleep, and never woke up at once.

"Ah, you were wrong to call me, Henri. I dreamed you had a son."

"Listen!" said Henri; "listen!"

"What do you want me to hear? I think you talk enough nonsense all day without taking my nights!"

"Do you not hear?" cried the king, extending his hand in the direction whence came the noise.

"Oh, oh," cried Chicot, "I do hear cries!"

"'What will the king say? What will the king say?' Do you hear?"

"You may believe either one of two things: either your hound Narcissus is ill or the Huguenots are taking their revenge and making a Saint-Bartholomew of Catholics."

"Help me to dress, Chicot."

"I am willing, but first help me to rise, Henri."

"What a misfortune! what a misfortune!" was repeated in the ante-chambers.

"The devil! this is becoming serious," said Chicot.

"We had better arm ourselves," said the king.

"It would be even better to go out at once through the little door and see for ourselves the extent of the misfortune instead of simply hearing about it."

Henri followed Chicot's advice, and found himself in the corridor leading to the Duc d'Anjou's apartments.

There they saw arms uplifted towards heaven and heard exclamations of despair.

"Oh, oh," said Chicot, "I can guess! Your unfortunate

prisoner has probably hanged himself. *Ventre de biche!*
Henri, I congratulate you; you are a better politician than
I thought."

"Ah, no!" cried Henri, "it cannot be that."

"So much the worse."

"Come, come!" and they entered the duke's chamber.
The window was open, and a crowd had assembled and was
gazing at the rope ladder still suspended from the balcony.
Henri grew pale as a corpse.

"Eh, my son," said Chicot, "you are not yet so *blasé* as I
thought."

"Fled! escaped!" said Henri, in such thundering tones
that all the gentlemen turned round. The king's eyes
flashed as his hand sought the hilt of his sword.

Schomberg tore his hair; Maugiron and Quélus struck
their heads and faces. As to D'Epernon, he had disappeared
under the specious pretext of going in pursuit of the Duc
d'Anjou. The sight of the martyrdom which, in their
despair, his favorites were inflicting on themselves, suddenly quieted the king.

"Hey! gently my sons!" he said, holding on to Maugiron.

"No, *mordieu!* I will kill myself!" said Maugiron, preparing to strike his head against the wall.

"Help me while I hold him," cried Henri.

"Ho, friend!" said Chicot, "there is a pleasanter death
than that. Run your sword through your body."

"Hold your tongue, you brute!" said Henri, with tears
in his eyes. During this time Quélus was bruising his
cheeks.

"Oh, Quélus, my child," said Henri, "you will look like
Schomberg when he had been dipped in the vat of indigo!
You will be horrible."

Quélus stopped.

Schomberg alone continued to tear his hair and weep from
rage.

"Schomberg, Schomberg! a little reason, I beg!"

"I shall go mad!"

"Pshaw!" said Chicot.

"It is, indeed, a terrible misfortune, and you must preserve your reason, Schomberg. Yes, it is a horrible
misfortune; I am lost! This means civil war in my
kingdom. Ah, who furnished the ladder? *Par la mordieu!* I will hang the whole city!" A great terror spread
among the spectators. "Where is the guilty one?" continued Henri. "Ten thousand crowns to the one who will
tell me his name, and one hundred thousand to whomsoever
will bring him to me, dead or alive."

"Who can it be if not some Angevin?" cried Maugiron.

"*Pardieu!* you are right," cried Henri. "Ah, the
Angevins, *mordieu!* they shall pay for it."

As if that word had been a spark lighting a train of
powder, a frightful explosion of cries and threats broke
out against the Angevins.

"Oh, yes, the Angevins!" cried Quélus.

"Where are they?" roared Schomberg.

"Rip them open!" vociferated Maugiron.

"A hundred gibbets for a hundred Angevins," resumed
the king.

Chicot could not remain silent in this universal fury; he
drew his sword, and striking right and left with the flat
side, he attacked the favorites and beat the walls.

"Oh, *ventre de biche!* oh, noble rage! ah, damnation
to the Angevins, *mordieu!*" he repeated, as he glared
about him.

This cry, "Death to the Angevins!" was heard throughout the city, as the cry of the Hebrew mothers was heard
throughout Rama.

Henri had disappeared. He had thought of his mother,
and slipping out of the room without saying a word, had
gone to see Catherine, whom he had somewhat neglected of

late.   She, apparently indifferent, awaited some suitable occasion which would again bring her policy to the front.

When Henri entered, she was half lying in a large arm-chair, and with her fat, yellowish cheeks, her bright staring eyes, her plump, pale hands, she resembled a wax statue of meditation rather than a living creature.   But at the news of François' escape, which Henri announced without any preparation whatever, filled as he was with anger and hatred, the statue seemed suddenly awake, though she merely leaned a little further back and shook her head without speaking.

"Well, mother, do you not speak ? " asked Henri.   " Does not this flight of your son seem to you criminal, and worthy of punishment ? "

" My dear son, liberty is well worth a crown ; and remember that I, too, advised you to escape when you could reach that crown."

" Mother, I am insulted."

Catherine shrugged her shoulders.

" He braves me."

" Oh, no ; he saves himself, that is all."

" Ah," said Henri, " see how you take my part ! "

" What do you mean, my son ? "

" I mean that feelings grow dull with age ; I say — "

He stopped.

" What are you saying ? " resumed Catherine, with her usual calmness.

" I say that you no longer love me as you did."

" You are mistaken," said Catherine, with increasing coldness, " you are still my beloved son ; but the one of whom you complain is also my son."

" Ah, a truce to moral sentiments, madame," said Henri, furiously ; " we know their value."

" Ah, you should know it better than any, my son, for with you my moral has always been weakness."

"And as this is the time to repent, you repent."

"I felt that we would come to that, my son," said
Catherine, "therefore I remained silent."

"Adieu, madame, adieu. I know what I have to do
since even my mother has no compassion for me; I shall
find advisers capable of feeling for me and helping me in
this case."

"Go, my son," quietly replied the Florentine. "May God
guide your counsellors; they will need his assistance to aid
you in this strait," and she let him go without a gesture,
without saying a word to keep him.

"Adieu, madame," repeated Henri, but he stopped near
the door.

"Adieu, Henri," said the queen. "I do not pretend to
advise you, — you do not need me, I know, — but beg your
counsellors to think well before they advise, and even better
before they act."

"Oh, yes," said Henri, taking advantage of this not to go
away, "the position is difficult, is it not, madame?"

"Very grave, Henri," said Catherine, slowly raising her
hands and eyes to heaven. The king, struck by the expression of his mother's eyes, returned to her.

"Who are those who planned his escape? Have you
any idea?" he asked.

Catherine did not reply.

"I think it was the Angevins," continued the king.

Catherine smiled that fine smile which always showed in
her the superior and ever watchful mind.

"The Angevins?" she repeated.

"You do not believe it," said Henri, "yet every one does."

Catherine again shrugged her shoulders.

"The others may believe that, — but you, my son?"

"What do you mean, madame? I beg you to explain."

"Why should I?"

"To enlighten me."

"Enlighten you! Come Henri, I am only an old woman in her dotage, whose only influence lies in her prayers and repentance."

"No, speak, speak, mother, I am listening. Oh, you are still, and will always be, the cleverest of us all."

"It is useless, I have only the ideas of another century, and the distrustfulness of old age. That I should still be able to offer you advice, — impossible, my son."

"Very well, mother, keep your advice and deprive me of your assistance. But within an hour, I shall hang all the Angevins in Paris."

"Hang all the Angevins!" exclaimed Catherine, with the amazement of superior minds when something extraordinary is said before them.

"Yes, hang, slay, massacre, burn. At this very moment my friends are scouring the city to break the bones of those cursed rebels!"

"Let them beware, unhappy man!" cried Catherine, carried away by the gravity of the situation. "They would ruin themselves, — that is nothing, — but they would also ruin you."

"How so?"

"Blind!" murmured Catherine. "Will kings eternally have eyes not to see?" And she clasped her hands.

"Kings are kings only on condition that they will avenge the injuries inflicted on them; because in that case vengeance is justice; and in this case, my whole kingdom will rise to avenge me."

"Foolish child!"

"Why so?"

"Do you think that men like Bussy, Antraguet, Livarot, and Ribeirac can be hanged, burned, or slain, without causing rivers of blood to flow?"

"No matter, provided they are killed."

"Yes, no doubt if they are killed. Show them to me

dead, and by Notre-Dame ! I will say that you did right. But they will not be killed, they will raise the standard of revolt, and draw their swords, — a thing they would not have done for François, — and your kingdom will rise in arms not for you but against you."

"But if I do not avenge myself they will think I am afraid."

"Did any one ever say I was afraid ?" asked Catherine, frowning, and biting her thin red lips.

"Yet, if it is the Angevins, they deserve punishment."

"Yes, but it was not they."

"Who could it be if not my brother's friends ? "

"It is not your brother's friends, for he has none."

"But who is it ? "

"Your enemy."

"Which one ? "

"My son, you have never had but one, as your brother Charles never had but one, — who is the same as mine, always the same."

"You mean Henri de Navarre ? "

"Yes."

"He is not in Paris."

"Eh, do you know who is or who is not in Paris ? Do you know something ? Have you eyes and ears ? Have you any one around you who sees and hears ? No, you are all deaf and blind."

"Henri de Navarre ! " repeated the king.

"My son, in every disappointment you meet with, in every misfortune that happens to you, the author of which is unknown, do not seek, hesitate, or inquire ; that is useless. Say, 'It is Henri de Navarre,' and you are sure to be right. Strike on the side where he is, for that is the right side to strike. Oh, that man, that man ! he is the sword suspended by God over the house of Valois."

"Then you think I ought to countermand the order about the Angevins ? "

"At once!" cried Catherine, "without losing a minute or a second. Hasten, it may now be too late; recall your orders; go, or you are lost."

And seizing her son by the arm, she pushed him to the door with incredible force and energy. Henri rushed out of the Louvre to try and assemble his friends, but he found only Chicot sitting on a stone and drawing geometrical figures on the sand.

CHAPTER XXIII.

HOW CHICOT AND THE QUEEN-MOTHER BEING OF THE SAME
OPINION, THE KING BEGAN TO AGREE WITH THEM.

HENRI looked at the Gascon, who seemed to have made
up his mind not to turn around, even if Paris were taken
by storm.

"Ah, wretch!" he said, in a thundering voice, "is this
how you defend your king?"

"I defend him after my own fashion, which I consider
a good one."

"A good one, indeed!"

"I maintain it, and I prove it."

"I am curious to see this proof."

"It is easy; but first of all, we have committed a great
blunder."

"In doing what?"

"In doing what we have done."

"Ah, ah!" said Henri, struck by the agreement between
these two minds who had had no communication.

"Yes," replied Chicot, "your friends are howling
through the city, 'Death to the Angevins!' and now that
I reflect upon it, I find it was never proved that the
Angevins had anything to do with the case. As I said,
your friends, in crying through the town 'Death to the
Angevins!' will simply raise that nice little civil war of
which MM. de Guise are so greatly in need, and which they
could not raise of themselves. Now at this moment,
Henri, your friends are either dead — which would not
displease me, I confess, but which would cause you sor-

row — or else they have driven all the Angevins from the city — which would greatly displease you, but would delight that dear M. d'Anjou."

" *Mordieu !* " cried the king, " do you think that matters are already so bad as that ? "

" If not a little worse."

" But all this does not explain what you are doing here on this stone."

" I am doing very important work, my son."

" What is it ? "

" I am tracing a plan of all the provinces that will rise in rebellion at your brother's call, and I am counting up the number of men that each one will furnish to the revolt."

" Chicot, Chicot," said the king, " am I only surrounded by birds of ill-omen ? "

" The owl sings at night, my son, because that is his hour. Now, it is dark, Henriquet, — so dark, in fact, that one might mistake night for day ; and I sing what you ought to hear. Look ! "

" At what ? "

" At my map, and judge. First we have Anjou, which rather resembles a pie, — you see ? That is where your brother has taken refuge, so I have given it the first place. Anjou, well managed by your master of the hounds Monsoreau and your friend Bussy, can alone furnish ten thousand men to your brother."

" You think so ? "

" That is the minimum. Let us pass on to Guyenne : here it is, a figure like a calf walking on one leg. Well, you must not be surprised to find some malcontents in Guyenne. It is an old focus of revolt, and the English have only just left it. Guyenne will be quick to rise, not against you, but against France. You can count on eight thousand men from there ; that is little, but you may be sure they are well disciplined and trained troops. Then to the left of Guyenne, we have Béarn and Navarre, — these two divisions, which resemble an ape on the back of an elephant. Navarre has been greatly cut up, but, with Béarn, it still has a population of about three or four hundred thousand men. Suppose that Béarn and Navarre, pressed by Henri, should furnish five per cent of their population, that will be sixteen thousand men. Let us therefore recapitulate: ten thousand for Anjou."

And Chicot continued to draw the numbers on the sand with his stick.

```
" Anjou . . . . . . . . . . 10,000
  Guyenne . . . . . . . .  8,000
  Béarn and Navarre  . . . . 16,000

       Total . . . . . . . 34,000 "
```

"You think," said Henri, "that Navarre will form an alliance with my brother?"

"Pardieu!"

"Do you think he had anything to do with his escape?"

Chicot looked straight at the king.

"Henriquet," he said, "that was not your own idea."

"Why not?"

"It is too clever, my son."

"No matter whose it is; I question you: answer. Do you think Henri of Navarre had anything to do with my brother's escape?"

"Well, I heard in the Rue de la Ferronnerie, a ' Ventre saint-gris!' which seems to me rather conclusive."

"You heard a ' ventre saint-gris'?" cried the king.

"Yes," said Chicot, "and I have only just remembered it."

"So he was in Paris?"

"I believe so."

"What can make you believe it?"

"My eyes."

"You saw the King of Navarre?"

"Yes."

"And you did not come and tell me that my enemy had braved me even here in my capital."

"A man is a gentleman or he is not," said Chicot; "if he is a gentleman, he is not a spy, — that's all."

Henri became thoughtful.

"So," he said, "Anjou and Béarn, my brother François and my cousin Henri."

"Without counting the three Guises."

"What! do you think they will join the alliance?"

"Thirty-four thousand men on one side," said Chicot, counting on his fingers, — "ten for Anjou, eight for Guyenne, sixteen for Béarn, plus twenty or twenty-five thousand under the orders of M. de Guise, as lieutenant-general of your armies; total, fifty-nine thousand men. Let us reduce them to fifty thousand on account of gout, rheumatism, sciatica, and other infirmities. It is still, as you see, my son, a very nice total."

"But Henri de Navarre and the Duc de Guise are enemies."

"That will not prevent their uniting against you, even if they should exterminate each other after they have exterminated you."

"You are right, Chicot; my mother is right; you are both right. You must prevent a scandal; help me to assemble the Swiss."

"Ah, yes, the Swiss! Quélus has taken them."

"My guards."

"Schomberg has taken them."

"But my own attendants."

"They have gone with Maugiron."

"What!" cried Henri, "without my orders?"

"And since when do you give orders, Henri? Ah, in the matter of processions and flagellations, I do not say you are not given full sway over your own skin and even that of others. But all questions of war and government, — why, they concern M. de Schomberg, M. de Quélus, and M. de Maugiron. As to D'Epernon, I say nothing about him, since he is hiding."

"*Mordieu!*" said Henri, "is this the way that things are going on?"

"Allow me to tell you, my son," replied Chicot, "that you are very late in perceiving that you are only the seventh or eighth king of your kingdom."

Henri bit his lip and stamped his foot.

"Eh," said Chicot, trying to peer through the darkness.

"What is the matter?" asked the king.

"*Ventre de biche!* here are your men, Henri," and he pointed out to the king three or four horsemen who galloped up, followed at a distance by some other horsemen and a great many men on foot. The horsemen were about to enter the Louvre without having noticed the two men standing near the ditch, half concealed in the dim light.

"Schomberg!" cried the king, "Schomberg, come here!"

"Who calls me?" said Schomberg.

"Come, my child, come."

Schomberg thought he recognized the voice, and drew near.

"Eh," he said, "God damn me! it is the king."

"In person; I was running after you, and not knowing where to join you, I was impatiently waiting. What have you done?"

"What have we done?" asked a second horseman, approaching.

"Ah, come Quélus," said the king, "and do not go off again in this way without my permission."

"There is no need of it," said a third, whom the king recognized as Maugiron; "all is over."

"All is over ? " repeated the king.

" Heaven be praised ! " said D'Epernon, suddenly appearing. " Hosanna ! " cried Chicot, raising his hands to heaven.

" Then you have killed them ? " asked the king; and he added in a low voice, "after all, the dead do not return."

" Have you killed them ? " asked Chicot. " Ah, if you have done that, there is nothing to say."

" We did not have that trouble," said Schomberg. " The cowards had flown away like a flock of pigeons; we scarcely had time to cross our swords with them."

Henri grew pale.

" With whom ? " he asked.

" With Antraguet."

" I hope you killed that one."

" On the contrary, he killed one of Quélus' valets."

" They were, then, on their guard ? "

"*Parbleu!* I should think they were," cried Chicot. " You cry, 'Death to the Angevins,' you fire cannon, ring bells, and you expect honest people to be more deaf than you are foolish."

" Oh," murmured the king, "this means a civil war ! "

Quélus started at these words.

" The devil ! " he said, "that is true."

" Ah, you are beginning to see," said Chicot; " how fortunate ! Here are MM. de Schomberg and Maugiron who do not even suspect the fact."

" We reserve ourselves," said Schomberg, "to defend the person and crown of his Majesty."

" Eh, *pardieu !* " said Chicot, "for that we have M. de Crillon, who makes less noise but who is worth quite as much."

" But you, Monsieur Chicot, who have been criticising us right and left, — you thought like the rest of us, and cried out as we did," said Quélus.

"I ?" said Chicot.

"Certainly, and you were beating the walls and crying out, 'Death to the Angevins!'"

"With me," said Chicot, "it is a very different matter. I am a fool and every one knows it, but you are clever men."

"Come, gentlemen," said Henri, "peace; we shall soon have enough war."

"What are your Majesty's orders?" asked Quélus.

"That you should make the same efforts to calm the people that you made to excite them; that you should bring back to the palace the Swiss, guards, and members of my household and close the gates, so that to-morrow the *bourgeois* may take the whole thing for a drunken brawl."

The young men went away rather crestfallen, and transmitted the king's orders to the officers who had accompanied them. As for Henri, he returned to his mother, who, anxious and gloomy, was busy giving orders.

"Well," she asked, "what has taken place?"

"What you had foreseen."

"Have they fled?"

"Alas! yes."

"What else?"

"Nothing. That seems to me quite sufficient."

"The city?"

"Is excited; but that does not trouble me, I have it under control."

"Yes," said Catherine, "but the provinces?"

"They will rise in rebellion," replied Henri.

"What do you intend to do?"

"I see but one thing."

"What is that?"

"To accept the position openly."

"How so?"

"I give my orders to the colonels and to my guards, I

arm the militia, summon the troops from La Charité, and
march against Anjou."

"And M. de Guise?"

"Well, M. de Guise! I shall have him arrested if necessary."

"And you think violent measures will succeed?"

"What am I to do?"

Catherine looked down and reflected for a moment.

"All that you propose is impossible, my son."

"Ah," cried Henri, "am I so badly inspired to-day?"

"No, but you are agitated; calm yourself and we shall
see."

"Well, mother, think for me; we must act and do something."

"You see, my son, I was giving orders."

"What orders?"

"For the departure of an ambassador."

"To whom shall we send one?"

"To your brother."

"An ambassador to this traitor! You humiliate me."

"This is not the time for pride," said Catherine, severely.

"An ambassador who will ask for peace?"

"And even buy it if necessary."

"For what advantage, *mon Dieu!*"

"Eh, my son," said the Florentine, "if only to give us
later on the power of securing those who escaped to make
war. Did you not say a while ago that you would like to
secure their persons?"

"Oh, I would give four provinces of my kingdom for
that, — one for each man!"

"Who wishes the end, wishes the means," replied Catherine, in a voice which stirred the desire for hatred and
vengeance in Henri's heart.

"I think you are right, mother. But whom shall we
send?"

"Seek among your friends."

"I do not see a single man to whom I could entrust such a mission."

"Give it to a woman, then."

"To a woman! Mother, would you consent?"

"My son, I am very old and weak, and death may perhaps await me on my return; but I shall make this journey so rapidly that I shall arrive in Angers before your brother and his friends have had time to understand all their power."

"Oh, mother, my good mother!" cried Henri, effusively, kissing her hands, "you are ever my support, my benefactress, my providence!"

"That means that I am still Queen of France," murmured Catherine, and the glance which rested on her son contained as much pity as tenderness.

CHAPTER XXIV.

IN WHICH IT IS PROVED THAT GRATITUDE WAS ONE OF M. DE SAINT-LUC'S VIRTUES.

On the day following the one when M. de Monsoreau's dismal expression had obtained for him the Duc d'Anjou's permission to retire, that gentleman rose early and descended into the palace courtyard. His object was to find the groom to whom he had already spoken, and obtain from him, if possible, some information concerning Roland's habits. The count succeeded. He entered beneath a vast shed where forty magnificent horses were devouring the best oats and hay of Anjou. Monsoreau's first glance went in search of Roland. The horse was in its place, and eating with appetite. The second glance was for the groom.

He recognized him standing near the wall and watching the horses as they ate.

" Eh, my friend," said the count, " are Monseigneur's horses taught to return to their stable alone ? "

" No, Monsieur le Comte," replied the groom. " Why do you ask this question ? "

" About Roland."

" Ah, he returned alone yesterday. But that does not surprise me ; he is a very intelligent animal."

" Yes," said Monsoreau, " I noticed that. Has he done so before ? "

" No, monsieur ; he is generally used by Monseigneur the Duc d'Anjou, who is an excellent rider, not easily unhorsed."

"Roland did not throw me," said the count, unwilling that even a groom should suspect him of such bad horsemanship. "Without having Monseigneur's skill, I am a good rider. No, I had tied him to a tree while I entered a house; when I returned, he had disappeared. I thought he had been stolen, or that some gentleman had played me a trick by carrying him away. That was my reason for asking how he had returned."

"He came alone, as the major-domo had the honor of telling Monsieur le Comte yesterday."

"That is strange," said Monsoreau. He paused for a moment, then changing the conversation, "Does Monseigneur often ride this horse?" he asked.

"He rode him nearly every day until the arrival of the equipages."

"Did his Highness come in late last night?"

"About one hour before you, Monsieur le Comte."

"What horse did the duke ride? Was it not a bay with white stockings and a star on its forehead?"

"No, monsieur," said the groom; "he rode Isolin, whom you see here."

"Was there no one in the prince's escort riding a horse answering to the description I gave you?"

"I know no one having such a horse."

"Very well," said Monsoreau, impatient at the lack of success of his discoveries. "Thank you. Saddle Roland for me."

"Monsieur le Comte desires Roland?"

"Yes. Has the prince given any orders against it?"

"No, monsieur; on the contrary, I was told to say that the whole stable is at your disposal."

There was no way of showing anger against a prince so full of delicate attentions. Monsoreau nodded to the groom, who immediately saddled the horse. When this was done, and the groom had led Roland to the count, —

"Listen," said the latter, as he took the bridle, "and answer me."

"Certainly, monsieur."

"What are your wages for the year?"

"Twenty crowns, monsieur."

"Would you like to earn ten times that sum at one stroke?"

"*Pardieu !* but how?"

"Find out who rode yesterday a horse answering to the description I gave you."

"Ah, monsieur!" said the groom; "this is a very difficult task. So many gentlemen come to visit his Highness."

"Yes, but two hundred crowns is a large sum to earn when you have no risks to run."

"I know it, Monsieur le Comte, and I shall do my best."

"Come," said the count; "I see you are willing. Here are ten crowns as an encouragement. You see you will not have lost everything."

"Thank you, Monsieur le Comte."

"Well, tell the prince that I have gone to reconnoitre the woods for the chase."

The count had scarcely uttered these words, when he heard footsteps behind him. He turned round.

"M. de Bussy!" he cried.

"Eh, good-morning, M. de Monsoreau," said Bussy. "You, in Angers; what a miracle!"

"And you, monsieur, — I thought you were ill."

"So I am," said Bussy. "My physician orders absolute rest, and I have not left the city for a week. Ah, ah, it seems you are about to ride Roland. I sold him to M. le Duc d'Anjou, who is so pleased that he rides him nearly every day."

Monsoreau turned pale.

"Yes," he said, "I can understand that. Roland is an excellent horse."

202 LA DAME DE MONSOREAU.

" You are very fortunate in making so good a choice from the first," said Bussy.

" Oh, this is not my first acquaintance with him. I rode him, yesterday."

" Which made you wish to try him again to-day ? "

" Yes," replied the count.

" Pardon me," said Bussy, " did you not speak of preparing a chase ? "

" The prince has expressed that wish."

" I am told there are a great many deer in the vicinity."

" A great many."

" And which side will you drive the animal ? "

" In the neighborhood of Méridor."

" Ah ! " said Bussy, growing pale in spite of himself.

" Will you accompany me ? " asked Monsoreau.

" No, I thank you," replied Bussy. " I am going to bed ; I feel the fever coming on."

" Ah," cried a ringing voice from the stable door ; " here is M. de Bussy, up without my permission."

" Le Haudoin ! " said Bussy ; " now, I am sure to be scolded. Adieu, count ; I recommend Roland to you."

" Have no fear."

Bussy walked away, and Monsoreau mounted the horse.

" What is the matter ? " asked Rémy. " You are so pale that I believe you are really ill."

" Do you know where he is going ? "

" No."

" To Méridor."

" Well, did you expect him to avoid it ? "

" What will happen, *mon Dieu!* after what took place yesterday ? "

" Madame de Monsoreau will deny."

" But he saw her."

" She will insist that he is dreaming."

" Diane will not have the strength."

"Oh, M. de Bussy, is it possible that you do not know women any better?"

"Rémy, I feel very ill."

"I should think so. Go home. I prescribe for this morning —"

"What?"

"A fowl, a slice of ham, and a bisque."

"But I am not hungry."

"All the more reason for me to order you to eat."

"Rémy, I have a feeling that this wretch will make a scene at Méridor. I really ought to have accompanied him as he proposed."

"What for?"

"To sustain Diane."

"Madame Diane will sustain herself unaided; and as you must do the same, I beg you to come. Besides, you must not be seen up and about. Why did you go out notwithstanding my injunctions?"

"I was too uneasy and could stand it no longer."

Rémy shrugged his shoulders, led Bussy away, and having closed all the doors, seated him before a well served table while M. de Monsoreau rode out of Angers through the same gate as the day before. The count had his object in wishing to ride Roland a second time: he wished to ascertain whether chance or habit had led the animal to carry him to the park wall. Therefore, as he left the palace, he dropped the reins; Roland did exactly what his rider expected. He was no sooner out of the gates than he turned to the left, then to the right; M. de Monsoreau allowed him to follow his own direction, and passed through the path, then the fields, and through the forest. As Roland approached Méridor, his speed increased, his trot became a gallop, and at the end of forty minutes, M. de Monsoreau found himself before the wall at the very spot he had reached the day before. Only silence and solitude reigned;

there was no horse around. M. de Monsoreau dismounted;
but this time, to escape the risk of having to walk home,
he slipped Roland's bridle over his arm and climbed up
the wall.

But all was silent within and without the park. The
long alleys extended before him and a few deer gambolled
on the green sward.

The count concluded that it would be useless to waste
any more time watching people who had, no doubt, been
frightened into giving up their meetings, or into selecting
another spot. He accordingly mounted his horse, took a
little path, and within fifteen minutes had reached the
gate.

The baron was busy whipping his dogs to keep them in
good training when the count passed over the drawbridge.
He caught sight of his son-in-law and advanced ceremoni-
ously to meet him. Diane, seated beneath a magnificent
sycamore, was reading Marot's poems; Gertrude, her faithful attendant, was embroidering beside her.

The count, after having greeted the baron, perceived the
two women. He dismounted and approached them. Diane
rose, advanced to meet him, and bowed.

"What calmness, or rather what perfidy!" murmured
the count. "What a tempest I shall cause on these sleeping
waters."

A footman approached; the master of the hounds threw
him the bridle of his horse, then turning to Diane, —

"Madame," he said, "will you kindly grant me a few
moments' conversation?"

"Willingly, monsieur," replied Diane.

"Will you do us the honor to remain at the castle, Monsieur le Comte?" asked the baron.

"Yes, monsieur, until to-morrow at least."

The baron went away to see that his son-in-law's room
was prepared according to all the laws of hospitality.

Monsoreau invited Diane to resume her seat, and took the
chair that Gertrude had occupied; then with a look which
would have intimidated the bravest men, —

"Madame," he said, "who was with you in the park, last
evening ? "

Diane looked at her husband with a clear and limpid
glance.

"At what time, monsieur ? " she asked, in a voice from
which she had succeeded in banishing all emotion.

"At six o'clock."

"Where ? "

"Near the copse."

"It must have been one of my friends, and not I, who
was walking in that part."

"It was you, madame," insisted Monsoreau.

"How do you know ? " asked Diane.

Monsoreau, taken by surprise, did not have a word to
say; but anger soon followed this amazement.

"Tell me the name of that man."

"Of what man ? "

"The one who was walking with you."

"I cannot tell you as I was not walking."

"It was you, I tell you ! " cried Monsoreau, stamping his
foot on the ground.

"You are mistaken, monsieur," coldly replied Diane.

"How dare you deny that I saw you."

"Ah, it was you, monsieur ? "

"Yes, madame. How dare you deny it was you when
there is no other woman at Méridor ? "

"You are again mistaken, monsieur, for Jeanne de
Brissac is here."

"Madame de Saint-Luc ? "

"Yes, Madame de Saint-Luc, my friend."

"And M. de Saint-Luc ? "

"He does not leave his wife, as you know; theirs

was a love match. You saw M. and Madame de Saint-Luc."

" It was not M. de Saint-Luc nor Madame de Saint-Luc. It was you, — for I recognized you, — with a man whom I do not know, but whom I shall know, I swear to you."

" So you persist in saying it was I, monsieur ? "

" I tell you I recognized you, and heard your scream."

" When you have recovered your senses, monsieur," said Diane, " I shall consent to listen to you; but for the present, I think I had better retire."

" No, madame," said Monsoreau, holding Diane by the arm, " you shall remain."

" Monsieur," said Diane, " here are M. and Madame de Saint-Luc. I hope you will control yourself before them."

Indeed, Saint-Luc and his wife were seen approaching, summoned by the dinner-bell, which had just been rung, as if they only had waited for Monsoreau to take their places at table. Both recognized the count, and guessing that their presence would perhaps relieve Diane from an unpleasant situation, they quickly approached.

Madame de Saint-Luc bowed to Monsoreau, and her husband cordially extended his hand. All three exchanged a few remarks, and Saint-Luc, pushing his wife towards the count, offered his arm to Diane.

They went to the house.

Nine o'clock was the dinner hour at the Château de Méridor; this was an old custom from the reign of King Louis XII. to which the baron still adhered.

M. de Monsoreau was placed between Saint-Luc and his wife. Diane, separated from her husband by a skilful manœuvre of her friend, sat between Saint-Luc and the baron.

The conversation was general and turned naturally on the arrival of the king's brother in Angers and on the movement which this arrival would cause in the province.

Monsoreau would have liked to converse on other topics, but he could not direct the conversation. Not that Saint-Luc refused to answer him; on the contrary, he cajoled the furious husband with his wittiest sallies, and Diane, who could thus remain silent, thanked her friend with eloquent glances.

"That Saint-Luc is a fool who chatters like a magpie," said the count to himself; "here is the man from whom I shall worm the secret I wish to know."

M. de Monsoreau did not know Saint-Luc, having entered the court just as the latter left it. With this belief, he joined the young man, thus increasing Diane's joy and giving satisfaction on all sides. Besides, Saint-Luc gave Madame de Monsoreau glances which meant, —

"Do not be worried, madame; I have a plan."

In the next chapter we shall see M. de Saint-Luc's plan.

CHAPTER XXV.

THE PROJECT OF M. DE SAINT-LUC.

WHEN the meal was over, Monsoreau took his new friend
by the arm and led him out of the castle.

"Do you know," he said, "that I am very happy to find
you here; the solitude of Méridor frightened me."

"Why," said Saint-Luc, "have you not your wife? As
for me, in such company, I would find a desert too
populous."

"I do not deny that," replied Monsoreau, biting his lips,
"yet — "

"Yet what?"

"Yet I am very glad to find you here."

"Monsieur," said Saint-Luc, picking his teeth with a
little gold sword, "you are really very polite; but I shall
never believe that you could fear *ennui* with such a wife
and in such a beautiful country."

"Pshaw!" said Monsoreau, "I have spent half of my
life in these woods."

"All the more reason for you not to be bored," said Saint-
Luc. "It seems to me that the more we see the forests, the
more we love them. See this admirable park; I know I
shall be in despair when I have to leave it. Unfortunately,
I fear this will soon happen."

"Why should you leave it?"

"Eh, monsieur, is man master of his fate? He is like
the leaf of a tree, blown about by the winds without even
knowing whither. You are happy."

" In what way ? "

" In living beneath these beautiful trees."

" Oh," said Monsoreau, " I shall probably not remain here very long."

" What makes you say that ? I think you are mistaken."

" No," said Monsoreau.   " I am not such a fanatical admirer of Nature, and I distrust this park which you admire so much."

" What ? " asked Saint-Luc.

" Yes," repeated Monsoreau.

" You say you distrust this park ?   In what way ? "

" Because I do not consider it safe."

" Not safe ! Really ? " said Saint-Luc, surprised.   " Ah, I understand, — on account of its isolated position."

" No, not exactly on that account, for I presume you have visitors at Méridor."

" Faith ! no," said Saint-Luc, with perfect simplicity, " not a soul."

" Ah, really ? "

" As I had the honor of telling you."

" What ! have you no visitors from time to time ? "

" Not since I have been here."

" Not a single gentleman from the brilliant court at Angers ? "

" Not one."

" Impossible ! "

" It is so, nevertheless."

" Ah, fie ! you slander the Angevin gentlemen."

" I do not know whether I slander then, but the devil take me if I have so much as spied one of their plumes."

" Then I am wrong on that point."

" Yes, absolutely wrong. Let us return to what you were just saying about the park being unsafe. Are there any bears ? "

" Oh, no."

"Wolves ? "

" No."

" Robbers ? "

"Perhaps. Tell me, my dear monsieur, Madame de Saint-Luc is very pretty, is she not ? "

" Why, yes."

" Does she often walk in the park ? "

" Very often ; she is like me and adores the country. But why do you ask this question ? "

" When she walks do you always accompany her ? "

" Always," said Saint-Luc.

" Nearly always," said the count.

" What the devil are you driving at ? "

" Oh, *mon Dieu !* nothing, — or almost nothing."

" I am listening."

" I have been told — "

" What ? Speak."

" You will not be angry ? "

" I never get angry."

" Besides, between husbands, these confidences are right. I have been told that a man was seen wandering in the park."

" A man ? "

" Yes."

" Who came for my wife ? "

" Oh, I do not say that."

" You would be very wrong not to say it, my dear M. de Monsoreau ; this is most interesting. And who saw him ? Pray tell me."

" Why should I ? "

" We are talking, are we not ? Well, we might as well talk about that as anything else. You say that this man came for Madame de Saint-Luc. How very queer ! "

" Listen, and I shall confess the whole thing ; I do not think it was really for Madame de Saint-Luc."

" And for whom, then ? "

" I fear that it was for Diane."

" Ah," said Saint-Luc, " I would like that better."

" What ! you would like that better ? "

" No doubt; you know that husbands are the most selfish race of beings. Each one for himself, and God for all."

" Or rather, the devil," added Monsoreau.

" So you think a man entered ? "

" I do better than believe it, — I saw him."

" You saw a man in the park ? "

" Yes," said Monsoreau.

" Alone ? "

" With Madame de Monsoreau."

" When ? "

" Yesterday."

" Where ? "

" Here, to the left." As Monsoreau had conducted his companion to the copse, he was able to point out the spot.

" Ah," said Saint-Luc, " here is a wall in very bad condition; I must tell the baron."

" And whom do you suspect ? "

" Whom do I suspect ? "

" Yes," said the count.

" Of doing what ? "

" Of climbing over the wall to come in the park and talk with my wife."

Saint-Luc seemed buried in a profound meditation; the result of which Monsoreau awaited with impatience.

" Well ? " he said.

" Well," said Saint-Luc, " I only see — "

" Whom ? " quickly asked the count.

" You," said Saint-Luc, facing him.

" Are you jesting, my dear M. de Saint-Luc," said the count, petrified.

"Why, no. In the early part of my marriage I did such things. Why should you not do the same ? "

"Come, you do not wish to answer me ; confess it, my dear friend, and fear nothing. I have courage. Come, help me to discover the man; you would greatly assist me."

Saint-Luc scratched his ear.

" I can only think of you," he said.

" A truce to jests ; take the thing seriously, monsieur, for I warn you it is of importance."

" You think so ? "

" I tell you I am sure."

" That is another matter; but how does this man come ? Do you know ? "

" He comes by stealth. *Parbleu !* "

" Often ? "

" I should think so; his footsteps have left tracks in the soft stone of the wall ; look, now."

" Yes, true."

" Had you never perceived what I have just told you ? "

" Oh," said Saint-Luc, " I suspected it."

" Ah, you see !" said the count, breathless. "What next ? "

" I never troubled myself : I thought it was you."

" But when I assure you — "

" I believe you, my dear monsieur."

" You believe me ? "

" Yes."

" Well, then ? "

" Then it is some one else."

The master of the hounds glared at Saint-Luc, who was displaying his most coquettish nonchalance.

" Ah !" he said, in such an angry tone that the young man raised his head.

" I have another idea," said Saint-Luc.

" Really ? "

"Supposing it were—"

"Whom?"

"No."

"Speak."

"Supposing it were M. le Duc d'Anjou."

"I had thought of him," replied Monsoreau, "but on inquiring, I found that it could not be."

"The duke is very cunning."

"Yes, but it was not he."

"You always tell me that it is not," said Saint-Luc, "and you want me to insist that it is."

"No doubt; you live in the castle, you ought to know."

"Stop!" cried Saint-Luc.

"Have you an idea?"

"Yes; if it was neither you nor the duke, it must have been me."

"You, Saint-Luc?"

"Why not?"

"You come to the park on horseback, when you are already in it?"

"Eh, *mon Dieu!* I am such a whimsical creature."

"You would have taken flight on seeing me appear over the wall?"

"One would fly for less."

"Then you were doing wrong," said the count, losing control of himself.

"I do not say I was not."

"You are laughing at me," cried the count, "and this has been going on for fifteen minutes."

"You are mistaken, monsieur," said Saint-Luc, drawing his watch and looking at Monsoreau with a fixity which made the latter shudder in spite of himself. "It has been going on for twenty minutes."

"You insult me, monsieur!" cried the count.

"And do you imagine, monsieur, that you are not insulting me with your pointed questions?"

"Ah, I see it all clearly, now."

"What a miracle at ten o'clock in the morning! Well, tell me what you see."

"I see that you have an understanding with the traitor and coward whom I came near killing yesterday."

"*Pardieu!*" said Saint-Luc, "he is my friend."

"In that case, I will kill you in his stead."

"What! in your own house, so suddenly, without warning?"

"Do you expect me to stand on ceremony to punish a wretch?" cried the exasperated count.

"Ah, M. de Monsoreau," replied Saint-Luc, "how ill-bred you are! Living among wild beasts has spoiled your manners. Fie!"

"But do you not see that I am furious?" shrieked the count, placing himself before Saint-Luc with folded arms and features contracted by the expression of the frightful despair in his heart.

"Yes, *mordieu!* I see it, and fury is not in the least becoming to you; you are horrible to behold, my dear M. de Monsoreau."

The count, beside himself, placed his hand on his sword.

"Ah, take care," said Saint-Luc, "you are provoking me. I beg you to see that I am perfectly calm."

"Yes, fop, coxcomb, I do provoke you!"

"Take the trouble to pass over to the other side of the wall, M. de Monsoreau; there we shall be on neutral ground."

"What do I care?" cried the count.

"I care," replied Saint-Luc. "I do not wish to kill you in your own house."

"Very well," said Monsoreau, climbing hastily over the wall.

"Take care! go carefully, count; this stone is loose. Do not hurt yourself. I should be greatly grieved."

And Saint-Luc climbed over.

"Come, be quick!" said the count, drawing his sword.

"As I came to the country for pleasure, I can boast of having had a great deal of amusement," said Saint-Luc, talking to himself as he reached the other side.

CHAPTER XXVI.

IN WHICH M. DE SAINT-LUC SHOWED M. DE MONSOREAU THE THRUST HE HAD LEARNED FROM THE KING.

M. DE MONSOREAU awaited Saint-Luc, sword in hand.

"Are you ready ? " he asked.

"Ah," replied Saint-Luc, "you did not take the worst place with your back to the sun."

Monsoreau moved a little to one side.

"This is better," said Saint-Luc; "I shall at least see what I am about."

"Do not spare me," said Monsoreau; "I am in earnest."

"Ah," said Saint-Luc, "do you really wish to kill me ? "

"Do I wish it ? — oh, yes, I do ! "

"Man proposes and God disposes," said Saint-Luc, drawing his sword in turn.

"What are you saying ? "

"Look at that tuft of poppies and dandelions."

"Well ? "

"Well, I mean to lay you there," and he laughingly placed himself in posture of defence. Monsoreau began the combat furiously, and made several thrusts which Saint-Luc parried with equal agility.

"*Pardieu!* M. de Monsoreau," he said, as he toyed with his enemy's weapon, "you use your sword very skilfully, and any man but Bussy or myself would have been killed by that thrust."

Monsoreau turned pale as he realized what an adversary he had to deal with.

"You are perhaps surprised," said Saint-Luc, "to see how well I use my sword; but the king, who is very fond of me, as you know, took the trouble to give me lessons, and among other things, taught me a thrust which I shall show you presently. I tell you this, because if you are killed, you will have the pleasure of knowing you are killed by the king's method; it will be very flattering to you."

"You are very witty, monsieur," said Monsoreau, exasperated, and dealing a thrust which would have gone through a wall.

"Well, we do our best," modestly replied Saint-Luc, jumping to one side and forcing his antagonist to turn in such a way that he had the sun full in his eyes.

"Ah, ah," he said, "you are just where I wanted to see you, until I put you on another spot. I brought this about very neatly, did I not? I am pleased, — really quite pleased. A while ago you had only fifty chances out of a hundred of being killed, now you have ninety-nine." And with a suppleness, vigor, and rage such as Monsoreau had never seen and which would have seemed impossible in this effeminate young man, Saint-Luc rushed at the master of the hounds, who parried five thrusts, but received the sixth full in the chest.

Monsoreau remained standing for another second, but like an uprooted oak that awaits a breath to know on which side to fall.

"Now," said Saint-Luc, "you have the hundred chances complete; and observe, monsieur, that you will fall on the very tuft I had pointed out to you."

The count's strength suddenly gave way; he stretched out his hands while his eyes grew dim; his knees bent, and he fell on the tuft of poppies, over which his blood flowed.

Saint-Luc quietly wiped his sword and looked at the different tints of the face, which gradually changed from that of a dying man to that of a corpse.

"You have killed me, monsieur," said Monsoreau.

"I tried," replied Saint-Luc; "but now that I see you lying there, ready to die, the devil take me if I am not sorry for what I have done. You are now sacred to me, monsieur. You are horribly jealous, but you were brave."

And satisfied with this funeral oration, Saint-Luc knelt beside Monsoreau, and said to him, —

"Have you any last wish, monsieur? Tell me, and upon my word as a gentleman, it shall be executed. I know that a wounded man is generally thirsty; shall I get you a drink?"

Monsoreau did not reply. He was lying face downwards, biting the grass, and struggling in a pool of blood.

"Poor devil!" said Saint-Luc, rising. "Ah, friendship, thou art a very exacting divinity."

Monsoreau opened his fading eyes, tried to raise his head, and fell back with a hollow groan.

"Come, he is dead," said Saint-Luc. "Let us think no more about him. That is easy to say — In all this I have killed a man. No one will accuse me of wasting my time in the country."

He jumped over the wall and ran through the park to the castle. The first person he saw was Diane; she was conversing with her friend.

"Black will be becoming to her," thought Saint-Luc, as he approached the charming group formed by the two women.

"Pardon me, madame," he said to Diane, "but I should like to exchange a few words with Madame de Saint-Luc."

"Certainly, my dear guest," replied Madame de Monsoreau. "I shall join my father in the library; when you will have finished with M. de Saint-Luc," she added, turning to her friend, "come and join me; I shall be there."

"I shall not be long," said Jeanne, as Diane walked away with a smile. The husband and wife remained alone.

"What is the matter?" asked Jeanne, with her sunniest smile; "you look gloomy, dear husband."

"Yes, yes," replied Saint-Luc.

"What has happened ? "

"Oh, *mon Dieu !* an accident."

"To you ? " asked Jeanne, in terror.

"Not exactly to me, but to a person who was near me."

"To whom ? "

"The one with whom I was walking."

"M. de Monsoreau ? "

"Alas! yes. Poor dear man ! "

"What has happened to him ? "

"I believe he is dead."

"Dead ! " cried Jeanne, in an agitation most natural to conceive, " dead ! "

"Exactly."

"He who was here just now, talking and looking."

"That is just the cause of his death; he looked, and, above all, talked too much."

"Saint-Luc, my friend —" said the young woman, seizing her husband's hands.

"What ? "

"You are keeping something from me."

"Absolutely nothing, I swear, — not even the spot where he died."

"And where did he die ? "

"There, behind the wall, on the very spot where our friend Bussy was in the habit of tying his horse."

"You killed him, Saint-Luc ? "

"*Parbleu !* who else can it be ? We were only two, and I come back alive to tell you that he is dead. It is not very difficult to guess which of the two killed the other."

"Unhappy man ! "

"Well, my dear friend, he provoked me, insulted me, and drew his sword."

"This is horrible, horrible ! Poor man ! "

"Now," said Saint-Luc, "I was sure of it. You will

see that before a week every one will call him Saint Monsoreau."

"But you cannot remain here," cried Jeanne; "you cannot dwell any longer beneath the roof of the man you have killed."

"I said that to myself at once, dearest, and hastened here to ask you to make preparations for our departure."

"He did not wound you, at least?"

"At last; though it comes rather late, this question reconciles me with you. No, I am perfectly whole."

"Then we start —"

"At once. You understand that the accident may be discovered at any moment."

"What accident?" cried Madame de Saint-Luc, coming back to her first thought. "But now, I am thinking, Madame de Monsoreau is a widow."

"That is exactly what I said to myself."

"After having killed him?"

"No, before."

"Then, while I tell her —"

"Spare her feelings."

"How bad you are! While I tell her, saddle the horses yourself as for a ride."

"An excellent idea! You would do well to have a great many of the same kind, dear friend, because I confess that my brain is not so clear as it might be."

"But where are we going?"

"To Paris."

"To Paris! And the king?"

"The king will have forgotten all; so many things have occurred since last we met. As there will probably be a war, my place is beside him."

"Very well; let us, then, leave for Paris."

"Yes; but I must have a pen and ink."

"To write to whom?"

"To Bussy. You understand that I cannot leave Anjou without telling him why I go."

"Of course. You will find everything you need in my room."

Saint-Luc went upstairs at once, and with a hand which, in spite of himself, trembled a little, he wrote the following lines : —

DEAR FRIEND, — You will soon hear, by report, of the accident which befell M. de Monsoreau. We had near the old copse a discussion on the causes and effects of crumbling walls, and the objections to horses who find their way home alone. In the heat of the discussion, M. de Monsoreau fell on a tuft of poppies and dandelions in such a manner that he was killed on the spot.

Your friend for life,   SAINT-LUC.

P. S. — As you might find this rather improbable, I shall add that when the accident happened we both held our swords in hand. I leave at once for Paris, with the intention of paying my respects to the king, Anjou not seeming to me very safe after what has occurred.

Ten minutes later, one of the baron's servants was on the road to Angers with this letter, while M. and Madame de Saint-Luc went out of the park through a little side-door which opened on a cross-road, leaving Diane very much agitated and embarrassed how to tell the baron about the accident. She had turned away her eyes when Saint-Luc passed.

"Serve your friends," said the latter to his wife. "Men are selfish; I am the only grateful one."

CHAPTER XXVII.

THE QUEEN-MOTHER MAKES HER ENTRANCE INTO THE
GOOD CITY OF ANGERS, BUT NOT TRIUMPHANTLY.

AT the very moment when M. de Monsoreau fell beneath
the sword of Saint-Luc, there was a great flourish of trumpets at the gates of Angers, which were closed with the
greatest care. The guards, who had been notified, raised
the standard, and replied with similar symphonies. It
was Catherine de Medicis who was entering Angers with
a rather imposing retinue. The arrival was announced to
Bussy, who rose from his bed and went to the prince, who
immediately got into his. The airs played on the Angevin
trumpets were very beautiful ones, but they had not the
virtues of those which caused the walls of Jericho to fall:
the gates of Angers did not open.

Catherine then leaned out of the litter to show herself to
the guards, hoping that the majesty of a royal countenance
would have more effect than the sound of trumpets.

The militiamen of Angers saw the queen, and saluted her
with courtesy, but the gates remained closed. Catherine
sent a gentleman to the barriers and he was treated with
great courtesy; but when he demanded the right of entrance for the queen-mother, and insisted that her Majesty
should be received with honor, he was told that Angers
being in a state of siege the gates could not be opened
without certain indispensable formalities.

The gentleman returned very crestfallen to his mistress,
and Catherine uttered these words, which Louis XIV. modi-

fied later on in accordance with the proportions taken by royal authority.

" I shall wait," she said.

Her gentlemen stood around her, trembling with rage. Finally Bussy, who had spent nearly half an hour lecturing his Highness and giving him a hundred state reasons, each one more peremptory than the last, made up his mind.

He had his horse saddled with gaudy trappings, chose five gentlemen whom he knew to be most disagreeable to the queen-mother, and placing himself at their head, went slowly to meet her Majesty.

Catherine was growing weary, not of waiting, but of plotting vengeance against the authors of this trick. She remembered the Arab tale in which it is said that a genii, imprisoned in a copper vase, promised, during the first ten centuries of his captivity, to give wealth to whoever would deliver him; then, furious at having waited so long, he swore to kill the imprudent one who would break the cover of the vase.

Catherine had reached that point.

She had first decided to be gracious to the one who would come to meet her. She then made up her mind to vent her anger on the first one she would see.

Bussy, all plume-bedecked, appeared at the gates and looked out like a night-watchman who hears rather than sees. " Who is there ? " he cried.

Catherine expected genuflections at least. Her attendant officer looked at her to learn her wishes.

" Go to the barrier," she said. "They have asked, 'Who is there ?' Reply, monsieur ; it is a formality."

The gentleman advanced to the end of the drawbridge.

" It is her Majesty the Queen-mother who comes to visit the good city of Angers," he replied.

"Very well, monsieur," replied Bussy. "Turn to the left, and about eighty feet from here, you will find the postern."

"The postern!" cried the gentleman. "A small door for her Majesty!"

Bussy was no longer there to hear. Followed by his friends, who were laughing in their sleeve, he had advanced towards the place where, in obedience to his instructions, the queen-mother was to alight.

"Has your Majesty heard?" asked the gentleman. "The postern."

"Ah, yes, monsieur, I heard. Let us enter there since that is necessary."

The flash from her eyes terrified the blunderer who had emphasized her humiliation. The *cortége* turned to the left, and the postern was opened.

Bussy dismounted, and with drawn sword, advanced through the little door. He bowed to Catherine with great respect, while around him the hat-plumes swept the ground.

"Your Majesty is welcome in Angers," he said.

Beside him were drums that did not beat, and soldiers who did not present arms. The queen descended from her litter, and leaning on the arm of one of her gentlemen, advanced towards the door after having spoken these words, —

"Thank you, M. de Bussy."

This was the result of all the meditations she had had time to make. She advanced with her head erect, but Bussy stopped her, and even caught her arm.

"Take care, madame, the door is low and your Majesty might hurt herself."

"I must then stoop; but how? It is the first time I have entered a city thus." These words, uttered with perfect calmness, had for clever courtiers, a depth of meaning which gave food for thought to more than one spectator of this scene, and Bussy himself pulled his moustache as he looked away.

"You went too far," whispered Livarot, in his ear.

"Pshaw!" said Bussy, "she will have to go through a great many more."

Her Majesty's litter was hoisted over the wall so that she could resume her place in it to go to the palace. Bussy and his friends mounted their horses and rode on either side of the litter.

"My son!" suddenly exclaimed Catherine. "I do not see my son D'Anjou."

She would have liked to keep back these words, which were forced from her by an irresistible anger. François' absence at such a moment was the height of insult.

"Monseigneur is ill in bed, madame, otherwise your Majesty does not doubt that his Highness would have hastened to do the honors of his good city of Angers."

Here Catherine was sublimely hypocritical.

"Ill,—my poor child is ill?" she cried. "Ah, gentlemen, let us hasten! He is well cared for, I hope?"

"We are doing our best," said Bussy, looking at her with surprise, to ascertain if this woman were really a mother.

"Does he know that I am here?" resumed Catherine, after a pause which she employed in examining all the gentlemen.

"Yes, madame, certainly."

Catherine pressed her lips together.

"He must be suffering greatly," she said in a tone of compassion.

"Horribly," said Bussy. "His Highness is subject to these sudden spells."

"Is it a sudden illness, M. de Bussy?"

"*Mon Dieu!* yes, madame."

They reached the palace. A great crowd lined the street on either side. Bussy hurried in and reached the duke's room out of breath.

"Here she is," he said; "take care!"

"Is she furious?"

"Exasperated."

"Does she complain?"

"No, she smiles, which is much worse."

"What do the people say?"

"They have not moved. They look upon this woman with mute terror; if they do not know her, they have an instinctive fear."

"And she?"

"She sends kisses, and bites her fingers."

"The devil!"

"That is what I thought, monseigneur. Now play a close game."

"We insist on war."

"*Pardieu!* ask a hundred to get ten, and with her you will only get five."

"Pshaw!" said the duke, "you must think me very weak. Are you all there? Why did not Monsoreau return?"

"I believe he is at Méridor. Oh, we can do without him."

"Her Majesty the queen-mother!" cried the usher, from the threshold of the room.

Catherine immediately appeared, pale, and dressed in black according to her wont. The Duc d'Anjou made a motion to rise, but Catherine, with an agility which no one would have suspected in this body enfeebled by age, threw herself in the arms of her son and covered him with kisses.

"She will smother him," thought Bussy; "these are real kisses, *mordieu!*"

She did more, she wept.

"Let us beware," said Antraguet to Ribeirac; "every tear will cost us a pint of blood."

Catherine, having finished her embraces, seated herself at the duke's bedside; Bussy made a sign, and the assistants withdrew. He, doing as he would in his own house, leaned against the bedpost and waited.

"Will you not see to the comforts of my poor followers, dear M. de Bussy," suddenly said Catherine. "After my son, you are our dearest friend and the master of the house, are you not? I ask this favor of you."

There could be no hesitation.

"I am caught," thought Bussy. "Madame," he said, "I am only too happy to be agreeable to your Majesty, and I hasten to obey. Wait," he murmured to himself, "you do not know the doors here as you do at the Louvre; I shall return." And he went out without even being able to make a sign to the duke; Catherine suspected him, and did not lose sight of him for a moment.

She then tried to find out whether her son were really ill or only pretending. That was to be the base of all her diplomatic operations. But François, who was the worthy son of such a mother, played his part to perfection.

She had wept; he had fever. Catherine was deceived, and believed him ill; she hoped to have more influence on a mind weakened by suffering. She overwhelmed the duke with tenderness, embraced him again, and wept to such an extent that the duke inquired the reason of these tears.

"You have run so great a danger, my child," she replied.

"In escaping from the Louvre, mother?"

"No, after having escaped."

"How so?"

"Those who aided you in this escape — "

"Well?"

"They were your worst enemies."

"She knows nothing," he thought, "but she would like to know."

"The King of Navarre," she said brusquely, "the eternal scourge of our race, — I know him well."

"Ah, ah," he said to himself, "she knows all!"

"Would you believe that he boasts of it?" she asked. "He thinks he has gained everything."

"It is impossible," he replied; "you have been deceived."

"Why so?"

"Because he had nothing to do with my escape, and even if he did, I am safe, as you see. I have not seen the King of Navarre for two years."

"I am not speaking of that danger only," said Catherine, seeing that the blow had been parried.

"What next, mother?" he asked, looking at the tapestry of his alcove, which moved behind the queen.

Catherine approached François, and in a voice which she made as solemn as possible, "The king's anger," she said, — "that furious anger which threatens you."

"This danger is like the other, madame; I believe the king, my brother, to be furiously angry, but I am safe."

"You think so," she said, in a tone which could strike terror to the boldest heart.

The tapestry moved.

"I am sure of it," replied the duke, "and this is so true that you have come in person to tell me so, my good mother."

"How?" said Catherine, uneasy at this calmness.

"Because," he said, after another glance at the partition, "if you had been charged only with threats, you would not have come; the king would have hesitated to furnish me with a hostage like your Majesty."

Catherine was frightened, and raised her head.

"I, a hostage!" she said.

"The holiest and most venerable of all," he replied with a smile; and as he kissed Catherine's hand, he glanced triumphantly at the woodworks.

Catherine dropped her arms, crushed; she could not guess that Bussy was watching his master through a secret door, holding him beneath his glance, and sending him courage and boldness at every hesitation.

" My son," she said, "you are perfectly right; I bring you words of peace."

" I am listening, mother, and you know my respect," said François. "I think we are beginning to understand each other."

CHAPTER XXVIII.

LITTLE CAUSES AND GREAT EFFECTS.

DURING this first part of the conversation, Catherine had been under a visible disadvantage.

This species of failure was not foreseen, and was so unusual that she was beginning to ask herself if her son would be as firm in his refusal as he seemed, when a very small event suddenly changed the face of things.

We have seen battles nearly lost, and then won by a change of wind, and *vice versa*; Marengo and Waterloo are a double example. A grain of sand impedes the action of the most powerful machines.

Bussy, in a secret corridor which opened into M. le Duc d'Anjou's alcove, was placed so as to be seen by the duke alone; from his hiding-place, he put his head through the tapestry whenever he thought his cause was endangered.

His cause, we can understand, was war at any price; he had to remain in Anjou as long as M. de Monsoreau would be there, to watch the husband and visit the wife. This policy, though very simple, greatly complicated that of France: great effects have little causes. For this reason, Bussy, with many furious grimaces, violent gestures, and a frightful play of the eyebrows, urged his master to obstinacy.

The duke, who was afraid of Bussy, suffered himself to be urged, and was, as we have seen, extremely ferocious.

Catherine was therefore defeated on all sides, and already thinking of making an honorable retreat, when a little event, almost as unexpected as M. le Duc d'Anjou's strength of will, came to her rescue.

While the conversation between the mother and son was most lively, and the duke's resistance most energetic, Bussy suddenly felt his cloak pulled. Anxious to lose nothing of the conversation, he put his hand to the place and felt a wrist; going along the wrist, he felt an arm, then a shoulder, then a man. This was of sufficient importance to make him turn around, and he did so. The man was Rémy.

Bussy wished to speak, but Rémy placed his finger on his lips, and gently drew his master into the neighboring room.

"What is the matter, Rémy?" asked the count, very impatiently, "and why do you disturb me at such a moment?"

"A letter?" whispered Rémy.

"The devil take you! for a letter you disturb me from a most important interview with the Duc d'Anjou."

Rémy seemed in no way disturbed by this greeting.

"There are letters and letters," he said.

"No doubt," said Bussy. "Where is this one from?"

"From Méridor."

"Oh," said Bussy, "from Méridor! Thank you, my good Rémy, thank you."

"So I did not do wrong?"

"Can you do wrong? Where is that letter?"

"Ah, this made me think it was most important; the messenger will deliver it only into your own hands."

"He is right. Is he here?"

"Yes."

"Bring him."

Rémy opened a door, and made a sign to a sort of groom.

"Here is M. de Bussy," he said, pointing to the count.

"Give it to me; I am the one whom you seek," said Bussy, and he slipped a half-crown into his hand.

"Oh, I know you well," said the groom, as he handed the letter.

"Did she send it?"

"No, not she, — he."

"Who?" quickly asked Bussy, as he glanced at the writing.

"M. de Saint-Luc."

"Ah, ah!"

Bussy had grown slightly pale, because he imagined that the word *he* referred to the husband, and M. de Monsoreau enjoyed the privilege of making Bussy turn pale every time Bussy thought of him.

The count therefore turned aside to read, and, while reading, conceal that emotion which every one must fear to exhibit on receipt of an important letter, when one is neither Cæsar Borgia, Catherine de Medicis, Machiavelli, nor the devil.

Poor Bussy was right to turn away, because scarcely had he read the letter we already know than the blood rushed to his brain like an angry sea; from pale he became crimson, and felt so dizzy that his strength gave way, and he dropped on a chair near the window.

"Go," said Rémy to the groom, who was amazed at the effect produced by the letter he had brought, and he pushed the man by the shoulders. The groom fled swiftly; he feared the news was bad and he might be forced to give up his half-crown. Rémy returned to the count.

"*Mordieu!*" he said, "answer me at once, or by the holy Æsculapius, I will bleed you."

Bussy rose; he was no longer pale, he was no longer dizzy; he was gloomy.

"See what Saint-Luc has done for me," he said, and he handed the letter to Rémy, who read it eagerly.

"Well," he said, "all this seems very fine, and M. de Saint-Luc is a gallant friend. Trust a man of sense for sending a soul to purgatory; he goes at it the right way."

"This is incredible," murmured Bussy.

"Of course, it is incredible, but never mind. Here is your position. Within a year, I shall have a Comtesse de Bussy for my patient, and *mordieu!* you can trust me as you would Ambroise Paré."

"Yes," said Bussy, "she will be my wife."

"It seems to me," replied Rémy, "that you will not have much to do to bring that about, as she is already more your wife than she was the wife of her husband."

"Monsoreau dead!"

"Dead," repeated Le Haudoin; "it is written."

"Oh, it seems like a dream, Rémy. What! I shall no longer see that kind of spectre always ready to rise between me and my happiness? Rémy, we are mistaken."

"We are not in the least mistaken. Read it over, *mordieu!* — fallen on the poppies, and so heavily that he is dead! I had already observed that it is very dangerous to fall on poppies; but I thought this danger existed only for women."

"But then," said Bussy, following his own train of thought, and not listening to his friend's witticisms, "Diane cannot remain at Méridor. I do not wish it. She must go where she can forget."

"I think Paris would do very well for that," said Le Haudoin; "one forgets very well in Paris."

"You are right. She will return to her little house of the Rue des Tournelles, and we shall pass the ten months of her widowhood in obscurity, if happiness can be obscure, and marriage will be for us only a continuation of bliss."

"True," said Rémy, "but to go to Paris —"

"Well?"

"We must have something."

"What?"

" Peace in Anjou."

"Ah, yes," said Bussy. "*Mon Dieu!* how much time has been uselessly wasted."

"That means that you will mount your horse and rush to Méridor."

"Not I, but you; I am kept here, and besides, at such a moment, my presence would be almost indecent."

"How shall I see her? Shall I present myself at the castle?"

"No; go first to the old copse. She may be walking there, expecting me; then if you do not see her, go to the castle."

"What shall I tell her?"

"That I am nearly mad," and pressing the hand of the young man on whom experience had taught him that he could depend as on his second self, he hastened to resume his place behind the tapestry in the alcove. During Bussy's absence, Catherine was trying to regain the advantage which his presence had made her lose.

"My son," she said, "it seemed to me that a mother and child could never fail to understand each other."

"Yet you see that it sometimes happens, mother," replied the Duc d'Anjou.

"Never, when she wishes it."

"Madame, you mean when they wish it," replied the duke, delighted with himself and seeking Bussy's glance of approbation for this bold speech.

"But I wish it!" cried Catherine. "Do you hear François? I wish it." The tone of her voice contrasted with the words, for they were imperative while the voice was almost supplicating.

"You see!" said the Duc d'Anjou, smiling.

"Yes," said Catherine, "I wish it, and every sacrifice to attain that end will be made."

"Ah, ah," said François, "the devil!"

"Yes, dear child; tell me, what do you require? What do you wish? Speak, command!"

"Oh, mother!" said François almost embarrassed at this easy victory which did not give him the opportunity to show himself exacting.

"Listen, my son," said Catherine, in her most caressing voice. "You do not wish to drown the kingdom in blood; that is impossible. You are neither a bad Frenchman nor a bad brother."

"My brother has insulted me, madame, and I owe him nothing more, — nothing as a brother and nothing as a king."

"But I, François? You have no cause to complain of me."

"Yes, madame, for you abandoned me!" replied the duke, thinking that Bussy was still there to hear him.

"Ah, you wish to kill me!" said Catherine, in a gloomy voice. "Well I shall die as a woman should, when she sees her sons thirsting for each other's blood." Needless to say that Catherine had not the slightest desire to die.

"Oh, do not say that, madame; you break my heart!" cried François, who was not moved in the least.

Catherine burst into tears. The duke took her hands and tried to pacify her, while he cast uneasy glances towards the alcove.

"But what do you wish?" she asked. "Express your demands, that we may at least know how we stand."

"What do you wish, mother?" replied François. "Speak. I am listening."

"I desire that you should return to Paris, dear child; that you should return to the court of the king, your brother, who will receive you with open arms."

"Eh, *mordieu!* Madame, I see it but too well. He will not receive me in his arms but in the Bastille."

"No; return, and on my honor, on my love as a mother, on the blood of our Lord Jesus Christ," here Catherine made the sign of the cross, "you will be received by the king as though you were the king and he the Duc d'Anjou."

The duke's gaze was obstinately directed towards the alcove.

"Accept," continued Catherine, — "accept, my son. Do you desire other provinces; do you wish guards?"

"Eh, madame, your son gave me some, and even a guard of honor, since he chose his four favorites."

"Come, do not reply in this manner. You will choose the guards yourself; you will have a captain, and if you wish, this captain will be M. de Bussy."

The duke, shaken in his resolution by this offer, which he thought would please Bussy, threw another glance towards the alcove, half fearful of finding flashing eyes and white teeth glittering in the darkness. But oh, surprise! he beheld Bussy laughing, joyous, and nodding in approbation.

"What can this mean?" he asked himself. "Was Bussy anxious for war only to become captain of my guards?"

"Then I must accept?" he said aloud, as though talking to himself.

"Yes, yes!" said Bussy, with his hands, his shoulders, and his head.

"Leave Anjou, and return to Paris?" continued the duke.

"Yes, yes!" motioned Bussy, with increased energy.

"No doubt, my child," said Catherine; "but is it, then, so difficult to return to Paris?"

"Faith," said the duke to himself, "I am all at sea! It was agreed that I should refuse everything, and now he urges me to friendship and peace."

"Well," said Catherine, anxiously, "what is your answer?"

"I shall reflect," said the duke, who wished to consult Bussy about this sudden change; "and to-morrow — "

"He is yielding," thought Catherine. "Well, I have won the battle."

"Bussy may be right, after all," said the duke, who parted with his mother after an affectionate embrace.

CHAPTER XXIX.

HOW M. DE MONSOREAU OPENED AND SHUT HIS EYES, WHICH PROVES THAT HE WAS NOT QUITE DEAD.

A GOOD friend is a comfort, all the greater because very rare. Rémy was saying this to himself as he galloped across the fields mounted on one of the prince's best horses. He would have taken Roland; but as M. de Monsoreau had had that same idea earlier in the day, he was forced to be satisfied with another.

"I love M. de Bussy," said Le Haudoin to himself, "and I also think that he loves me. I am so joyful to-day because I feel happy for two." Then he added, as he drew a deep breath, "Really, I do not find my heart wide enough. What shall I say to Madame Diane? If she is stiff, ceremonious, and funereal, silent salutations with my hand on my heart; if she smiles, a *pirouette* and a *polonaise*, which I shall dance all alone. As for M. de Saint-Luc, if he be still at the castle, which I doubt, I shall compliment him in Latin. He will not be funereal. Ah, I approach."

The horse, after having turned to the left, then to the right, trotted down the path through the forest, and now entered the copse which led to the wall.

"Oh, the beautiful poppies!" said Rémy; "they remind me of our master of the hounds; those upon which he fell could not be more beautiful than these, poor dear man!"

Rémy was nearing the wall. All at once the horse stopped, with open nostrils and staring eyes. Rémy, who had been galloping, nearly went over the head of Mithri-

dates. (That was the name of the horse he had taken instead
of Roland.) Rémy, who had become a fearless rider, put
spurs into his horse's sides, but Mithridates did not move.
He had no doubt received this name for his obstinate
character, which resembled that of the King of Pontus.

Rémy, greatly surprised, looked down to see what obstacle
lay in the way; but he only saw a large pool of blood gradually being absorbed by the earth and the flowers.

"Well," he cried, "this must be the spot where M. de
Saint-Luc ran M. de Monsoreau through with his sword."
He looked down, then all around. Ten paces before him
he perceived two stiff legs and a body even stiffer. The
legs were stretched out, and the body leaned against a
wall.

"It is Monsoreau!" exclaimed Rémy. "*Hic obiit Nimrod!* Come, come, if the widow leaves him thus exposed
to the crows and vultures, this is a good sign for us, and
the funeral oration will take the form of *pirouettes* and the
polonaise." And Rémy, having dismounted, took a few
steps in the direction of the body.

"This is queer," he said; "here he is, dead, — perfectly
dead. Yet the blood is over there. Ah, here is the track!
He must have come here; or rather, that good M. de Saint-
Luc, who is charity personified, placed him near this wall
that the blood might not rush to his head. Yes, that is it.
He is dead, with his eyes wide open, — stark dead!"

All at once he stepped back in horror. The two eyes that
he had seen wide open had closed again, and a pallor even
more livid than the first had spread over the dead man's
face. Rémy became almost as pale as M. de Monsoreau;
but as he was a physician, and something of a materialist,
he muttered as he scratched his nose, —

"*Credere portentis mediocre.* If he has shut his eyes, he
is not dead;" and as, in spite of his materialism, the position was a most unpleasant one, and the points of his knees

bent more than was comfortable, he sat, or rather dropped, at the foot of a tree, and found himself face to face with the corpse.

"I do not know where I read that after death certain phenomena take place which signify only a giving way of the matter, — that is, a beginning of decomposition. Devil of a man, who must worry us even after death! His eyes not only closed, but the pallor increased, — *chroma chlôron*, as Galien says; *color albus*, to quote Cicero, who was a very witty speaker. Besides, there is one way of ascertaining whether he is dead or no, and that is to bury my sword in his body; if he does not move, he will be really dead."

Rémy was preparing for this charitable action, and had already put his hand to his sword, when Monsoreau's eyes opened again. This accident produced an effect contrary to the first. Rémy bounded up, and a cold perspiration gathered on his brow. This time the dead man's eyes remained staring.

"He is not dead!" murmured Rémy, "he is not dead! Well, here we are in a nice position!" A thought came most naturally to the young man's mind: "He is alive; but if I kill him, he will be really dead." And he looked at Monsoreau, who seemed to read his very soul and understand his evil intentions.

"Fie!" suddenly cried Rémy; "what a hideous thought! Heaven knows that if he were standing before me brandishing his sword I would kill him without compunction; but such as he is now, without strength and three-quarters dead, it would be more than crime; it would be infamy."

"Help!" cried Monsoreau, "help! I am dying."

"*Mordieu!*" said Rémy, "the position is critical. I am a physician, and it is my duty to relieve my suffering neighbor. It is true that Monsoreau is so ugly that I might almost be excused for not calling him my neighbor, but he is of the same species, — *genus homo*. Come, let me forget that my name is Rémy, that I am M. de Bussy's friend, and let me do my duty as a physician."

"Help!" repeated the wounded man.

"Here I am," said Rémy.

"Get me a priest or a physician."

"The physician is here, and may enable you to dispense with the priest."

"Rémy," said Monsoreau, recognizing him, "by what chance?" As may be seen, Monsoreau was faithful to his character. Even in his agony, he was still suspicious, and asked questions. Rémy understood the bearing of his questions. This wood was not a beaten road, and no one came there without having business. The question was therefore almost natural.

"How did you come here?" asked Monsoreau, whose suspicions gave him strength.

"*Pardieu!*" replied Rémy. "I met M. de Saint-Luc about a league from here."

"Ah, my murderer!" murmured Monsoreau, turning pale with anger and suffering.

"He said to me, 'Rémy, go to the wood, and in the copse you will find a dead man.'"

"Dead!" repeated Monsoreau.

"Well, he thought so," said Rémy; "so I came, I saw, and you are conquered."

"Now, you are speaking to a man; fear nothing, and tell me if I am mortally wounded."

"The devil!" said Rémy, "you are asking a great deal, but I shall try; let me see."

We have said that the physician's conscience had vanquished his friendship. He therefore approached Monsoreau, and with the greatest precautions removed his cloak, his doublet, and his shirt. The sword had penetrated between the sixth and seventh ribs.

"Humph!" said Rémy, "are you suffering much?"

"Not in my chest, but in my back."

"Which portion of your back?"

"Beneath the shoulder-blade."

"The sword must have struck against a bone," said Rémy, "thence the suffering." And he examined the spot indicated by the count. "No, no," he said, "I was mistaken; the sword came against nothing at all, and went right through you. *Peste!* what a neat thrust! There is some pleasure in attending M. de Saint-Luc's victims. You are perforated."

Monsoreau fainted, but Rémy did not trouble himself about this weakness.

"Ah, that is it; syncope and weak pulse." He felt the hands and feet; they were cold. He placed his ear on the chest; absence of noise and no hollow sound. "The devil!" he murmured, "Madame Diane's widowhood may after all be a question of time."

At this moment a reddish foam appeared on the wounded man's lips. Rémy quickly drew a lancet from his pocket, then he tore a strip from Monsoreau's shirt and compressed his arm.

"We shall see," he said; "if the blood flows, Madame Diane may not be a widow. But if it should not flow — Ah, ah, it flows! Pardon me, my dear M. de Bussy, but I am a physician first and foremost."

The blood after hesitating, spurted from the vein; the wounded man opened his eyes almost at the same moment.

"Ah," he murmured, "I thought it was all over."

"Not yet, my dear monsieur; it is even possible —"

"That I may recover?"

"*Mon Dieu!* yes; but let us first close the wound. Wait, do not move. Nature at this moment is assisting me. I put a bandage and she makes a clot of blood. I make it flow and she stops it. Ah, monsieur, Nature is a great surgeon. Now, let me wipe your lips," and Rémy passed a handkerchief over the count's mouth.

" Now see," continued Rémy, "the hemorrhage has already stopped. You are better ; so much the worse."

" How ! so much the worse ? "

" So much the better for you, certainly; but so much the worse! I know what I am saying. My dear M. de Monsoreau, I fear I shall have the good fortune of curing you."

" How! you fear ? "

" Yes, I understand what I mean."

" You think I shall recover ? "

" Alas ! "

" You are a singular doctor, Monsieur Rémy."

" What do you care, provided I save you? Now let us see."

Rémy, having tied up the wound, rose.

" Do you abandon me ? " asked the count.

" Ah, do not talk too much, my dear monsieur. — I ought rather to advise him to scream."

" I do not understand you."

" Fortunately. Now, here you are, bandaged."

" Well ? "

" Well, I am going to the castle for assistance."

" And what shall I do during that time ? "

" Remain perfectly still, do not move, breathe gently, and try not to cough and disturb that precious clot. What is the nearest house ? "

" The Château de Méridor."

" What is the road ? " asked Rémy, affecting the most perfect ignorance.

" Climb over the wall into the park, or follow the wall until you reach the gate."

" I shall not be long."

" Thank you, generous man."

" If you knew how far I carried generosity, you would thank me even more," murmured Rémy ; and mounting his

horse, he galloped in the direction indicated. At the end
of five minutes, he reached the castle, all the inmates of
which were searching the thickets and walks without being
able to find their master's body, because Saint-Luc, to gain
time, had sent them on the wrong track.

Rémy fell in the midst of them like a meteor, and made
them follow his footsteps. He showed so much eagerness
that Madame de Monsoreau could not help looking at him
in surprise. A secret thought came to her, and in one
second tarnished the angelic purity of her soul.

"Ah, I thought him M. de Bussy's friend," she murmured as Rémy disappeared, taking with him a stretcher,
lint, cool water, and all that was necessary for the dressing.
Æsculapius could not have done better with the wings of
his divinity.

CHAPTER XXX.

HOW M. LE DUC D'ANJOU WENT TO MÉRIDOR TO CON-
GRATULATE MADAME DE MONSOREAU ON THE DEATH OF
HER HUSBAND, AND FOUND M. DE MONSOREAU THERE
TO RECEIVE HIM.

So soon as the duke had finished his conversation with his
mother, he hastened to join Bussy to inquire into the cause
of this incredible change. Bussy, having returned to his
apartment, was reading over for the fifth time Saint-Luc's
letter, which impressed him more pleasantly each time.

On the other hand, Catherine, having retired to her
rooms, was giving orders and making preparations for her
departure, which could take place, she thought, within a
day or two.

Bussy received the prince with a most gracious smile.

"What! monseigneur," he said, "does your Highness
deign to come and visit me?"

"Eh, *mordieu!*" said the duke. "I come to demand an
explanation."

"From me?"

"Yes, from you."

"I am listening."

"You tell me to steel myself against my mother's attacks
and sustain the shock valiantly; I do so, and in the hottest
of the fight, when none of the blows have told on me, you
come and say, 'take off your coat of mail and surrender.'"

"I made all these injunctions, monseigneur, because I
was ignorant of the object of Madame Catherine's visit;

but now that I see that she has come to promote your
Highness's honor and glory — "

"How ! " said the duke, — "to promote my honor and
glory ? What do you mean ? "

"No doubt," said Bussy. "What does your Highness
wish ? To triumph over your enemies, do you not ? I do
not believe, as certain persons say, that you dream of
becoming King of France."

The duke cast a furtive glance at Bussy.

" Some may perhaps advise you to do so, monseigneur,"
said the young man, " but believe me, those who do so are
your worst enemies. If they are too tenacious, and you do
not know how to get rid of them, send them to me. I shall
convince them that they are on the wrong track."

The duke made a face.

" Besides," continued Bussy, " consider yourself. Have
you a hundred thousand men, ten million crowns, foreign
allies, and above all, do you wish to go against your lord
and master ? "

" My lord and master did not hesitate to go against me,"
said the duke.

" Ah, if you take it on that footing, you are right. Well,
declare yourself, get crowned, and take the title of King of
France. I ask for nothing better than to see you succeed;
for if you rise, I shall rise with you."

" Who talks of being King of France ? " angrily asked
the duke. " You are discussing a question which I have
never asked any one to settle, not even myself."

" Then all is settled, monseigneur, and there can be no
more discussion between us, since you have settled the
principal point."

" Do we agree ? "

" It seems so to me. Let them give you a guard and five
hundred thousand crowns. Before the peace is signed,
demand a subsidy for Anjou in case of war. Once you

have it, keep it. In this manner we shall have men, money, power, and we shall go — God knows where! "

" But once in Paris near them, when they have me there, they will laugh at me," said the duke.

"Come, monseigneur, you are not thinking of what you say. They laugh at us! Did you not hear what the queen-mother offered you ? "

" She offered me a great deal."

" I understand; and this troubles you ? "

" Yes."

"But among other things, she offered you a company of guards, even if I were to command them."

"Yes, she did."

" Well, accept. Appoint Bussy your captain, Antraguet and Livarot, lieutenants, and Ribeirac, ensign. Let us get up this company as we see fit, and you will see that with this escort at your heels, no one will dare laugh at you and not salute you; not even the king."

" Faith!" said the duke, " I think you are right, Bussy, and I shall think about it."

" Think over it, monseigneur."

" Yes, but what were you reading there so attentively when I came in ? "

" Ah, pardon me. I forgot. A letter."

" A letter ? "

"Which must interest you even more than me. What the devil was I thinking of that I did not show it to you at once!"

"Was it a great piece of news ? "

"*Mon Dieu!* yes, and rather sad news at that; M. de Monsoreau is dead."

"What ? " cried the duke, with a movement of such marked surprise that Bussy, who had his eyes fixed on the prince, thought he detected signs of joy.

" Dead, monseigneur."

" M. de Monsoreau ? "

" Eh, *mon Dieu!* yes ; are we not all mortal ? "

" Yes, but we do not die thus suddenly."

" That depends. If one is killed — "

" Was he killed ? "

" It seems so."

" By whom ? "

" By Saint-Luc, with whom he picked a quarrel."

" Ah, that dear Saint-Luc ! " cried the prince.

" Why," said Bussy, " I was not aware of your friendship for that dear Saint-Luc ! "

" He is my brother's friend," said the duke, " and since we are to be reconciled, my brother's friends are mine."

" Ah, very well, monseigneur, and I am charmed to see you in this mood."

" And you are sure ? "

" As sure as I can be. Here is a note from Saint-Luc announcing this death, and as I am as incredulous as you, I sent Rémy to ascertain the fact and present my compliments of condolence to the old baron."

" Dead, — Monsoreau dead ! " repeated the duke, " dead, by himself."

These words and the " dear Saint-Luc " betrayed his thoughts. Both were horribly plain.

" He did not die by himself, since Saint-Luc killed him," said Bussy.

" Oh, I understand myself."

" Had Monseigneur given him to some one else to kill ? " asked Bussy.

" No, had you ? "

" Oh, I, monseigneur, — I am not a great prince to have that work done by others, and I am obliged to do it myself."

" Ah, Monsoreau, Monsoreau ! " said the prince, with his frightful smile.

"Come, monseigneur, you seem to have had a grudge against that poor count."

"No, but you did."

"It was very simple that I should," said Bussy, blushing in spite of himself. "Did he not subject me to a most terrible humiliation on the part of your Highness?"

"Do you still remember that?"

"Yes, monseigneur, as you see; but you whose friend and tool he was —"

"Come, come," said the prince, interrupting the conversation, which was getting embarrassing for him, "have the horses prepared, Bussy."

"Horses? What for?"

"To go to Méridor and condole with Madame Diane. I planned this visit long ago, and cannot imagine why I did not pay it; but I shall delay no longer. *Corbleu!* I know not why, but I feel most complimentary to-day."

"Faith!" said Bussy to himself, "now that Monsoreau is dead, I have no more fear that he will sell his wife to the duke; so I do not care if he does see her. Should he attack her, I am quite able to defend her; and as I have this good opportunity to see her again, I shall avail myself of it."

And he went out to give orders about the horses.

A quarter of an hour later, while Catherine slept, or pretended to sleep, after the fatigue of her journey, the prince, Bussy, and ten gentlemen, mounted on fine horses, wended their way towards Méridor with that vigor and spirit which fine weather, green grass, and youth, always inspire in men and horses.

At the sight of this magnificent cavalcade, the porter of the castle came to inquire the names of the visitors.

"The Duc d'Anjou!" cried the prince.

The porter blew his horn, and at this sound all the servants of the castle hastened to the drawbridge. They were then seen rushing through the apartments and corridors;

the turret-windows were opened; there was a sound of clashing iron and the old baron appeared on the threshold, holding in his hand the castle keys.

"It is amazing how little Monsoreau is regretted," said the duke; "see, Bussy, how unconcerned they all seem to be."

A woman appeared on the porch.

"Ah, here is the fair Diane," cried the duke. "Do you see her, Bussy?"

"Certainly, monseigneur, I see her," replied the young man; "but," he added in a low voice, "I do not see Rémy."

Diane came out of the house, but immediately behind her was a stretcher on which lay Monsoreau. His eyes were bright with fever or jealousy, and he resembled a sultan of India on his palanquin rather than a dead man on his funeral couch.

"Oh, oh, what is this?" cried the duke to his companion, who had turned whiter than the handkerchief behind which he was trying to conceal his emotion.

"Long live Monseigneur the Duc d'Anjou!" cried Monsoreau, raising his hand in the air by a violent effort.

"Gently," said a voice behind him, "take care, or you will open the wound." It was Rémy who, faithful to his duty as a physician, watched over the wounded man. Astonishment does not last long at court, — on the face, at least; the Duc d'Anjou quickly changed amazement into a smile.

"Oh, my dear count," he cried, "what a happy surprise! Do you know we had heard that you were dead?"

"Come near, monseigneur," said the wounded man, "that I may kiss your hand. Thank God, I am not only alive, but I shall live, I hope, to serve you with more ardor and fidelity than ever."

As for Bussy, who was neither husband nor prince, — the two stations in life in which dissimulation is most necessary, — he felt a cold perspiration gather on his brow, and dared not even look at Diane. The sight of this treasure which he was losing for the second time, hurt him, when so near its possessor.

"And you, M. de Bussy," said Monsoreau, "let me thank you, for I nearly owe you my life."

"How to me?" stammered the young man, thinking that the count spoke in jest.

"Yes, indirectly it is true, but my gratitude is none the less great; here is my saviour," he added, pointing to Rémy, who raised his arms to heaven in despair and would have liked the earth to open and swallow him. "My friends owe it to him that I am still with them."

And in spite of the signs which the poor doctor was making for him to remain silent, and which he took for hygienic recommendations, he emphatically related the care, skill, and zeal which Rémy had shown him.

The duke knit his brow, and Bussy glared at Rémy with a frightful expression. The poor fellow, hidden behind Monsoreau, replied with a gesture which said, "Alas! it is not my fault."

"I hear," continued the count, "that Rémy one day found you dying as he found me. It is a tie of friendship between us. Count on mine, M. de Bussy. When Monsoreau loves, he loves well; but when he hates, it is also with his whole heart."

Bussy thought the count's eyes flashed as he glanced at the duke, but M. d'Anjou saw nothing.

"Come," he said, dismounting and offering his hand to Diane, "deign, fair lady, to do us the honors of this house which we had expected to find in grief, but which, on the contrary, continues to be the abode of joy. As for you, Monsoreau, take the rest you need."

"Monseigneur," said the count, "it shall not be said that you came to Monsoreau's house and that while he lived he allowed any one else to do the honors of the place; my servants will carry me, and wherever you will go, I shall follow."

The duke seemed to divine Monsoreau's real thought this time, for he let go of Diane's hand. The husband breathed again.

"Go near her," whispered Rémy to Bussy.

Bussy approached Diane, and Monsoreau smiled on them; Bussy took her hand, and Monsoreau still smiled.

"This is a great change, Monsieur le Comte," said Diane, in a low voice.

"Alas!" said Bussy, "why is it not even greater?"

It is needless to say that in receiving the prince, the old baron displayed the greatest hospitality.

CHAPTER XXXI.

THE INCONVENIENCE OF WIDE LITTERS AND NARROW DOORS.

Bussy did not leave Diane; Monsoreau's smiles gave him a liberty of which he was only too glad to avail himself. Jealous persons have this privilege, that, after they have made a brave fight to keep their property, they are not spared when once poachers have set foot on their estates.

"Madame," said Bussy to Diane, "I am really the most unfortunate of men. At the news of his death, I advised the prince to return to Paris and make peace with his mother; he consented, and now you remain in Anjou."

"Oh, Louis," replied the young woman, pressing Bussy's hand with the tips of her slender fingers, "how dare you say that we are miserable? Do you forget those beautiful days, those unspeakable joys, the mere memory of which thrills my very being?"

"I forget nothing, madame; on the contrary, I remember only too well, and this is why I suffer at the thought of losing this happiness. Think of my torture if I must return to Paris far from you. It breaks my heart, Diane, and makes me a coward."

Diane looked at Bussy, and saw so much grief in his eyes that she lowered her head and reflected. The young man waited for a moment with a pleading glance and clasped hands.

"Well," finally said Diane, "you will go to Paris, Louis, and so shall I."

"What!" cried the young man, "you will leave M. de Monsoreau?"

"Were I to leave him, he would not leave me," replied Diane. "No, believe me, Louis, it is best that he should come with us."

"Wounded! ill as he is, impossible!"

"He will come, I tell you," and leaving Bussy's arm, she approached the prince, who, in a very bad humor, was replying to Monsoreau, while Ribeirac, Antraguet, and Livarot clustered around the litter. As Diane drew near, the count's brow cleared. But this moment of calm was not of long duration; it vanished like a ray of sunshine between two storms. Diane went to the duke, and Monsoreau frowned.

"Monseigneur," she said, with a charming smile, "I am told that your Highness is passionately fond of flowers. Come, and I shall show you the most beautiful ones in Anjou."

François gallantly offered his hand.

"Whither are you taking Monseigneur, madame?" asked Monsoreau, uneasily.

"Into the conservatory, monsieur."

"Ah," said Monsoreau, "very well, carry me into the conservatory."

"Faith!" said Rémy, "I think I was quite right not to kill him, thank God! He will kill himself now."

Diane gave Bussy a smile full of promise.

"Let M. de Monsoreau be ignorant of the fact that you are leaving Anjou," she whispered, "and I shall manage the rest."

"Very well," said Bussy, and he approached the prince, while Monsoreau's litter passed around a clump of trees.

"Monseigneur," he said, "be very guarded in what you say. Do not let Monsoreau know that you are about to make peace."

" Why so ? "

" Because he might tell Madame Catherine, to make a
friend of her; and if she knew you had made up your mind,
she might be less inclined to generosity."

" You are right," said the duke.   " So you distrust him ? "

" Monsoreau ?   *Parbleu !* "

" Well, so do I.   I believe he pretended to be dead, only
to deceive us."

"No, upon my word, he really received a sword thrust,
and that idiot, Rémy, who pulled him through, really
thought him dead for a moment.   His soul must be riveted
to his body."

They had reached the conservatory.   Diane continued to
smile charmingly on the prince.

The duke went in first, then Diane; Monsoreau wished
to come next, but he soon saw that his litter could not
possibly pass through the door, which was high and narrow,
whereas his litter was six feet wide.   At the sight of this
narrow door he uttered a groan.

Diane entered the conservatory without noticing her husband's desperate gestures.   Bussy, for whom her smile was
perfectly clear, — he could read her heart so well, —
remained near Monsoreau and said to him with perfect
calmness, —

" It is useless to try, Monsieur le Comte.   The door is
too narrow and you will never go through."

" Monseigneur, monseigneur," cried Monsoreau, "do not
go into that conservatory.   The air is poisonous; some
strange flowers exhale deadly perfumes, monseigneur."

But François did not listen; he was so happy to feel
Diane's hand within his own that he forgot his usual prudence, and lost himself beneath the verdant shadows.
Bussy exhorted Monsoreau to bear his sufferings with
patience; but in spite of what he could say, the count,
unable to endure the mental torture, fainted away.

Rémy resumed his authority as a physician, and ordered that the wounded man should be taken to his room.

"And now," he asked the young man, "what am I to do?"

"Eh, *pardieu!*" said Bussy, "finish the work you have so well begun. Remain with him, and cure him."

Then he told Diane of the accident which had happened to her husband. Diane immediately left the duke, and went towards the castle.

"Have we succeeded?" asked Bussy, as she passed.

"I believe so; at all events, do not leave without having seen Gertrude."

The duke, who loved flowers only when he could visit them with Diane, now remembered the count's words, and left the conservatory. Livarot, Ribeirac, and Antraguet followed him.

In the mean time, Diane joined her husband, to whom Rémy was attending. The count soon opened his eyes. His first movement was to rise hastily, but Rémy had foreseen this first movement, and Monsoreau was tied to his mattress. He roared, but as he looked around, he saw Diane beside him.

"Ah, you are here, madame," he said. "I am very glad to see you and tell you that we start for Paris to-night."

Rémy exclaimed, but Monsoreau paid not the slightest attention to him.

"Can you think of such a thing with your wound?" asked Diane, with her usual calmness.

"Madame," said the count, "my wound does not matter in this case, and I prefer death to suffering. Even if I am to die on the way, we start to-night."

"As you please, monsieur," said Diane.

"This is my wish, and I beg you to make your preparations."

"My preparations will soon be made, monsieur; but may I inquire into the cause of this sudden resolution?"

"I shall tell it to you, madame, when you will have no more flowers to show the prince, or when the doors will be wide enough for my litter to go everywhere."

Diane bowed.

"But, madame," said Rémy.

"Monsieur le Comte wishes it," replied Diane; "my duty is to obey."

Rémy understood from a sign that he must cease his observations. He did so, but muttered to himself, —

"They will kill him, and say that my medicine was at fault."

During this time, the Duc d'Anjou was preparing to leave Méridor. He thanked the baron for his warm welcome, and mounted his horse. Gertrude appeared at this moment. She came to announce that her mistress, being detained near her husband, regretted she could not have the honor of bidding farewell to the prince, and whispered to Bussy that Diane was to leave that night.

They went.

The duke had an unstable will, or rather, he bent it to satisfy his whims. While Diane was cruel to him, she made his stay in Anjou seem distasteful, but her smiles made him unwilling to depart.

As he was in ignorance of the resolution taken by the master of the hounds, he meditated all the way home on the danger there might be in yielding too easily to the desires of the queen-mother. Bussy had foreseen all this, and counted on his desire to stay.

"You see, Bussy," said the duke to him, "I have reflected."

"Well, monseigneur, and what about?" asked the young man.

"That it might not be advisable to yield at once to my mother's wishes."

"You are right. She thinks herself clever enough without that."

"Whereas you see, if we ask for one week, or rather delay one week, if we give a few fêtes to which we shall summon all the nobility of the province, we shall show our strength."

"This is well reasoned, monseigneur, yet —"

"I shall remain here one week," said the duke, "and thanks to this delay I shall draw new concessions from the queen; you may depend upon me."

Bussy seemed buried in thought.

"Very well, monseigneur," he said; "obtain what you can, but try not to lose instead of profiting by this delay. The king for instance —"

"What of the king?"

"Well, if he does not know your intentions, he may be angry; he is very irascible, as you are aware."

"You are right; I should send him some one who will announce my return. That will give me the eight days I need."

"Yes, but that some one runs a great risk," said Bussy.

The Duc d'Anjou smiled his evil smile.

"You mean that I might change my mind?" he asked.

"Eh, in spite of the promise to your brother, you would change your mind if you found it to your interest to do so, would you not?"

"Perhaps."

"In that case your ambassador will be sent to the Bastille."

"He will not know the contents of the letter he will carry."

"On the contrary," said Bussy, "give him no letter, and tell him."

"Then no one will undertake the task."

" Why not ? "

" Do you know any one who would ? "

" Yes, I know one."

" Who ? "

" Myself, monseigneur."

" You ? "

" Yes, I like difficult negotiations."

" Bussy, my dear Bussy," said the duke, "if you do that you can count on my everlasting gratitude."

Bussy smiled ; he knew the measure of this gratitude. The duke thought he hesitated.

" I shall give you ten thousand crowns for your journey," he added.

" Come, monseigneur," said Bussy, " such things cannot be paid."

" So you will go ? "

" Yes."

" To Paris ? "

" To Paris."

" When ? "

" Why, when you wish."

" The sooner the better."

" Well, to-night if you say so."

" Good Bussy, dear Bussy, so you really consent ? "

" Do I consent ? Why, your Highness is well aware that I would go through fire to serve you. It is, then, agreed ; I set out to-night, lead a joyous life, and get some fat abbey for me from the queen-mother."

" I had already thought of it, my friend."

" Then good-by, monseigneur."

" Good-by, Bussy, and do not forget one thing."

" What is that ? "

" Take leave of my mother."

" I shall have that honor."

CHAPTER XXXII.

WHAT MOOD KING HENRI III. WAS IN WHEN M. DE.
SAINT-LUC REAPPEARED AT COURT.

AFTER Catherine's departure, the king, though relying on the ambassador he had sent to Anjou, thought only of arming himself against the attacks of his enemies. He knew from experience the genius of his family, and all the possibilities that lay in the way of a pretender to the crown, — that is to say, of the new man against the lawful possessor.

He amused himself like Tiberius in drawing up long lists of proscriptions with the assistance of Chicot, on which were written down, in alphabetical order, all those who did not show themselves zealous for the defence of the king.

These lists were becoming longer every day, and under S and L, — that is to say, twice over, — he inscribed the name of Saint-Luc. The king's anger against his former favorite was, moreover, stimulated by the court commentaries, the perfidious insinuations of the courtiers, and bitter recriminations based on Saint-Luc's flight to Anjou, — a flight which became treason on the day when the duke himself had fled to that province.

In fact, Saint-Luc's escaping to Méridor could be considered M. d'Anjou's quarter-master going to prepare lodgings in Angers.

In the midst of all this agitation and movement, Chicot, encouraging the favorites to sharpen their daggers and swords to cut and slash at his Most Christian Majesty's enemies, was magnificent to behold; all the more so because though he seemed to play a very useless part, he really had a very important one. Little by little, man by man, so to speak, Chicot was assembling an army for his master's service.

One afternoon, while the king was supping with the queen, whose society he always cultivated in all political disturbances, Chicot entered suddenly with legs and arms extended like those of a jumping-jack.

"Ouf!" he said.

"What?" asked the king.

"M. de Saint-Luc," said Chicot.

"M. de Saint-Luc?" exclaimed his Majesty.

"Yes."

"In Paris?"

"Yes."

"In the Louvre?"

"Yes."

After that triple affirmation, the king rose from the table, pale and trembling. It was difficult to say what sentiments agitated him.

"Pardon me," he said to the queen, after wiping his moustache and throwing his napkin on his chair, "but these are affairs of state which do not concern women."

"Yes," said Chicot, raising his voice, "these are affairs of state."

The queen wished to retire but Henri said to her, —

"I beg you to remain, madame, and I shall go into my room."

"Oh, sire," said the queen, with that tender interest she always showed in her ungrateful husband, "I entreat you not to get angry."

"May God spare me!" said Henri, without observing the quizzical way in which Chicot twirled his moustache. Henri rushed out of the room; Chicot followed him.

"Why has the traitor come?" asked the king, in an agitated voice.

" Who knows ? " replied Chicot.

" I am sure he comes as deputy from the assembly of Anjou as envoy from my brother; for this is the course of rebellions. The rebels fish, in muddy waters, all sort of advantages which, though sordid and precarious, gradually become fixed and permanent. This one has scented the rebellion, and taken the opportunity to come here and insult me."

" Who knows ? " said Chicot.

The king looked at this laconic individual.

" It may be," said Henri, walking down the gallery at a pace that betrayed his agitation, "that he has come to ask for his estates, the revenues of which I withhold from him; this may be rather excessive abuse as, after all, he has not committed any real crime."

" Who knows ? " continued Chicot.

" Ah," said Henri, "you are always repeating the same thing, like a parrot. *Mort de ma vie !* you irritate me with your eternal ' who knows ? ' "

" Eh, *mordieu !* do you think yourself amusing with your eternal questions ? "

" You might at least answer something."

" What can I answer ? Do you take me for an oracle ? For Jupiter, Apollo, or Manto ? You irritate me with your foolish suppositions."

" Monsieur Chicot — "

" Well, Monsieur Henri."

" Chicot, my friend, you see my sorrow, and you laugh at me."

" Have no sorrow, *mordieu !* "

" But every one betrays me."

" Who knows ? *Ventre de biche !* who knows ? "

Henri, losing himself in conjectures, descended to his room, where the news of Saint-Luc's return had caused all the courtiers to assemble. Among them was Crillon, who, with flaming eyes, a red nose, and bristling moustache, looked like a dog ready to fight.

Saint-Luc was standing there surrounded by all these threatening faces, feeling the anger seething around him and yet not in the least concerned. He had brought his wife and seated her on a stool near the balustrade of the bed. He was walking about and returning the glances that were levelled at him.

Out of consideration for the lady, some of the nobles had moved aside, in spite of their desire to insult Saint-Luc and to speak disagreeable words to him. The ex-favorite was moving about amid this silence.

Jeanne, modestly wrapped in her travelling-cloak, was waiting with downcast eyes. Saint-Luc, proudly wrapped in his cloak, was also waiting. Finally, the whole assembly was waiting to know the reason of Saint-Luc's reappearance at court where all were trying to divide among themselves some portion of his past favor and where his presence was considered most useless.

Expectation had reached its height when the king appeared.

Henri entered, very agitated, and busy working himself up; it is this very breathlessness which often constitutes what is known as the dignity of princes. He entered, followed by Chicot, who had the calm dignity which the King of France should have shown; he at once observed Saint-Luc's attitude, a thing which Henri III. should have done.

"You here, monsieur?" cried the king, without heeding those around him, like the Spanish bull who rushes into the arena and sees only the red rag.

"Yes, sire," simply and modestly replied Saint-Luc as he bowed with respect.

This answer made so little impression on the king, so little did this dignified attitude convey to his mind a corresponding sense of dignity, that he continued at once, —

"Really, your presence at the Louvre surprises me."

At this brutal aggression, a death-like silence reigned around the king and his favorite. It was the silence which reigns around the lists when two adversaries are about to settle a supreme question. Saint-Luc was the first to break it.

"Sire," he said, with his habitual elegance and without being moved in the least by the royal anger, "I am surprised that under the existing circumstances your Majesty did not expect me."

"What do you mean, monsieur?" replied Henri, with royal pride and raising his head with an expression of great dignity.

"Sire," replied Saint-Luc, "your Majesty is in danger."

"In danger?" cried the courtiers.

"Yes, gentlemen, a serious, great, and real danger, — a danger in which the king will have need of all those who are devoted to him; and being convinced that in a danger like this one, there is no small assistance, I come to lay at his feet my humble services."

"Ah, ah, my son," said Chicot, "you see I was right to say, 'Who knows?'"

Henri III. did not reply at first. He looked around, and all those present seemed agitated and offended; but Henri soon discovered the jealousy which agitated all the hearts. He concluded that Saint-Luc had done something of which the majority would have been incapable, — that is, something noble; yet he would not yield at once.

"Monsieur," he said, "you have only done your duty; you owe us your services."

"All the subjects owe their services to the king, — I know it, sire," replied Saint-Luc; "but in these times many people forget to pay their debts. I have come, sire, to pay mine, only too happy if your Majesty will deign to number me among your creditors."

Henri, disarmed by this continuous gentleness and humility, took a step towards Saint-Luc.

"Then," he said, "you return without any other motive save the one you mentioned, — without any mission or safe-conduct?"

"Sire," quickly said Saint-Luc, who saw there was neither anger nor reproach in his master's tone, "I have returned simply and purely for the reason I gave. Now your Majesty can throw me into the Bastille or have me shot, but I shall have done my duty. Sire, Anjou is on fire; Touraine is about to revolt; Guyenne is rising beside them; M. le Duc d'Anjou is working the west and south of France."

"And he is well seconded, is he not?" cried the king.

"Sire," said Saint-Luc, who understood the meaning of the royal words, "neither counsel nor argument can stay the duke; and M. de Bussy, firm as he is, cannot reassure your brother under the terror with which your Majesty inspires him."

"Ah, ah," said Henri, "he is trembling, the rebel!"

And he smiled under his moustache.

"*Tudieu!*" said Chicot, as he stroked his chin, "here is a clever man," and pushing the king with his elbow, —

"Make way, Henri," he said, "and let me shake M. de Saint-Luc's hand."

This movement was followed by the king. He let Chicot pay his compliment to the new-comer, then going slowly to his old friend, he placed his hand on his shoulder and said, —

"You are welcome, Saint-Luc."

"Ah, sire," cried Saint-Luc, kissing the king's hand, "I find again my beloved master."

"Yes, but you are no longer the same," said the king, "or rather, you have grown so thin, my poor Saint-Luc, that I would not have recognized you."

At this moment a feminine voice was heard.

"Sire," said this voice, "it is from grief at having incurred your Majesty's displeasure."

Though this voice was gentle and respectful, Henri started, for its sound was almost as disagreeable to him as thunder was to Augustus.

"Madame de Saint-Luc!" he murmured. "Ah, true; I had forgotten — "

Jeanne fell on her knees.

"Rise, madame," said the king. "I love all those who bear the name of Saint-Luc."

Jeanne quickly seized the king's hand and carried it to her lips, but Henri as quickly drew it away.

"Go and convert the king," said Chicot to the young woman, " *ventre de biche!* you are pretty enough for that."

But Henri turned his back on Jeanne, and throwing his arm around Saint-Luc's neck, led him into the next room.

"Then we have made peace," he said.

"Say rather, that the pardon is granted, sire," replied the courtier.

"Madame," said Chicot to Jeanne, who hesitated, " a good wife must not leave her husband, — particularly, when her husband is in danger," and he pushed her after the king and Saint-Luc.

CHAPTER XXXIII.

IN WHICH WE MEET TWO IMPORTANT CHARACTERS IN THE
STORY, WHO HAVE NOT BEEN SEEN FOR SOME TIME.

THERE is one character in this story, — there are even two,
— about whose fate the reader has a right to inquire. With
the humility of the author of an ancient preface, we hasten
to reply to these questions, all the importance of which we
understand.

We mean first an enormous monk, with heavy brows,
thick red lips, large hands, broad shoulders, and the
length of whose neck daily decreases in inverse propor-
tion to the development of his chest and cheeks. We
next have a large donkey, whose sides are gradually
swelling out like a balloon. The monk is fast getting like
a hogshead; the ass resembles a child's crib supported on
four posts.

The one inhabits a cell in the convent of Sainte-Genevieve, where all the blessings of the Lord come and visit
him; the other, the stable of the same convent. The one
answers to the name of Gorenflot, the second to the name
of Panurge.

For the moment, both were enjoying themselves beyond
their wildest dreams. The monks of Sainte-Genevieve took
all possible care of their illustrious companions; and like
the divinities of the third rank, who attended Jupiter's
eagle, Juno's peacock, and Venus' doves, the lay brothers
devoted their energies to fattening Panurge for his master's sake. Savory odors came from the kitchen, while
the choicest Burgundy wines filled the largest glasses.

If there came a missionary who had travelled in distant
lands for the propagation of the faith, or a legate bearing
indulgences from the Pope, they showed him Brother
Gorenflot, that model churchman who preaches like Saint
Luke, and uses his sword like Saint Paul. They showed
him Gorenflot in all his glory, — that is to say, seated at
a table in which a hollow had been cut out for his sacred
stomach; and they took great pride in saying that he could
consume the rations of eight ordinary persons. And when
the new-comer had piously contemplated that marvel, the
prior would clasp his hands and say to him, "What an
admirable nature ; Brother Gorenflot loves the pleasures of
the table and cultivates the arts. You see how he eats !
Ah, if you had heard the sermon he preached one famous
night, when he offered to devote himself for the triumph
of the faith ! His is a mouth which speaks like Saint John
Chrysostom's, and swallows like that of Gargantua."

Sometimes, however, in the midst of all these splendors,
a cloud passes over Gorenflot's brow. The capons smoke
uselessly before his wide nostrils, the little Flemish
oysters yawn in vain in their pearly shells. The bottles
stand before him untouched. Gorenflot is gloomy ; he is
no longer hungry ; he dreams.

The report spreads at once that the worthy monk is in
an ecstasy like Saint Francis, or in a swoon like Saint
Theresa, and the admiration increases. He is no longer
a monk ; he is a saint, a demi-god, and others even go so
far as to liken him to a God.

"Hush !" they murmur, "let us not disturb Brother
Gorenflot's meditation."

And all move aside. The prior then awaits the moment
when Brother Gorenflot will make some sign. He
approaches the monk, takes his hands, and questions him.
Gorenflot raises his head, and looks vacantly at the prior,
and seems to come from another world.

"What were you doing, worthy brother?" asked the prior.

"I?" said Gorenflot.

"Yes, you; you were doing something."

"Yes, Father, I was composing a sermon."

"In the style of the one you gave us on the night of the League?"

Every time that this sermon is mentioned, Gorenflot bewails his infirmity.

"Yes," he says with a sigh, "in the same style. Ah, what a pity I did not write that one!"

"Does a man like you need to write, my dear brother? No, you are inspired; you open your mouth, and as the word of God is within you, it flows from your lips."

"You think so?" said Gorenflot.

"Happy is the man who doubts," replied the prior.

From time to time, Gorenflot, who understands the necessities of his position, meditates a sermon.

Away with Marcus Tullius, Cæsar, Saint Gregory, Saint Augustine, Saint Jerome, and Tertullian; the revival of sacred eloquence will begin with Gorenflot!

From time to time, when he has finished a meal, Gorenflot rises, and drawn by an invincible force, wends his way to the stables; there he looks lovingly at Panurge, who brays with pleasure; then he passes his fat hand over the thick hair, in which it almost disappears. This is no longer pleasure, it is happiness; and Panurge not only brays, but rolls himself.

The prior and three or four dignitaries usually accompany him in these excursions, and pet Panurge; they give him cakes, biscuits, macaroons, like those who gave honey-cakes to Cerberus in order to win Pluto's favor.

Panurge, having a most amiable disposition, suffers these attentions; besides, as he has neither ecstasies nor sermons to meditate, and no reputation to sustain save that of obsti-

nacy and laziness, he finds nothing more to desire, and is
the happiest of donkeys.

The prior looks tenderly at him.

"Simple and gentle," he said; "those are the attributes
of strength."

Gorenflot had learned that *ita* is the Latin for "yes."
He made marvellous use of this word, replying *ita* to all that
was said to him, and always producing a fine effect.   Encouraged by this perpetual agreement with all he said, the
abbot would sometimes say to him, —

"You work too much, my dear brother, and your heart
grows sad."

And Gorenflot replied to Joseph Foulon as Chicot sometimes replied to his Majesty King Henri III., —

"Who knows?"

"Our meals are perhaps a little coarse," added the prior;
"you might like the cook changed.   You know, my dear
brother, *Quædam saturationes minus succedunt.*"

"*Ita*" was Gorenflot's invariable answer as he patted his
donkey.

"You caress Panurge a great deal, good brother," said
the prior; "are you longing to travel again?"

"Oh!" Gorenflot would answer with a sigh.

The fact is that Gorenflot was tormented by memories.
He had first left his convent with great reluctance; but he
discovered in his exile infinite and unknown joys, the source
of which is freedom.   In the midst of his happiness he felt
this longing for freedom, — freedom with Chicot, that gay
companion whom he loved without knowing why; perhaps
because Chicot beat him from time to time.

"Alas!" timidly said a young brother who had followed
the play of Gorenflot's features, "I think you are right,
worthy prior, and that convent life is burdensome to him."

"Not exactly," said Gorenflot; "but I feel that I am
born to lead a life of activity in the midst of political strug-
gles and campaigns."

As he spoke these words Gorenflot's eyes sparkled. He was thinking of Chicot's omelets, of the wine of Anjou in Maître Claude Bonhomet's cellar, and of the public-room of the Corne d'Abondance.

Since the night of the League, or rather, since the morning which followed his return to the convent, he had not been allowed to go out; since the king had appointed himself chief of the Union, the Leaguers acted with great reserve. Gorenflot was so simple-minded that he had not even thought of taking advantage of his position to have the door opened. He had been told, "Brother, you are forbidden to go out," and he had not gone. No one suspected this inward fire which caused the happiness of the convent to weigh upon him.

But as his sadness daily increased, the prior said to him one morning, —

"Dear brother, no one should fight against his vocation. Yours is to fight for Christ. Go, then, and fulfil the mission for which the Lord has sent you, only be careful of your precious life and return for the great day."

"What great day?" asked Gorenflot, absorbed in his joy.

"That of the Fête Dieu"

"*Ita*," said the monk, with an air of profound wisdom; "but," added Gorenflot, "give me some money that I may bestow alms in a Christian manner."

The prior hastened to fetch a large purse, which he opened. Gorenflot plunged in his great hand.

"You will see what I shall bring back to the convent," he said, as he transferred to his own the contents of the prior's purse.

"You have the text, have you not, dear brother?"

"Yes, certainly."

"Confide it to me."

"Willingly; but to you alone."

The prior approached Gorenflot and listened attentively.

" 'The flail which beats the corn beats itself,' " said the monk.

" Oh, magnificent! oh, sublime!" cried the prior; while all the others, sharing his enthusiasm, repeated with him, "Magnificent! sublime!"

"And now, Reverend Father, am I free?" humbly asked Gorenflot.

" Yes, my son; go and walk in the path of the Lord."

Gorenflot saddled Panurge, mounted him with the aid of two vigorous monks, and left the convent at about seven o'clock in the evening. It was the same day on which Saint-Luc arrived from Méridor. The news from Anjou held Paris in a state of ferment.

Gorenflot, after having followed the Rue Saint-Étienne, had just turned to the right and passed the Jacobins, when Panurge started suddenly. A heavy hand had been laid on his back.

"Who is there?" cried Gorenflot, frightened.

"A friend," replied a voice which Gorenflot thought he recognized. The monk was very anxious to turn round; but, like the sailors who must get accustomed to the motion of the ship every time they go to sea, every time he mounted his ass it took some time for him to find his centre of gravity.

"What do you want?" he asked.

"Worthy monk, would you kindly show me the way to the Corne d'Abondance?" replied the voice.

"*Morbleu!* it is M. Chicot in person!" cried Gorenflot, with delight.

"Exactly," replied the Gascon. "I was going to seek you at the convent when I saw you come out. I followed you for some time, as I would not compromise myself by being seen talking to you. But now that we are alone, how are you? *Ventre de biche!* I think you have grown thin!"

"And you, M. Chicot, have grown fat."

"I think we are flattering each other."

"What have you there, M. Chicot?" asked the monk; "you seem laden."

"I have a haunch of venison which I have stolen from his Majesty," said the Gascon; "we shall have it cooked."

"Dear M. Chicot!" cried the monk. "And under the other arm?"

"A flask of Cyprus wine sent by another king to my king."

"Let me see," said Gorenflot.

"That is the wine I love. Do you not like it, worthy brother?" asked Chicot, opening his cloak.

"Oh, oh," cried Gorenflot, jumping about in such glee that Panurge bent beneath the load. In his joy, the monk raised his hands to heaven and in a voice which made the windows rattle, he sang to Panurge's accompaniment, —

> "La musique a des appas,
> Mais on ne fait que l'entendre,
> Les fleurs ont le parfum tendre,
> Mais l'odeur ne nourrit pas.
> Sans que noire main y touche,
> Un beau ciel flatte nos yeux ;
> Mais la vie coule en la bouche,
> Mais le vin se sent, se touche
> Et se boit ; je l'aime mieux
> Que musique, fleurs et cieux."

It was the first time he had sung for a month.

CHAPTER XXXIV.

HOW MONSOREAU AND DIANE JOURNEYED TO PARIS.

LET us leave the two friends at the Corne d'Abondance (whither, as the reader may have observed, Chicot never conducted Gorenflot without intentions which the poor monk was far from suspecting) and let us return to M. de Monsoreau, who was travelling to Paris in his litter, and to Bussy, who had left Angers with the intention of following the same road.

It is not difficult for a well-mounted rider to overtake foot travellers, and he even runs the risk of passing them. This happened to Bussy.

It was towards the end of May and the heat was great, particularly about noon. M. de Monsoreau ordered a halt in a little wood which was near the road; and as he wished M. le Duc d'Anjou to remain as long as possible in ignorance of his departure, he saw that his whole suite entered the thicket, where they remained until the heat of the day was over; and as they had a horse laden with provisions there was no necessity to go to an inn.

During this time, Bussy passed them. But as we may imagine, he did not travel without inquiring if horses and riders and a litter carried by peasants had been seen. Until he reached the village of Durtal, he obtained positive and satisfactory information; and certain that Diane was before him, he went on very slowly, rising in his stirrups at the top of each hill, in the hope of perceiving the party he was following.

But all information suddenly ceased; the travellers whom he met had seen no one, and on reaching La Flèche he became convinced that instead of following, he was now preceding. He then remembered the little wood he had passed and understood why his horse had neighed and sniffed the air as they rode by.

He made up his mind at once, and put up at the worst inn of the street, after having seen that his horse would be well attended to (he was more careful of it than of himself, for he knew he must be able to rely on its strength in case of necessity); then he settled himself near a window, carefully concealed behind the strip of cloth that served as a curtain. Bussy had been guided in his choice by the fact that this tavern was situated directly opposite the best hostelry in the town, and he did not doubt that Monsoreau would stop there. He had guessed rightly. Towards four o'clock there came a courier who stopped at the door of the inn. Half an hour later came the rest of the party, composed of the count, countess, Rémy, and Gertrude, and of eight carriers who were relayed at every five leagues. The courier's duty was to prepare these relays of peasants.

Now, as Monsoreau was too jealous not to be generous, this mode of travelling suffered neither difficulty nor delay.

The principal travellers entered the hostelry one after the other; Diane was the last, and Bussy thought she glanced anxiously around. His first impulse was to show himself, but he had the courage to repress it; the slightest imprudence might ruin them.

Night came; Bussy hoped that during the night Rémy might come out or Diane might show herself at some window, so he wrapped himself up in his cloak and went down into the street. He waited there until nine o'clock; at that hour the courier left the inn, and five minutes later eight men approached the door; four of them entered.

"Oh," said Bussy to himself, "are they going to travel by night? That would be an excellent idea on the part of M. de Monsoreau."

All concurred for the plausibility of this supposition, — the night was balmy and the stars shone brightly; a soft breeze, laden with freshness and perfumes, cooled the air. The litter came out first, followed by Diane, Rémy, and Gertrude on horseback. Diane looked around, but the count called her and she was obliged to go beside his litter. The four men for the relay walked on either side of the road with lighted torches.

"Good!" said Bussy, "had I commanded the details of this march, I could not have done better." He returned to his inn, saddled his horse, and set out in pursuit of the travellers.

This time there was no danger of his taking the wrong road and losing sight of them; the torches clearly indicated the direction they followed. Monsoreau scarcely allowed Diane to move from his side. He talked to her, or rather, scolded her. Her visit to the conservatory served as a text for innumerable comments and malicious questions.

Rémy and Gertrude sulked, or rather, Rémy reflected and Gertrude sulked. The cause of this behavior could be easily explained. Rémy no longer found it necessary to be in love with Gertrude since Diane was in love with Bussy.

The *cortége* advanced, some disputing, others sulking. At last Bussy, who followed the cavalcade at a safe distance, gave a long shrill whistle with which he was in the habit of summoning his attendants in the *hôtel* of the Rue de Grenelle-Saint-Honoré, and thus notified Rémy of his presence. This sound, which always echoed from one end of the house to the other, would bring men and beasts, at the call. We say men and beasts, because Bussy, like all strong men, took pleasure in training fighting dogs, wild horses, and falcons. Now, at the sound of this whistle, the dogs started in their kennels, the horses in their stalls and the falcons on their perches. Rémy recognized it at once. Diane started, and looked at the young man, who nodded in the affirmative. As he passed beside her, he whispered, —

"It is he."

"What is it?" asked Monsoreau. "Who was speaking to you, madame?"

"To me? No one, monsieur."

"Yes, I saw a shadow and I heard a voice."

"The voice was Monsieur Rémy's," replied Diane. "Are you also jealous of him?"

"No, but I prefer that those around me should speak aloud; it would amuse me."

"There are certain things which cannot be said aloud before Monsieur le Comte," said Gertrude, coming to the rescue.

"Why so?"

"For two reasons."

"What are they?"

"Because the things either do not interest Monsieur le Comte or interest him too much."

"And of which kind were the things which Monsieur Rémy has just whispered to Madame?"

"Of the kind which interest Monsieur too much."

"What was Rémy saying to you, madame? I must know."

"I was saying, Monsieur le Comte, that if you excite yourself in this way, you will be dead before you have gone one third of the way."

By the pale light of the torches, Monsoreau was seen to grow deadly white. Diane, breathless and pensive, was silent.

"He is waiting for you behind," said Rémy, in a scarcely audible voice; "ride slowly and he will overtake you."

Rémy had spoken so low that Monsoreau heard only a murmur; he made an effort, threw back his head, and saw Diane riding near.

"Another movement like that, Monsieur le Comte," said Rémy, "and you will bring on a hemorrhage."

Diane had now become courageous. Her love had given birth to that audacity which a woman truly in love usually carries beyond the limits of prudence. She turned her horse's head and waited.

At the same moment, Rémy dismounted, threw his bridle to Gertrude, and approached the litter to occupy the sick man's attention.

"Let me feel your pulse," he said; "I am sure you have fever."

Five seconds later Bussy was beside Diane. They needed no speech to understand each other, and remained for some moments locked in a tender embrace.

"You see," said Bussy, who was the first to break the silence, "that when you go, I follow you."

"Oh, Bussy, what happiness for me in the days and nights if I know that you are near!"

"But by day he will see us."

"No, you will follow from a distance, and I alone shall see you, my Louis. At the turn of the road or the top of a hill your waving plume or your handkerchief floating in the breeze will speak to me in your name and tell me that you love me. If at the fall of day I can see your shadow bend to send me a kiss, I shall be so happy."

"Speak on, my beloved Diane; you do not know what harmony there is in the sound of your voice."

"And when we travel by night, — which we shall often do, for Rémy told him that the night air would cool the fever of his wounds, — I can sometimes stay behind as I am doing now; from time to time, I shall be able to press you in my arms and tell you how I shall have thought of you all day."

"Oh, how I love you! how I love you!" murmured Bussy.

"Do you know," said Diane, "I think our souls are so closely united that even at a distance, without speaking or even seeing each other, we can be happy in our thoughts."

"Oh, yes; but to be near you, to see you, and hold you in my arms, — oh, Diane! Diane!"

The horses came together, while their silver-mounted bridles jingled, and the two lovers forgot the world in a long embrace. Suddenly was heard a voice which made them both start, Diane with fear and Bussy with anger.

"Madame Diane!" it cried. "Where are you? Answer."

This call sounded through the air like a death-knell.

"Oh, it is he! I had forgotten him," murmured Diane. "It is he; I was dreaming; sweet dream and bitter awakening."

"Listen!" cried Bussy, "listen, Diane; we are together. Speak but one word and nothing can separate us. Let us fly. What prevents us? Before us is happiness and liberty. One word, and we shall go: one word, and you are lost to him and belong to me forever."

The young man was gently holding her.

"And my father?"

"When the baron will know how I love you, —" he murmured.

"Oh, a father? What are you saying there?"

This single word recalled Bussy to himself.

"I will do nothing by violence, dear Diane," he said. "Order, and I shall obey."

"Listen," said Diane, "our destiny is there; let us be stronger than the demon who persecutes us. Fear nothing, and you will see if I know how to love."

"Must we then separate?"

"Countess," cried the voice, "answer or I will jump from this infernal litter, even if it kill me to do so."

"Adieu," said Diane; "he would do it and kill himself."

"You pity him?"

"Jealous!" said Diane, with an adorable smile.

Bussy let her go. In two bounds she had reached the litter, and found the count half fainting.

"Stop!" he murmured, "stop!"

"*Morbleu!*" said Rémy, "do not stop, he is mad; if he wishes to kill himself, let him."

And the litter went on.

"After whom are you crying?" said Gertrude. "Madame is here, beside me. Come, madame, speak to him; Monsieur le Comte is surely delirious."

Diane, without uttering a word, entered the circle of light.

"Ah," said Monsoreau, exhausted, "where were you?"

"Where could I be, monsieur, if not behind you?"

"At my side, madame; and do not leave me again."

Diane had no other motive for remaining behind; she knew that Bussy was following her. Had there been any moonlight, she could have seen him.

They reached a halting-place. Monsoreau rested a few hours, and wished to go on. He was anxious, not to reach Paris, but to be far from Angers. From time to time, the scene we have just described was renewed. Rémy said to himself, —

"If he dies of rage, the physician's honor will be safe."

But Monsoreau did not die; on the contrary, at the end of ten days, they reached Paris and he was much better. Rémy was positively a very able physician, more so even than he wished.

During these ten days Diane had gradually demolished all Bussy's great pride. She had urged him to visit Monsoreau and take advantage of the latter's friendship for him. He had an excuse for his visit, — the count's health about which he came to inquire. Rémy attended the husband and carried notes to the wife.

" Æsculapius and Mercury," he said; "my functions are complex."

CHAPTER XXXV.

HOW THE DUC D'ANJOU'S AMBASSADOR REACHED PARIS, AND THE RECEPTION HE MET WITH.

IN the mean time, neither Catherine nor the Duc d'Anjou appeared at the Louvre, and the report of a dissension between the two brothers became every day more important. The king had received no message from his mother, and instead of believing, according to the proverb, "No news, good news," he shook his head and said, "No news, bad news."

The favorites added : "François, ill-advised, must have kept your mother."

François, ill-advised. In fact, all the singular policy of this singular reign and of the three preceding ones could be summed up in these words: Ill-advised was King Charles IX. when he had — if not ordered — at least authorized the massacre of Saint-Bartholomew. Ill-advised was Francis II. when he ordered the massacre of Amboise. Ill-advised was Henri II., the father of this perverted race, when he burned so many heretics and conspirators before he was killed by Montgomery, who was also said to have been ill-advised when his lance penetrated so awkwardly beneath the king's visor : no one dared say to the king :

"Your brother has bad blood in his veins ; he is trying, according to the custom in your family, to dethrone or poison you ; he wishes to do to you what you did to your elder brother, what your elder brother did to his, and what your mother taught you all to do to one another."

No, a king in those days, particularly in the sixteenth century, would have taken these remarks for insults; for a king was a man in those days; civilization alone has been able to make of him a fac-simile of God like Louis XIV., or an irresponsible myth like a constitutional king.

The favorites therefore said to Henri III., —

"Sire, your brother is ill-advised."

And as there was only one person possessing the power and mind to advise François, it was against Bussy that the storm was raised, and was becoming each day more violent. The public councils were seeking modes of intimidation, and the privy councils were seeking modes of extermination, when the news suddenly came that the Duc d'Anjou was sending an ambassador.

Whence came this report? Who carried it and spread it? It would be as easy to say that as to say how the clouds of dust are raised on the plains or the whirlwinds of noise in the cities.

There is a demon who puts wings to certain reports and lets them fly through space like eagles. When this one reached the Louvre, it produced a general conflagration. The king became pale with anger, and the courtiers, who always exaggerated their master's passions, became livid. They swore. It would be difficult to say all they swore, but they swore among other things, that if the ambassador were an old man he would be scoffed at, derided, and thrown into the Bastille. If he were a young man he would be cut into small pieces, which would be sent to all the provinces of France as a sample of the royal anger.

The favorites, according to their custom, polished their swords, took fencing lessons, and buried their daggers in the wall. Chicot left his sword in its scabbard, his dagger in its sheath, and began to reflect. The king, seeing Chicot reflect, and remembering that Chicot had once been of the same opinion as the queen-mother on a subject of great moment, and that this opinion had been justified by events, understood that the wisdom of the kingdom was embodied in Chicot, and he questioned him.

"Sire," he replied, after mature reflection, "Monseigneur the Duc d'Anjou will either send an ambassador, or will not send one."

"*Pardieu!*" said the king, "what was the use of burying your fist in your cheek to find this dilemma?"

"Patience, patience, as your august mother is always saying in the language of Machiavelli."

"You see that I have some, since I am listening to you."

"If he send you an ambassador, it is because he thinks he can do it; if he, who is prudence itself, think he can do it, it is a proof that he feels himself strong. Therefore, you must temporize with him. We must respect powers and deceive them, but we must not play with them; we must receive their ambassador and show great pleasure at seeing him. That means nothing at all. You remember how your brother Charles IX. embraced that good Admiral Coligny who came as an ambassador from the Huguenots, who also thought themselves a power?"

"Then you approve of the policy of my brother Charles IX.?"

"Not at all; I am simply giving an example. If, later on, you find means, not of hurting a poor devil of an ambassador, or envoy, but of seizing the master, the motor, the chief, the high and mighty prince, Monseigneur the Duc d'Anjou, the real and only culprit, together with the three Guises, and locking them up in a fortress stronger than the Louvre, do so by all means."

"I like this beginning," said Henri III.

"*Peste!* you are not hard to please. I shall continue."

"Go on."

"But if he should not send an ambassador, why do you allow all your friends to bellow?"

" Bellow ? "

" You understand. I would say roar if there was any way
of comparing them to lions. I say bellow — because —
Come Henri, it makes me ill to see these fellows — more
bearded than the monkeys of your menagerie — playing
ghost like little boys and trying to frighten men by crying,
' Hoo, hoo,' without counting that if the Duc d'Anjou send
no one, they will imagine it is on their account, and think
themselves great personages."

"Chicot, you forget that the persons of whom you speak
are my friends, my only friends."

" Will you let me win a thousand crowns from you, oh,
king ? " asked Chicot.

"Speak."

" Bet with me that these fellows will remain faithful
through every trial, and I will bet that before to-morrow
night I will have gained over three of the four, body and
soul."

Chicot's assurance made the king reflect. He did not
reply.

"Ah ! " said Chicot, "so you too are thinking, and burying your charming fist in your pretty mouth. You are
more clever than I thought, my son, for you are beginning
to see the truth."

" Then what do you advise me to do ? "

"Wait. Half of Solomon's wisdom lies in that word. If
an ambassador should come, receive him well; if no one
come, do as you choose, but believe me, do not sacrifice
your brother to your scamps. *Cordieu !* I know he is a
great rascal, but he is a Valois. Kill him if you like, but
for the honor of the name, do not disgrace him; he is
attending very diligently to that himself."

" That is true, Chicot."

" One more lesson that you owe me. Fortunately we do
not keep account. Now let me sleep, Henri. A week ago

I found it necessary to intoxicate a monk, and when I perform such feats I am tipsy for a week."

"Is it that good monk of Sainte-Genevieve of whom you have already spoken ? "

"Exactly; you promised him an abbey."

"I ? "

"*Pardieu !* it is the least you might do for him after all he did for you."

"Is he still devoted to me ? "

"He adores you. By the way, my son."

"What ? "

"The Fête Dieu is in three weeks."

"Well ? "

"I hope you are preparing some nice little procession."

"I am the most Christian king, and it is my duty to give my people the example of religion."

"And you will stop as usual in all the great convents of Paris ? "

"Yes."

"At the Abbey of Sainte-Genevieve ? "

"No doubt; it is the second one I intend to visit. But why do you ask ? "

"Oh, nothing! I was only curious. Now, I know what I wanted. Good-night, Henri."

At this moment, as Chicot was preparing to take a nap, a great noise was heard in the Louvre.

"What is this ? " asked the king.

"Come," said Chicot, "it is said that I shall not sleep, Henri."

"Well ? "

"My son, you must rent a room for me, or I shall leave you. Upon my word, the Louvre has become uninhabitable."

At this moment, the captain of the guards entered. He looked very frightened.

" What is it ? " asked the king.

" Sire," replied the captain, " it is the Duc d'Anjou's envoy who is dismounting at the gate."

" With a suite ? "

" No, all alone."

" Then you must receive him doubly well, Henri, for he is a brave man."

" Come," said the king, whose face was pale, though he tried to look calm, " assemble my whole court in the great hall, and let me dress in black. One must dress in mourning to treat with one's brother through an ambassador."

CHAPTER XXXVI.

WHICH IS ONLY THE CONTINUATION OF THE LAST.

KING HENRI III.'s throne was in the great hall. Around this throne was an excited and tumultuous throng. The king took his seat, sad and frowning. All eyes were turned towards the gallery, through which the captain of the guards was to introduce the envoy.

"Sire," whispered Quélus, in the king's ear, "do you know the name of the ambassador?"

"No, what do I care?"

"Sire, it is M. de Bussy. Is not the insult trebled?"

"I do not see any insult," said Henri, trying to be calm.

"Your Majesty may not see it," said Schomberg, "but we see it."

Henri did not reply. He felt anger and hatred at work around his throne, and congratulated himself on being able to place two barriers of this strength between himself and his enemies.

Quélus, growing alternately red and pale, had placed both hands on the hilt of his sword. Schomberg took off his gloves, and drew his dagger half out of the sheath. Maugiron took his sword, which was held by a page, and fastened it to his belt; D'Epernon twirled his moustache, and stood behind his companions. As for Henri, like a hunter who hears his dogs barking at a boar, he let his favorites do as they would and smiled.

"Let the ambassador enter," he said.

At these words, a deathlike silence reigned throughout the room, and it almost seemed as if the dull murmur of the king's wrath could be heard. Then a quick, firm step was heard, and the spurs jingled proudly on the marble floor. Bussy entered with head erect, and a calm countenance, holding his hat in his hand.

He advanced directly to Henri, made a profound bow, and waited to be questioned, standing proudly before the throne, but with a pride wholly personal, — the pride of a gentleman, not at all offensive to the Royal Majesty.

"You here, M. de Bussy? I believed you to be in the depths of Anjou."

"Sire," said Bussy, "I was there, but I have returned as you see."

"And what brought you to our capital?"

"The desire of presenting my humble respects to your Majesty."

The king and the favorites looked at one another. They evidently expected something else from the impetuous young man.

"And — nothing more?" said the king.

"I will add, sire, the orders I received from his Highness, Monseigneur the Duc d'Anjou, to join his respects to mine."

"And the duke said nothing else?"

"He told me that being on the point of returning with the queen-mother, he wished me to apprise your Majesty of the return of one of his most faithful subjects."

The king, almost suffocated by surprise, could not continue his questions. Chicot took advantage of the interruption to approach the ambassador.

"How do you do, M. de Bussy?" he asked.

Bussy turned round, surprised to find a friend in that assembly.

"Ah! Monsieur Chicot, I greet you with all my heart," he replied. "How is M. de Saint-Luc?"

"Very well; he is now walking near the aviary with his wife."

"And this is all you had to say to me, M. de Bussy?" asked the king.

"Yes, sire, if there is anything else of importance, Monseigneur the Duc d'Anjou will have the honor of telling you himself."

"Very well," said the king, and rising silently from his throne he descended the two steps. The audience was at an end; the groups broke up. Bussy noticed out of the corner of his eye that he was surrounded by the four favorites, and almost locked in a living circle full of agitation and menace.

At the end of the hall the king was conversing in a low tone with his chancellor. Bussy pretended to see nothing, and continued to converse with Chicot; but the king called him away as if he too were in the plot to isolate Bussy.

"Come here, Chicot," he said, "I have something to tell you."

Chicot saluted Bussy with great courtesy, and Bussy bowed in return with no less elegance, and remained alone within the circle. Then he changed his expression; he had been calm with the king, polite with Chicot; he now became gracious, seeing Quélus approach.

"Ah, how are you, M. de Quélus?" he said to him; "may I have the honor of asking you how your household is?"

"Not very well, monsieur," replied Quélus.

"Ah, *mon Dieu!*" said Bussy, as though this reply grieved him personally; "what has happened?"

"There is something which greatly annoys us," replied Quélus.

"Something?" asked Bussy, in astonishment, "are you not sufficiently powerful to rid yourself of this something?"

"Pardon me, monsieur," said Maugiron, pushing aside Schomberg who had advanced to take part in this conversation which promised to be interesting, "it is not something but some one that M. de Quélus means."

"If there is some one in M. de Quélus' way, let him push him aside as you have done."

"I have given him the same advice, M. de Bussy," said Schomberg, "and I think he has made up his mind to follow it."

"Ah, is this you, M. de Schomberg? I did not have the honor of recognizing you."

"Perhaps not; is my face still blue?"

"No, you are, on the contrary, very pale; are you in poor health, monsieur?"

"Monsieur," said Schomberg, "if I am pale, it is with anger."

"Ah, so you are like M. de Quélus, annoyed by something or some one?"

"Yes, monsieur."

"Like me," said Maugiron. "I too have some one who annoys me."

"Always witty, my dear M. de Maugiron," said Bussy, "but the more I look at you, the more concerned I am about your preoccupied expressions."

"You forget me, monsieur," said D'Epernon, proudly planting himself before Bussy.

"Pardon me, M. d'Epernon, you were behind the others, according to your habit, and I have so little the pleasure of knowing you that it was not my place to speak first."

It was a curious sight to see Bussy's smile and his unconcerned manner, placed as he was between these four madmen, whose eyes spoke with only too much eloquence, and he must have been blind or stupid who did not understand their meaning; but Bussy seemed not to understand. He remained silent with the same smile on his lips.

"Well," said Quélus, who was the first to lose his patience, and stamped with his foot. Bussy raised his eyes to the ceiling and looked around him.

"Monsieur," he said, "do you notice the echo in this room ? Nothing reverberates the sound like marble walls, though the voices are doubly sonorous beneath arches of stucco; on the contrary, on a plain the sound divides itself, and, on my honor, I believe the clouds take their share. I advance this proposition according to Aristophanes. Have you read Aristophanes, gentlemen ? "

Maugiron thought he understood Bussy's invitation, and approached the young man to whisper in his ear; but Bussy stopped him.

"No confidences here, monsieur, I beg of you," he said. "You know that his Majesty is jealous, and would believe that we are gossiping."

Maugiron went away, more furious than ever. Schomberg took his place, and said in a pompous tone, —

"I am a German, very heavy, very obtuse, but very frank; I speak loud, that those who listen may have every chance of hearing. But when my words, which I try to make clear, are not understood by the one to whom they are addressed, or when that one is deaf, because he does not wish to hear, then I — "

"You ? " asked Bussy, fixing on the young man one of those looks that the tigers send forth from their fathomless orbs, those looks that seem to well up from an abyss and shed torrents of fire, "you — "

Schomberg stopped. Bussy shrugged his shoulders and turned on his heel. He found himself face to face with D'Epernon; D'Epernon was started and could not possibly withdraw.

"See, gentlemen," he said, "how provincial M. de Bussy has become during the expedition he has just made with the Duc d'Anjou; he wears his beard and has no bow on his sword; he has black boots and a gray felt hat."

"I was making the same reflection, my dear M.

d'Epernon. When I saw you so well dressed, I asked myself where absence could lead a man. Here am I, Louis de Bussy, lord of Clermont, obliged to take a little Gascon gentleman as a model of taste. But will you please let me pass? You are so near me that you have stepped on my foot, and so has M. de Quélus whom I felt through my boots," he added with a charming smile, and passing between D'Epernon and Quélus, he held out his hand to Saint-Luc who had just entered. Saint-Luc found this hand dripping with perspiration. He understood that something extraordinary was taking place, and dragged Bussy away from the group, then out of the room.

A strange murmur arose among the favorites and spread through the other groups of courtiers.

"It is incredible," said Quélus; "I insulted him and he did not reply."

"I provoked him," said Maugiron, "and he did not reply."

"I raised my hand on a level with his face," said Schomberg, "and he did not reply."

"I stepped on his foot," cried D'Epernon, "and he did not reply," and he seemed to grow the length of Bussy's foot.

"It is clear that he did not wish to hear," said Quélus; "there is something under that."

"There is," said Schomberg, "and I know what it is."

"What is it?"

"He feels that we four will kill him, and he does not wish to be killed."

At this moment the king approached the four young men, while Chicot whispered in his ear.

"Well," said the king, "what was M. de Bussy saying? I heard loud talking in this corner."

"You wish to know what M. de Bussy was saying, sire?" asked D'Epernon.

"Yes, you know that I am curious," replied Henri with a smile.

" Faith, nothing good," said Quélus; "he is no longer a Parisian."

" What is he ? "

" A countryman ; he is reforming."

" Oh, oh ! " said the king, " what does this mean ? "

" It means that I am going to train a dog to bite his legs," said Quélus, " and who knows if he will even feel it through his boots."

" I," said D'Epernon, " will go straighter and further. To-day, I stepped on his foot. To-morrow, I shall slap his face. He is a sham hero, a hero of vanity who says to himself, ' I have fought enough for honor, now I wish to be prudent for life.' "

" What, gentlemen," said Henri, with feigned anger, " do you dare to ill-treat here in my house a gentleman of my brother's suite ? "

" Alas, yes," said Maugiron, replying with feigned humility to the king's feigned anger; "and though we treated him very ill, sire, I assure you he said nothing."

The king looked at Chicot with a smile, and leaning towards him, —

" Do you still think that they bellow, Chicot ? " he asked; " I think they have roared."

" Eh ! " said Chicot, " they have perhaps mewed. I know people whose nerves are horribly affected by the cry of a cat. M. de Bussy may be one of those people, and that is why he went out without replying."

" You think so ? "

" Those who live will see," replied Chicot, sententiously.

" Come now," said Henri, " like master, like man."

" If you mean to say that Bussy is your brother's servant, you are very much mistaken, sire."

"Gentlemen," said the king, "I dine with the queen; later in the evening the Gelosi[1] are coming to play a farce, and I invite you all to come."

The assembly bowed respectfully, and the king went out through the large door. At the same moment Saint-Luc entered through the small door. He made a sign to the four gentlemen who were about to go out.

"Pardon me, M. de Quélus," he said with a bow, "do you still reside on the Rue Saint-Honoré ? "

" Yes, my dear friend, why do you ask ? "

" I have a few words to say to you."

" Ah, ah ! "

" And you, M. de Schomberg, may I inquire for your address ? "

" I live on the Rue Béthisy," replied Schomberg with surprise.

" I know yours, D'Epernon."

" Rue de Grenelle."

" You are my neighbor, and you, Maugiron ? "

" Near the Louvre."

" I shall therefore begin with you; or, rather, no — with Quélus."

"Ah, I think I understand. You come from M. de Bussy."

" I do not say from whom I come, gentlemen ; I wish to speak to you, that is all."

" To all four ? "

" Yes."

" Well, if as I presume, you do not wish to speak to us in the Louvre, we can all go to the house of one of us. May we not all hear what you have to say to each one ? "

" Perfectly."

"Let us go to Schomberg's, on the Rue Béthisy. It is the nearest."

[1] Italian Comedians who gave performances at the Hôtel de Bourgogne.

"Very well, gentlemen," said Saint-Luc, and he bowed again.

"Show us the way, M. de Schomberg."

"Willingly."

The five gentlemen left the Louvre arm-in-arm, and took up the whole width of the street. Behind them came their attendants, armed to the teeth. They reached the *hôtel*, and Schomberg ordered the main hall to be opened.

Saint-Luc stopped in the ante-chamber.

CHAPTER XXXVII.

HOW M. DE SAINT-LUC ACQUITTED HIMSELF OF THE COMMISSION GIVEN HIM BY BUSSY.

LET us leave Saint-Luc for a while in Schomberg's ante-chamber, and see what had taken place between him and Bussy.

Bussy had left the audience chamber with his friend, bowing to those who, despite the wind of court favor, would not neglect so powerful a man as Bussy. In those days when brute force or personal power were everything, a man, if he were strong and clever, could make for himself a little physical and moral kingdom in that beautiful land of France. Thus it was that Bussy reigned at the court of King Henri III. But that day he had not been warmly welcomed in his kingdom.

Once out of the hall, Saint-Luc stopped and looked anxiously at his friend.

"Are you ill?" he asked; "you are so pale that you look as if you were about to faint."

"No," said Bussy, "I am only choking with anger."

"Do you pay any attention to the remarks of those fellows?"

"*Corbleu!* you shall see if I do."

"Come, Bussy, be calm."

"You are charming with your injunctions. If you had heard half of the things I have had said to me, there would have been a dead man ere this."

"Well, what do you wish?"

"You are my friend, Saint-Luc, and you have given me a terrible proof of this friendship."

"Ah, my dear friend," said Saint-Luc, who believed Monsoreau dead and buried, "that was a mere trifle for which I deserve no thanks. The thrust was surely a neat one and succeeded admirably; but I deserve no praise, for the king showed it to me while he kept me prisoner at the Louvre."

"My dear friend — "

"Let us leave Monsoreau where he is, and speak of Diane. Was she a little pleased? Has she forgiven me? When is the wedding to take place?"

"Oh, my dear friend, we must wait for Monsoreau's death."

"What?" cried Saint-Luc, starting up as if he had walked on a sharp nail.

"Poppies are not so dangerous as you had first thought, and he did not at all die from his fall on them. On the contrary, he is alive and more furious than ever."

"What, really?"

"Yes, he thinks of nothing but his vengeance, and has sworn to kill you at the earliest opportunity."

"So he lives?"

"Alas, yes!"

"And who then is the ass of a physician who cured him?"

"Mine, dear friend."

"What? I cannot get over it," replied Saint-Luc, crushed by this revelation. "Why, I am dishonored, *ventrebleu!* I had announced his death to all, and he will find his heirs in mourning. Oh, but he shall not give me the lie. I shall find him again, and instead of one sword thrust, he shall have four if necessary."

"Calm yourself in turn, my dear Saint-Luc," said Bussy. "Monsoreau serves me better than you think. I imagine that he suspects the duke of having despatched you against

him; it is the duke of whom he is jealous. I am an angel,
a precious friend, a Bayard; I am his dear Bussy. That is
most natural, for it was that fool Rémy who cured him."

"What a stupid idea that was!"

"What will you have? It is the idea of an honest man.
He imagines that because he is a physician he must cure
people."

"The fellow is visionary."

"In short, he pretends that he owes me his life, and confides his wife to my care."

"Ah! I understand that under the circumstances you
should await his death with more patience, but nevertheless
I am completely amazed."

"Dear friend."

"Upon my honor, I cannot realize it."

"You see that for the moment I am not thinking of M.
de Monsoreau."

"No, let us enjoy life while he is still wounded. But
the moment he becomes convalescent, I warn you that I
shall order a coat of mail, and have iron blinds put to my
windows. You might ask the Duc d'Anjou if his good
mother has not given him some antidote. In the mean
while let us have a good time."

Bussy could not help smiling; he passed his arm through
Saint-Luc's.

"So you see, my dear Saint-Luc, you have rendered me
only half a service."

Saint-Luc looked at him in surprise.

"Very true," he said, "would you like me to finish him
up? That would be rather hard; but for you, my dear
Bussy, I would do a great deal, particularly if he looks at
me with his yellow eye."

"No; as I said before, let us not think of Monsoreau.
If you owe me anything I wish you would make some other
use of it."

"Speak, I am listening."

"Are you on very good terms with those favorites?"

"Faith, we are something like cats and dogs in the sun: as long as the same ray heats us all we say nothing; but let one try to take more than his share of light and heat, and I do not answer for the consequences. Teeth and claws would be brought into play."

"I am delighted to hear you speak in this way."

"So much the better."

"Let us admit that the ray of light has been intercepted."

"Very well."

"Now show your white teeth and long claws, and let us open the game."

"I do not understand."

Bussy smiled.

"Will you go to M. de Quélus for me?"

"Ah, ah," said Saint-Luc.

"Are you beginning to understand?"

"Yes."

"Very well. Will you ask him what day he would be pleased to cut my throat, or allow me to cut his?"

"I shall do so."

"You do not object?"

"Not in the least. I shall go at once if you like."

"Wait a second. On your way to M. de Quélus, will you make the same proposition to M. de Schomberg?"

"Ah, ah," said Saint-Luc, "to M. de Schomberg, too? The devil! how you go on."

Bussy made a gesture which admitted of no reply.

"Very well," said Saint-Luc, "your wishes shall be obeyed."

"Then, my dear Saint-Luc," replied Bussy, "since you are so amiably disposed, you will go to the Louvre and speak to M. de Maugiron. I saw by his gorget that he is on duty to-day; will you ask him to join the other two?"

"Oh, oh," said Saint-Luc, "three; are you thinking of it, Bussy? Is that all?"

"No."

"How no?"

"From there you will go to M. d'Epernon. I need not lay much stress on him, because I do not consider him of great importance; but he will add to the number."

Saint-Luc let his arms fall, and stared at Bussy.

"Four!" he murmured

"Exactly, dear friend," said Bussy, nodding his head; "it is needless to recommend to a man of your breeding to proceed with all the politeness and courtesy which you possess to such a degree."

Saint-Luc bowed.

"I rely on you to do it in gallant fashion."

"You shall be satisfied."

Bussy held out his hand to Saint-Luc.

"Very well; now, gentlemen, it will be our turn to laugh."

"Now, dear friend, what are your conditions?"

"I make none; I shall accept theirs."

"Your arms?"

"The arms of those gentlemen."

"The time and place —"

"Which they shall appoint."

"But still —"

"Let us leave these trifles; go quickly. I shall wander in the little garden of the Louvre; you will find me there on your return."

"Then you will wait?"

"Yes."

"I may be a long while."

"I have time."

We now know how Saint-Luc found the four young men in the audience chamber, and how he opened preliminaries. Let us therefore join him in the ante-chamber of Schom-

berg's *hôtel*, where in accordance with the laws of etiquette
then in vogue, he waited, while the four favorites, who suspected the object of his visit, stationed themselves in the
four corners of the room.

This having been done, the doors were opened wide, and
Saint-Luc, with his left hand on the hilt of his sword and
his hat in his right hand, appeared on the threshold, where
he stopped.

"M. d'Espinay de Saint-Luc!" cried the usher.

Saint-Luc entered. Schomberg, being the host, rose to
meet his guest who, instead of bowing, placed his hat on his
head. This formality gave color and intention to the visit.
Schomberg replied with a bow, and, turning towards Quélus,
said, —

"I have the honor of presenting M. Jacques de Levis,
comte de Quélus."

Saint-Luc advanced towards Quélus and made a deep bow.

"I was seeking Monsieur," he said.

Schomberg then turned towards another corner of the
room.

"I have the honor of presenting M. Louis de Maugiron."

Same salutation on the part of Saint-Luc, and same reply
from Maugiron. The same ceremony was gone through for
D'Epernon. Then Schomberg gave his own name and
received the same compliment.

Having done this, the four friends resumed their seats,
while Saint-Luc remained standing.

"Monsieur le Comte," he said to Quélus, "you have
insulted M. le comte Louis de Clermont d'Amboise, lord of
Bussy, who presents you his very humble respects, and
challenges you to fight in single combat, on any day and
hour, and with such weapons as you may select until death
should follow. Do you accept?"

"Most certainly," calmly replied Quélus, "and M. de
Bussy does me a great honor."

"What is your day, Monsieur le Comte ? "

" I have no choice, only I prefer the earliest time."

" Your time ? "

" The morning."

" Your weapons ? "

" The dagger and sword, if M. de Bussy accepts these two instruments."

Saint-Luc bowed.

"All that you may decide is sure to be accepted by M. de Bussy." He then turned to Maugiron, who made the same replies, and passed on to the other two.

"But," said Schomberg, who being the host was the last one addressed, "we have not thought of one thing, M. de Saint-Luc."

" What is that ? "

"If it should so happen that through some strange chance we all chose the same day and hour, M. de Bussy would be greatly embarrassed."

Saint-Luc bowed with his most courteous smile.

"Certainly," he said, "M. de Bussy would be embarrassed as every brave man should be, before four such gallant men as you; but he says the case would not be a new one for him, as it already occurred at the Tournelles, near the Bastille."

" And he would fight us all four ? " asked D'Epernon.

" All four," replied Saint-Luc.

"Separately ? " asked Schomberg.

"Separately or together; the challenge is at once individual or collective."

The four young men looked at one another. Quélus was the first to break the silence.

"This is very fine on the part of M. de Bussy," he said, purple with anger; "but however little we may be worth, we can each attend to our business alone : we shall accept the count's proposition, one after the other, or what would be even better — "

Quélus looked at his friends who understood him and nodded assent, so he continued, —

"As we are not trying to assassinate a brave man, chance shall decide which of us is to fight M. de Bussy."

" But the other three ? " quickly said D'Epernon.

" M. de Bussy has too many friends, as we have too many enemies, for the other three to remain idle. Do you agree to this ? " he asked, turning to his companions.

"Yes," was the unanimous reply.

"It would be very agreeable to me," said Schomberg, "if M. de Bussy would invite M. de Livarot to take part in this little game."

" If I may be allowed to express an opinion," said Maugiron, " I would like the company of M. Balzac d'Entragues."

" The party would be complete if M. de Ribeirac will accompany his friends," said Quélus.

" Gentlemen," replied Saint-Luc, "I shall transmit your wishes to M. de Bussy, who is too courteous not to satisfy them. I have but to thank you in Monsieur le Comte's name."

Saint-Luc bowed again, and the four gentlemen returned his bow. They conducted Saint-Luc to the door. In the last ante-chamber he found the four lackeys assembled. He drew his purse full of gold and threw it to them.

" This is to drink the health of your masters," he said.

CHAPTER XXXVIII.

IN WHICH M. DE SAINT-LUC WAS MORE CIVILIZED THAN
M. DE BUSSY, THE LESSONS WHICH HE GAVE HIM AND
THE USE WHICH M. DE BUSSY MADE OF THEM.

SAINT-LUC returned very proud of the manner in which he
had executed his commission. Bussy was waiting for him
and thanked him. Saint-Luc found him very sad; this was
very unnatural for a man who had just received the news
of a fine and brilliant duel.

"Have I done wrong?" said Saint-Luc.

"Really, my dear friend, I regret that you did not say,
'At once,' instead of waiting for a delay."

"Have patience; the Angevins have not yet returned.
The devil! give them time to come; then, where is the
necessity of surrounding yourself so soon with a heap of
dead and dying?"

"I would like to die as soon as possible."

Saint-Luc looked at Bussy with that astonishment felt by
all well-organized persons at the news of some strange
misfortune.

"Die! at your age, with your name and your mistress?"

"I am sure I shall kill four, and receive some good thrusts
which will give me eternal peace."

"What gloomy thoughts, Bussy."

"I would like to see you in my place. A husband who
was thought dead and who comes to life; a wife who cannot leave the bedside of this dying man. Not to see her,
smile on her, touch her hand! *Mordieu!* I should like to
have some one to tear to pieces —"

Saint-Luc replied to this by a burst of laughter which put to flight a flock of sparrows.

"Ah," he cried, "what an innocent man! To think that women love this Bussy, — a tyro. But, my dear fellow, you are losing your senses; there is no other lover so happy as you."

"Ah, very good! prove that to me, married man."

"*Nihil facilius,* as the Jesuit Triquet, my pedagogue, used to say to me: you are M. de Monsoreau's friend."

"Yes; for the honor of human intelligence I am ashamed to confess it; that brute calls me his friend."

"Well, be his friend."

"Oh, and abuse that title."

"*Prorsùs absurdum!* to quote Triquet. Is he really your friend?"

"He says he is."

"No, since he makes you unhappy. Now the object of friendship is to make men happy through one another: at least, this is his Majesty's definition, and he is learned."

Bussy began to laugh.

"I continue," said Saint-Luc: "if he makes you unhappy you are not friends; therefore, you may treat him either as an indifferent person and take his wife, or as an enemy and kill him if he does not like it."

"The fact is, I hate him," said Bussy.

"And he fears you."

"You think he does not like me?"

"Well, try him. Take his wife and you will see."

"Is this still Father Triquet's logic?"

"No, it is mine."

"I congratulate you."

"Does it satisfy you?"

"No, I prefer being a man of honor."

"And let Madame de Monsoreau complete her husband's physical and moral cure? Because, if you let yourself be killed, she will certainly devote herself to the only remaining man."

Bussy frowned.

"At all events," continued Saint-Luc, "here comes my wife. She always gives good advice. After having gathered flowers in the queen-mother's garden, she will be in a very good humor. Listen to her."

Jeanne appeared, radiant with happiness and sparkling with mischief. There are some happy natures which make all around them seem full of promise for the future.

Bussy met her as a friend. She held out her hand to him, a fact which proves that the plenipotentiary Dubois did not import the fashion from England with the treaty for the quadruple alliance.

"How are your love affairs?" she inquired, as she tied her flowers with a gold chain.

"Dying," replied Bussy.

"No, they are wounded and faint," said Saint-Luc, " but I am sure you can call them back to life, Jeanne."

"Come, show me the wound," she said.

"Here it is in brief," replied Saint-Luc: "M. de Bussy does not like smiling on the Comte de Monsoreau and has made up his mind to withdraw."

"And leave Diane?" cried Jeanne in terror.

"Oh! madame, Saint-Luc has not told you that I wish to die."

Jeanne looked at him for a moment with a glance which was anything but evangelical.

"Poor Diane," she murmured, "what is the use of loving men? They are all ungrateful."

"Listen to my wife's principles."

"I am ungrateful!" cried Bussy, "because I do not wish to debase my love by practising a disgraceful hypocrisy."

"Ah, monsieur, that is but a poor excuse," said Jeanne.

"If you really loved, you would fear but one thing, — to be loved no more."

"Ah, ah!" said Saint-Luc.

"But, madame," said Bussy, "there are some sacrifices — "

"Not another word. Confess that you no longer love Diane; that would be more worthy of a man of honor."

Bussy turned pale at the mere thought.

"You dare not say it, but I shall."

"Madame, madame!"

"You men are very amusing with your sacrifices. And do you suppose that we make none? What! she exposes herself to be massacred by that tyrant Monsoreau; she lets a man keep his rights by displaying a courage and strength of will of which Samson and Hannibal would have been incapable. Oh! Diane is sublime, and I would not have done one fourth of what she has."

"Thank you," replied Saint-Luc, with a ceremonious smile which caused Jeanne to burst out laughing.

Bussy hesitated.

"And he reflects!" cried Jeanne; "he does not fall on his knees, and say '*meâ culpâ.*'"

"You are right," replied Bussy. "I am only a man, an imperfect creature, inferior to the least noble of women."

"It is very fortunate that you are at last convinced," said Jeanne.

"What are your orders?"

"That you go at once to visit — "

"M. de Monsoreau?"

"Who speaks of him? — Diane."

"But they are always together."

"When you went so often to visit Madame de Barbezieux, did she not always have near her a big ape who would bite you because he was jealous?"

Bussy laughed. Saint-Luc and Jeanne did the same;

their mirth brought to the windows all the courtiers who were walking in the galleries.

"Madame," at length said Bussy, "I am going to see M. de Monsoreau. Adieu!"

Thereupon they separated. Bussy begged Saint-Luc to say nothing of his intended duel with the favorites.

He went at once to see M. de Monsoreau whom he found in bed. The count uttered cries of joy when he perceived him. Rémy had just promised that his wound would be healed within three weeks.

Diane placed her finger on her lips; it was her mode of greeting. Bussy had to tell the count the whole story of the mission which the Duc d'Anjou had intrusted to him, his visit to court, the king's uneasiness, and the cold demeanor of the favorites.

Cold demeanor was the word he used. Diane merely laughed. Monsoreau became thoughtful, asked Bussy to come nearer, and whispered to him, —

"Are there not other projects on foot?"

"I think so," replied Bussy.

"Believe me," said Monsoreau, "do not compromise yourself for this mean man. I know him; he is perfidious. I can assure you that he never hesitates to betray one."

"I know it," said Bussy with a smile, as he recalled the circumstances in which he had been betrayed by the duke.

"You see," said Monsoreau, "you are my friend, and I wish to put you on your guard. Moreover, every time that you will find yourself in a difficult position, ask my advice."

"Monsieur, you must sleep after the dressing of your wound," said Rémy.

"Yes, dear doctor. My friend, take a turn in the garden with Madame de Monsoreau. I am told it is charming this year."

"As you please," replied Bussy.

CHAPTER XXXIX.

M. DE MONSOREAU'S PRECAUTIONS.

SAINT-LUC was right; Jeanne was right. At the end of a week, Bussy had found it out, and did them full justice.

To be like the ancient Romans would have been great and beautiful in the eyes of posterity; but Bussy, forgetful of Plutarch who had ceased to be his favorite author since love had corrupted his heart, — Bussy, handsome as Alcibiades, and thinking only of the present, cared little for an article in history, which would place him on a level with Scipio and Bayard.

Diane was more simple and natural. She gave herself up to the two instincts which the cynical Figaro recognizes as inborn in the race, — to love and to deceive. She never thought of carrying her ideas of honesty to speculative philosophy.

To love Bussy was her logic; to be his alone was her moral; to thrill with pleasure at the mere touch of his hand was her metaphysic.

M. de Monsoreau, whose accident was now a fortnight old, was getting better and better. He had avoided fever, thanks to cold water applications, — that remedy which chance, or rather Providence had enabled Ambroise Paré to discover, — when suddenly he received a great shock. He heard that M. le Duc d'Anjou had just arrived in Paris with the queen-mother and his Angevins.

The count had every reason to be uneasy, for on the day following his arrival, the prince, under pretext of inquiring about his health, presented himself at the *hôtel* of the Rue des Petits-Pères. There was no possibility of denying himself to a Royal Highness who took such a tender interest in him. M. de Monsoreau received the prince, who was charming to the master of the hounds, and more especially so to his wife.

No sooner had the prince left than M. de Monsoreau called Diane, and leaning on her arm, walked three times around the room, in spite of Rémy's expostulations.

After that, he seated himself in that same armchair; he seemed very pleased, and Diane saw by his smile that he must be meditating some scheme. But this belongs to the private history of the house of Monsoreau.

Let us, therefore, return to M. le Duc d'Anjou's arrival which belongs to the narrative of this book.

The day when Monseigneur François de Valois returned to the Louvre was not without interest to the lookers-on; and this is what they observed: much haughtiness on the part of the king, great indifference on the part of the queen-mother, an humble insolence on the part of the Duc d'Anjou who seemed to say, —

"Why the devil did you recall me if you meant to receive me in this way?"

This whole reception was accompanied by angry looks on the part of MM. de Livarot, De Ribeirac, and D'Entragues who, warned by Bussy, were very glad to make their future antagonists understand that they would offer no opposition to the proposed duels.

Chicot, that day, made more marches and counter-marches than Cæsar on the eve of the battle of Pharsalia. Then all became peaceful once more.

Two days after his arrival, the Duc d'Anjou paid a second visit to his wounded friend. Monsoreau, informed of the slightest detail of the interview between the king and his brother, humored the Duc d'Anjou, and encouraged his hostile intentions.

As he was getting better and better, after the duke's departure, he took the arm of his wife and walked once around the room. After that he sat down with an even more satisfied look than the first time.

That same evening, Diane told Bussy that M. de Monsoreau was surely meditating something. A moment later, Monsoreau and Bussy were left alone.

"When I think," said Monsoreau to Bussy, "that this prince who smiles on me so pleasantly is my mortal enemy and had me assassinated by M. de Saint-Luc — "

"Oh, assassinated," said Bussy; "take care, Monsieur le Comte, Saint-Luc is a gentleman, and you confessed yourself that you provoked him and were the first to draw the sword, and that he wounded you in a duel."

"Very well; but it is none the less true that he only acted in obedience to the Duc d'Anjou's instigations."

"Listen," said Bussy, "I know the duke, but I also know M. de Saint-Luc; I must tell you that M. de Saint-Luc is devoted to the king, and not at all to the duke. Ah, if you had been wounded by Antraguet, Livarot, or Ribeirac, I do not say — but Saint-Luc — "

"You do not know French history as I do, my dear M. de Bussy," said Monsoreau, clinging to his opinion.

Bussy might have told him that if he did not know French history, he was particularly well acquainted with that of Anjou, particularly that portion where the Château de Méridor is situated.

Monsoreau was at last able to get up and walk in the garden.

"That is sufficient," he said. "To-night we shall move."

"Why so?" asked Rémy, "are you not comfortable on the Rue des Petits-Pères, or do you find lack of amusement?"

"On the contrary," said Monsoreau, "I have too much. M. d'Anjou fatigues me with his visits. He is always accompanied by thirty gentlemen, and the noise of their spurs grates on my nerves."

"But where are you going ? "

" I have ordered my little house at the Tournelles to be prepared for me."

Bussy and Diane — for Bussy was always there — exchanged a fond glance of memories.

"What ! that hovel ? " cried Rémy, heedlessly.

" Ah, ah, you know it ? " said Monsoreau.

"Pardieu !" said the young man, " who does not know the houses of the master of the hounds, particularly when one has lived Rue Beautreillis."

Monsoreau, from force of habit, had some vague suspicion in his mind.

" Yes, I shall go there," he said, " and I shall be comfortable. We cannot receive more than four persons at a time. It is a fortress, and from the window one can see visitors at a distance of three hundred paces."

" So that — " asked Rémy.

" So that it is possible to avoid them," said Monsoreau, " particularly when one is in good health."

Bussy bit his lips. He feared that the day might come when Monsoreau would avoid him also; Diane sighed. She remembered that in this little house she had seen Bussy lying fainting on her bed. Rémy reflected; so he was the first of the three who spoke.

" You cannot go," he said.

" And why not, if you please ? "

" Because the master of the hounds must hold receptions, and keep servants and hounds. He may have a palace for his hounds, but he cannot have a kennel for himself."

" Humph ! " said Monsoreau, in a tone that meant, " That is true."

" And as I am doctor of the mind as of the body, it is not your stay here which worries me."

" What is it, then ? "

" That of Madame."

" Well ? "

" Well, send her away."

" Separate myself from the countess!" cried Monsoreau, fixing on Diane a look in which there was surely more anger than love.

" Then give up your position as master of the hounds. I think that would be wise, as you must either fulfil or not fulfil your duties. If you do not, you will displease the king; if you do — "

" I shall do all I have to do," said Monsoreau, grinding his teeth; " but I will not leave the countess."

The count had just spoken these words when a great noise of horses and voices was heard in the courtyard. Monsoreau started.

" Again the duke!" he murmured.

" Exactly," said Rémy, going to the window. He had not finished speaking when the duke, taking advantage of the privilege of princes to enter unannounced, appeared at the door.

Monsoreau was on the alert; he saw that François' first glance was for Diane. The duke's overflowing gallantry enlightened him even better. He brought to her as a present one of those rare jewels, a masterpiece, such as the patient and generous artists of that day produced, three or four, during their lifetime; yet masterpieces were more frequent in those days than they are now.

This was a charming poniard, with a dagger of chased gold. The handle was a scent bottle. On the blade was a whole chase carved with admirable skill, — dogs, horses, hunters, game, trees, and sky, mingled together in harmonious confusion, and kept the eye fixed on the blade of azure and gold.

" Let me see," cried Monsoreau, who feared there might be some note concealed in the handle. The prince at once separated the two parts.

"To you who are a hunter," he said, "I give the blade; the handle is for the countess. Good morning, Bussy; I see you have become the count's intimate friend."

Diane blushed; but Bussy remained very self-possessed.

"Monseigneur," he said, "you forget that you sent me yourself to inquire after M. de Monsoreau's health. I obeyed your Highness's orders as usual."

"That is true," said the duke, who seated himself near Diane and spoke to her in a low voice. After a few minutes, —

"Count," he said, "I find it horribly warm in this sickroom. I see that the countess feels it, and I shall offer her my arm to take a turn in the garden."

The husband and the lover exchanged an angry look. Diane, being thus invited, rose and placed her hand on the duke's arm.

"Give me your arm," said Monsoreau to Bussy, and he followed his wife.

"Ah, ah," said the duke, "you seem to be quite well!"

"Yes, monseigneur, and I hope I shall soon be able to accompany Madame de Monsoreau wherever she goes."

"Very good; but in the mean time you must not over-exert yourself." Monsoreau himself felt the justness of this remark, so he sat on a bench whence he could not lose sight of them.

"Here, count," he said to Bussy, "if you were very amiable you would escort Madame de Monsoreau to my little *hôtel* near the Bastille. I would really prefer to have her there. Having snatched her from the claws of this vulture at Méridor, I shall not have her devoured in Paris."

"Not at all, monsieur," said Rémy to his master, "you cannot accept."

"Why not?" asked Monsoreau.

"Because you belong to M. d'Anjou, who would never forgive you if you helped to play such a trick on him."

"What do I care?" cried the impetuous young man, when a glance from Rémy told him that he should be silent. Monsoreau was reflecting.

"Rémy is right," he said; "I cannot ask you to do this for me. I shall conduct her myself, for within two or three days I shall be in condition to dwell there myself."

"Folly!" said Bussy; "you will lose your office."

"Possibly, but I shall keep my wife." And he accompanied these words with a frown which made Bussy sigh. That very night the count conducted his wife to the little house of the Tournelles which our readers know so well.

Rémy aided the convalescent in making himself comfortable. Then, as he was a most devoted man, he understood that in this small house Bussy would be in need of every assistance, so he made peace with Gertrude, who began by beating him and ended by forgiving him. Diane resumed possession of her old room with the white and gold damask hangings.

Only a narrow passage separated this room from that of the count. Bussy pulled out his hair by the handfuls. Saint-Luc pretended that rope ladders had reached such a point of perfection that they could replace stairs. Monsoreau rubbed his hands and smiled when he thought of the Duc d'Anjou's annoyance.

CHAPTER XL.

A VISIT TO THE LITTLE HOUSE.

WITH some men excitement takes the place of real passion, as hunger gives the wolf and hyena the appearance of courage. M. d'Anjou, whose annoyance cannot be described when he found that Diane had left Méridor, had returned to Paris filled with this sentiment. He was almost in love with this woman just because she was taken from him.

The result was that his hatred of Monsoreau, which had begun on the day when he first discovered that Monsoreau had betrayed him, changed into a sort of fury, all the more dangerous that, having learned to know the count's energetic character, he wished to be able to strike without receiving any blow in return.

On the other hand, he had not renounced his political aspirations, while he had grown in his own estimation. He had scarcely reached Paris when he resumed his underhand machinations.

The moment was favorable. A large number of wavering conspirators, encouraged by the sort of triumph which the king's weakness and Catherine's cunning had afforded to the Angevins, gathered around the Duc d'Anjou, uniting by strong, but invisible, threads the prince's cause with that of the Guises, who remained prudently in the shadow, greatly alarming Chicot by their silence.

However, the duke no longer confided his political projects to Bussy; he manifested towards him a friendly hypocrisy and nothing more. The prince was vaguely uneasy at having seen him in Monsoreau's house, and begrudged him the confidence which Monsoreau, usually so distrustful, seemed to have in him.

He was also frightened at the joy and happiness which shone on Diane's face, and made her even more charming than before. The prince knew that flowers get color and perfume only in the sunlight, and women in the light of love. Diane was visibly happy, and for this evil-minded and ever suspicious prince the happiness of others seemed a kind of hostility.

Born a prince he had attained power by dark and crooked means; he had made up his mind to resort to force for his love or vengeance, since force had succeeded so well. Advised by D'Aurilly, he thought it would be shameful to be balked in his purpose by such ridiculous obstacles as the jealousy of a husband or the repugnance of a woman.

One day, after spending a bad night haunted by evil dreams, he felt that he was in the proper mood, and ordered his equipages to visit Monsoreau.

Monsoreau, as we know, had left for his little house. The prince smiled as he heard this. He inquired about the situation of the house, and hearing it was on the Place Saint-Antoine, he turned to Bussy who accompanied him, and said, —

"Since he is on the Place Saint-Antoine, let us go thither."

The escort set out in that direction, and the neighborhood was soon excited over the presence of twenty-four gentlemen who composed the duke's usual retinue, and who had each two lackeys and three horses. The prince knew the house and door, and Bussy knew them no less well.

Both stopped before the door, entered the alley, and mounted the stairs; only the prince entered the apartments, while Bussy remained on the landing. The result of this arrangement was, that the prince who seemed to be the privileged character saw only Monsoreau, lying on a couch, while Bussy was received in the arms of Diane who pressed him to her heart, while Gertrude kept watch.

Monsoreau, naturally pale, became livid when he perceived the prince, — his dreaded vision.

"Monseigneur," he cried, "you here in this humble house! This is too much honor for me."

The irony was visible. The count scarcely took the trouble to disguise it, yet the prince pretended not to observe it, and approached with a smile.

"Wherever a sick friend goes," he said, "I go to inquire about his health."

"I believe your Highness spoke the word 'friend.'"

"I did, my dear count; how are you?"

"Much better, monseigneur. I can get up and walk about. Within a week, I shall be quite well."

"Was it your physician who prescribed the air of the Bastille for you?" asked the prince, with an innocent air.

"Yes, monseigneur."

"Were you not comfortable on the Rue des Petits-Pères?"

"No, monseigneur, I received too much company; they made too much noise."

The count uttered these words in a firm tone which did not escape the prince, yet he affected not to notice it.

"But you seem to have no garden here," he said.

"The garden did me no good, monseigneur."

"But where did you walk?"

"That is just it, monseigneur, I did not walk."

The prince bit his lip and leaned back in his chair.

"Do you know, count," he said after a pause, "that many people are applying to the king for your position?"

"Indeed, and on what pretext, monseigneur?"

"A great many pretend that you are dead."

"Oh! monseigneur, I am sure you reply that I am not?"

"I reply nothing at all, you bury yourself, therefore you are dead."

Monsoreau now bit his lips.

"Well then, monseigneur, I must lose my position."

"Really?"

"Yes, there are other things which I prefer to it."

"Ah," said the prince, "you are very disinterested."

"Such is my nature, monseigneur."

"In that case you should not object to allow the king to become acquainted with your nature."

"Who would tell him of it?"

"Why, if he question me, I shall be compelled to repeat our conversation."

"Faith, monseigneur, if all that is said in Paris were repeated to the king, two ears would not suffice to listen."

"What is said in Paris, monsieur?" said the prince, turning as though he had been stung.

Monsoreau saw that the conversation had gradually drifted to subjects far too serious to be discussed by a convalescing man not yet at liberty to act; he calmed the anger of his soul, and assuming an indifferent look, —

"What should I, a poor invalid, know?" he said; "I only see the shadow of passing events. If the king is displeased at the manner in which I discharge my duties, he is wrong."

"How so?"

"Why, my accident proceeds a little from him."

"Explain yourself."

"Well, M. de Saint-Luc who struck the blow, is he not among the king's dearest friends? The king himself taught him the thrust by which he wounded me, and nothing tells me that the king did not prompt him."

The Duc d'Anjou almost made a sign of approbation.

"You are right," he said, "but the king is the king."

"Until he ceases to be," said Monsoreau.

The duke started.

"By the way," he said, "is not Madame de Monsoreau here ? "

"Monseigneur, she is now ill, or she would have come to present her respects to your Highness."

"Ill ? Poor woman ! "

"Yes, monseigneur."

"From grief at seeing you suffer ? "

"Together with the fatigue attending on this change of abode."

"I trust her illness will be short, my dear count. You have a clever physician," and he rose.

"The fact is," said Monsoreau, "that dear Rémy took admirable care of me."

"But you are naming Bussy's physician."

"The count has in fact given him to me."

"Are you then so intimate with Bussy ? "

"He is my best, I may almost say, my only friend," coldly replied Monsoreau.

"Adieu, count," said the prince, raising the damask curtain. Just as he stepped out, he fancied he saw a woman's dress disappear into the next room, while Bussy suddenly appeared at his post in the hall. The duke's suspicions increased.

"We are going," he said to Bussy, who did not reply, but went down at once to prepare the escort, and perhaps also, to hide his blushing face. The duke, left alone, tried to penetrate in the direction where he had seen the dress disappear ; but on turning round, he observed that Monsoreau had followed him, and was standing pale and trembling on the threshold.

"Your Highness mistakes the way," he said, coldly.

"True," stammered the duke. "Thank you," and he went down with rage in his heart. On the way home, which was long, he and Bussy did not exchange a single

word. Bussy left the duke at the door of his *hôtel.*
When François had entered, and was alone in his cabinet,
D'Aurilly mysteriously glided in.

"Well," said the duke, "I am flouted by the husband."

"And perhaps also by the lover, monseigneur," said the
musician.

"What are you saying?"

"The truth."

"Then finish."

"Listen, monseigneur; I hope your Highness will pardon
me; it was in your service."

"That is settled; you are pardoned in advance."

"Well, I watched from under a shed in the yard, while
you were upstairs."

"Ah, ah, and what did you see?"

"I saw a woman's dress. I saw that woman lean forward, and I saw two arms thrown around her neck, after
which I heard distinctly the sound of a long and tender
kiss."

"But who was the man?" asked the duke. "Did you
recognize him?"

"I cannot recognize arms," said D'Aurilly; "gloves
have no faces, monseigneur."

"Yes; but you might recognize the gloves."

"In fact, it seemed to me —"

"That you recognized them? Eh?"

"But this is a mere supposition."

"No matter, speak."

"Well, monseigneur, they looked like M. de Bussy's."

"Buff, embroidered in gold?" asked the duke, from whose
eyes was torn the veil which concealed the truth.

"Yes, monseigneur, buff, embroidered in gold," said
D'Aurilly.

"Ah, Bussy! yes, Bussy! it is Bussy!" cried the duke.
"Blind that I was, or rather, no, I was not blind, only
I could not believe in so much audacity."

"Take care," said D'Aurilly. "Your Highness is speaking very loud."

"Bussy!" again repeated the duke, recalling to mind a thousand circumstances unnoticed before, but which now became so significant.

"Yet, monseigneur," said D'Aurilly, "you must not believe too lightly. Might there not have been some man concealed in Madame de Monsoreau's chamber?"

"Yes, no doubt; but Bussy, who was in the corridor, must have seen him, too."

"Very true, monseigneur."

"And then the gloves! the gloves!"

"Quite true; and then, besides the sound of the kiss I heard something else —"

"What?"

"Three words."

"Which ones?"

"'Till to-morrow evening.'"

"Ah, *mon Dieu!*"

"Now, if you were willing to go through the same exercises as on former occasions, we might make sure."

"D'Aurilly, we shall begin to-morrow evening."

"Your Highness knows that I am at his orders."

"Ah, Bussy!" repeated the duke, between his teeth; "Bussy, traitor to his lord! Bussy, that bugbear to all! Bussy, that man of honor who does not wish me to be King of France!"

And the duke, smiling with infernal joy, dismissed D'Aurilly to reflect more at ease.

CHAPTER XLI.

THE WATCHERS.

D'AURILLY and the Duc d'Anjou kept word with each other. The duke kept Bussy near him all day, so as not to lose sight of his movements. Bussy asked nothing better than to attend the prince during the day; in this manner he had his evenings free.

This was his method, and he put it into practice. At ten o'clock he wrapped himself in his cloak, and with his rope ladder started towards the Bastille. The duke, who did not know that Bussy had his ladder with him, and who could not believe that he would go thus alone through the streets of Paris, supposed he would stop at his *hôtel* for a horse and an attendant: so he lost ten minutes in preparations. During these ten minutes Bussy, who was active and in love, had gone three fourths of the way.

He was fortunate, as all bold men usually are ; he met no one on the way, and when he approached he saw a light at the window. That was the signal agreed upon with Diane.

He threw his ladder on to the balcony. That ladder, furnished with six hooks, was sure to fasten on something. At the noise, Diane extinguished the light, and opened her window to secure the ladder. This was done in a moment. Diane glanced at the square and peered into all the nooks and corners. The street seemed deserted.

She then made a sign to Bussy to mount; he climbed up two steps at a time. There were ten, so it took him five seconds.

The moment was happily chosen; for while he entered through the window, M. de Monsoreau, who had been patiently listening for more than ten minutes at his wife's door, painfully descended the stairs, leaning on the arm of a confidential valet who replaced Rémy in all cases where medical skill was not needed. This double manœuvre was so cleverly executed that M. de Monsoreau opened the street door just as Bussy drew up his ladder and Diane closed her window.

Monsoreau found himself in the street, but, as we have said, the street was deserted and he saw nothing.

"You have been ill-informed," he said to the servant.

"No, monseigneur," replied the latter, "I have just come from the Hôtel d'Anjou, where one of the grooms, who is my friend, told me that Monseigneur had positively ordered two horses for this evening. Now, monsieur, it may have been to go somewhere else."

"Where else can he go?" asked Monsoreau, in a gloomy voice. The count was like all jealous men, who believe that the rest of humanity has no other thought than to torment him. He looked around a second time.

"I would perhaps have done better to remain in Diane's · room," he muttered. "But they may have signals to correspond; she would have warned him of my presence, and I would have seen nothing. It is better to watch outside as we first decided. Come, take me to the hiding-place which you tell me is so good."

"Come, monsieur," said the valet. Monsoreau advanced, leaning on the man's arm.

In fact, within twenty-five feet of the door was an enormous pile of stones used by the children as fortifications in their mock combats, the popular remains of the feuds of the Burgundians and Armagnacs.

The valet had arranged these stones in a way to shelter two persons. He spread a cloak on them, and the count crouched upon it. The servant placed himself at his feet. A loaded musket was laid beside him. The man was about to light the match, but Monsoreau prevented him.

"There will always be time for that. We are scenting royal game, and the penalty is a heavy one for whoever lays hands on him."

His eyes, shining like those of the wolf hidden near the sheepfold, wandered from Diane's window to the adjacent streets and back again, for he wished to see, yet feared to be seen.

Diane had prudently drawn her heavy damask curtains, so that scarcely a ray of light filtered around the edges and betrayed the life in that otherwise silent house. Monsoreau had not been watching ten minutes, when two horsemen came down the Rue Saint-Antoine. The servant did not speak, but pointed silently in their direction.

" Yes," said Monsoreau, " I see."

The two men dismounted at the corner of the Hôtel des Tournelles, and tied their horses to the iron rings placed in the wall for that purpose.

"Monseigneur," said D'Aurilly, "I think we are too late ; he must have come directly from your *hôtel*. He had an advance of ten minutes, and must already have entered."

" Very well," said the prince, " but if we did not see him go in, we shall see him come out."

" Yes, but when ? " said D'Aurilly.

" When we wish," said the prince.

" May I ask how you intend to go about it, monseigneur ? "

"Nothing is more simple. We have but to knock at the door, one of us, that is you, under pretext that you come to inquire after M. de Monsoreau's health. All lovers are afraid of noise, so while you enter the house, he will come out through the window, and I shall see him depart."

" And Monsoreau ? "

" What the devil can he say ? He is my friend ; I am

uneasy; I send to inquire because I found him looking badly to-day, nothing more."

"This is most ingenious, monseigneur," said D'Aurilly.

"Do you hear what they are saying?" asked Monsoreau.

"No, monsieur, but if they continue to talk, we are sure to hear them as they are coming this way."

"Monseigneur," said D'Aurilly, "here is a pile of stones which seems to have been placed there on purpose to conceal your Highness."

"Yes, but wait; there may be some way of seeing through the curtains."

As we have said before, Diane had lit the lamp, and a little ray of light shone through the cracks. The Duke and D'Aurilly walked up and down for upwards of ten minutes, in search of a place whence they could look into Diane's chamber. During these evolutions, Monsoreau was burning with impatience, and his hand often wandered to the barrel of the musket.

"Oh, shall I suffer this?" he murmured; "shall I also swallow this affront? No, no, I cannot; my patience is worn out; *mordieu!* to think that I can neither sleep nor wake, nor even suffer in peace, because a shameful caprice has lodged itself in the idle brain of that miserable prince. No, I am not a complaisant valet, I am the Comte de Monsoreau, and if he comes this way, on my honor, I shall blow his brains out. Light the match, René."

At this moment, the prince finding fruitless his attempts to see, returned to his first idea, and was about to conceal himself among the stones, when all at once, D'Aurilly, forgetting the distance between them, laid his hand on the prince's arm.

"Well, monsieur," said the prince in surprise, "what is it now?"

"Come, monseigneur, come," said D'Aurilly.

"Why so?"

"Do you see something shining on the left? Come, monseigneur."

"Yes, I see a spark among those stones."

"That is the match of a musket or an arquebuse."

"Ah, ah!" cried the duke, "and who can be there?"

"Some friend or servant of Bussy's. Let us go away and come back from another direction. The servant will give the alarm, and we shall see Bussy descend from the window."

"You are right," said the duke. "Come," and they crossed the street going to the place where they had tied their horses.

"They are going away," said the valet.

"Yes," said Monsoreau, "did you recognize them?"

"To me they looked like the prince and D'Aurilly."

"Exactly; but I shall soon be even more certain."

"What is Monsieur about to do?"

"Come."

During that time, the duke and D'Aurilly turned down the Rue Sainte Catherine, with the intention of coming back through the boulevard of the Bastille. Monsoreau entered and prepared his litter. At this noise, Bussy took fright; the light was again extinguished, the window opened, the ladder fastened, and Bussy to his great regret was obliged to flee like Romeo, but without having, like Romeo, seen the sun rise, and heard the song of the lark. Just as he reached the ground, and Diane threw the ladder after him, the duke and D'Aurilly appeared at the corner of the Bastille.

Right below the fair Diane's window, they saw a shadow suspended between heaven and earth, but the shadow disappeared immediately round the corner of the Rue Saint Paul.

"Monsieur," said the valet to Monsoreau, "we shall wake up the whole household."

"What does it matter?" replied Monsoreau, furious. "I think I am master here, and I have the right to do in my own house what M. le Duc d'Anjou wished to do."

The litter was ready. Monsoreau sent for two of his attendants who lived on the Rue des Tournelles, and when these people who were in the habit of accompanying him had taken their places, the machine started off at once, drawn by two vigorous horses, and had reached the Hôtel d'Anjou in less than fifteen minutes. The duke and D'Aurilly had so recently returned that their horses were not even unsaddled.

Monsoreau, who had the privilege of entering the duke's apartment at all times, appeared on the threshold just as the duke, after having thrown his hat on a chair, was holding out his boots for a valet to remove them. Another valet announced the master of the hounds. A clap of thunder would not have startled the prince more than did this announcement.

"M. de Monsoreau!" he cried, and his emotion was perceptible in the pallor which overspread his face and in the tremulousness of his voice.

"Yes, monseigneur, in person," replied the count, repressing, or rather trying to repress, his emotion. The effort was so violent that he felt his knees bend beneath him as he fell upon a seat near the door.

"You will kill yourself, my dear friend," said the duke; "you are so pale that you seem about to faint."

"Oh, no, monseigneur. For the moment I have things of great importance to communicate to your Highness; I may faint afterwards."

"Speak, my dear count," said François, greatly agitated.

"But not before your attendants, I suppose," said Monsoreau.

The duke dismissed every one, even D'Aurilly, and the two men remained alone.

"Has your Highness just come in?" asked Monsoreau.

" As you see, count."

" Your Highness is very imprudent to wander through the streets in this manner."

" Who tells you I have been in the streets ? "

" Why, judging from the dust on your clothes — "

" M. de Monsoreau," said the prince in a sharp tone, "have you any other employment besides that of the 'master of the hounds'? "

" That of spy ? Yes, monseigneur. All the world follows it more or less, and I do like the rest."

" And what does this profession bring you, monsieur ? "

" A knowledge of what is going on."

" That is curious," said the prince, drawing nearer the bell in order to be able to summon help.

" Very curious," said Monsoreau.

" Then tell me what you have to say."

" I came for that purpose."

" Will you permit me to sit down ? "

" No irony, monseigneur, towards an old and faithful friend who comes at this hour and in this state to do you a great service ! If I sat down, monseigneur, on my honor, it is because I could not stand."

" A service ? " repeated the duke, — " a service ? "

" Yes."

" Speak, then."

" Monseigneur, I come on the part of a powerful prince."

" From the king ? "

" No, from Monseigneur the Duc de Guise."

" Ah, that is a very different thing. Come near, and speak lower."

CHAPTER XLII.

HOW M. LE DUC D'ANJOU SIGNED, AND HOW AFTER HAVING SIGNED HE SPOKE.

THERE was a momentary pause; then the duke said, —

"Well, Monsieur le Comte, what have you to say to me from MM. de Guise?"

"A great many things, monseigneur."

"Have they written to you?"

"Oh, no; the duke writes no more since the strange disappearance of Maître Nicolas David."

"Then you have been to the army?"

"No, monseigneur; they have come to Paris."

"MM. de Guise in Paris?"

"Yes, monseigneur."

"And I have not seen them?"

"They are too prudent to expose themselves and your Highness at the same time."

"And I have not been notified?"

"I am telling you now."

"Why have they come?"

"They come, monseigneur, to the rendezvous you have given them."

"I have given them a rendezvous?"

"No doubt. The very day on which your Highness was arrested, you had received M. de Guise's letter, and sent him a verbal reply that he need only be in Paris from the 31st of May to the 2d of June. This is the 31st of May; if you have forgotten MM. de Guise, they have not forgotten you, monseigneur."

François turned pale. So many events had occurred since then, that this meeting, important though it was, had entirely escaped his memory.

"True," he said, "but the relations which then existed between me and MM. de Guise no longer exist."

"In that case, monseigneur," said the count, "you would do well to notify them, because they think differently."

"How so?"

"Yes, you may perhaps consider yourself in no way bound to them, but they still consider themselves bound to you."

"A trap, my dear count, — a trap in which I shall not be caught a second time."

"And where was Monseigneur caught the first time?"

"In the Louvre, *mordieu!*"

"Was it the fault of MM. de Guise?"

"I do not say that," murmured the duke, "I only say that they did nothing towards my escape."

"That would have been difficult, as they were flying themselves."

"True," murmured the duke.

"But after you had safely reached Anjou, did they not send you word, through me, that you could still count on them as they counted on you, and that the day you marched on Paris they would do the same?"

"That is still true," said the duke, "but I did not march on Paris."

"You did, monseigneur, you are here."

"Yes, but as my brother's ally."

"Monseigneur, you will permit me to observe that you are more than their ally."

"What am I, then?"

"Their accomplice."

The Duc d'Anjou bit his lips.

"And you are sent by them to announce their arrival?"

"I have that honor."

"Have they communicated to you the motives of their return ? "

"Knowing me to be the trusted follower of your Highness, they have communicated their plans and motives."

"They have plans ?   What are they ? "

"Always the same."

"They believe them to be practicable ? "

"They look upon them as certain."

"And the object of these plans is still —"   The duke stopped, not daring to utter the words which were the natural consequence of what he had just said; Monsoreau finished for him.

"To make you King of France; yes, monseigneur."

The duke felt his blood rush madly to his face.

"But is the moment favorable ? " he asked.

"Your wisdom must decide."

"My wisdom ? "

"Yes; here are the true and visible facts."

"Speak."

"The appointment of the king as Chief of the League was but a comedy, quickly seen through and appreciated. The reaction has now begun, and the entire country is rising against the tyranny of the king and his creatures.   Sermons are calls to arms, and the churches are places where they curse the king instead of praying to God.   The army is trembling with impatience ; the *bourgeois* are organizing themselves ; our emissaries are continually getting new signatures and new adherents to the League ; the reign of the Valois is at last reaching its close.   Under the circumstances, MM. de Guise had to select a serious candidate for the throne, and their choice naturally fell upon you. Now, do you renounce your former ideas ? "

The duke did not reply.

"Well," said Monsoreau, "what does your Highness think ? "

"Why," replied the prince, "I think —"

"Monseigneur knows that he may speak openly to me."

"I think," said the duke, "that my brother has no children. After his death, the throne will come to me. And his health is poor; why should I plot with all these people, compromise my name, my dignity, and my affection in a useless struggle? Why should I run any risks to obtain a thing which will come to me without any danger?"

"Your Highness is in error," said Monsoreau. "Your brother's throne will only come to you if you take it. MM. de Guise cannot reign themselves, but they will only allow a king of their own choice to do so. They had counted on your Highness to be this king, but if you refuse, they will get another."

"Who?" cried the Duc d'Anjou, frowning, — "who else would dare sit on the throne of Charlemagne?"

"A Bourbon instead of a Valois, one son of Saint Louis instead of another."

"The King of Navarre!" cried François.

"Why not? He is young and brave. It is true that he has no children, but we know that he could have some."

"He is a Huguenot."

"Was he not converted at the Saint-Bartholomew?"

"But he has recanted since then."

"Oh! he will do to get the throne what he did to save his life."

"Do they think I will give up my rights without defending them?"

"The case is provided for."

"I shall fight them."

"Pooh! they are soldiers."

"I shall put myself at the head of the League."

"They are the soul of it."

"I shall unite with my brother."

"Your brother will be dead."

"I shall call on all the kings of Europe to assist me."

"The kings of Europe will willingly make war against kings, but they will think twice before making war against a people."

"How against a people ? "

"No doubt, MM. de Guise have decided to do anything, even to forming a confederation or a republic."

François clasped his hands in inexpressible anguish. Monsoreau was frightful with his ready answers for everything.

"A republic ! " he murmured.

"*Mon Dieu !* yes ; like Switzerland, Genoa, or Venice."

"But my party will not suffer France to be made a republic."

"Your party ? " said Monsoreau. "Eh! monseigneur, you have been so disinterested and magnanimous that upon my word your party consists of M. de Bussy and myself."

The duke could not repress a sinister smile.

"Then I am tied," he said.

"Very nearly, monseigneur."

"Then why need you have recourse to me, if I am, as you say, destitute of all power ? "

"I mean, monseigneur, that you can do nothing without MM. de Guise, but you can do everything with them."

"I can do all with them ? "

"Yes ; speak but one word and you shall be king."

The duke rose in a very agitated state, walked about the room, touching everything around him, — the curtains, tables, chairs, — and finally stopped before Monsoreau.

"You spoke the truth, count, when you said I had but two friends, — you and Bussy ; " and he uttered these words with a bland smile which had replaced the look of fury.

"Therefore ? " said Monsoreau, whose eyes glittered.

"Therefore, faithful friend, speak, I am listening."

"Are these your orders, monseigneur ? "

"Yes."

"Then here is the plan."

The duke grew pale, but stopped to listen. The count continued, —

"The Fête Dieu will take place in a week; for some time past the king has planned for that day a grand procession to the principal convents."

"It is his habit to have a procession every year at that time."

"At these times, as your Highness will remember, the king is without his guards, as they remain outside. The king stops before each altar, kneels and recites five *Paters* and five *Aves,* followed by the Seven Psalms."

"I know all that."

"He will also go to the Abbey of Sainte-Genevieve."

"No doubt."

"Only as an accident will have happened just before the gate — "

"What accident?"

"A sewer will have given way during the night; the altar will not be on the porch, but within the courtyard. The king will enter with four or five persons, and the gates will be closed behind him."

"And then?"

"Your Highness knows the monks who will do the honors of the Abbey to his Majesty."

"They will be the same — "

"Who were there at the coronation of your Highness."

"And they will dare to lay hands on the Lord's anointed?"

"Only to cut his hair; you know the verse, —

> " 'De trois couronnes, la première,
> Tu perdis, ingrat et fuyard;
> La seconde court grand hasard;
> Des ciseaux feront la dernière.' "

"They will dare to do that?" cried the duke, with sparkling eyes; "they will touch the king's head?"

"He will no longer be king then."

"How so?"

"Have you not heard of a holy monk who preaches sermons until the time shall come for him to perform miracles?"

"Brother Gorenflot?"

"Exactly."

"The same one who wished to preach to the League with his arquebuse on his shoulder?"

"The same."

"The king will be taken to his cell; once there, the monk will ask him to sign his abdication, and that being done, Madame de Montpensier will enter with her scissors which are bought and which she wears suspended from her belt. They are charming scissors of pure gold and admirably chased."

François remained silent; his eyes shone like those of the cat that watches its prey in the shadow.

"You understand, monseigneur," continued the count. "We announce to the people that the king, frightened at the weight of his iniquities, has made a vow never to leave the convent where he is repenting. If there are any who doubt the sincerity of this vocation, M. de Guise has the army, M. le Cardinal the Church, and M. de Mayenne the bourgeoisie: with this trinity, the people can be made to believe anything."

"But I shall be accused of violence," said the duke, after a pause.

"You are not obliged to be there."

"They will look upon me as an usurper."

"Monseigneur forgets the abdication."

"The king will refuse."

"It seems that Brother Gorenflot is not only very eloquent but very strong."

" The plan is settled ? "

" Absolutely."

" And they have no fear of my betraying them ? "

" No, monseigneur ; there is another plan, no less perfect, in case you betray them."

"Ah, ah ! " cried François.

"I am not acquainted with that plan, being too well known as your friend ; I am simply aware of its existence."

" Then I yield.   What must I do ? "

" Approve."

" Well, I approve."

" But verbal approbation does not suffice."

" How must I approve ? "

" In writing."

" It is folly to suppose that I would consent to that."

" Why so ? "

" Supposing the plot should fail — "

" That is just the case for which your signature is needed."

" They wish to shelter themselves behind my name ? "

" Nothing else."

" Then I refuse a thousand times."

" You cannot."

" I cannot refuse ? "

" No."

" Are you mad ? "

" To refuse is to betray."

" How so ? "

" Because I was not anxious to speak, and only did so at your command."

" Very well, let those gentlemen take it as they wish ; I shall at least have chosen my danger."

" Monseigneur, take care you do not choose wrong."

"I shall risk it," said François, a little agitated, but trying, nevertheless, to retain his composure.

"In your own interest, monseigneur, I do not advise you to do so."

"But I compromise myself by signing."

"In refusing you assassinate yourself."

François shuddered.

"They would dare?" he asked.

"They would dare anything, monseigneur. The conspirators have gone so far that they must succeed at any price."

The duke fell into a state of indecision easily understood.

"I shall sign," he said.

"When?"

"To-morrow."

"No, monseigneur; if you sign, you must do so at once."

"But MM. de Guise must at least draw up the agreement I am to sign."

"It is already drawn up, monseigneur, and I have it with me."

Monsoreau drew a paper from his pocket. It was a full and entire adhesion to the plan. The duke read it through, and as he read, the count could see him turn pale; when he finished, his knees gave way beneath him, and he sat, or rather fell, on a chair.

"Here, monseigneur," said Monsoreau, giving him a pen.

"Must I then sign?" said François, leaning his head on his hand.

"If you wish to do so; no one forces you."

"I am forced, since I am threatened with assassination."

"God is my witness that I do not threaten; I only warn you."

"Give it here," said the duke, and making an effort, he

took, or rather snatched, the pen from his hands and signed.

As he watched his movements, Monsoreau's eye glittered with hope and hatred; when he saw · him put the pen to the paper, he was obliged to lean on the table, and his eyes dilated as the duke's hand traced the letters of his name.

"Ah," he said, after François had signed; and seizing the paper, he placed it between his shirt and the garment of woven silk which took the place of the vest in those days, carefully buttoned his doublet and closed his cloak over the whole. The duke watched him in astonishment, not understanding the expression of this pale face and its flash of ferocious joy.

" And now, monseigneur, be prudent," said the count.

" How so ? "

" Yes; do not go through the streets with D'Aurilly as you did just now."

"What do you mean ? "

" I mean that this evening you pursued a woman whom her husband adores, and of whom he is so jealous that he will kill whoever approaches her without his permission."

" Do you happen to speak of your wife ? "

" Yes, monseigneur, since you have made such a good guess, I shall not deny. I married Diane de Méridor, and so long as I live, none shall have her, not even a prince ; and to convince you, monseigneur, I swear by my name and on this dagger," and he placed the blade so near the prince's breast that the latter stepped back.

" You are threatening me, monsieur," said François, pale with rage and anger.

"No, prince, as I said just now, I am only warning you."

" Of what ? "

" That no one will have my wife."

"And I warn you that you are too late, as some one already has her," cried D'Anjou, beside himself.

Monsoreau uttered a terrible cry, and buried his two hands in his hair.

"It is not you, monseigneur," he stammered, and his hand which still held the dagger had but to reach out to strike the prince. François stepped back.

"You are mad," he said, preparing to ring the bell.

"No, I see, I talk reason, and I hear well: you said that some one has my wife; you said it."

"I repeat it."

"Name the person and prove the fact."

"Who was ambushed near your door with a lighted musket?"

"I, myself."

"Well, count, during that time, a man was in your house, or rather with your wife."

"You saw him enter?"

"I saw him come out."

"Through the door?"

"Through the window."

"You recognized this man?"

"Yes," said the duke.

"Name him," cried Monsoreau, "name him, or I do not answer for myself."

The duke passed his hand over his brow, and a kind of smile flitted over his lips.

"Monsieur le Comte," he said, "on my word as a prince, on my soul, within a week, I shall make known to you the name of this man."

"You swear!" cried Monsoreau.

"I swear."

"Very well, monseigneur," said the count, striking his breast over the place where the paper lay, "you understand, in one week —"

" Return in one week. I have nothing more to say."

"This may be better," said Monsoreau; "in one week I shall have regained all my strength, and he who wishes to avenge himself has need of it all."

And as he went out he made a gesture which might have been taken for a menace, as well as a farewell.

LA DAME DE MONSOREAU.

CHAPTER XLIII.

A PROMENADE AT LES TOURNELLES.

In course of time, the Angevin gentlemen returned to Paris, though no one will believe that they did so with much confidence. They knew the king, his brother, and his mother too well to hope that all would terminate in a family embrace. They still remembered their pursuit by the king's friends, and could not bring themselves to believe that they were to have a triumph to compensate for this rather unpleasant ceremony. They therefore returned timidly, and slipped into the city armed to the teeth, ready to fire at the least suspicious gesture; and before reaching the Hôtel d'Anjou, drew their swords fifty times against the *bourgeois* who had committed no other crime than watching them go by. Antraguet showed himself particularly ferocious, and attributed all his disgraces to the king's favorites with whom he was longing to exchange a few significant remarks.

He told Ribeirac of this plan, and was told that to carry it into execution he would need one or two frontiers within easy reach.

"I shall arrange that," said Antraguet.

The duke gave them a cordial welcome. They were his own men, as MM. de Maugiron, Quélus, Schomberg, and D'Epernon belonged to the king. He therefore began by telling them, —

"My friends, there is a plan for killing you. These sorts of receptions are in the air, so look to yourselves."

"We are doing so, monseigneur," said Antraguet, "but should we not present our very humble respects to his

Majesty ? If we hide ourselves, we will do little honor to Anjou. What do you think ? "

"You are right," said the duke; "go if you will, and I shall accompany you."

The three young men exchanged a glance. At this moment, Bussy entered the hall and embraced his friends.

"Ah," he said, "you were late in coming. But what do I hear? — his Highness proposes to go and have himself killed in the Louvre, like Cæsar in the Roman senate. Remember that each one of the favorites would gladly carry away beneath his cloak a small piece of Monseigneur."

"But, my dear friend, we wish to rub against these gentlemen a little."

Bussy began to laugh.

"We shall see," he said, — "we shall see."

The duke gave him a searching look.

"Let us go to the Louvre," said Bussy, "but alone. Monseigneur can remain in his own garden knocking off poppy heads."

François affected to laugh very gayly. The fact is he was glad to dispense with the disagreeable task. The Angevins donned their richest costumes. They were great lords who gladly spent the whole of their income for silks, velvets, and embroidery. They presented a glittering mass of gold, precious stones, and brocade ; and on their way to the palace, the people cried, "Noël," for the popular instinct felt them to be enemies of the favorites.

Henri III. would not receive these gentlemen from Anjou, and they waited vainly in the gallery. This news was brought by MM. de Quélus, Maugiron, Schomberg, and D'Epernon, who all bowed with great politeness and expressed their regrets.

"Ah, messire," said Antraguet, for Bussy held himself aloof ; "the news is sad, but coming from your lips, it loses half of its bitterness."

"Gentlemen," said Schomberg, "you are the very flower of courtesy. Would you be pleased to change this reception into a little promenade?"

"We were about to ask you to do so," quickly replied Antraguet, whose arm Bussy touched as though to say, —

"Hush, and let them act."

"Where shall we go?" asked Quélus.

"I know a charming spot near the Bastille."

"Gentlemen, we follow you," said Ribeirac; "you have but to lead the way."

The four friends of the king left the Louvre, followed by the four Angevins, and walked along the quay to the old inclosure of the Tournelles, which was then the horse market, a kind of open place planted with a few straggling trees, and here and there some posts to which the horses could be tied. The eight gentlemen walked arm-in-arm, and on the way conversed most amicably on various subjects, to the surprise of the *bourgeois* who seeing this unexpected friendship regretted their acclamations, and said that the Angevins had made some compact with Herod. They reached the place, and Quélus spoke first, —

"This is a good, lonely place," he said; "see what a good footing there is on this saltpetre."

"Yes," said Antraguet, trying in various places.

"Well," continued Quélus, "these gentlemen and I thought that one of these days you would be willing to accompany us hither to assist M. de Bussy who has invited us all four to meet him."

"That is true," said Bussy to his astonished friends.

"He said nothing about it," said Antraguet.

"Oh! M. de Bussy is a man who knows the value of things. Will you accept, gentlemen?"

"Certainly, and we rejoice at the honor," replied the three Angevins in one breath.

"This is well," said Schomberg, rubbing his hands. "Shall we now select our antagonists?"

"I like that arrangement," said Ribeirac, with flaming eyes, "therefore — "

"No, no," said Bussy, "that would not be fair. We all have the same feelings, therefore we are inspired by God. Let us leave to Him the care of choosing the opponents. You know that is most important, if we agree that the first who is free can join the others."

"That must be, that must be!" cried the favorites.

"All the more reason then to do as the Horatiis : let us draw lots."

"Did they draw lots ? " asked Quélus, reflecting.

"I have every reason to think so," replied Bussy.

"Let us then do likewise."

"Wait a moment," said Bussy. "Before knowing our antagonists, let us settle the rules of the game. It would be most unjust to have the rules follow the selection."

"These are most simple," said Schomberg ; "we will fight till death ensues, as M. de Saint-Luc has said."

"Of course, but how shall we fight ? "

"With the sword and dagger," said Bussy.

"On foot ? " asked Quélus.

"Yes ; on horseback one's movements are not so free."

"Then on foot."

"What day ? "

"The earliest possible."

"No," said D'Epernon. "I have a thousand things to settle ; my will to make: pardon me, but I prefer waiting. Five or six days will whet our appetites."

"That is speaking like a brave man," said Bussy, rather ironically.

"Is this settled? "

"Yes ; we always agree on all subjects."

"Then let us draw lots," said Bussy.

"Stop a moment," said Antraguet. "I have a proposition to make. Let us divide the ground. As the names will be coupled two by two, let us have four divisions, one for each pair."

" Very good."

" I propose for number one the long square between the lindens ; that is a fine place."

"Agreed."

" But the sun ? "

" So much the worse for the second one of the pair; he will face the east."

"Not at all, gentlemen; that would be unjust," said Bussy. " Let us kill, but not assassinate one another. Let us make a semicircle, and have the sun sideways."

Bussy showed the position, which was accepted; after which they drew for the names.

Schomberg came out first, Ribeirac, second. They were the first pair.

Quélus and Antraguet were second.

Livarot and Maugiron, third.

At the name of Quélus, Bussy, who hoped to have him as adversary, knit his brow. D'Epernon, who saw himself with Bussy, turned pale, and was obliged to pull his moustache to bring a little color to his cheeks.

" Now, gentlemen," said Bussy, "until the day of the combat, we belong to one another. We are friends for life or death. Will you accept a dinner at the Hôtel de Bussy."

All bowed in assent, and went to Bussy's *hôtel*, where a sumptuous repast kept them until morning.

CHAPTER XLIV.

WHERE CHICOT GOES TO SLEEP.

ALL these movements of the Angevins had been observed by the king and by Chicot. Henri was walking up and down, impatiently awaiting the return of his friends. Chicot had followed them from a distance and examined their actions, which he could understand better than any one. Having satisfied himself as to the intentions of Bussy and Quélus, he went on to visit Monsoreau.

The master of the hounds was a wily man, but he could not pretend to deceive Chicot. The Gascon brought him the king's greetings ; how could he help receiving him well! Chicot found Monsoreau in bed.

The visit of the night before had completely unnerved him. Rémy, resting his chin on his hand, watched uneasily for the first symptoms of fever which threatened to seize its victim. Monsoreau was nevertheless able to sustain the conversation and conceal his anger against the Duc d'Anjou in such a manner that none but Chicot could have suspected it. But the more discreet and reserved he was, the better the Gascon read his thoughts.

" The fact is," he said to himself, " no man can be so fond of M. d'Anjou unless he has some plan in his head."

Chicot wished to know whether the count's fever was not a comedy like the one which Nicolas David had played some weeks before. But Rémy was not mistaken. "This man is ill and unable to do anything," thought Chicot. " There remains M. de Bussy. Let us see what he can do."

And he ran to the Hôtel de Bussy, which he found glittering with lights, and giving forth vapors which would have caused Gorenflot to utter exclamations of joy.

"Is M. de Bussy getting married ? " he asked a lackey.

"No, monsieur," replied the latter. " M. de Bussy has become reconciled with several gentlemen of the court, and is celebrating this reconciliation with a famous banquet."

" Unless he poison them, and I know he is incapable of doing that," said Chicot, "his Majesty may be at rest on his side."

He returned to the Louvre, and found Henri walking up and down and grumbling. He had sent three messengers for Quélus, and as these messengers did not understand the king's uneasiness, they had simply stopped on the way at M. de Birague's, where every man wearing the king's livery was always sure to find a full glass, some ham, and preserves. The Biragues made use of this method to remain in favor. When Chicot appeared at the door, the king uttered a loud exclamation.

" Oh, dear friend, do you know what has become of them ? " he asked.

" Of whom ? your favorites ? "

" Alas, yes, my poor friends."

" They must be very low at this moment," replied Chicot.

"Have they killed them ? " asked Henri, with flashing eyes. "Are they dead ? "

"Dead ! I am afraid they are — "

" Dead, and you laugh, pagan."

"Wait, my son, yes, dead, but dead drunk."

"Ah, fool, how you frightened me ! But why do you slander those gentlemen ? "

" I glorify them, on the contrary."

" You are always jesting, — come, be serious. Do you know they went out with the Angevins ? "

"*Pardieu!* of course I know it."

"Well, what has been the result?"

"Well, the result was what I have told you: they are dead drunk, or very nearly?"

"But Bussy, Bussy?"

"Bussy is making them drink; he is a very dangerous man."

"Chicot, have pity."

"Well, yes; Bussy has given a dinner to your friends; do you approve of that?"

"Bussy has given them a dinner? Oh, impossible; they are sworn enemies."

"Exactly; if they were friends they would not find it necessary to get drunk together. Listen, have you good legs?"

"What do you mean?"

"Would you go as far as the river?"

"To witness such a sight, I would go to the end of the world."

"Well, only go to the Hôtel de Bussy, and you will witness that prodigy."

"Will you come with me?"

"Thanks, I have just been there."

"But Chicot —"

"Oh, no; you should understand that I have seen, so there is no necessity of my being convinced. I have walked so much that my legs are three inches shorter. If I walked any more, they would stop at the knees. Go, my son, go."

The king shot him an angry glance.

"You are very good to worry about those people," continued Chicot. "They are laughing, feasting, and making opposition to the government. Reply to all these things as a philosopher; they are laughing, let us laugh; they are dining, let us have something nice and warm; they are making opposition, let us go to bed after supper."

The king could not help smiling.

"You can flatter yourself that you are a true sage," said Chicot. "Other kings of France have had long hair, one was brave, one was great, some were lazy. I am sure you will be called Henri the patient. Ah, my son, that is a great virtue, when one has no other."

"Betrayed," said the king, — "betrayed; those people have not even the manners of gentlemen."

"Ah, you are worried about your friends," cried Chicot, pushing the king into the dining-room, where supper had just been served. "You pity them as if they were dead, and when you are told that they are not dead, you weep — Henri, you are always whining."

"You wear out my patience, Monsieur Chicot."

"Come, would you prefer that they should have five or six inches of steel through their body? Be consistent."

"I would like to be able to count on my friends," said Henri, in a gloomy voice.

"Oh, *ventre de biche!*" said Chicot, "count on me. I am here, my son, only you must feed me. I want some pheasant and truffles," he added, holding out his plate.

Henri and his only friend went to bed early, the king sighing because his heart was empty, and Chicot breathless because his stomach was full. The next morning MM. de Quélus, Schomberg, Maugiron, and D'Epernon presented themselves at the king's levee, the usher always let them in, so he opened the door for them.

Chicot was still asleep, but the king had been unable to close his eyes. He jumped furiously out of bed, and snatching off the perfumed apparatus from his face and hands, —

"Out of here!" he cried, "out of my sight!"

The astonished usher explained to the young men that the king was dismissing them. They looked at one another with equal surprise.

"But, sire," stammered Quélus, "we wished to tell your Majesty — "

"That you are no longer intoxicated, I suppose," vociferated Henri.

Chicot opened one eye.

"Pardon me, sire," gravely said Quélus, "your Majesty is in error — "

"And yet I have not drunk the wine of Anjou!"

"Ah, very well," said Quélus with a smile, "I understand, yes, well — "

"Well what?"

"Will your Majesty remain alone with us, that we may have a little conversation?"

"I hate drunkards and traitors."

"Sire!" cried the four gentlemen.

"Patience, gentlemen," said Quélus, stopping them. "His Majesty has spent a bad night and had unpleasant dreams; one word will put him in a better humor."

This impertinent excuse, given by a subject to his king, caused the king to stop and think that any man bold enough to say such things had done nothing dishonorable.

"Speak," said he, "and be brief."

"That is possible but difficult."

"Yes, it is difficult to get around certain accusations."

"No, sire, we go straight to meet them," said Quelus, looking at Chicot and the usher as though to reiterate his request for a private audience. The king made a gesture. The usher went out; Chicot opened his other eye and said, —

"Pay no attention to me, I am asleep;" and closing both eyes, he began to snore with all his might.

CHAPTER XLV.

WHERE CHICOT WAKES.

WHEN Chicot was seen to be so conscientiously asleep, no one paid any more attention to him. Besides, they were all accustomed to consider him as part of the furniture in the king's chamber.

"Your Majesty," said Quélus with a bow, "knows only one half of the matter, and I make bold to say the least interesting half. We surely do not intend to deny that we dined at M. de Bussy's, and I shall even add in praise of his cook, that we dined very well."

"There was also a certain Austrian, or rather Hungarian, wine which I found marvellous," said Schomberg.

"Oh, the horrid German," interrupted the king; "he likes wine; I always suspected that."

"I was always sure of it," said Chicot; "I have seen him drunk twenty times." Schomberg turned towards him. "Pay no attention, my son," said the Gascon, "the king will tell you that I always dream aloud."

Schomberg returned to Henri.

"Faith, sire," he said, "I conceal neither my likes nor my dislikes; good wine is very good."

"Let us not apply the name of good to a thing which makes us forget our lord," said the king, sententiously.

Schomberg was about to reply, being no doubt unwilling to abandon so good a cause, when Quélus made him a sign.

"You are right," said Schomberg, "go on."

"I was saying, sire," resumed Quélus, "that during the repast, and particularly before it, we had most serious and interesting conversations concerning the interests of your Majesty."

"Your introduction is very long," said Henri; "that is a bad sign."

"*Ventre de biche!* how that Valois talks!" cried Chicot.

"Oh, oh! Master Chicot," said the king with much haughtiness, "if you are not asleep you must go."

"*Pardieu!* I do not sleep because I cannot; your tongue wags the whole time."

Quélus, seeing that it was impossible to talk seriously on any subject, in this palace where every one had become so frivolous, shrugged his shoulders and rose angrily.

"Sire," said D'Epernon, "these are grave matters."

"Grave matters?" repeated the king.

"No doubt, if the lives of eight brave men deserve any attention from your Majesty."

"What do you mean?" asked the king.

"I am waiting for the king to be willing to listen to me."

"I am listening, my son, I am listening," said Henri, laying his hand on Quélus' shoulder.

"I was telling you, sire, that we had conversed seriously, and here is the result of our conversations; royalty is imperilled and weakened."

"That is to say, every one seems to conspire against it," cried Henri.

"It resembles," continued Quélus, "those strange gods who, like those of Tiberius and Caligula, reached old age but could not die, and in their immortality followed the course of mortal infirmities. The gods, having reached that point in their ever increasing decrepitude, can only be saved by the noble sacrifice of some devotee who will give them new life. Being then regenerated by the transfusion

of youthful, ardent, and generous blood, they live again,
and become once more strong and powerful. Well, sire,
your royalty resembles those gods : it can live only by
sacrifices."

"His words are golden," said Chicot. "Quélus, my son,
go and preach through the streets of Paris, and I will
wager an egg against an ox, that you will excel Lincestre,
Cahier, Cotton, and even that renowned Gorenflot."

Henri replied nothing. A great change was evidently
taking place in his mind. He had first received the
favorites with haughty glances, but as he gradually realized
the truth, he became thoughtful and gloomy.

"Go on, Quélus," he said, "you see that I am listening."

"Sire," replied the latter, "you are a very great king,
but you have no horizon before you. The nobility places
so many barriers in your way, that you can see nothing
unless it be the greater barriers of the people. Well, sire,
you who are a brave man, tell me what is the rule in war
when one battalion places itself like a threatening wall
before another ? The cowards look behind, and seeing an
open space, they flee; the brave men lower their heads and
rush on."

"Well, forward, then!" cried the king. "*Mordieu!* am
I not the first gentleman of my kingdom? Has any one
fought greater battles than those of my youth ? Can this
century now drawing to a close boast of greater names
than those of Jarnac and Moncontour? Forward, gentlemen! and I shall lead you, as I have always done, into the
thickest of the fray."

"Yes, sire, forward!" cried the young men, carried away
by the king's warlike demonstration.

Chicot sat up.

"Be quiet," he said, "and let my orator continue. Go
on, Quélus; you have already said great and good things,
and doubtless have others to say; so continue, my friend."

"Yes, Chicot, you too are right, as you often are. I shall continue, and tell the king that the time has now come when royalty must have one of those sacrifices of which I spoke just now. Against these ramparts, which are now closing around your Majesty, four men will march, sure of your approval, and of that of posterity."

"What are you saying, Quélus?" asked the king, in whose eyes shone joy, tempered by solicitude. "Who are those four men?"

"Those gentlemen and I," said the young man, with that feeling of lawful pride which exalts every man who risks his life for a principle or a passion, — "those gentlemen and I will devote ourselves, sire."

"For what?"

"For your safety."

"Against whom?"

"Against your enemies."

"Private animosities of young men!" cried Henri.

"Oh, sire, this is the expression of a vulgar prejudice, and your Majesty's tenderness for us is so great that it consents to disguise itself beneath this trivial cloak. Speak like a king, sire, and not like a *bourgeois* of the Rue Saint-Denis. Do not affect to believe that Maugiron hates Antraguet, that Schomberg dislikes Livarot, that D'Epernon is jealous of Bussy, or that Quélus has a grudge against Ribeirac. No, they are all young, handsome, and brave; friends and enemies, they could all love one another like brothers. But it is no rivalry of man against man that puts the sword in our hands, — it is the quarrel of France against Anjou, the quarrel of popular right against divine right. We present ourselves as the champions of royalty in the lists where we shall meet the champions of the League, and we came to say, 'Bless us, sire.' Smile on those about to die for you. Your blessing will perhaps make them victorious. Your smile will make them die happy."

Henri, overcome with emotion, opened his arms to Quélus and the others. He clasped them to his heart; and it was not a spectacle without interest, a picture without expression, but a scene where manly courage was allied to feelings of profound tenderness, sanctified by devotion.

Chicot, sombre and gloomy, with his hand on his brow, looked on from the alcove; and his face, usually indifferent or sardonic, was not the least eloquent of the six.

"Ah, my brave friends," finally said the king, "this is great devotion. This is a noble task, and I am proud to-day, not of reigning over France, but of being your friend. However, as I know my interests better than any one, I shall not accept a sacrifice, noble though it may be, the result of which may deliver me into the hands of my enemies if it should fail. France is sufficient to fight against Anjou. I know my brother, the Guises, and the League. Oftentimes during my life have I tamed horses more fiery and more obstinate."

"But, sire," cried Maugiron, "soldiers do not reason thus. They cannot admit ill-luck among the considerations of so serious a question, — questions of honor, questions of conscience, in which man follows his convictions rather than his reason."

"Pardon me, Maugiron," said the king, "a soldier may act blindly, but a captain reflects."

"Reflect, sire, and let us act, who are only soldiers," said Schomberg. "Besides, I do not know ill-luck. I always win."

"Friend," interrupted the king, "I cannot say as much; true, you are only twenty."

"Sire," said Quélus, "your Majesty's kind words only increase our ardor. What day shall we cross swords with MM. de Bussy, Livarot, Antraguet, and Ribeirac?"

"Never, I absolutely forbid it! Never! do you understand?"

"I beg you to excuse us, sire," replied Quélus; "but the rendezvous was arranged yesterday before the dinner. We have given our word, and cannot take it back."

"Excuse me, monsieur," said Henri. "The king absolves from promises and oaths, by saying, 'I wish, or I do not wish;' for the king is all-powerful. Send word to those gentlemen that I threatened you with my anger if you came to blows, and that you may not doubt my word, I swear to exile you, if—"

"Stop, sire," said Quélus, "for if you can release us from our promises, God alone can release you from yours. Do not swear, then, because if for such a cause we have deserved your anger, — and this anger takes the form of exiling us, — we shall gladly go into exile; for being no longer on your Majesty's territories, we shall be able to meet our adversaries in foreign lands."

"If those gentlemen approach within musket range of you, I shall have them thrown into the Bastille."

"Sire," said Quélus, "on the day when your Majesty behaves in this manner, we shall go barefooted, with a halter around our necks, and present ourselves to Maître Laurent Testu that he may imprison us with those gentlemen."

"I shall have their heads cut off, *mordieu!* I am the king."

"If such a thing happened to our enemies, sire, we would cut our throats at the foot of their scaffold."

Henri remained silent for a long time, then raising his black eyes, —

"Well," said he, "these are good and brave nobles. If God did not bless a cause defended by such people —"

"Do not be impious, do not blaspheme," said Chicot solemnly, rising from his bed and advancing towards the king. "Yes, these are noble hearts; do what they wish, and name a day for these young men. That is your business, and not to dictate his duty to the Almighty."

"Oh! *mon Dieu! mon Dieu!*" murmured Henri.

"Sire, we beseech you," said the four young men, bowing their heads and bending their knees.

"Well, so be it! If God is just he will give us the victory, but we shall also know how to prepare for it by Christian and judicious measures. Remember, dear friends, that Jarnac performed his devotions before meeting La Chateigneraie: the latter was a great swordsman, but he forgot himself in feasts and banquets and went to see the women, which was an abominable sin. In short he tempted God, who would perhaps have looked favorably on his youth, beauty, and strength, and wished to save his life. Yet Jarnac cut his leg. Listen, we will enter upon a devotion; if I had time I would send your swords to Rome and have them blessed by Our Holy Father. But we have the shrine of Sainte-Genevieve which is worth the very best of relics. Let us fast, macerate ourselves, and sanctify the day of the Fête Dieu; then on the following day —"

"Ah! thanks, sire; it is in a week," cried the four young men. They rushed on the king's hands, and he embraced them all once more, then entered his oratory bathed in tears.

"Our challenge is all drawn up," said Quélus; "there only remains for us to write the name and hour. Write on that table, Maugiron, with the king's pen; write the day after the Fête Dieu."

"It is done," replied Maugiron. "Where is the herald who will carry this letter?"

"I shall carry it, if you please," said Chicot, approaching, "but I wish to give you a piece of advice. His Majesty speaks of fasts, macerations, and shrines. These are all very good after a victory; but before the fight I prefer the effects of good food, generous wines, and eight hours' sleep. Nothing gives strength and agility like a three hours' sitting at table without intoxication. But I approve of the king's views on the subject of love; that is too enervating, and you had best dispense."

"Bravo, Chicot!" cried the young men.

"Adieu, my little lions," replied the Gascon. "I am going to the Hôtel de Bussy." He walked three steps, then came back. "By the way," he said, "do not leave the king on that beautiful day of the Fête Dieu. Do not go to the country, any of you, but remain at the Louvre like a handful of paladins. Now that you have agreed to that, I will do your commission," and holding the letter in his hand, he made use of his long legs, and was soon out of sight.

CHAPTER XLVI.

DURING this week the coming events were being prepared
as the storm gathers in the heavens during the calm and
sultry summer days. Monsoreau, who had now recovered
from his two days of fever, busied himself watching the
thief of his honor; but as he discovered no one, he remained
more than ever convinced of the Duc d'Anjou's hypocrisy
and of his evil intentions with regard to Diane.

Bussy did not discontinue to visit the house of the
master of the hounds by day; but having been warned by
Rémy of the husband's watchfulness, he came no more at
night through the window.

Chicot divided his time into two parts : one was given
up to his beloved master Henri de Valois, whom he left as
little as possible, and watched as a mother does her child;
the other was for his tender friend Gorenflot, whom he had
persuaded to return to his cell, whither he had conducted
him, and where he had received from the abbot messire
Joseph Foulon, the most charming welcome.

During this visit the king's piety was praised, and the
prior seemed most grateful to his Majesty for the honor
that would be conferred upon him by his proposed visit to
the abbey.

This honor was even greater than had been expected.
Henri, urged by the venerable abbot, had consented to
spend the day and night in retreat in the convent. Chicot
confirmed the abbot in this expectation, and as he was
known to have the king's ear, he was warmly invited to

return, and promised to do so. As for Gorenflot, he had grown ten cubits in the estimation of the monks. It was a masterly stroke to have won Chicot's confidence. Machiavelli could not have done better.

Being invited to return, Chicot returned; and as he carried in his pockets under his cloak, in his wide boots, flagons of the rarest and choicest wines, Brother Gorenflot received him even better than Messire Joseph Foulon. He would then remain for hours in the monk's cell, sharing his studies and ecstasies, according to the general report. The night but one, preceding the Fête Dieu, he spent in the convent; the next day the report was circulated that Gorenflot had persuaded him to embrace monastic life.

As for the king, he was constantly giving fencing lessons to his friends, teaching them new thrusts, and above all, exercising D'Epernon, to whom fate had given such a formidable adversary, and who, as the time drew near, became visibly uneasy.

Any one wandering in the neighborhood of the Abbey of Sainte-Genevieve, at certain hours of the night, would have met those strange monks of whom we have given a description in the first chapters of our book, and who resembled soldiers more than monks. We might also add, that the Hôtel de Guise had become at once mysterious and turbulent, peopled within, and deserted without; that meetings were held every evening in the great hall, when all the blinds were hermetically closed, and that these meetings were preceded by dinners to which none but men were invited, and which were presided over by Madame de Montpensier.

All these details are to be found in the memoirs of that period, and we are forced to give them to our readers because they are not found in the archives of the police. In fact, the police of the times did not even suspect what was going on, though the plot was one of importance and the worthy *bourgeois* who went the rounds with helmet and spear, were quite as unsuspecting, not being able to imagine any dangers save those resulting from fire, burglars, mad dogs, or drunken brawls.

From time to time a patrol would stop before the Hôtel de la Belle-Étoile, Rue de l'Arbre-Sec; but Maître La Hurière was known to be such a zealous Catholic that all were certain that the noise which took place in his hostelry was all for the greater good of religion.

This was the condition of Paris when dawned the solemnity of the Fête Dieu, which has, since then, been abolished by the constitutional government.

The day was beautiful, and the flowers which filled the streets sent their perfumes through the air.

On that morning, Chicot, who, for the past fortnight had slept regularly in the king's chamber, awakened the king very early; no one had yet entered the royal chamber.

"Ah, my poor Chicot," cried Henri, "a plague on you! I have never seen a man choose his time so ill. You have awakened me from the sweetest dream of my life."

"What were you dreaming, my son?"

"I dreamed that Quélus had run Antraguet through and through with his sword, and that this dear friend was swimming in his adversary's blood. But here is the day; let us pray to God for the realization of my dream. Call, Chicot."

"What do you want?"

"My haircloth and scourge."

"Would you not prefer a good breakfast?" asked Chicot.

"Pagan!" said Henri. "Who would hear mass on the Fête Dieu, with a full stomach?"

"Even so."

"Call, Chicot."

"Patience," said Chicot, "it is barely eight o'clock, and you will have plenty of time to scourge yourself. Let us

talk first. Converse with your friend, Valois, and you will
not regret it, on the word of Chicot."

"Let us talk then, but be brief."

"How do we divide our day, my son?"

"Into three parts."

"In honor of the Holy Trinity. Very good. Let us see
these parts."

"First, mass at Saint-Germain-l'Auxerrois."

"Good."

"Return to the Louvre for a collation."

"Very good."

"Then a procession through the streets, stopping at the
principal convents of Paris, beginning with the Jacobins
and ending with Sainte-Genevieve, where I promised the
prior I would remain in retreat until to-morrow, in the
cell of a saint who will spend the time in prayers for
the success of our cause."

"I know him."

"The saint?"

"Yes, perfectly."

"So much the better; you will accompany me, Chicot:
we shall pray together."

"Yes, you may be sure."

"Then dress yourself and come."

"Wait."

"What for?"

"I have a few more details to ask."

"Can you not ask them during my toilet?"

"I prefer to ask them while we are alone."

"Then be quick, for time passes."

"What is the court to do?"

"Follow me."

"And your brother?"

"Will accompany me."

"Your guards?"

" The French guards with Crillon will wait for me at the Louvre; the Swiss, at the door of the abbey."

"Very good," said Chicot; "I am now informed."

" I can now call ? "

" Yes."

Henri rang the bell.

" The ceremony will be magnificent," continued Chicot.

" I trust God will receive it favorably."

"We shall see that to-morrow. But tell me, Henri, before any one comes, have you nothing else to tell me ? "

" No. Have I forgotten some detail of the ceremony ? "

" I am not speaking of that."

" Of what, then, are you speaking ? "

" Of nothing."

" But you were asking — "

"If you have quite decided to stop at the Abbey of Sainte-Genevieve ? "

" No doubt."

" And you will spend the night ? "

" I have promised to do so."

" Well, if you have nothing more to tell me, I shall tell you that this ceremonial does not suit me."

" How so ? "

"No; and when we shall have dined, I shall tell you of another arrangement I wish to propose."

"Very well, I consent to it."

"Whether you consent or not, my son, it comes to the same."

" What do you mean ? "

"Hush! here are your attendants." As he spoke, the ushers opened the doors and admitted his Majesty's barber, perfumer, and valet, who, taking possession of the king's person, began to execute one of those toilets we have described in the early part of this book. When his Majesty was nearly dressed, his Highness, Monseigneur the Duc d'Anjou, was announced.

Henri turned and prepared to greet him with his best smile. The duke was accompanied by MM. de Monsoreau, D'Epernon, and D'Aurilly. D'Epernon and D'Aurilly remained in the background. Henri, at the sight of the count whose pale face was more frightful than ever, could not repress a movement of surprise. The duke perceived this movement, as also did the count.

"Sire," said the duke, "here is M. de Monsoreau who has come to pay homage to your Majesty."

"Thank you, monsieur," said Henri, "and I appreciate your visit all the more as I heard you had been wounded."

"Yes, sire."

"At the chase, I was told."

"Yes, sire."

"But you are better now, are you not?"

"I have quite recovered."

"Sire," said the Duc d'Anjou, "after we have made our devotions, would you not be pleased to have M. le Comte de Monsoreau go and prepare a fine chase for us in the woods of Compiègne?"

"But," said Henri, "do you not know that to-morrow —" He was about to say, "Four of my friends are about to meet four of yours," but he remembered that it had been kept secret, and stopped short.

"I know nothing, sire," replied the Duc d'Anjou; "but if your Majesty will inform me —"

"I was about to say that as I am to spend the night in devotions at the Abbey of Sainte-Genevieve, I may not be ready. But let Monsieur le Comte go. If it be not for to-morrow, the chase will take place on the day after to-morrow."

"Do you hear?" said the duke to Monsoreau who bowed. "Yes, monseigneur," he replied.

At this moment Quélus and Schomberg entered. The king received them with open arms.

"One more day," said Quélus, saluting the king.

"Luckily, only one," said Schomberg.

During this time, Monsoreau was saying to the duke:

"You are sending me into exile, monseigneur."

"It is the duty of the master of the hounds to prepare the chase for the king," replied the duke, laughing.

"I understand," said Monsoreau, "and I see how it is. To-night expires the week which your Highness had asked me to wait, and you prefer sending me to Compiègne to keeping your promise. But take care; before to-night I can by a single word —"

François caught the count by the wrist.

"Hush!" he said; "on the contrary, I am keeping this promise which you ask."

"Explain yourself."

"Your departure for the chase will be known to all since the order is official."

"Well!"

"You will not go, but you will hide near your house. The man whom you wish to know, believing you to be gone, will come; the rest concerns you. I believe I promised nothing more."

"Ah, ah! if that be so," said Monsoreau.

"You have my word," said the duke.

"Better still, monseigneur, I have your signature."

"Ah! *mordieu!* I know it only too well."

The duke left Monsoreau to join his brother; D'Aurilly touched D'Epernon's arm.

"It is done," he said.

"What is done?"

"M. de Bussy will not fight to-morrow."

"M. de Bussy will not fight to-morrow?"

"I can answer for it."

"Who will prevent him?"

"What matters it, provided he does not fight."

"If that should be so, my dear wizard, you shall have one thousand gold crowns."

"Gentlemen," said Henri, who had now completed his toilet, "to Saint-Germain-l'Auxerrois."

"And from there to the Abbey of Sainte-Genevieve?" asked the duke.

"Certainly," replied the king.

"Count upon it," said Chicot, buckling on the belt of his sword, while Henri passed into the gallery where his whole court awaited him.

CHAPTER XLVII.

WHICH WILL EXPLAIN THE LAST CHAPTER.

THE night before, after everything had been arranged and settled between the Guises and the Angevins, M. de Monsoreau returned home and found Bussy there. On seeing that brave gentleman for whom he felt great friendship, he realized that as Bussy knew nothing of the anticipated events, he might greatly compromise himself the next day. So taking him to one side, M. de Monsoreau said, —

"My dear friend, would you permit me to give you a piece of advice ? "

"Why, certainly," replied Bussy, " I beg you to do so."

"In your place, I would leave Paris to-morrow."

"I ? And why so ? "

" I can only tell you that your absence will probably save you from great embarrassment."

"Embarrassment ? " said Bussy, giving the count a searching look.

" Are you ignorant of what is to take place to-morrow ? "

"Completely."

" On your honor ? "

" On my word as a gentleman."

" M. d'Anjou has confided nothing to you ? "

" M. d'Anjou confides to me only those things which he can tell aloud to every one."

" Well, I who am not the Duc d'Anjou, I who love my friends for their own sakes and not for my own, I shall tell you, my dear count, that grave events will take place to-morrow, and that the parties of Guise and Anjou are meditating a stroke which may result in the fall of the king."

Bussy looked at M. de Monsoreau with a little suspicion; but the latter's face expressed such absolute sincerity that no mistake could possibly be made.

"Count," he replied, "I belong to the Duc d'Anjou as you already know, — that is to say, my life and my arm are at his command. The king, against whom I have done nothing, dislikes me, and never loses an opportunity to insult me by word or deed. Even to-morrow," added Bussy, in a low voice, "and I say this to you alone, — to-morrow I am going to risk my life in order to humiliate Henri de Valois in the person of his favorites."

"So you are willing to bear the consequences of your attachment to the Duc d'Anjou?" asked Monsoreau.

"Yes."

"Do you know where that may lead you?"

"I know where I shall stop; whatever may be my reasons to complain of the king, I shall never raise my hand against the Lord's anointed. I shall let the others act, and without striking or provoking any one I shall simply follow M. le Duc d'Anjou to defend him in case of danger."

M. de Monsoreau reflected for a moment, then laying his hand on Bussy's shoulder, —

"My dear count," he said, "the Duc d'Anjou is perfidious and treacherous; a coward, capable, from jealousy or fear, of sacrificing his most faithful servant, his most devoted friend. Follow the advice of a friend, abandon him, spend the day to-morrow at your little house of Vincennes, go where you will, but do not go to the procession of the Fête Dieu."

Bussy looked at him and said, —

"Then why do you follow the duke yourself?"

"For certain reasons which concern my honor, I have need of him for some time yet."

"Well, I am in the same case," replied Bussy; "for certain questions of honor, I too must follow the duke."

The Comte de Monsoreau pressed Bussy's hand, and they parted.

We have related, in a preceding chapter, the events which took place at the king's levee.

Monsoreau returned home and announced to his wife his departure for Compiègne; at the same time he gave orders to have everything in readiness. Diane heard the news with joy. She knew, through her husband, of the proposed duel between Bussy and D'Epernon, but D'Epernon was the one of the king's favorites who had the least reputation for courage and skill; she therefore thought of the fight only with fear mingled with pride.

Bussy had gone to the Duc d'Anjou in the morning, and had accompanied him to the Louvre, but had remained in the gallery. He followed the duke when the latter left his brother, and the whole *cortége* went to Saint-Germain-l'Auxerrois.

When he saw Bussy so frank, so loyal, and so devoted, the prince felt some remorse; but two causes combated in his mind this return to better feelings, — the great influence which Bussy had acquired over him, as every strong nature has over a weak one, and which made him fear that Bussy, standing so near the throne, might eventually be the real king; then Bussy's love for Madame de Monsoreau awakened all the pangs of jealousy in the heart of the prince.

Yet, as Monsoreau inspired him with as much terror as Bussy, he had said to himself, —

"Bussy will either accompany me, and by his support win victory to our side, — then if I triumph, what do I care for Monsoreau, — or Bussy will abandon me, in which case I too shall abandon him."

In consequence of this double reflection, of which Bussy was the object, the prince did not once remove his eyes from the young man. He saw him enter the church with a calm and smiling face, after having courteously made way for M. d'Epernon his antagonist, and kneel down a little way behind him.

The prince then made a sign to Bussy to come nearer. In his present position he was obliged to turn completely round, whereas, if Bussy were on his left he had but to turn his eyes.

About fifteen minutes later, Rémy entered the church and knelt near his master. The duke started when he saw the young physician whom he knew to be the confidant of Bussy's secret thoughts. After having exchanged a few words in a low tone, Rémy slipped a note into the count's hand. The prince felt a thrill through his whole body; the address was written in a charming feminine hand.

"It is from her," he said; "she sends him word that her husband is about to leave Paris."

Bussy put the note into his hat, opened it, and read it. The prince could not read the note, but he could see Bussy's face radiant with joy and love.

"Ah, woe to you if you do not accompany me," he murmured.

Bussy raised the note to his lips, then placed it over his heart. The duke looked around; if Monsoreau had been there, François might not have had the patience to wait until evening to denounce Bussy to him. Mass being over, they returned to the Louvre, where a collation awaited the king in his apartments, and the gentlemen in the gallery. The Swiss stood in line at the gates of the Louvre. Crillon and the French guards were in the courtyard.

Chicot watched the king as closely as the Duc d'Anjou watched Bussy. On entering the Louvre, Bussy approached the duke. ·

"Pardon me, monseigneur," he said, bowing, "I should like to say two words to your Highness."

"Is there any need for haste?"

"Great haste."

"Can you not tell me during the procession? We shall walk side by side."

"Monseigneur must pardon me, but I wish to be excused· from going."

"How so?" asked the duke, in a voice from which he was unable to banish all emotion.

"Monseigneur, to-morrow is a great day, since we are to settle the quarrel between France and Anjou; I should therefore like to retire to my little house of Vincennes, and spend the day in retreat."

"So you will not join the procession with the king and the court?"

"No, monseigneur, if you will excuse me."

"You will not even join me at Sainte-Geneviève?"

"Monseigneur, I wish to have the whole day to myself."

"Supposing something should occur during the day when I shall have need of my friends —"

"As Monseigneur would only need them to draw their swords against the king, I have a double reason for being excused," replied Bussy; "my sword is engaged to M. d'Epernon."

The night before, Monsoreau had told the duke that he might count on Bussy. All was changed since the night before, and the change was caused by the note which Le Haudoin had brought to the church.

"So you abandon your lord and master," said the duke, through his closed teeth.

"Monseigneur," said Bussy, "the man who is about to risk his life in a bloody, mortal duel, as ours will be, has but one master, and that master will have my last devotions."

"You know that I am playing for a throne, and you leave me."

"Monseigneur, I have worked enough for you, and I shall work again to-morrow. Do not ask me for more than my life."

"Very well," said the duke, in a hollow voice, "you are free ; go, M. de Bussy."

Bussy, not heeding this sudden coldness, saluted the prince, descended the steps of the Louvre, and once out of the palace, went quickly towards his house. The duke called D'Aurilly, who appeared at once.

"Well, monseigneur? " asked the lute player.

"Well, he has condemned himself."

"He does not accompany you ? "

"No."

"He goes to the rendezvous of the note ? "

"Yes."

"Then it is for this evening ? "

"Yes, for this evening."

"Is M. de Monsoreau notified ? "

"Of the rendezvous, yes, — but not of the man."

"Then you have decided to sacrifice the count ? "

"I have determined to avenge myself," said the prince. "I now fear but one thing."

"What is that ? "

"That Monsoreau will trust to his strength and skill, and allow Bussy to escape him."

"Reassure yourself, monseigneur."

"Why ? "

"Is M. de Bussy positively condemned ? "

"Yes, *mordieu !* A man who dictates to me ; who takes my will from me and substitutes his own ; who takes my mistress and makes her his own ; a sort of lion of whom I am less the master than the keeper, — yes, D'Aurilly, he is condemned without mercy, and without appeal."

"Well, as I was telling you, monseigneur, be not uneasy ; if he escape Monsoreau, he will not escape another."

"Who is this other?"

"Does your Highness command me to name him?"

"Yes, I command you."

"That other is M. d'Epernon."

"D'Epernon who is to fight with him to-morrow?"

"Yes, monseigneur."

"Tell me about it."

D'Aurilly was about to begin the account, when the duke was called. The king was at table, and was surprised at the duke's non-appearance, or rather, Chicot had called his attention to it, and the king summoned his brother.

"You will tell me the whole thing during the procession," said the duke, as he followed the usher. As we shall not have the leisure to follow the duke and D'Aurilly through the streets of Paris, let us tell our readers what had taken place between D'Epernon and the lute player.

One morning, at about daybreak, D'Epernon had presented himself at the Hôtel d'Anjou, and asked for D'Aurilly. The gentleman had long known the musician. The latter had been called to teach him how to play on the lute, and master and pupil frequently played together according to the fashion of those days, both in France and Spain. The result was that the two musicians were quite intimate. Besides, D'Epernon, who was a subtle Gascon, practised the method of insinuation which consists in reaching the masters through their servants, and there were few secrets in the Duc d'Anjou's household of which he was not informed through his friend D'Aurilly. Let us add that he flattered the king and the duke, floating between the two, fearing to have the future king for an enemy, and wishing to keep the reigning king as his friend.

The object of this visit was to talk about the approaching duel with Bussy. This duel greatly agitated him.

During the whole of his long life courage never was D'Epernon's strongest point. He would have needed more than courage to look forward to this duel with calmness. Fighting with Bussy meant almost certain death. Those who had dared it had fallen, never to rise again.

At the first word spoken by D'Epernon on the subject which he had most at heart, the musician, who knew his master's silent hatred of Bussy, entered into sympathy, and pitied his pupil, telling him that for the past week, Bussy had practised fencing for two hours every morning with a trumpeter of the guards, — the most skilful swordsman in Paris; a sort of artist in sword thrusts who, a traveller and philosopher, had borrowed from the Italians their close and prudent game; from the Spaniards their subtle and brilliant feints; from the Germans firmness of wrist and method of parry and thrust; and finally, from the savage Poles, who were then called Sarmatians, their turns, bounds, sudden prostrations and close embrace, man to man. During this long enumeration of disasters D'Epernon, in his terror, ate all the carmine off his finger-nails.

"Then I am a dead man," he said, half laughing and turning pale.

"Why, yes," replied D'Aurilly.

"But this is absurd," cried D'Epernon; "the idea of going to fight with a man who is sure to kill me. It is just as if one were to play dice with a man who is sure to throw double sixes every time."

"You should have thought of that before accepting, Monsieur le Duc."

"Peste," said D'Epernon, "I will break the engagement. I am not a Gascon for nothing. A man is a fool if he willingly gives up his life at twenty-five. But now I think of it, mordieu! yes, it is good logic. Listen."

"Speak."

"You say that M. de Bussy is sure to kill me?"

"I do not doubt it for one moment."

"Then if he is sure, it is no longer a duel, but an assassination."

"Apparently."

"The devil! if it is an assassination — "

"Well?"

"It is lawful to prevent an assassination by — "

"What?"

"By a murder."

"No doubt."

"Since he wishes to kill me, who can prevent my killing him beforehand?"

"Nothing at all; I had even thought of that."

"Is my reasoning clear?"

"Clear as day."

"Natural?"

"Very natural."

"Only instead of killing him with my own hands, as he intends to do with me, I shall leave the task to others, as I abhor blood."

"That is to say, you will hire assassins?"

"Yes, as M. de Guise and M. de Mayenne did for Saint Mégrin."

"It will cost you dear."

"I will give three thousand crowns."

"When your assassins will know with whom they are to deal, you will hardly have more than six men for three thousand crowns."

"Are not six enough?"

"Six men! M. de Bussy will have killed four before he is even touched. Do you remember the fight in the Rue Saint-Antoine where he wounded you and Schomberg, and nearly broke Quélus' head?"

"I shall give six thousand crowns if necessary," said D'Epernon. "*Mordieu!* If I attempt it, I want the thing done well, so that he may not escape."

"Have you your men?" asked D'Aurilly.

"Oh!" said D'Epernon, "I have plenty of innocent men,

brave old soldiers, who are well worth those of Venice and
Florence."

"Very well, but take care."

"Of what ? "

"If they fail, they will denounce you."

"I have the king on my side."

"That is something, but the king cannot prevent your
being killed by M. de Bussy."

"This is very true," said D'Epernon, thoughtfully.

"I might suggest a combination," said D'Aurilly.

"Speak, my friend."

"But you might object to an auxiliary."

"I would object to nothing which would double my
chances of getting rid of this mad dog."

"Well, a certain enemy of your enemy is jealous."

"Ah, ah ! "

"And is now laying a snare for him."

"Well."

"But he needs money. With the six thousand crowns he
would settle your business and his own at the same time.
You are not anxious to have the credit of the thing, I
presume ? "

"No, I only wish to remain in the background."

"Send your men to the place of meeting, and he will
make use of them without telling your name."

"But if my men do not know me, I should at least know
that man."

"I shall point him out to you this morning."

"Where ? "

"At the Louvre."

"Then he is a gentleman ? "

"Yes."

"D'Aurilly, the six thousand crowns shall be yours on
the spot."

"It is settled ? "

" Irrevocably."

" To the Louvre, then ! "

" To the Louvre."

We have seen in the preceding chapter how D'Aurilly said to D'Epernon, " Be not uneasy ; M. de Bussy will not fight to-morrow."

CHAPTER XLVIII.

THE PROCESSION.

So soon as the collation was over, the king, accompanied by Chicot, entered his room to put on the penitent's robe, and came out a few moments later with bare feet, a rope around his waist, and his hood pulled down over his face. The courtiers had made the same toilet.

The weather was magnificent; the pavement strewn with flowers. All spoke of the altars, each one of which was more beautiful than the last, particularly the one prepared by the monks of Sainte-Genevieve in the crypt of their church. An immense crowd lined the roads leading to the four places where the king was to stop, and which were the convents of the Jacobins, the Carmes, the Capuchins, and Sainte-Genevieve.

The clergy of Saint-Germain-l'Auxerrois led the way. The Archbishop of Paris carried the Blessed Sacrament. Between the clergy and the archbishop were young boys carrying censors and young girls strewing flowers. These walked backwards. Then came the king, followed by his four friends, barefooted and frocked like himself.

The Duc d'Anjou followed in his ordinary dress; his whole Angevin court accompanied him, mingling with the great dignitaries of the crown, who walked behind the prince, each occupying the place assigned to him by etiquette.

Then came the *bourgeois* and the people.

It was after one o'clock in the afternoon when they left the Louvre. Crillon and the French guards wished to follow the king, but he made them a sign to remain at the palace. It was nearly six o'clock in the evening when, after having stopped at the different stations, the head of the *cortége* first perceived the porch of the old abbey; and the monks of Sainte-Genevieve, with the prior at their head, stood on the threshold to receive his Majesty. After leaving the last station, M. le Duc d'Anjou, who had been on his feet since morning, pleaded fatigue. He asked the king's permission to retire to his *hôtel*, and his request was granted at once.

His gentlemen also left the *cortége*, and followed him, thus showing very plainly that they accompanied him and not the king. But the fact is, that as three of them were to fight the next morning, they were anxious not to over-tire themselves.

At the door of the abbey the king, thinking that Quélus, Maugiron, Schomberg, and D'Epernon were quite as much in need of rest as Livarot, Ribeirac, and Antraguet, dismissed them. The archbishop, who was officiating since morning, and had eaten nothing, was exhausted with fatigue, as well as the priests. The king took pity on these holy martyrs, and dismissed them all. Then turning to the prior, Joseph Foulon, —

"Here I am, father," he said, in a nasal voice, "and I come as a sinner to seek rest in your solitude."

The abbot bowed. Then turning to those who had stood by him the whole day and accompanied him so far, the king said, —

"Thank you, gentlemen, you may go in peace."

They all bowed, and the royal penitent slowly mounted the steps of the abbey, striking his breast as he went. No sooner had Henri crossed the threshold of the abbey than the doors were closed behind him.

The king was so buried in thought that he did not seem to observe this circumstance, which was in no way extraordinary, since he had dismissed his suite.

"We shall first conduct your Majesty to the crypt, which we have ornamented as best we could to do honor to the king of heaven and earth," said the prior.

The king merely made a gesture of assent, and followed the abbot. But he had no sooner passed through the sombre arch beneath which stood two rows of monks, he had no sooner turned the corner of the yard leading to the chapel, than twenty hoods were thrown back, and eyes were seen gleaming with joy and pride.

These were no faces of lazy and cowardly monks; the thick moustaches and bronzed skins denoted strength and activity. A great many of the faces were scarred, and beside the proudest and most illustrious of all appeared the triumphant and happy face of a woman dressed in a monk's robe. This woman, shaking a pair of golden scissors which hung from her belt, cried, —

"Ah, my brothers, we have the Valois at last!"

"Upon my word, sister, I believe it," said the Balafré."

"Not yet, not yet," murmured the cardinal.

"How so?"

"Yes, shall we have enough troops to resist Crillon and his guards?"

"We have better than troops," replied the Duc de Mayenne, "and, believe me, we shall not exchange a single shot."

"How will you arrange that?" asked the Duchesse de Montpensier; "I should have liked a little noise."

"Well, sister, I regret to say that you will have to do without it. When the king is taken he will cry out, but no one will reply to his cries; then, by persuasion or violence, but without showing ourselves, we will make him sign an abdication. The news will then spread through the city, and dispose the soldiers and *bourgeois* in our favor."

"The plan is a good one, and cannot fail now," said the duchess.

"It is a little brutal," said the Cardinal de Guise, shaking his head.

"The king will refuse to sign the abdication," said the Balafré; "he is brave and will prefer death."

"Then let him die!" cried Mayenne and the duchess.

"Not at all," firmly replied the Duc de Guise, "not at all. I am willing to succeed to a prince who abdicates and who is despised; but I do not wish to take the place of a murdered man who will be pitied. Besides, in your plans you seem to forget that if the king is killed, M. le Duc d'Anjou will claim the crown."

"Let him claim it, *mordieu!*" said Mayenne; "our brother the cardinal had anticipated that difficulty. M. le Duc d'Anjou is included in his brother's abdication; M. le Duc d'Anjou has had relations with the Huguenots; he is unworthy of reigning."

"With the Huguenots? Are you sure?"

"*Pardieu!* did he not escape with the aid of the King of Navarre?"

"Well?"

"Then follows another clause in favor of our house; this clause makes my brother lieutenant of the kingdom, and from lieutenancy to royalty there is but one step."

"Yes, yes," said the cardinal; "I have foreseen all that; but in order to ascertain that the abdication is a genuine and voluntary one, the French guards may storm the abbey. Crillon does not understand jests, and he is the kind of man to say to the king, 'Sire, there may be danger of life, but first of all we must save our honor.'"

"This concerns the general," said Mayenne, "and the general has taken his precautions. To sustain a siege, we have here eighty gentlemen, and I have distributed arms to one hundred monks. We could resist an army for one month, without counting that in case of defeat there is the subterranean passage through which we can escape with our prey."

"What is the Duc d'Anjou doing at this moment?"

"At the hour of danger he always weakens. The Duc
d'Anjou has returned home, and is no doubt waiting for
news from us through Bussy or Monsoreau."

"Eh, *mon Dieu!* he should be here and not at home."

"I think you are mistaken, brother," said the cardinal;
"the people and nobles would have seen in that union
of the two brothers a snare to entrap the family. As I
said just now, we must above all be careful not to play the
part of usurpers: we inherit, and nothing more. In leaving
the Duc d'Anjou free, and the queen-mother independent,
we shall win approbation and admiration from all sides, and
no one will have a word to say. Otherwise, we should have
Bussy and a hundred very dangerous swords against us."

"Pshaw! Bussy is going to fight against the king's favorites to-morrow."

"*Pardieu!* he will kill them, and then join us," said the
Duc de Guise; "as for me, I shall make him general of an
army in Italy, where war is sure to break out. The lord
of Bussy is a superior man whom I greatly esteem."

"And as a proof that I do not esteem him less than you
do, if I become a widow I shall marry him," said the
Duchesse de Montpensier.

"Marry him!" cried Mayenne.

"Yes, women of nobler birth have done even more for
him, and at that time he was not even a general."

"Come, come," said Mayenne, "we shall see about this
later; to work now!"

"Who is with the king?" asked Guise.

"The prior and Brother Gorenflot, I believe," said the
cardinal; "he must first be surrounded only by familiar
faces, otherwise he would be frightened."

"Yes," said Mayenne, "we can eat the fruits of the
conspiracy, but we must not pluck them."

"Is he already in the cell?" asked Madame de Montpensier, anxious to give the king the third crown she had so long been promising him.

"Oh, no! he will first visit the crypt, then the relics."

"And then?"

"The prior will speak a few high sounding words on the vanity of worldly goods; after which, Brother Gorenflot, you know the one who preached the magnificent sermon on the evening of the League — "

"Yes, yes."

"Brother Gorenflot will try to obtain from his conviction what we are reluctant to wrest from his weakness."

"That would indeed be much better," said the duke, thoughtfully.

"Pshaw!" said Mayenne, "Henri is weak and superstitious; I am sure he will yield to the fear of hell."

"I am less sure," said the duke, "but we have burned our ships, and can no longer retreat. After the prior's attempt and Gorenflot's speech, if both fail we will try the last resort,— intimidation."

"And then I shall shear my Valois," said the duchess, who always returned to her favorite hobby. At this moment a bell sounded.

"The king is descending to the crypt," said the Duc de Guise; "call your friends, Mayenne, and let us again become monks."

The hoods immediately concealed the bold faces, sparkling eyes, and well-known scars; then thirty or forty monks, led by the three brothers, went towards the opening of the crypt.

CHAPTER XLIX.

CHICOT I.

THE king was absorbed in a meditation which promised an easy success to the projects of MM. de Guise. He visited the crypt with the whole community, kissed the shrine, and struck his breast while he muttered the most doleful psalms. The prior began his exhortations, to which the prince listened with the same signs of fervent contrition. Presently, on a signal from the Duc de Guise, Joseph Foulon bowed before the king, and said, —

"Sire, will it please you now to come and lay your terrestial crown at the feet of your eternal father ? "

" Let us go," said the king, simply ; and followed by the whole community, he wended his way towards the cells, to which a passage on the left conducted. Henri seemed very much affected. He continued to beat his breast, and the chaplet of death heads rattled at his side. They finally reached the cell, on the threshold of which stood Gorenflot with a flushed face and eyes shining like carbuncles.

" Here ? " asked the king.

"Right here," replied the fat monk. The king could hesitate because at the end of the corridor was a door, or rather, a mysterious grating, opening into darkness. Henri entered the cell.

" Hic portis salutis ? " he murmured.

" Yes," replied Foulon, "this is the haven."

"Leave us," said Gorenflot, with a majestic gesture. The door was immediately closed, and retreating footsteps

were heard. The king spied a stool, and seated himself
with both hands on his knees.

"Ah, here you are, Herod, Pagan, Nebuchadnezzar!"
said Gorenflot, suddenly, as he placed his fat hands on his
hips. The king seemed surprised.

"Are you speaking to me, brother?" he asked.

"Yes, to you. Can I call you by any name that will not
become you?"

"Brother," murmured the king.

"There is no brother here. I have long been meditating
a sermon, and you shall have it. I divide it into three
parts, like every good preacher. First, you are a tyrant;
secondly, you are a satyr; thirdly, you are dethroned. I
shall speak on these subjects."

"Dethroned, brother!" exclaimed the king.

"Neither more nor less. This is not like Poland, and
you shall not escape — "

"Ah, a snare!"

"Oh, Valois, learn that a king is but a man!"

"You are violent, brother."

"*Pardieu!* do you think we imprison you to flatter
you?"

"You abuse the cloak of religion."

"Is there a religion?" asked Gorenflot.

"Oh, you are a saint, and you say such things!"

"Never mind; I have spoken."

"You will be damned."

"Is there any damnation?"

"You speak like an infidel, brother."

"Come, no preaching. Are you ready, Valois?"

"To do what?"

"To give up your crown. I am sent to demand that of
you."

"You are committing a mortal sin."

"Oh," said Gorenflot, "I have the right of absolution,

and I absolve myself in advance. Come, renounce, Brother Valois."

"To what ?"

"To the throne of France."

"I would rather die than do that."

"Then you will die. Here is the prior, make up your mind."

"I have my guards, my friends. I shall defend myself."

"That may be, but you will first be killed."

"Give me, at least, a moment for reflection."

"Not one minute, not one second."

"Your zeal carries you away, my friend," said the prior, and with his hand he made a gesture that meant, —

"Sire, your request is granted," and he closed the door. Henri fell into a profound meditation.

"I accept the sacrifice," he said, after reflecting about ten minutes. Some one knocked at the door.

"It is done," said Gorenflot; "he accepts."

The king heard a murmur of joy and surprise in the corridor.

"Read the act to him," said a voice which startled the king to such a degree that he looked through the grating. A roll of parchment passed from the monk's hand to that of Gorenflot, who read the act. The king, whose sorrow was great, listened, with his head buried in his hands.

"And if I refuse to sign?" he asked in a tearful voice.

"You will doubly ruin yourself," replied the Duc de Guise, from under his hood. "Consider yourself as dead to the world, and do not compel subjects to shed the blood of a man who has been their king."

"I will not be forced."

"I feared this," murmured the duke to his sister, who frowned while her eyes glittered with a sinister light.

"Go, brother," he said to Mayenne, "let every one arm and prepare."

"For what ? " asked the king, in a plaintive tone.

"For everything," replied Joseph Foulon.

The king's despair increased.

"*Corbleu!* " cried Gorenflot; "I hated you, Valois, but now I despise you. Sign, or you shall perish from my hand."

"Have patience," said the king. "Let me pray to my divine master for resignation."

"He wishes to reflect longer," cried Gorenflot.

"Give him until midnight," said the cardinal.

"Thanks, charitable Christian," said the king, in a paroxysm of grief. "May God reward you ! "

"His brain was really enfeebled," said the Duc de Guise, "we are serving France in deposing him."

"No matter," said the duchess, "enfeebled as he is, I shall take pleasure in clipping him."

During this dialogue, Gorenflot, with folded arms, was uttering the most violent insults, and reproaching the king with all his disorders. Suddenly a dull noise was heard outside of the convent.

"Silence," cried the Duc de Guise. The most profound silence now reigned, and regular blows could be heard to strike against the resounding door of the abbey. Mayenne came running as quickly as his rotundity would permit.

"Brothers," he said, "there is a troop of armed men outside."

"They have come for him," said the duchess.

"All the more reason for him to sign quickly," said the cardinal.

"Sign, Valois, sign," said Gorenflot, in a thundering voice.

"You gave me until midnight," piteously said the king.

"Ah, you retract because you hope to be rescued."

"No doubt, I have a chance — "

"To die if he does not sign at once," said the shrill and imperious voice of the duchess.

Gorenflot caught the king by the wrist and gave him a pen. The noise outside increased.

"A new troop," cried a monk, "they are surrounding the abbey on the left."

"Come," said Mayenne and the duchess impatiently.

The king dipped the pen in the ink.

"The Swiss," cried the prior, "are occupying the cemetery on the left. The whole abbey will soon be surrounded."

"Well, we shall defend ourselves," resolutely replied Mayenne. "With such a hostage in our hands, we shall never be forced to an unconditional surrender."

"He has signed," ejaculated Gorenflot, tearing the paper from Henri, who buried his face in his hands.

"Then you are king," said the cardinal to the duke. "Take away that precious paper."

The king, yielding to a paroxysm of despair, overturned the only lamp which lighted the scene ; but the duke already held the parchment.

"What shall we do ?" asked a monk, beneath whose robe was visible the costume of a gentleman, completely armed. "Crillon is here with the French guards and threatens to break open the doors. Listen — "

"In the king's name!" cried Crillon's powerful voice.

"There is no more king," cried Gorenflot, through a window.

"Who says that, scoundrel ?" asked Crillon.

"I, I," said Gorenflot, proudly.

"Let some one see this rascal and send a few bullets into his carcass," said Crillon ; and Gorenflot, seeing the muskets aimed at him, fell back into the room.

"Break in the doors, Monsieur Crillon," said a voice, the sound of which made the hair of all the monks, real or pre-tended, stand on end. It was the voice of a man who left the ranks and advanced to the steps of the abbey.

"Yes, sire," said Crillon, striking a terrific blow in the door with his axe. The door groaned.

"What do you want?" said the prior, appearing at the window in great agitation.

"Ah, it is you, Messire Foulon," said the same calm and haughty voice, "I want my jester who came to spend the night in one of your cells. I want Chicot; I am lonely at the Louvre."

"And I am greatly amused my son," replied Chicot, throwing back his hood and passing through the crowd of monks who recoiled with a cry of terror. At this moment, the Duc de Guise, who had sent for a lamp, read the signature obtained with so much labor.

"Chicot I.!"

"I, Chicot I.!" he cried, "a thousand damnations."

"Ah," said Chicot, turning to Gorenflot who was nearly fainting, and he began to strike him with the cord he had around his waist.

CHAPTER L.

PRINCIPAL AND INTEREST.

As the king spoke, and as the conspirators recognized him, they passed from amazement to terror. The abdication signed " Chicot I." changed this terror into rage. Chicot threw back his hood upon his shoulders, folded his arms, and while Gorenflot fled at his utmost speed, sustained, firm and smiling, the first shock. The furious gentlemen advanced on the Gascon, fully determined to be revenged on him for the cruel mystification of which they had been the victims.

But this man without weapons, whose breast was covered only by his arms; this mocking face which seemed to defy so much strength with its very weakness, arrested their steps even more than the remonstrances of the cardinal who made them observe that Chicot's death could serve no end, but, on the contrary, would be terribly avenged by the king who was the jester's accomplice in this scene of terrible buffoonery.

The daggers and swords were accordingly lowered before Chicot who continued to laugh at them, either from devotion, a thing of which he was quite capable, or because he read their secret thoughts. However, the king's threats and Crillon's blows became more pressing. It was evident that the door could not long resist such an attack which no attempt was made to repel: therefore, after a moment's pause, the Duc de Guise gave the orders for retreat. This order made Chicot smile.

During the nights he had spent in meditation with Gorenflot, he had examined the cellar. He had found the outlet, and pointed it out to the king, who had placed there Tocquenot, lieutenant of the Swiss guards. It was evident that the Leaguers would go, one after another, and throw themselves into the trap.

The cardinal was the first to disappear, followed by about twenty gentlemen. Then Chicot saw the duke pass with about the same number, and then Mayenne, whose corpulence naturally assigned to him the task of bringing up the rear-guard. When the Duc de Mayenne had passed the door of the cell, Chicot no longer smiled: he laughed outright. Ten minutes elapsed, during which Chicot listened attentively, expecting at every moment to hear the noise of the Leaguers as they were repulsed in the cellar; but to his great surprise, the noise instead of growing louder, seemed to die away.

All at once a thought flashed through his mind, and changed his smile into anger. The Leaguers did not return. Had they found the door guarded, and discovered some other outlet? Chicot was about to rush from the cell, when the door was suddenly blocked by an enormous mass which fell at his feet and began to tear its hair.

"Oh, wretch that I am!" cried the monk. "Oh, my good Monsieur Chicot, forgive me, forgive me!"

Why did Gorenflot, who was the first to go, now return alone, when he should already have been far away? This question naturally presented itself to Chicot's mind.

"Oh, my good Monsieur Chicot!" he continued to cry, "pardon your unworthy friend who repents at your feet."

"But why did you not escape with the others?" asked Chicot.

"Because in his anger, the Lord has struck me with obesity, and I could not get through where the others did. Oh, cursed belly! oh, miserable paunch!" cried the monk,

striking with his clinched fist that part of his anatomy
which he thus addressed. " Oh ! why am I not thin like
you, Monsieur Chicot ? How beautiful, and above all, how
lucky it is to be thin ! "

Chicot could understand nothing of the monk's lamentations.

" Are the others escaping somewhere ? " he asked, in a
voice of thunder.

" *Pardieu !* " said the monk, " what should they do, —
wait to be hanged ? Oh, wretched paunch ! "

" Silence, and answer me."

Gorenflot raised himself on his knees. " Question me,
Monsieur Chicot," he said, "you surely have the right to
do so."

" How are the others escaping ? "

" As fast as they can."

" I understand, but where ? "

" Through the ventilator."

" *Mordieu !* through what ventilator ? "

" The one that opens into the graveyard vault."

" Is that what you call the cellar ? Answer quickly."

" No, my dear Monsieur Chicot, the cellar door was
guarded on the outside. Just as he was about to open it,
the great cardinal heard a Swiss outside say, ' *Mich durstet,*'
which means, ' I am thirsty.' "

" *Ventre de biche !* " cried Chicot, " I know what that
means ; so the fugitives have taken some other way ? "

" Yes, dear Monsieur Chicot, they are escaping through
the graveyard vault."

" Which opens ? "

" On one side into the crypt; on the other, under the
Porte Saint-Jacques."

" You lie."

" I, dear lord ? "

" If they had escaped through the vault opening into

the crypt, I should have seen them pass before your cell."

"Exactly, dear Monsieur Chicot; they thought they had no time for that, so they crept through the air-hole."

"Which one?"

"The one that opens into the garden, and serves to light the passage."

"So that you —"

"I was too big and could not get through, and they drew me back by the legs because I intercepted the passage for the others."

"But," cried Chicot, whose face suddenly expressed strange joy, "if you were unable to pass —"

"I made every effort. See my shoulders and breast."

"Then he who is bigger than you —"

"He! who?"

"Oh, *mon Dieu!*" said Chicot, "if you help me in this matter, you shall have my eternal gratitude. Neither will he be able to pass."

"Monsieur Chicot."

"Get up."

The monk rose as quickly as he could.

"Now take me to the air-hole."

"Wherever you wish, dear friend."

"Then lead the way."

Gorenflot trotted as fast as he was able, from time to time raising his arms to Heaven, while Chicot stimulated his pace by striking him with the cord. They both traversed the corridor and descended into the garden.

"This way," said Gorenflot.

"Hold your tongue, and go on."

Gorenflot made a last effort, and reached a clump of trees whence came the sound of groans.

"There it is," he said, as he fell exhausted on the grass. Chicot advanced three steps, and saw something wriggling on the ground. By the side of this something, which resembled the animal called by Diogenes a rooster with two feet and no feathers, was a frock and sword. It was evident that the individual so unfortunately placed in the hole had gradually divested himself of all objects which could increase his size. He was now reduced to his utmost simplicity; yet, like Gorenflot, he made fruitless efforts to disappear completely.

"*Morbleu! ventrebleu! sangdieu!*" cried the smothered voice of the fugitive. "I would rather pass through the guards. Do not pull so hard, my friends; I shall come through gradually; I feel that I am advancing, not quickly, — but I am advancing."

"*Ventre de biche!* it is M. de Mayenne," murmured Chicot with delight.

"I have not been surnamed Hercules for nothing," resumed the voice; "I shall raise that stone," and he made such a violent effort that the stone shook.

"Wait," said Chicot, "just wait," and he made a noise with his feet like some one running fast.

"They are coming," said several voices in the cellar.

"Ah," said Chicot, as if out of breath, — "ah, here you are, wretched monk."

"Do not speak, monseigneur," said several voices; "they take you for Gorenflot."

"Ah, here you are, heavy mass, — *pondus immobile;* take this, *indigesta moles*, take this."

And at each apostrophe, Chicot, who had now found the long-wished-for opportunity for vengeance, used with all his might the rope with which he had already chastised Gorenflot.

"Silence," said the voices, "they take you for the monk."

Mayenne only gave vent to smothered groans, while he made frantic efforts to raise the stone.

"Ah, conspirator," continued Chicot, "unworthy monk,

this is for your drunkenness, your laziness, your bad tem·
per, your greediness. I regret that there are only seven
capital sins. This is for all your vices."

"Monsieur Chicot," said Gorenflot, dripping with perspiration, — "Monsieur Chicot, have pity on me!"

"Ah, traitor!" cried Chicot, striking harder, "this is
for your treason."

"Spare me," murmured Gorenflot, who thought he felt
all the blows received by Mayenne, — "spare me, dear Monsieur Chicot."

But Chicot, intoxicated by vengeance, only increased his
blows. However great his power of self-control, Mayenne
could not repress his groans.

"Ah," continued Chicot, "why did it not please God to
substitute for your vulgar, plebeian carcass the high and
mighty shoulders of the Duc de Mayenne to whom I owe a
volley of blows, the interest of which has been accumulat-
ing for seven years."

Gorenflot sighed and fell.

"Chicot!" vociferated the duke.

"Yes, it is I, in person. I, unworthy servant of the king,
weak man who would like to have a hundred arms for this
occasion." Chicot, becoming more and more excited, repeated
the blows with such violence that the sufferer made a tre-
mendous effort, and in a paroxysm of pain raised the stone
and fell torn and bleeding into the arms of his friends.
Chicot's last blow fell into empty space. He then turned
round. The real Gorenflot had fainted from terror, if not
from pain.

CHAPTER LI.

WHAT WAS TAKING PLACE NEAR THE BASTILLE WHILE
CHICOT WAS PAYING HIS DEBTS AT THE ABBEY OF SAINTE-
GENEVIEVE.

IT was eleven o'clock at night, the Duc d'Anjou was in his
study, whither he had retired on his return from the procession, and was impatiently awaiting a messenger from the
Duc de Guise to announce the downfall of the king his
brother. He walked up and down, from the door to the
window, and from the window to the door, watching the
great clock whose hands moved slowly in their gilded
frame.

Suddenly he heard the gallop of a horse in the courtyard;
he thought it might be his messenger, and ran to the balcony, but this horse was held by a groom, and awaited its
master. The master came out of the apartments; it was
Bussy, who as captain of the guards came to give the password for the night before going to his rendezvous.

The duke, on perceiving the brave and handsome young
man who had never given him any cause for complaint, felt
a moment's remorse; but as Bussy came near the torch held
by the groom, his face expressed so much joy, happiness,
and hope that all the duke's jealousy returned.

But Bussy, ignorant of the fact that François was watching him and reading the expression of his face, gave the
password, rolled his cloak over his shoulders, jumped on his
horse, put spurs into its sides, and galloped away.

The duke, who was uneasy at seeing no one come, thought
for one instant of sending after him, because he was very

sure that before going to the Bastille, Bussy would stop at his *hôtel ;* but he pictured to himself the young man laughing with Diane at his love, and placing him, the prince, on the same level with the despised husband; and this time again his evil instincts conquered the good ones.

Bussy had smiled happily as he rode away; this smile was an insult to the prince who let him go; had he looked sad and dejected, the prince might have called him.

Bussy was no sooner out of the Hôtel d'Anjou than he moderated his pace as if he had feared the sound of his own footsteps, and stopping at his own house, gave his horse in charge to a groom who was patiently listening to a demonstration by Rémy.

"Ah, ah," said Bussy, recognizing the young doctor, "is this you, Rémy ? "

"Yes, monseigneur, in person."

"And not yet in bed ? "

"I shall be there in ten minutes, monseigneur; I have just come home. Indeed, since I no longer have a patient, it seems to me that the days have forty-eight hours."

"Are you bored ? "

"I am afraid so."

"And love ? "

"Ah, I have often told you that I am wary of love. In general, I only try it for the sake of experiments."

"So Gertrude is abandoned ? "

"Entirely."

"You wearied of her ? "

"I rather wearied of being beaten. That was my amazon's method of showing love."

"And your heart does not speak for her to-night ? "

"Why to-night, monseigneur ? "

"Because I would have taken you with me."

"To the Bastille ? "

"Yes."

"You are going there?"

"Yes."

"And Monsoreau?"

"Is at Compiègne, my dear fellow, preparing a hunt for his Majesty."

"Are you sure, monseigneur?"

"The order was publicly given this morning."

"Ah!"

Rémy became thoughtful.

"Well then?" he asked, after a pause.

"Then I spent the day in thanking God for the happiness he sent me for to-night, and I shall spend the night in the enjoyment of that happiness."

"Get my sword, Jourdain," said Rémy. The groom disappeared into the house.

"Have you changed your mind?" said Bussy.

"How so?"

"You are taking your sword."

"Yes, I shall accompany you as far as the door for two reasons."

"What are they?"

"First, lest you should meet enemies."

Bussy smiled.

"Eh, *mon Dieu!* yes. Laugh, monseigneur, I know you do not fear evil encounters, and that Rémy is but a poor companion; but two men are less easily attacked than one. The second is that I have a great deal of good advice for you."

"Come, my dear Rémy, we shall talk of her. Next to seeing the woman we love, I know no greater happiness than to speak of her."

"There are even people who put the pleasure of talking about her above that of seeing her."

"The weather looks very doubtful," said Bussy.

"All the more reason; the sky is alternately clear and

cloudy. I like variety. Thank you, Jourdain," he said
to the groom who gave him his sword. Then turning to
the count, " I am at your orders, monseigneur."

Bussy took the young doctor's arm and both went
towards the Bastille. Rémy had told the count that he had
a great deal of advice to give him, and no sooner had they
started than the young doctor began to make a number of
high-sounding Latin quotations, the object of which was to
persuade Bussy that instead of visiting Diane, he had better
spend a good night in bed, because a man usually fights
poorly when he has slept badly. Then he changed
to mythology, and proved how Venus usually disarmed
Mars.

Bussy smiled ; Rémy insisted.

" You see, Rémy," said the count, " when my arm holds a
sword it becomes so identified with it that the fibres of the
flesh take the hardness and spring of steel; while on the
other hand, the steel seems to warm and vivify into living
flesh. From that moment, my sword is an arm and my
arm is a sword. So you see, this is no question of mood or
strength ; a blade cannot be tired."

"No, but it can become dull."

" Fear nothing."

"Ah! my dear master," continued Rémy, "to-morrow
you enter into a combat which must rank like that of
Hercules against Anteus, that of Theseus against the
Minotaur, that of Bayard, — something Homeric, gigantic,
impossible. In future times Bussy's fight must be taken as
the typical one, and I do not want your skin to be even
scratched."

"Be not uneasy, my good Rémy, you shall see won-
ders. This morning I put swords in the hands of four
fencers, who during eight minutes did not touch me once
while I tore their doublets to pieces. I bounded like
a tiger."

WHAT TOOK PLACE NEAR THE BASTILLE.   403

"I do not deny that; but will your muscles of to-day be your muscles of to-morrow ?"

Here Bussy and his surgeon began a Latin dialogue which was frequently interrupted by bursts of laughter. They thus reached the end of the Rue Saint-Antoine.

"Farewell," said Bussy, "here we are."

"Suppose I should wait for you ?"

"Why so ?"

"To be sure that you will be home within two hours, that you may have at least five or six good hours' sleep before your duel."

"If I give you my word ?"

"Oh! that will be sufficient, *Peste!*   I should never think of doubting Bussy's word."

"Well, you have it.   In two hours I shall be at the *hôtel.*"

"Then adieu, monseigneur."

"Adieu, Rémy."

The two young men separated; but Rémy remained on the spot.   He saw the count approach the house, and, as Monsoreau's absence gave him great security, enter through the door which was opened by Gertrude, and not through the window.   Then he turned to go home, looking philosophically down the deserted streets.   As he came to the Place Beaudoyer, he saw five men enveloped in cloaks, and seeming entirely armed under these cloaks.

Five men at this hour, — it was an event; and he wisely hid in the corner of a house.   When they arrived within ten feet of him they stopped, and after exchanging a cordial good-night four took one road, while the fifth remained motionless and thoughtful.   At this moment the moon came out from behind a cloud, and its rays fell upon the man's face.

"M. de Saint-Luc!" cried Rémy.

Saint-Luc raised his head on hearing his name, and saw a man coming towards him.

"Rémy!" he cried in turn.

"In person, and I am happy to say not at your service, because you seem to enjoy perfect health. Is it an indiscretion to inquire what your lordship is doing at this hour, so far from the Louvre?"

"No, in obedience to the king's orders, I am examining the physiognomy of the city. He said to me, 'Saint-Luc, walk through the streets of the city, and if you happen to hear that I have abdicated, you may boldly deny it.'"

"Have you heard anything of that?"

"No one has mentioned it to me. Now, as it is nearly midnight and I met no one but Monsoreau, I dismissed my friends, and was about to go home when you saw me reflecting."

"What? M. de Monsoreau!"

"Yes."

"You met M. de Monsoreau?"

"With a troop of armed men, ten or twelve at least."

"M. de Monsoreau! Impossible."

"Why is it impossible?"

"Because he must be at Compiègne."

"He should have been, but he is not."

"But the king's order?"

"Pshaw! who obeys the king?"

"You met M. de Monsoreau with ten or twelve men?"

"Certainly."

"Did he recognize you?"

"I believe so."

"You were only five?"

"My four friends and I, no more."

"And he did not throw himself upon you?"

"On the contrary, he avoided me, and this surprised me. When I recognized him, I expected a horrible fight."

"Which way was he going?"

"Towards the Rue de la Tixeranderie."

"Ah! *mon Dieu!*" cried Rémy.

"What?" asked Saint-Luc, frightened by the young man's tone.

"Monsieur de Saint-Luc, a great misfortune is about to happen."

"A great misfortune! To whom?"

"To M. de Bussy."

"To Bussy! *mordieu!* speak Rémy, I am his friend as you know."

"What a misfortune! M. de Bussy believed him to be at Compiègne."

"Well?"

"He thought he could take advantage of his absence."

"So that —"

"He is now at Madame Diane's."

"Ah!" said Saint-Luc, "this becomes complicated."

"Yes. Do you understand?" said Rémy. "He suspected something or was warned, and feigned to depart that he might appear suddenly."

"Wait a second," said Saint-Luc, striking his forehead.

"Have you an idea?"

"There is the Duc d'Anjou under all this."

"But the Duc d'Anjou suggested M. de Monsoreau's departure this morning."

"All the more reason. Have you good lungs, my brave Rémy?"

"*Corbleu!* like bellows."

"In that case, let us run without losing a moment. You know the house?"

"Yes."

"Then lead the way." And the two young men started through the streets at a pace which would have done honor to hunted deer.

"Has he much advance?" asked Rémy.

"Who, Monsoreau?"

" Yes."

" About fifteen minutes," said Saint-Luc, vaulting over a pile of stones five feet high.

" Provided we get there in time," said Rémy, drawing his sword to be ready for any emergency.

CHAPTER LII.

THE ASSASSINATION.

Bussy, himself free from uneasiness or hesitation, had been fearlessly received by Diane who was sure of her husband's absence. Never had the beautiful young woman been so joyous; never had Bussy been so happy. At certain moments, the gravity of which is felt by the soul or the instinct of self-preservation; man unites his moral faculties to all that his senses can furnish him in the way of physical resources; he concentrates and multiplies himself. With all his energies he enjoys life which he may lose at any moment, though he cannot guess through what catastrophe.

Diane was agitated, all the more so because she tried to conceal her agitation. Moved by her fears for the threatening morrow, she seemed more tender, because sadness coming into love gives to this love the poetry that it lacks. True passion is never gay, and the eyes of a woman truly in love are more often tearful than brilliant. So she began by checking the amorous young man. What she had to tell him that evening was that her life was his; what she had to discuss with him was the surest way to escape.

It was not sufficient to conquer; after having conquered, the king's anger was to be feared, as it was not probable that Henri would ever pardon the defeat or death of his favorites.

"And then," said Diane, with her arms round Bussy's neck, while her eyes rested on his face, "are you not the bravest man in France? Why should you take pride in the increase of your honor? You are already so superior to others that it would not be generous to try and win greater fame. You do not wish to please other women, for you love me, and would fear to lose me. Louis, defend your life! I do not say, Think of death; because I do not think there exists a man strong enough to kill my Louis, except by treason. But think of the wounds; you may be wounded, and you know it, since it is to a wound received in fighting these same men that I owe your acquaintance."

"Do not be uneasy," said Bussy, laughing. "I shall guard my face. I do not wish to be disfigured."

"Oh, take care of your whole self, as if you were I. Think of the grief you would feel if you saw me brought back wounded and bleeding. Well, I would feel the same pain at the sight of your blood. Be prudent, my brave lion. This is my recommendation. Do like that Roman whose story you read to me the other day. Let your three friends do their fighting; aid the one who needs it most; but if two or three men attack you at once, fly. You will turn like Horatius and kill them one after the other."

"Yes, dearest Diane," said Bussy.

"Oh, you answer without hearing me, Louis; you look at me, and do not listen to me."

"Yes, but I see you, and you are very beautiful."

"Do not think of my beauty, now. *Mon Dieu!* I am thinking of your life, — of our life. What I am about to say is very dreadful, but I want you to know it; you will be more prudent. I shall have the courage to witness this duel."

"You?"

"Yes."

"How so? It is impossible."

"No, listen; in the room next to this, there is a window opening into a little court and with a side view of the Tournelles."

"Yes, I remember; it overlooks an iron railing, and from there I threw crumbs to the birds the other day."

"From there I shall see you. Above all, place yourself in a way for me to see you; you will know that I am there, and you can see me yourself. But no, foolish woman that I am, do not look at me lest your enemy should profit by it."

"And kill me while my eyes are fixed on you. If I could choose my death, Diane, that is the one I would take."

"Yes, but you are not condemned. This is no time for death; you must think of living."

"And I shall live, you may be sure. Besides, I shall be well seconded; you do not know my friends, but I know them. Antraguet uses his sword as well as I do. Ribeirac is so cool that the only living things about him seem to be his eyes with which he watches his antagonist, and the arm with which he strikes. Livarot has the activity of a tiger. The advantage is ours; I wish there were more danger, to win more glory."

"Well, I believe you, and I smile because I hope; but listen to me, and promise to obey me."

"Yes, provided you do not order me to leave you."

"That is just what I mean to do, and I appeal to your reason."

"Then you should not have made me mad."

"No nonsense, but obedience, — that is the way to prove your love."

"Order then."

"Your eyes are heavy, dearest; you need a good night's rest; leave me."

"What, already?"

"I shall say my prayers, and you will kiss me."

"But one ought to pray to you as to the angels."

"And do you think that the angels do not pray to

God?" said Diane, kneeling down. And looking upwards with a gaze which must have reached Heaven: "Lord," she prayed, "if thou art willing that thy servant should live happily and not die of despair, protect him whom thou hast sent on my path, and let me love him, and him alone."

She had just finished these words, and Bussy had thrown his arm around her to raise her face to his, when a window-pane was suddenly smashed in, then the window itself was broken, and three armed men appeared on the balcony, while a fourth one stepped over the balustrade. This one had his face concealed by a mask; in his left hand he held a pistol, and in his right a naked sword.

Bussy remained for a moment paralyzed by the frightful scream which Diane uttered at this sight. The masked man made a sign, and his three companions advanced. One of the men carried a musket. Bussy pushed Diane aside with his left hand, and drew his sword with his right. Then bending backwards he slowly lowered it without once losing sight of his adversaries.

"Come, my brave fellows," said a sepulchral voice from beneath the mask, "he is already half dead with fear."

"You are wrong," said Bussy, "I never feel fear."

Diane made a movement to draw near him.

"Stand aside, Diane," he said firmly; but Diane, instead of obeying, threw herself a second time on his neck.

"You will get me killed, madame." Diane moved away. She understood that she could only aid her lover by passive obedience.

"Ah!" said the hollow voice, "it is M. de Bussy; I would not believe it, fool that I am. Really, what a good and excellent friend."

Bussy bit his lips and remained silent; he was looking around for the best means of defence when it came to blows.

"He hears," continued the terrible voice, in a mocking tone which made it seem even more terrible, — "he hears that the master of the hounds is absent, leaving his wife alone; he fears she may be afraid and comes to keep her company. And when does he come? On the eve of a duel. I repeat, what a good and excellent friend he is."

"Ah! it is you, M. de Monsoreau," said Bussy. "Well, remove your mask. Now, I know with whom I have to deal."

"I shall do so," said the master of the hounds, and he threw away the velvet mask.

Diane uttered a feeble cry. The count's pallor was that of a corpse, while his smile was that of a demon.

"Let us put an end to this, monsieur," said Bussy. "I do not like noisy ways. It was very well for Homer's heroes to speak before acting: they were demi-gods; but I am a man, and not afraid. Attack me or let me pass."

Monsoreau replied by a hoarse, shrill laugh, which made Diane start, but which roused Bussy's anger.

"Let me pass," repeated the young man, whose blood now left his heart and rushed to his head.

"Oh, oh!" said Monsoreau; "let you pass! how you ask for that!"

"Then draw your sword and have done. I wish to be home, and have far to go."

"You had come to sleep here, monsieur, and you shall do so," replied the master of the hounds.

During this time two more men appeared over the bacony and took their places beside their companions.

"Four and two are six," said Bussy. "Where are the others?"

"They are waiting at the door," said Monsoreau.

Diane fell upon her knees, and notwithstanding her efforts, Bussy could hear her sobs. He gave her a rapid glance, then looking at the count, —

"My dear monsieur," he said, after a short pause, "you know that I am a man of honor."

"Yes," said Monsoreau, "you are a man of honor, as madame is a faithful wife."

"Well, monsieur," said Bussy, slightly bending his head, "this is severe, but it is deserved, and all will be settled at once. Only, as I have an engagement for to-morrow with four gentlemen whom you know, and their claim is prior to yours, I beg to be allowed to retire to-night, pledging my word that you will find me when and where you may wish."

Monsoreau shrugged his shoulders.

"Listen," said Bussy. "I swear before God, monseiur, that after I have satisfied MM. de Schomberg, D'Epernon, Quélus, and Maugiron, I shall be at your service. If they kill me, well, you will be paid by their hands; if, on the contrary, I am in condition to pay my debts — "

Monsoreau turned to his men.

"On, my brave fellows," he said.

"Ah!" said Bussy, "I was mistaken. This is not a duel: it is an assassination."

"*Parbleu!*" said Monsoreau.

"Yes, I see. We had misunderstood each other. But consider, monsieur, — the Duc d'Anjou will take this very ill."

"He sent me," said Monsoreau.

Bussy shuddered. Diane raised her hands to Heaven with a groan.

"In that case," said the young man, "I must rely on Bussy alone. Stand well, my men." In one second he had overturned the *prie-dieu*, drawn up a table, and thrown a chair upon the whole, thus improvising a kind of rampart between himself and his enemies. This movement had been so rapid that a bullet fired from the musket buried itself in the soft padding of the *prie-dieu*. Bussy also threw down a magnificent credence-table of the time of Francis

I. and added it to his fortifications. Diane was concealed behind this last rampart. She understood that she could aid Bussy only by her prayers, and she prayed. Bussy glanced at her, then at his assailants, then at his intrenchments.

"Come on, now," he said, "but take care. My sword is sharp."

The men, urged onward by Monsoreau, advanced, and one of them tried to seize the *prie-dieu* and draw it down; but before his hand had touched it, Bussy's sword, passing through a crack, had ripped open his arm from the elbow to the shoulder. The man uttered a cry and fell back. Bussy then heard rapid footsteps in the corridor, and thought he was caught between two fires. He rushed to the door to bolt it, but ere he could reach it, it was opened. The young man stepped backwards to be in a position of defence against his old and new enemies.

"Ah! dear master," said a well-known voice. "Are we in time?"

"Rémy!" cried the count.

"And I!" cried a second voice; "it seems they are trying to assassinate here."

Bussy recognized this voice, and made a joyful exclamation.

"Saint-Luc," he said.

"In person."

"Ah, ah!" said Bussy, "I think now, my dear M. de Monsoreau, that you would do well to let us pass. If you do not stand aside, we shall pass over you."

"Three more men!" cried Monsoreau, and three more heads appeared above the balcony.

"Ah, is it then an army?" asked Saint-Luc.

"Oh, God protect him!" prayed Diane.

"Wretch!" cried Monsoreau, and he advanced to strike her. Bussy saw the movement. Agile as a tiger, he bounded over his rampart. His sword met Monsoreau's, and he touched him on the throat; but the distance was too great. The wound was only a scratch.

Five or six men fell at once on Bussy. One of them fell beneath Saint-Luc's sword.

"Forward!" cried Rémy.

"No, not forward," said Bussy; "carry away Diane."

Monsoreau uttered a yell, and snatched a pistol from one of the new-comers. Rémy hesitated.

"But you," he said.

"Away, away!" cried Bussy, "I confide her to you!"

"Come, madame," said Rémy.

"Never! No, I shall never abandon him!"

Rémy picked her up in his arms.

"Bussy!" cried Diane; "come to me, — help!"

The poor woman was wild; she no longer distinguished her friends from her enemies. All that separated her from Bussy was fatal and mortal.

"Go!" cried Bussy; "I shall join you."

"Yes," shrieked Monsoreau, "you will join her, I hope."

Bussy saw Le Haudoin totter and fall, dragging Diane with him. He uttered a cry and turned.

"It is nothing, master," said Rémy; "I received the bullet; she is safe."

Three men threw themselves on Bussy. Just as he turned, Saint-Luc passed between Bussy and the three men. One of the three fell; the other two stepped back.

"Saint-Luc," said Bussy, "in the name of the woman you love, save Diane."

"But you?"

"I am a man."

Saint-Luc flew to Diane, who had already risen on her knees, picked her up in his arms, and disappeared through the door.

"Here, my men, from the staircase," shouted Monsoreau.

"Ah, wretch!" cried Bussy; "ah, coward!"

Monsoreau retreated behind his men. Bussy gave a back stroke and a thrust; with the first he cut open a head, and with the second he pierced a breast.

"That makes room," he said, as he took his place behind his rampart.

"Fly, master, fly!" murmured Rémy.

"I, fly, — fly from assassins!" Then bending over the young man, "Diane must escape," he said; "but what is the matter with you?"

"Take care," said Rémy, — "take care!"

Four men had just come in through the door from the staircase. Bussy was taken between the two bands; but his only thought was for Diane; and without losing a second, he flew at these four men. They were taken unawares and two fell, — one wounded, and the other dead. Then, as Monsoreau advanced, he stepped back and found himself behind his rampart.

"Draw the bolts!" cried Monsoreau; "turn the key; we have him; we have him!"

During this time, Rémy, by a last effort, had dragged himself before Bussy, and added his body to the rampart. There was a pause. Bussy, with his legs bent, his body placed against the wall, and his sword pointed, threw a rapid glance around him.

Seven men were lying on the ground and nine remained standing. Bussy counted them with his eyes. But when he saw the nine swords gleaming; when he heard Monsoreau encourage his men, and felt the blood beneath his feet, this brave man, who had never known fear, saw the image of death rising from the depths of the chamber and summoning him with her wan smile.

"I may kill five of the nine," he said, "but the other four will kill me. I have strength to fight for ten more minutes; well, during these ten minutes I shall do what man has never done before."

Removing his cloak, which he wound round his left arm like a buckler, he bounded into the middle of the room, seeming to consider it unworthy of his fame to fight any longer under cover. There his sword slipped like a snake among the other swords. Three times he saw an opening and extended his arm; three times he felt the leather doublets yield, and three times he felt the warm blood flow on his hands. During this time he had parried twenty thrusts with his left arm. His cloak was in shreds.

The assassins changed their tactics when they saw three men fall. They gave up the sword, and some fell upon him with the butt-end of their muskets, while others fired their pistols which they had not yet used. He avoided the bullets by jumping from side to side or stooping. In that supreme hour his whole being seemed to multiply itself. He not only saw, heard, and acted, but he seemed to divine his enemies' most secret thoughts. Bussy was in one of those moments where the creature reaches the height of its perfection. He was less than a god because he was mortal, but he was more than a man.

He then thought that by killing Monsoreau he would put an end to the fight. He looked for him among the assassins; but Monsoreau was behind his men, calmly loading the pistols or firing from his sheltered position. But it was an easy thing for Bussy to make an opening. He threw himself among the assailants and found himself face to face with Monsoreau. The latter, who held a loaded pistol, raised it and fired; and the bullet, striking against the sword, broke the blade within six inches of the hilt.

"Disarmed," cried Monsoreau, — "disarmed!"

Bussy stepped back, stooping as he did so to pick up his broken blade. In one instant he had tied it to his wrist with his handkerchief. The fight began again, presenting the prodigious spectacle of a man almost without weapons, but also almost without wounds, keeping six enemies at

THE ASSASSINATION. 417

bay, and with ten corpses as a rampart. The struggle
became more terrible than ever. While Monsoreau's men
rushed against Bussy, Monsoreau, who guessed that the
young man was seeking another weapon, drew to his side
all those that were within reach. Bussy was surrounded.
The blade of his sword was bent, twisted, and shook in his
hand; fatigue began to deaden his arm. He looked around,
and suddenly one of the bodies rose to its knees and handed
him a long, strong sword. This corpse was Rémy's, who
performed a last act of devotion.

Bussy uttered a cry of joy and bounded back to free his
hand from his broken blade. In the mean time, Monsoreau
approached Rémy and discharged his pistol at his head.
Rémy fell with a shattered skull, this time to rise no
more. Bussy roared.

His strength returned with the means of defence. He
whirled his sword round in a circle, cutting off a wrist and
opening a cheek. The way to the door was cleared by this
double stroke. He rushed against it, and tried to force it
open with an effort that shook the wall; but the bolts
resisted. Exhausted by the effort, Bussy let fall his right
arm, and with the left he tried to draw the bolts behind
him, while he faced his assailants.

During this second he received a bullet in the thigh and
two wounds in his side. But he had drawn the bolts and
turned the key. Sublime with rage, he repulsed the boldest
of the ruffians, and rushing on Monsoreau wounded him in
the chest. The master of the hounds uttered a curse.

"Ah!" said Bussy, opening the door, "I am beginning
to think that I shall escape."

The four men threw down their weapons and threw themselves on Bussy; they could not touch him with the sword,
for his marvellous skill made him invulnerable. They tried
to smother him, but Bussy knocked them with the hilt of
his sword, or slashed them, without mercy. Monsoreau

VOL. II. — 27

twice approached the young man, and was wounded twice
more. But the three men hung on the hilt of his sword,
and snatched it from his hands. Bussy picked up a tripod
of carved wood used as a footstool, and struck three blows;
two men fell, but the tripod broke on the shoulder of the
last who remained standing. He buried his dagger in
Bussy's breast, but Bussy seized his wrist, drew out the
dagger, and forced him to stab himself.

The last one jumped out of the window. Bussy advanced
to follow him; but Monsoreau, who was lying amongst the
corpses, rose in turn and ripped open his leg with a knife.
The young man uttered a cry, seized the nearest sword, and
plunged it into the master of the hounds so vigorously
that he nailed him to the ground.

"Ah," said Bussy, "I do not know if I shall live, but I
shall at least have seen you die."

Monsoreau made an effort to answer, but his last sigh
passed between his open lips. Bussy then dragged himself
to the corridor. He was losing all his blood from his wound
in the leg. He threw a last glance behind him. The moon
had just come from beneath a cloud; its light flooded this
room inundated with blood, and illumined the walls pierced
by bullets and hacked by blows, and lighted up the pale
faces of the dead, most of whom preserved in death the
fierce look of the assassin. Bussy, at the sight of this
field of battle peopled by himself, felt a thrill of pride,
wounded and dying though he was. As he had said, he
had done what no man could have done. There now
remained for him to fly and escape; he could fly from the
dead.

But all was not over for the unfortunate young man.
When he reached the staircase, he saw weapons gleaming
in the yard; a shot was fired, and he received a bullet in
his shoulder. The court was guarded. He then thought
of the little window through which Diane had promised to

watch the combat on the morrow, and he went to it as
rapidly as he could. It was open and looked out upon a
starlit sky. Bussy closed and locked the door behind him ;
then with great difficulty he succeeded in mounting on the
window, climbed over the railing, and measured with his eye
the distance to the iron trellis, so as to jump on the other
side.

"Oh, I shall never have the strength," he murmured; but
at that moment, he heard footsteps on the stairs. It was
the second troop coming up. Bussy was without means of
defence. He summoned all his strength, and, leaning on the
only arm and foot he could use, he made a spring. But as
he sprang, the sole of his boot slipped on the stone, he had
so much blood on his feet. He fell upon the iron trellis.
Some of the sharp points entered his body, while others
caught in his clothes, and he remained hanging. At that
moment he thought of his only friend.

"Saint-Luc!" he cried, "help! Saint-Luc!"

"Ah, it is you, M. de Bussy," said a voice, coming from
a clump of trees. Bussy started; it was not the voice of
Saint-Luc.

"Saint-Luc!" he cried again, "help! help! fear nothing
for Diane; I have killed Monsoreau."

"Ah, Monsoreau is killed?" said another voice.

"Yes."

"Very well."

Bussy saw two men come from beneath the trees; both
were masked.

"Gentlemen," said Bussy, "in the name of Heaven, help
an unfortunate man who may yet escape if you aid
him."

"What do you think, monseigneur?" asked one of the
men in an undertone.

"Imprudent!" said the other.

"Monseigneur," cried Bussy, who had heard through the

acuteness of his senses, "deliver me, and I will pardon you for betraying me."

"Do you hear?" asked the masked man.

"What do you order?"

"That you deliver him," — then he added, with a laugh which his mask partially concealed, — "from his sufferings."

Bussy turned his head towards the man who laughed at such a moment.

"Oh, I am lost," he murmured. At the same moment the barrel of a gun was placed against his breast and a shot was fired. Bussy's head fell upon his shoulder and his hands stiffened. "Assassin!" he said, "be accursed." He died with Diane's name on his lips. The drops of his blood fell from the trellis upon the one whom he called Monseigneur.

"Is he dead?" cried several men who had broken open the door and appeared at the window.

"Yes," cried D'Aurilly, "but fly. Remember that Monseigneur the Duc d'Anjou was M. de Bussy's friend and protector."

The men asked no more questions and disappeared. The duke heard the sound of their retreating footsteps.

"Now D'Aurilly," said the other masked man, "go up into that room and throw down Monsoreau's body." D'Aurilly went up, recognized the master of the hounds among the many corpses, took him up on his shoulders, and threw down the body which fell at the duke's feet, while the blood splashed on his clothes. François searched the dead man's doublet and drew out the paper signed by his royal hand.

"This is all I wanted," he said; "there is nothing more to be done here."

"And Diane?" asked D'Aurilly, from the window.

"*Ma foi!* I no longer care for her, and as she has not

recognized us, untie her and Saint-Luc and let them go where they please."

D'Aurilly disappeared.

"I shall not be King of France this time," said the duke, as he tore the paper to pieces; "but I escape being beheaded for high treason."

CHAPTER LIII.

HOW GORENFLOT FOUND HIMSELF MORE THAN EVER BETWEEN A GALLOWS AND AN ABBEY.

THE adventure of the conspiracy was a comedy to the very end; neither the Swiss placed at one end nor the French guards at the other had been able to lay hands on even the the smallest conspirator. All had fled through the subterranean passage. They saw nothing come out of the abbey. So soon as the door was broken in, Crillon placed himself at the head of about thirty men, and with the king, invaded Sainte-Genevieve.

A deathlike silence reigned throughout the vast and gloomy buildings. Crillon, a man of experience, would have preferred a great noise; he feared some ambush. But in vain did he send out scouts; in vain did they open doors and windows, and search the crypt, — all was deserted.

The king was among the first, and went sword in hand, crying out, "Chicot, Chicot!"

No one answered.

"Have they killed him?" asked the king. "*Mordieu!* they shall pay for my fool the price of a gentleman."

"You are right, sire," replied Crillon, "he was one, and of the bravest."

Chicot did not reply because he was busy beating M. de Mayenne, and he found so much pleasure in this occupation that he neither saw nor heard what was going on around him. However, when the duke had disappeared, and Gorenflot had fainted, and nothing remained to occupy his attention, he heard and recognized the royal voice.

"Here, my son, come this way," he cried with all his strength while trying to make Gorenflot sit up. He succeeded and placed him against a tree.

The strength he was obliged to use in this charitable work took away from his voice a portion of its volume, so that Henri imagined it came to him with a lamentable tone. This was not the case. Chicot was on the contrary, in the height of his triumph only as he watched the monk's pitiful condition, he asked himself if he must run the traitor through or be merciful towards this voluminous hogshead.

He therefore looked at Gorenflot for a moment as Augustus must have looked at Cinna. Gorenflot was gradually coming to his senses, and stupid though he was, he understood the peril of his situation. Besides, he rather resembled those animals who are incessantly threatened by men, and who feel instinctively that no hand is ever raised but to beat them. These were his inner feelings when he opened his eyes.

"Monsieur Chicot," he cried.

"Ah, ah," said the Gascon, "so you are not dead?"

"My good Monseiur Chicot," said the monk, trying to clasp his two hands over his enormous stomach, "is it possible that you will give me into the hands of my persecutors?"

"Wretch!" said Chicot, in a tone of ill-disguised tenderness.

Gorenflot began to howl. After having succeeded in joining his hands, he tried to wring them.

"I, who have made so many good dinners with you," he cried. "I who drank so neatly that you called me the king of sponges. I who was so fond of the capons you ordered at the Corne d'Abondance that I never left but the bones."

Chicot found this climax so sublime that he determined on clemency.

"Here they are, good God!" cried Gorenflot, making an unsuccessful effort to rise, — "here they are! they are coming. I am dead. Oh, good Monsieur Chicot, help me." And the monk, not being able to rise, threw himself face downwards. It was easier.

"Rise," said Chicot.

"Will you forgive me?"

"We shall see."

"You have beaten me so much that it might count for something."

Chicot burst out laughing. The poor monk was so upset that he really imagined he had received all the blows distributed to Mayenne.

"You laugh, Monsieur Chicot," he said.

"Yes, of course I laugh, animal."

"Then I shall live?"

"Perhaps."

"Well, you would not laugh if your Gorenflot were about to die."

"That does not depend upon me, but upon the king; the king alone has the right of life and death."

Gorenflot made an attempt and succeeded in getting upon his knees. At this moment the scene was brightly illuminated, and the two friends were surrounded by a number of men whose embroidered doublets and flaming swords glittered in the glare of the torches.

"Ah, Chicot, my dear Chicot," cried the king, "how glad I am to see you."

"You hear Monsieur Chicot, that great prince is happy to see you."

"Well?"

"Well, in his happiness, he will not refuse to grant what you request; ask for my pardon."

" From Herod ? "

" Oh, be silent, dear Monsieur Chicot."

" Well, sire," said Chicot, turning to the king, " how many have you ? "

" *Confiteor*," said Gorenflot.

" Not one," replied Crillon. " The traitors must have found some opening unknown to us."

" That is probable," said Chicot.

" But you saw them ? " asked the king.

" Certainly, I saw them."

" All ? "

" From the first to the last."

" *Confiteor*," repeated Gorenflot, who could get no further.

" You no doubt recognized them ? "

" No, sire."

" What ! you did not recognize them ? "

" That is to say, I only recognized one; and yet — "

" And yet ? "

" It was not his face."

" Which one did you recognize ? "

" M. de Mayenne."

" M. de Mayenne ! — the one to whom you owed ? "

" Exactly. We are quits, sire."

" Ah ! tell me about it, Chicot."

" Later, my son, later; let us attend to the present."

" Ah, you have made a prisoner ! " suddenly said Crillon, laying his hand on Gorenflot, who bent beneath the weight.

The monk began to speak, and Chicot took his time to reply, allowing all the anguish of fright to dwell within the heart of the unhappy man.

Gorenflot came very near fainting a second time when he felt all this anger seething around him. Finally, after a moment's silence, during which Gorenflot fancied he heard the trumpet of the last judgment blowing in his ears, —

" Sire," said Chicot, " look well at this monk."

One of the men raised a torch to Gorenflot's face. He closed his eyes to make easier the passage from one world to another.

"The preacher Gorenflot!" cried Henri.

"*Confiteor, confiteor, confiteor!*" quickly said the monk.

"In person," said Chicot.

"The one who —"

"Exactly," interrupted the Gascon.

"Ah, ah!" said the king, in a tone of satisfaction. The perspiration from Gorenflot's face might have filled a bucket, and with good cause, for the swords clashed in a most threatening manner; some even came dangerously near. Gorenflot felt them rather than saw them, and uttered a feeble cry.

"Wait," said Chicot, "the king must know all;" and taking Henri aside, —

"My son," he whispered to him, "thank God for having permitted this holy man to come into the world some thirty-five years ago, because he is the one who saved us all."

"How so?"

"Yes; he told me the whole plot from beginning to end."

"When?"

"About a week ago; so if ever your Majesty's enemies were to find him, he would be a dead man."

Gorenflot heard only the last words.

"A dead man!" and he fell on both hands.

"Worthy man!" said the king, throwing a kindly glance on that mass of flesh which, in the eyes of every sensible man, represented a mass of matter capable of absorbing and extinguishing every ray of intelligence, "we shall cover him with our protection."

Gorenflot caught this merciful glance in its flight, and like an ancient mask, smiled on one side while he wept on the other.

" And you will do wisely, my king," said Chicot; " for he is a most wonderful servant."

" What do you think I ought to do with him ? " asked the king.

" I think he will be in great danger so long as he remains in Paris."

"If I were to give him guards ? " said the king.

Gorenflot heard Henri make this proposition.

" Well," he said, " it seems I shall get off with imprisonment. I prefer that to beating, if they only feed me well."

"Not at all," said Chicot; "it will be needless if you allow me to take him with me."

" Where ? "

" Home."

" Well, take him and return to the Louvre, where I shall join my friends and prepare them for to-morrow."

" Rise, reverend father," said Chicot to the monk.

" He is jesting," murmured Gorenflot.

"Get up, you brute !" whispered the Gascon, giving him a kick.

" Ah, I deserved that ! " cried Gorenflot.

" What is he saying ? " asked the king.

" Sire," replied Chicot, " he enumerates all his fatigues, he recalls his tortures, and when I promise him your Majesty's protection, strong in the consciousness of his merits, he says, ' I deserved that ! ' "

" Poor devil ! " said the king, " well, take good care of him."

" Ah, be not uneasy, sire; when he is with me he lacks nothing."

" Ah, Monsieur Chicot," cried Gorenflot, " whither are you taking me ? "

" You shall soon know. In the mean time, thank his Majesty, you monster of iniquities !"

" What for ? "

"Thank him, I tell you!"

"Sire," stammered Gorenflot, "since your gracious Majesty —"

"Yes," said Henri, "I know all that you did during your journey to Lyons, during the evening of the League, and finally to-day. Receive the assurance that you shall be rewarded according to your merits."

Gorenflot breathed a sigh.

"Where is Panurge?" asked Chicot.

"In the stable, poor animal."

"Well, go and get him, mount him, and meet me here."

"Yes, Monsieur Chicot."

The monk went quickly away, very much surprised that the guards did not follow him.

"Now, my son," said Chicot, "keep twenty men for your escort, and detach ten others with M. de Crillon."

"Where shall I send them?"

"To the Hôtel d'Anjou, and let them bring your brother."

"What for?"

"That he may not escape a second time."

"Did my brother —"

"Do you repent of having followed my advice to-day?"

"No, *par la mordieu!*"

"Well, do as I tell you."

Henri ordered the colonel of the French guards to bring the Duc d'Anjou to the Louvre. Crillon, who had no feeling of tenderness for the prince, set out at once.

"And you?" said Henri.

"I am waiting for my saint."

"And you will join me at the Louvre?"

"Within one hour."

"Then I shall leave you."

"Go, my son!"

Henri set out with the rest of the troop. As for Chicot, he went towards the stable, and as he entered the yard he saw Gorenflot appear, mounted on Panurge. The poor fellow had not even thought of avoiding his impending fate.

"Come, come," said Chicot, leading Panurge by the halter; "we must hasten, for we are expected."

Gorenflot did not make a shadow of resistance, only he shed so many tears that he seemed to grow visibly thinner.

"When I said so," he murmured, — "when I said so!"

Chicot continued to lead Panurge, and shrugged his shoulders.

CHAPTER LIV.

WHERE CHICOT GUESSES WHY D'EPERNON HAD BLOOD ON HIS FEET, AND NONE IN HIS CHEEKS.

WHEN the king returned to the Louvre, he found his friends in bed and sleeping peacefully. Historical events have a singular influence, which consists in reflecting their greatness on preceding ones. Those who will consider the occurrences which were to take place that morning, for the king returned to the Louvre at about two o'clock, — those who will consider these occurrences with a knowledge of future results, will take some interest in seeing the king, who had just saved his crown, take refuge near his three friends who, in a few hours, were to risk their lives for him.

The poet who does not foresee, but who guesses, will find great charm in these young faces refreshed by sleep and smiling confidently as they lie in their beds placed side by side, like brothers in the paternal dormitory.

Henri advanced cautiously among them, followed by Chicot, who, having deposited his patient in a place of safety, had joined the king. One bed was empty: it was D'Epernon's.

"Not yet come in, the imprudent," murmured the king; "ah, the wretch, the fool! having to fight to-morrow with Bussy, the bravest man in France, the most dangerous in the world, and think no more of it than that!"

"Yes, very true," said Chicot.

"Send for him, bring him here," cried the king. "Then go for Miron; I wish him to make that madman sleep in spite of himself. I wish sleep to make him strong and vigorous, able to defend himself."

"Sire," said the usher, "here is M. D'Epernon who is just now returning."

D'Epernon had, in fact, just come in. Hearing of the king's return, and expecting his visit to the dormitory, he hoped to glide in unperceived. But his arrival was watched and immediately announced to the king. Finding there was no way to escape the scolding, he appeared on the threshold very much confused.

"Ah, here you are at last," said Henri; "come and look at your friends."

D'Epernon glanced around the room and made a sign intimating that he had seen.

"Look at your friends," continued Henri; "they are wise and understand the importance of the game they are to play to-morrow; but you wretch, instead of praying and sleeping like them, you have been running about the town. *Corbleu!* how pale you are, and what a good showing you will make to-morrow if you are already used up to-night!"

D'Epernon was indeed very pale, — so pale that at the king's remark he colored.

"Come," said Henri, "go to bed and sleep if you can!"

"Why not?" asked D'Epernon, and judging from his tone, he seemed to consider the question an insult.

"I ask you if you will have time to sleep. Do you know that you are to fight at daybreak, and at this time of the year the sun rises at four o'clock? It is now two; you have barely two hours."

"Two hours well employed can go a long way."

"Will you sleep?"

"Perfectly, sire."

"I do not think so."

"Why not?"

"Because you are agitated. You think of to-morrow. Alas! you are right, for to-morrow is to-day; but in spite of myself, I have a secret desire to say that we have not yet reached the fatal day."

"Sire," said D'Epernon, "I promise you I shall sleep, if your Majesty will only let me."

"That is just," said Chicot.

In the mean time, D'Epernon undressed himself and got into bed with a calm satisfaction that seemed to auger well both to the king and Chicot.

"He is brave as Julius Cæsar," said the king.

"So brave," said Chicot, scratching his ear, "that on my honor, I cannot understand it."

"See, he is already asleep."

Chicot approached the bed, doubting that D'Epernon's coolness could go so far.

"Oh, oh," he suddenly exclaimed.

"What is it?" asked the king.

"Look," and Chicot pointed to D'Epernon's boots.

"Blood!" murmured the king.

"He has been walking in blood, my son. The brave fellow."

"Can he be wounded?" asked the king, anxiously.

"Pshaw! he would have told you; and unless he has been wounded like Achilles, in the heel — "

"His doublet is also stained; and look at his sleeve. What has happened?"

"He may have killed some one," said Chicot.

"What for?"

"To keep his hand in."

"This is singular," said the king.

Chicot scratched his ear much more seriously.

"Hum, hum!" he said.

"You do not answer me."

" Yes; I said, 'Hum, hum!' That means a great deal, I think."

" *Mon Dieu!* " said Henri, " what is going on around me, and what has the future in store ? Luckily to-morrow — "

" To-day, my son, you always forget."

" Yes, that is true."

" Well, to-day ? "

" To-day I shall be tranquil."

" Why so ? "

" Because they will kill those cursed Angevins."

" You think so, Henri ? "

" I am sure of it; they are brave."

" I never heard that the Angevins were cowards."

" No doubt; but see how strong they are; see Schomberg's arms and their beautiful muscles."

" Ah, if you saw Antraguet's."

" Look at Quélus' proud lip and Maugiron's brow, haughty even in his sleep. With such faces, victory is certain. Ah! when those eyes flash the enemy is already half conquered."

" Dear friend," said Chicot, sadly shaking his head, "there are other brows as haughty and other eyes as bright. Is that all that reassures you ? "

" No, come and let me show you something."

" Where ? "

" In my room."

" Is it this thing that makes you confident of victory ? "

" Yes."

" Then come."

" Wait." Henri went towards the young men. "Listen," he said, "I do not wish to agitate them to-morrow or rather to-day, so I shall take leave of them at once."

Chicot shook his head. " Take leave, my son," he said.

The tone in which he uttered these words was so melancholy that the king felt a shudder through his frame, and tears came into his eyes.

"Farewell, my friends," he murmured, — "farewell, my dear friends."

Chicot turned away; his heart was not of stone any more than the king's, but in spite of himself, his eyes soon reverted to the young men. Henri leaned over them and kissed them on the forehead, one after another. A pale pink taper shed its light over this scene, and gave a funereal tint to the draperies of the room and to the faces of the sleepers.

Chicot was not superstitious; but when he saw Henri touch with his lips the brows of Maugiron, Quélus, and Schomberg, his imagination pictured a living man bidding a last farewell to the dead already lying in their graves.

"It is singular," he said, "I never felt so before. Poor children."

No sooner had the king finished embracing his friends than D'Epernon opened his eyes to see if he were really gone. He had just left the room leaning on Chicot's arm.

D'Epernon jumped out of bed, and began to efface as well as he could the bloodstains on his clothes and boots. This occupation caused his mind to revert to the scene near the Bastille.

"I never would have had enough blood for that man who has shed so much unaided," he murmured, as he returned to his bed.

As for Henri, he conducted Chicot to his room, and opened a long ebony coffer lined with white satin.

"Look," he said.

"Swords. Well, what of that?"

"Yes, but blessed swords, my friend."

"By whom?"

"By our Holy Father the Pope, who granted me this favor. Such as you see it, to send this box to Rome and get it back cost me twenty horses and four men; but I have the swords."

" Are they sharp ? "

" No doubt; but their principal merit is that they have been blessed."

" Yes, I know; but I should like to be sure that they are sharp."

" Pagan ! "

" Let us talk of something else."

" Very well, but make haste."

" Do you want to sleep ? "

" No, I want to pray."

" In that case, let us talk business. Have you sent for M. d'Anjou ? "

" Yes, he is waiting below."

" What do you intend to do with him ? "

" Throw him into the Bastille."

" That is very wise. Only choose a safe and deep dungeon, the one for instance which was occupied by the Constable de Saint-Pol or Jacques d'Armagnac."

" Oh, have no uneasiness."

" I know where you can buy fine black velvet, my son."

" Chicot, he is my brother."

" Exactly, and court mourning is purple. Will you speak to him ? "

" Yes, if only to show him that all his plots are discovered."

" Hum ! " said Chicot.

" Do you disapprove of my having an interview with him ? "

" No, but in your place I would cut short the conversation, and double the imprisonment."

" Let them bring here the Duc d'Anjou," said Henri.

" No matter," said Chicot, " I still maintain my first opinion."

The duke entered a moment later; he was very pale and disarmed. Crillon followed, holding his sword in his hand.

"Where did you find him?" asked the king, speaking to Crillon as if the duke had not been there.

"Sire, his Highness was not at home; but soon after I had taken possession of the *hôtel* in the king's name, his Highness returned, and we arrested him without resistance."

"That is fortunate," said the king, disdainfully; then turning to the prince, —

"Where were you, monsieur?" he asked.

"Wherever I was, your Majesty may be assured that I was attending to his business," replied the duke.

"I have no doubt of it," replied the king, "and your answer proves that I was quite right to do the same."

François made a respectful bow.

"Come, where were you?" asked the king, advancing toward his brother. "And what were you doing while your accomplices were being arrested?"

"My accomplices?" asked François.

"Yes, your accomplices," repeated the king.

"Sire, your Majesty is surely under an erroneous impression."

"Oh, this time you shall not escape, monsieur, and your criminal career is terminated. This time again, you shall not inherit from me."

"Sire, moderate yourself. There is surely some one who blackens my character to you."

"Wretch!" cried Henri, in a rage, "you shall die of hunger in the darkest dungeon of the Bastille."

"I await your orders, sire, and I bless them though you may order my death."

"But where were you, hypocrite?"

"Sire, I was saving your Majesty and working for the peace and glory of your reign."

"Oh," said the king, petrified with amazement, "upon my honor, your audacity is great."

"Bah!" said Chicot, leaning back, "tell us about it, prince; it must be curious."

"Sire, I would tell your Majesty at once had you treated me as a brother, but as you have treated me as a criminal, I shall let the event speak for me."

Having spoken these words, he bowed even more deeply than the first time; then turning to Crillon and the other officers who were present, —

"Now which of you gentlemen will conduct the first prince of the blood to the Bastille?" he said.

Chicot reflected, and a flash shot through his mind.

"Ah, ah," he murmured, "I think I can understand why M. D'Epernon had so much blood on his feet and so little in his cheeks."

CHAPTER LV.

THE MORNING OF THE COMBAT.

A BEAUTIFUL day rose over Paris; none of the *bourgeois* knew of the approaching event, but the royalist gentlemen and those of the Guise party, the latter still stupefied, awaited the result, and took cautious means to compliment the victors.

As we have seen in the last chapter, the king spent a sleepless night. He wept and prayed; but as he was after all a man of experience, particularly in all matters of duelling, at about three o'clock in the morning he set out, accompanied by Chicot, to do the only thing he could for his friends. He went to examine the ground where the combat was to take place. This was a very remarkable scene, but we must also add, very little remarked.

Dressed in clothes of a dark color, enveloped in a large cloak, his sword by his side, his hair and eyes hidden beneath the rim of his hat, he followed the Rue Saint-Antoine to within three hundred feet of the Bastille. Having reached that point, he saw a large concourse of people a little beyond the Rue Saint Paul, and not wishing to go through this crowd, he turned into the Rue Sainte-Catherine, and reached the inclosure of the Tournelles from the other side.

It may be easily guessed what that crowd was doing there: they were counting the dead. The king avoided it, and consequently remained in ignorance of what had taken place.

Chicot, who had witnessed the quarrel or rather the

agreement of the preceding week, explained to the king the
position of each combatant, and the conditions of the
combat. Henri, being thus informed, began immediately
to measure the ground, looking at the trees and calculating
the reflection of the sun.

"Quélus will be very much exposed; he will have the
sun on his right, just in his only eye,[1] whereas Maugiron
will have all the shade. Quélus should have taken Maugiron's place and Maugiron, who has excellent eyes, that of
Quélus. This is very badly managed. As for Schomberg,
who has weak legs, he will have a tree to rest against. I
am somewhat reassured for him, but Quélus, my poor
Quélus!"

And he sadly shook his head.

"You grieve me, my king," said Chicot. "Come, do not
torment yourself thus. The devil! they will get what
they can."

The king raised his eyes to Heaven and smiled.

"*Mon Dieu!* see how he blasphemes; but luckily, you
know he is but a fool."

Chicot shrugged his shoulders.

"And D'Epernon," continued the king, "I am unjust. I
did not even think of him; D'Epernon who is to fight with
Bussy; how he will be exposed! See the ground, Chicot,
to the left, a fence; to the right, a tree; behind, a ditch.
And he will have to move constantly, for Bussy is a tiger, a
lion, a serpent. Bussy is a living sword which bounds,
advances, and retreats."

"Pshaw!" said Chicot, "I am not uneasy about
D'Epernon."

"You are wrong; he will be killed."

"He is not such a fool; be sure he has taken precautions."

"What do you mean?"

---

[1] Quelus had lost his left eye in a former duel.

"I mean that he will not fight, *mordieu !* "

" Come, did you not hear him just now ? "

" Exactly."

" Well ? "

" Well, that is why I repeat that he will not fight."

" Incredulous and sceptical man."

" I know my Gascon, Henri; but believe me, let us return to the Louvre; it is now broad daylight."

" Do you believe I shall remain at the Louvre during the fight ? "

" *Ventre de biche!* you shall remain there ; for if you should be seen here, every one would say in case your friends were victorious, that you had forced the victory by the use of magic ; and in case they were conquered, that you brought them misfortune."

" What do I care for rumors and interpretations. I shall love them to the very end."

" You may have a strong mind, Henri, and I even pay you the compliment to say that you love your friends ; this is a rare virtue in a prince, but I do not wish you to leave M. d'Anjou alone in the Louvre."

" Is not Crillon there ? "

" Eh ! Crillon is only a buffalo, a rhinoceros, a boar, all that is brave and resolute, whereas your brother is a viper, a rattlesnake, any animal whose power resides less in its strength than in its venom."

" You are right. I should have had him thrown into the Bastille."

" I told you it was unwise to see him."

" Yes. I was conquered by his coolness, his audacity, and by the service he pretends to have rendered me."

" All the more reason for you to beware of him. Believe me, my son, let us go in."

Henri followed Chicot's advice and took his way to the Louvre, after having thrown a last glance at the field of combat.

Every one was up in the Louvre when the king and Chicot returned. The young men were among the first to wake up, and were being dressed by their lackeys. Henri asked what they were doing. Schomberg was bending his knees, Quélus was bathing his eye, Maugiron was drinking a glass of Spanish wine, and D'Epernon was sharpening his sword. He could be seen doing this work as he had had a stone carried up to their room.

"And you say he is not a Bayard?" asked Henri, giving him a loving glance.

"No; I say he is only a knife-grinder."

D'Epernon saw him and cried out, "The king."

And in spite of the resolution he had taken, and which under the circumstances he had not the strength to keep, Henri entered the room. We have already said that he was a very majestic king, and that he had great powers of self-control. His tranquil and almost smiling countenance betrayed none of the feelings of his heart.

"Good morning, gentlemen," he said. "I find you in excellent condition, it seems to me."

"Yes, thank Heaven," replied Quélus.

"You look gloomy, Maugiron."

"Sire, I am very superstitious, as your Majesty knows. I have had bad dreams, so I am drinking a little wine to keep up my spirits."

"My friend," said the king, "you must remember, — I am quoting Miron who is, as you know, a great doctor, — you must remember that dreams depend upon past impressions, but never influence coming actions, save with the will of God."

"Therefore, sire, you see me prepared," said D'Epernon. "I too had bad dreams last night. Nevertheless, my hand is firm and my eyes are bright." And he proved his words by making a lunge with his newly sharpened sword.

"Yes," said Chicot, "you dreamed that you had blood

on your shoes ; that dream is not a bad one. It means that some day you will be a great conqueror like Cæsar or Alexander."

"My friends," said Henri, "you know that you are defending my honor, but only my honor. Do not trouble yourselves about the safety of my person. Last night I settled my throne in such a manner that it will not be shaken again for some time. Therefore, fight for honor."

"Have no uneasiness, sire," said Quélus, "we may lose our lives, but our honor will be safe."

"Gentlemen," said the king, "I love you tenderly, and I also esteem you. Let me give you some advice. No false courage. You will aid my cause, not by dying, but by killing my enemies."

"Oh, as for me," said D'Epernon, "I shall give no quarter."

"I," said Quélus, "will promise nothing. I shall do what I can."

"And I," said Maugiron, "I assure your Majesty that if I am killed, I shall also kill my adversary, blow for blow."

"Do you fight with the sword alone ? "

"With the sword and dagger," replied Schomberg.

The king had one hand on his breast. It may be that that hand and heart communicated their fears through their pulsations ; but outwardly he was the king sending his soldiers to fight, and not his friends to their death.

"Really, my king," said Chicot, "you are truly magnificent at this moment."

The gentlemen were ready, and it only remained for them to take leave of their master.

"Are you going on horseback ? " asked Henri.

"No, sire, we shall walk," said Quélus. "Exercise is a good thing for the head, and your Majesty has told us a thousand times, that the head, rather than the arm, directs the sword."

"You are right," said the king. "Give me your hand."

Quélus bent over and kissed the king's hand, and the others followed his example. D'Epernon knelt down and said, —

"Sire, bless my sword."

"No, D'Epernon," said Henri, "give that sword to your page. I have better ones than those. Bring them, Chicot."

"No," said the Gascon, "give that task to your captain of the guards, my son. I am but a Pagan, and the blessings of Heaven might change to fatal spells, if my friend, tho devil, happened to see what I was carrying."

"What are these swords, sire?" asked Schomberg, glancing at the box which the officer had just carried in.

"Italian swords made in Milan. The hilts are good as you see; as with the exception of Schomberg, you all have delicate hands, and the first stroke would disarm you if you had not a good hold."

"Thank you, sire," unanimously exclaimed the four oung men.

"It is time for you to go," said the king, who could no longer control his emotions.

"Sire," asked Quélus, "shall we not have your Majesty's presence to encourage us?"

"No, that would not be right. You will fight without any one's knowing it, without my permission. Let us give no solemnity to the combat. Let it seem to be the result of a private quarrel."

And he dismissed them with a truly majestic gesture. When they had left his presence, when the last of the valets had crossed the threshold of the Louvre, when the jingling of their spurs had died away, the king flung himself down, and exclaimed, "Ah, I am dying!"

"And I wish to see that duel," said Chicot. "I do not know why, but I have an idea that something curious will happen about D'Epernon."

"You leave me, Chicot?" asked the king in a doleful voice.

"Yes," said Chicot, "for if one of them failed in his duty, I would be there to take his place, and sustain the honor of my king."

"Go," said Henri.

The Gascon had no sooner taken leave, than he was off like a flash. The king then retired to his room, closed the shutters, forbade any one to utter a word in the Louvre, and only said to Crillon, who knew what was about to take place, —

"If we are victorious, Crillon, you will tell me; if, on the contrary, we are defeated, knock three times."

"Yes, sire," replied Crillon, shaking his head.

CHAPTER LVI.

BUSSY'S FRIENDS.

IF the king's friends had spent the night sleeping quietly, those of the Duc d'Anjou had taken the same precaution. After a good supper, to which they had invited one another without the advice or presence of their patron who did not trouble himself about his favorites, they lay down in comfortable beds in Antraguet's house, which had been chosen as the one nearest to the field of battle. Ribeirac's squire, who was a great hunter and armorer, had spent the day cleaning, polishing, and sharpening the weapons. He was also to wake up the young men, — a duty which he always fulfilled on fête days or when they were to go hunting or fighting.

Before supper, Antraguet had gone to visit a little shop-girl, of the Rue Saint-Denis, whom he adored. Ribeirac had written to his mother, and Livarot had made his will. At three o'clock, when the king's friends were scarcely awake, they were already up, all armed and ready.

They wore red breeches and stockings that their enemies might not see their blood, and that they themselves might not be frightened at the sight. They wore doublets of gray silk, so that nothing might impede their movements if they fought all dressed. Finally, they wore shoes without heels, and their pages carried their swords in order that their shoulders and arms might feel no fatigue.

The weather was splendid for love, war, or walking. The sun gilded the gables on which sparkled the morning dew. A delightful and penetrating perfume rose from the adjoining gardens. The pavement was dry, and the air delightful. Before leaving the house, the young men had sent to the Duc d'Anjou for news of Bussy. They were told that he had gone out the night before at about ten o'clock, and had not yet returned. He had gone out with Rémy, and both had taken their swords.

There was no uneasiness felt concerning him. He frequently made similar absences; then he was known to be so strong, so skilful, and so brave that even a prolonged absence caused but little anxiety. The three friends listened to all these details.

"Well," said Antraguet, "did you not hear, gentlemen, that the king had commanded a grand chase in the forest of Compiègne, and that M. de Monsoreau must have set out yesterday?"

"Yes," replied the young men.

"Then 1 know where he is while the master of the hounds is stalking deer: he is hunting on Monsoreau's preserves. It is all right, gentlemen; you may be sure that he will precede us on the ground, as he is nearer than we."

"Yes," said Livarot, "but fatigued, harassed after a sleepless night."

Antraguet shrugged his shoulders.

"Does Bussy ever get tired?" he asked. "Come, gentlemen, let us be off; we shall call for him on the way."

They started. This was the moment when Henri distributed the swords to his friends; they had an advance of about ten minutes. As Antraguet lived near Saint Eustache, they took the Rue des Lombards, the Rue de la Verrerie, and finally, the Rue Saint-Antoine.

All these streets were deserted. The peasants coming from Montreuil, Vincennes, or Saint-Maur-les-Fossés with their milk and vegetables were alone permitted to see the three brave men with their three pages and three squires.

No more bravadoes, no more cries, no more threats; a mortal duel without mercy or quarter gives food for thought; and the most heedless of the three was that morning the most absorbed. On coming to the Rue Sainte-Catherine, all three glanced towards Monsoreau's little house with a smile that meant the same thought.

"One can have a good view from there," said Antraguet, "and I am sure that poor Diane will go more than once to the window."

"Look," said Ribeirac, "it seems that she has already been there."

"Why so?"

"It is open."

"Very true. But why is that ladder placed against the balcony when the house has doors?"

"That is very queer," said Antraguet.

They approached the house with the presentiment that they were on the brink of some serious discovery.

"We are not the only ones to be surprised," said Livarot; "see, those peasants stand up in their carts to get a better view."

The young men now stood in front of the house. A man was already there and seemed to examine the ground.

"Eh! M. de Monsoreau," cried Antraguet, "will you come and see us? In that case, make haste, for we wish to be the first on the field."

They waited in vain.

"No one answers," said Ribeirac, "but why the devil is this ladder here?"

"What are you doing there?" asked Livarot of the man.

"Did you put up that ladder?"

"God forbid, gentlemen," he answered.

"Why so?" asked Antraguet.

"Look up there."

All three raised their heads.

"Blood!" cried Ribeirac.

"Yes, blood," said the peasant, "and very black blood."

"The door has been broken open," said Antraguet's page at the same moment.

Antraguet glanced from the door to the window, and, seizing the ladder, reached the balcony in one second. He looked into the room.

"What is the matter?" asked the others who saw him totter and turn pale.

A terrible cry was his only answer. Livarot had climbed up behind him.

"Corpses! death everywhere!" cried the young man, and both entered the room. Ribeirac remained below to guard against a surprise. During this time, the peasant's exclamations caused all the passers-by to stop. The room showed everywhere the traces of the horrible struggle of the night. Stains or rather a river of blood covered the floor. The hangings were slashed with the swords or riddled by bullets. The furniture lay around, shattered and red, in the débris of flesh and garments.

"Oh, Rémy! poor Rémy!" suddenly cried Antraguet.

"Dead?" asked Livarot.

"Already cold."

"But a regiment of troopers must have passed through this room," cried Livarot. At this moment he saw the door leading into the corridor wide open. Tracks of blood indicated that the struggle had also taken place there; he followed the terrible vestiges and reached the staircase. The court was solitary and deserted. During this time Antraguet, instead of following him, went into the next room. There was blood everywhere; the blood led to the window. He leaned out and looked into the little garden. The iron spikes still held the stiff and livid corpse of the unfortunate Bussy. At this sight it was not a cry but a roar that Antraguet uttered. Livarot ran to him.

"Look!" said Antraguet, "Bussy dead!"

"Bussy assassinated, and thrown out of the window! Come in, Ribeirac, come in!"

In the mean time, Livarot rushed down into the court, met Ribeirac, and took him with him. A little door led from the court to the garden.

"It is really he," cried Livarot.

"His wrist is cut," said Ribeirac.

"He has two bullets in his breast."

"He is full of dagger wounds."

"Ah! poor Bussy," yelled Antraguet. "Vengeance! vengeance!"

As Livarot turned round he stumbled against another corpse.

"Monsoreau," he cried.

"What! Monsoreau, too?"

"Yes, Monsoreau shot through and through, and with his head broken on the pavement."

"Ah! they have assassinated all our friends to-night."

"And his wife, his wife," cried Antraguet, "Diane, Madame Diane!"

No one replied except the crowd which was beginning to gather around the house. This was the moment when the king and Chicot reached the Rue Sainte-Catherine and turned aside to avoid the people.

"Bussy! poor Bussy!" cried Ribeirac in despair.

"Yes," said Antraguet, "they wished to get rid of the most terrible of us all."

"This is cowardice! this is infamy," cried the other two young men.

"Let us complain to the duke," cried one of them.

"No," said Antraguet, "let us leave to none the task of avenging him; we would be but poorly avenged. Wait for me." In one second he had come down and joined Livarot and Ribeirac.

"Friends," he said, "see that noble face of the bravest of men. See the crimson drops of his blood; he sets us an example; he left to none the care of avenging him. Bussy, Bussy! we shall do as you did and be sure that we shall avenge you."

As he spoke these words, he removed his hat, touched Bussy's lips with his own, and drawing his sword dipped it in his blood.

"Bussy," he said, "I swear on your body that this blood will be washed in that of your enemies!"

"Bussy," said the others, "we swear to kill or die."

"Gentlemen," said Antraguet, sheathing his sword, "we shall show neither pity nor mercy."

"Neither pity nor mercy," they repeated as they extended their hands towards the corpse.

"But," said Livarot, "we are now only three against four."

"Yes, but we have assassinated no one," said Antraguet, "and God will give strength to the innocent. Adieu, Bussy."

"Adieu, Bussy!" repeated the other two companions, and they went, pale and horror-stricken from that cursed house. They had found there, with the image of death, that profound despair which multiplies strength; they had been inspired by that generous indignation which makes man superior to his mortal state.

They made their way through with difficulty, so great had the crowd increased during a quarter of an hour. On reaching the ground, they found their antagonists waiting for them, some seated on stones, the others picturesquely leaning against the wooden fences. They ran part of the way, ashamed of being the last ones. The four favorites were accompanied by four squires. Their four swords, lying on the ground, seemed to wait and rest like them.

"Gentlemen," said Quélus, rising and bowing with a sort

of disdainful pride, "we have had the honor of waiting for you."

"Excuse us, gentlemen," said Antraguet, "we would have been here before had we not been delayed by one of our companions."

"M. de Bussy?" asked D'Epernon. "I do not see him. He does not seem very eager this morning."

"We have waited so long that we might wait a little longer," said Schomberg.

"M. de Bussy will not come," said Antraguet.

Amazement was written on every face, save that of D'Epernon which expressed a different feeling.

"Ah, ah! he will not come," said he. "Is the brave of braves then afraid?"

"That cannot be the reason," said Quélus.

"You are right, monsieur," said Livarot.

"And why will he not come?" asked Maugiron.

"Because he is dead," replied Antraguet.

"Dead!" cried the favorites.

D'Epernon said nothing and even turned slightly pale.

"He died, assassinated!" continued Antraguet. "Did you not know it, gentlemen?"

"No," said Quélus, "and why should we know it?"

"Besides, is it certain?" asked D'Epernon.

Antraguet drew his sword.

"So certain," he said, "that here is his blood on my sword."

"Assassinated!" cried the king's three friends, "M. de Bussy assassinated!"

D'Epernon continued to shake his head with an air of doubt.

"This blood cries for vengeance," said Ribeirac, "do you not hear, gentlemen?"

"Ah!" said Schomberg, "your words seem to have a meaning."

"*Pardieu!*" said Antraguet.

"What is it?" cried Quélus.

"Seek who will profit by the crime," murmured Livarot.

"Ah! gentlemen, will you speak more clearly?" asked Maugiron, in a thundering voice.

"We have come for that gentlemen," said Ribeirac, "and we have more reasons than we need to kill you a hundred times."

"Then draw your swords and be quick," said D'Epernon, brandishing his own.

"Oh! you are in a great hurry, M. le Gascon," said Livarot; "you did not crow so loud when we were four against four."

"Is it our fault if you are only three?" replied D'Epernon.

"Yes, it is your fault," cried Antraguet. "He is dead because you would rather see him lying in his grave than standing here; he is dead with his wrist cut that that wrist might no longer hold a sword; he is dead, that you might not be frightened by the lightning flashing from those eyes. Do you understand me? Am I clear?"

Schomberg, Maugiron, and D'Epernon howled with anger.

"Enough, gentlemen," said Quélus. "Withdraw, M. d'Epernon; we shall fight three against three; these gentlemen will see that in spite of our right to do so, we are not the men to profit by a misfortune which we regret as much as they do. Come, gentlemen," added the young man, throwing off his hat and raising his left hand while he whirled his sword with the other, "when you see us fight beneath God's open heaven, you can judge if we are assassins."

"Ah! I hated you," said Schomberg, "and now I execrate you."

"And I," said Antraguet, "an hour ago would have killed you, but now I would tear you to pieces. On your guard, gentlemen."

" With or without doublets ? " asked Schómberg.

" Without doublets, without shirts," said Antraguet, " with bare breast and uncovered hearts."

The young men threw off their doublets and shirts.

" I have lost my dagger," said Quélus. " It was loose in the sheath, and must have fallen on the way."

" Or you left it at M. de Monsoreau's and did not dare draw it from its bloody sheath," said Antraguet.

Quélus yelled with rage and drew his sword.

" But he has no dagger, Monsieur Antraguet," cried Chicot, who had just reached the battlefield.

" So much the worse for him," said Antraguet ; " it is not my fault," and he drew his dagger with his left hand.

CHAPTER LVII.

THE COMBAT.

THE spot where this terrible encounter was about to take place was sequestered and shaded with trees. It was generally frequented only by children who came to play there during the day, or drunkards and thieves who came to sleep there by night. The barriers placed by the horse venders kept away the crowd, which, similar to the stream of a river, follows a current and is only arrested by an eddy. The passers-by went on their way and did not stop. Besides, it was too early, and the great concourse of people hurried towards Monsoreau's bloody house.

Chicot, his heart palpitating, though his was not a very tender nature, seated himself upon a wooden balustrade in front of the lackeys and pages. He did not like the Angevins. He hated the favorites, but they were all brave young men, and beneath their skin flowed generous blood soon to be shed. D'Epernon made a last bravado.

"What! they are afraid of me," he cried.

"Hold your tongue," said Antraguet.

"I have my rights," said D'Epernon; "we were to be eight in the game."

"Be off," said Ribeirac, impatiently.

He returned with his head in the air, and sheathed his sword.

"Come hither, bravest of men," said Chicot, "or you will lose another pair of shoes as you did yesterday."

"What do you mean?"

"I mean that there will soon be blood on the ground, and you will step in it as you did last night."

D'Epernon became deadly pale, and all his conceit fell before this terrible reproach. He seated himself within ten feet of Chicot, at whom he glanced with terror.

Ribeirac and Schomberg approached each other after the usual salutations. Quélus and Antraguet took one step forward and crossed swords. Maugiron and Livarot stood leaning against a barrier and made feints. The fight began as the Church of Saint Paul struck five. Fury was depicted on the faces of the combatants; but their closed lips, their threatening pallor, the involuntary trembling of their wrists indicated that this fury was controlled by prudence, and that, like a fiery horse, it would not escape without causing great damage.

For several minutes, which is an enormous length of time, nothing was heard but a clashing of swords. Not one stroke had taken effect. Ribeirac, wearied, or rather satisfied of having tried his adversary, lowered his hand and waited for a moment.

Schomberg advanced rapidly and touched him. His skin became livid, and the blood gushed from his shoulder; he drew back to ascertain the gravity of his wound. Schomberg wished to renew the stroke, but Ribeirac parried and wounded him in the side. Each one had his wound.

"We may now rest for a few seconds if you will," said Ribeirac.

Quélus and Antraguet had now warmed up, but Quélus, having no dagger, was under a great disadvantage; he was obliged to parry with his left arm, and as this arm was bare, every parry cost him a wound.

Without being seriously hurt, at the end of a few seconds, his hand was cut in many places. Antraguet, on the contrary, understood his advantage, and, no less skilful than Quélus, parried with extreme prudence.

The thrusts told, and without being dangerously hurt, he was losing blood through three wounds in the breast, but at each stroke he would repeat, —

" It is nothing."

Livarot and Maugiron were still untouched. Ribeirac, who was now maddened with pain, rushed against Schomberg. Schomberg did not move one step, and merely held out his sword. Ribeirac received a thrust in the breast, and wounded Schomberg in the neck.

Ribeirac, mortally wounded, placed his left hand on the spot and thus uncovered himself. Schomberg took advantage of this to inflict upon him a flesh wound. But Ribeirac seized his neighbor's hand with his right, and with his left buried the dagger up to its hilt. The sharp blade cut through the heart.

Schomberg uttered a dull cry and fell on his back, dragging down Ribeirac who still had the sword through his body.

Seeing his friend fall, Livarot rushed to the rescue, pursued by Maugiron. He gained a short distance in this way and aided Ribeirac in the efforts he was making to rid himself of Schomberg's sword. But he was then joined by Maugiron and obliged to defend himself on slippery ground with the sun in his eyes. At the end of a second, a blow of the sword opened Livarot's head, and he dropped his weapon and fell upon his knees. Quélus was closely pursued by Antraguet. Maugiron hastened to bury his sword once more in Livarot's body. Livarot fell down.

D'Epernon uttered a great cry.

Quélus and Maugiron remained alone against Antraguet. Quélus was covered with blood, but his wounds were slight. Maugiron was almost untouched.

Antraguet understood the danger. He had not received a single scratch, but he was beginning to feel fatigue. This was no time to ask for mercy from a wounded man and another fresh from carnage. He pushed aside Quélus' sword, and vaulted lightly over the barrier. Quélus returned the thrust, but found only wood. At this moment Maugiron attacked Antraguet, who turned round. Quélus took advantage of this to pass beneath the barrier.

"He is lost!" cried Chicot.

"*Vive le roi!*" cried D'Epernon; "go it, my lions."

"Silence, monsieur," said Antraguet; "do not insult a man who will fight even to the last breath."

"And one who is not yet dead," cried Livarot, of whom no one was thinking. He rose on his knees and buried his dagger between the shoulders of Maugiron, who dropped down sighing, —

"Jesus! my God! I am dying."

Livarot fell back fainting; the exertion and anger had exhausted all his remaining strength.

"M. de Quélus," said Antraguet, lowering his sword, "you are a brave man. Surrender, and I give you your life."

"And why should I surrender?" asked Quélus; "am I down?"

"No, but you are wounded and I am not."

"*Vive le roi!*" cried Quélus. "I have still my sword," and he rushed against Antraguet who parried the thrust.

"No, monsieur, you have it no longer," said Antraguet, seizing the sword near the hilt, and wrenching it away; but he slightly cut his finger in doing so.

"Oh! a sword, a sword!" cried Quélus, and bounding like a tiger on Antraguet, he threw both arms around him. Antraguet made no effort to shake him off, but taking his sword in his left hand and his dagger in the other, he began to strike Quélus right and left, covering himself with his enemy's blood, but unable to make him loose his hold.

At every stroke Quélus would cry, "*Vive le roi!*" He even managed to hold the hand that struck him, and twisted himself round his antagonist like a serpent. Antraguet, nearly suffocated, reeled and fell; but as he did so, he almost crushed the unfortunate Quélus.

"*Vive le roi!*" murmured the latter in agony.

Antraguet succeeded in disengaging his arm, and dealt him a last blow which entered his breast.

" There," he said, " are you satisfied ? "

" *Vive le r—* " whispered Quélus, his eyes fast closing.

This was all. The silence and terror of death reigned on this battlefield. Antraguet rose covered with blood, but it was the blood of his enemy. He had only a slight cut on the hand. D'Epernon made the sign of the cross and fled as though pursued by a ghost. Antraguet threw upon his friends and enemies, upon the dead and the dying, the same glance which Horatius must have thrown on the battlefield which decided the fate of Rome.

Chicot ran and raised Quélus, whose blood was pouring from nineteen wounds. The motion revived him. He opened his eyes.

" Antraguet," he said, "on my honor, I am innocent of Bussy's death."

" I believe you, monsieur," said Antraguet, greatly moved.

" Fly," murmured Quélus, " fly! the king would never forgive you."

" But I shall not abandon you thus, should the scaffold await me," said Antraguet.

" Save yourself, young man," said Chicot; " you have been saved by a miracle, but do not expect two in one day."

Antraguet approached Ribeirac, who was still breathing.

" Well ? " asked the latter.

" We are victorious," replied Antraguet, in a low tone, not to offend Quélus.

" Thank you," said Ribeirac, " now go," and he fainted away.

Antraguet picked up his own sword, which he had

dropped in the fray, then those of Quélus, Schomberg, and Maugiron.

"Kill me, monsieur, or leave me my sword," said Quélus.

"Here it is, Monsieur le Comte," said Antraguet, with a courteous bow. A tear shone in the eyes of the wounded man.

"We might have been friends," he murmured. Antraguet gave him his hand.

"You cannot be more chivalrous, Antraguet," said Chicot; "but fly, you are worthy of living."

"And my companions?" asked the young man.

"I shall take care of them, as well as of the king's friends."

Antraguet wrapped himself up in the cloak which his squire threw over him, thus concealing the blood with which he was covered; and leaving the dead and dying amid the pages and lackeys, he disappeared through the Porte Saint-Antoine.

CHAPTER LVIII.

THE END.

THE king, pale with anxiety, and starting at the slightest noise, was pacing his room and conjecturing with the experience of a practised man the time that his friends would take to join and fight their adversaries, as well as the good or bad possibilities afforded them by their character, their force, or their skill.

"Now," he said at first, "they are crossing the Rue Saint-Antoine; now they are entering the lists; now they draw their swords and begin."

At these words the poor king trembled and began to pray; but his heart was full of other feelings, and the prayers came only from his lips. At the end of a few moments, he rose.

"If Quélus will only remember the thrust I taught him. As for Schomberg, he is so cool that he ought to kill Ribeirac. If Maugiron is not unlucky, he will quickly rid himself of Livarot. But D'Epernon! oh, he is a dead man. Luckily he is the one I love the least. But alas! his death is not all, because after he is dead, Bussy, the terrible Bussy, will fall upon the others. Ah! my poor Quélus, my poor Schomberg, my poor Maugiron."

"Sire!" said Crillon at the door.

"What, already!" cried the king.

"No, sire, I bring no news, only the Duc d'Anjou wishes to speak to your Majesty."

"What for?" asked the king, still talking through the door.

"He says that the time has come for him to tell your Majesty the nature of the service he has rendered him, and that what he has to tell the king will greatly calm his fears."

"Well, let him come," said Henri.

Just as Crillon turned round, rapid footsteps were heard to approach, and a voice said, —

"I must speak to the king at once."

The king recognized the voice and opened the door.

"Come, Saint-Luc," he said, "what is the matter? What has happened, *mon Dieu!* are they dead?"

Saint-Luc rushed into the room, without hat or sword, pale and covered with blood.

"Sire," he said, throwing himself at the king's feet, "vengeance! I have come to ask for vengeance."

"What is the matter, my poor Saint-Luc? Speak, what can have caused this despair?"

"Sire, the noblest of your subjects, the bravest of your soldiers —" Here his voice failed him.

"What?" asked Crillon, who thought he had a right to the last title.

"Was murdered, treacherously murdered last night," continued Saint-Luc.

The king, who was absorbed by a single thought, was reassured when he heard this. It was not one of his four friends, since he had seen them all that morning.

"Murdered!" said the king. "Of whom are you speaking?"

"Sire, I know you do not love him," replied Saint-Luc; "but he was faithful and would have given his life for your Majesty; otherwise he would not have been my friend."

"Ah," said the king who was beginning to understand; and something like a flash, if not of joy at least of hope, illumined his face.

"Vengeance, sire, for M. de Bussy," cried Saint-Luc.

"For M. de Bussy," repeated the king, laying stress on each syllable.

"Yes, M. de Bussy, whom twenty assassins murdered last night. He killed fourteen of them."

"M. de Bussy dead!"

"Yes, sire."

"Then he cannot fight this morning," said the king, carried away by an irresistible impulse.

Saint-Luc gave the king a glance so reproachful that he turned away his head, and in doing so saw Crillon still standing near the door awaiting orders. He made him a sign to bring in the Duc d'Anjou.

"No, sire," added Saint-Luc in a severe tone. "M. de Bussy did not fight and that is why I come to ask not for vengeance, — I was wrong to say it, — but for justice. I love my king and my king's honor above all things, and I think that those who killed M. de Bussy have rendered a very poor service to your Majesty."

The Duc d'Anjou had just reached the door. He stood there, motionless as a bronze statue. Saint-Luc's words enlightened the king; they recalled to his mind the service which the duke pretended to have rendered him. He exchanged a glance with the duke who at the same slightly nodded his head in assent.

"Do you know what they will say?" asked Saint-Luc. "They will say that if your friends are victorious, it is because you murdered Bussy."

"And who will say this, monsieur?" asked tne king.

"Everybody, *pardieu*," said Crillon, who joined in the conversation as was his wont.

"No, monsieur," said the king, overcome by the opinion of the man, who since Bussy's death was the bravest in the land. "No, that shall not be said, for you will name the assassin."

Saint-Luc saw a shadow advance, and turning round recognized the Duc d'Anjou.

"Yes, sire, I shall name him," he said; "for I wish above all things to clear your Majesty from such a heinous accusation."

"Well, speak."

The duke stood quietly waiting. Crillon stood behind him shaking his head and glaring at him.

"Sire," said Saint-Luc, "last night they laid a snare for Bussy. While he was visiting a woman who loved him, her husband, warned by a traitor, entered the house with a troop of assassins. They were everywhere, — in the street, in the court, and even in the garden."

If the king's room had not been so dark, they would have seen the Duc d'Anjou turn pale, notwithstanding his powers of self-control.

"Bussy fought like a lion, sire, but numbers overwhelmed him — "

And he was killed, and justly," interrupted the king. "I shall certainly not avenge an adulterer."

"Sire, I have not finished my story. The unhappy man, after having defended himself for more than half an hour and triumphed over his enemies in the house, escaped, wounded, bleeding, mutilated; he only wanted some one to lend him a helping hand. I would surely have done so myself, had I not been seized and bound hand and foot by his assassins, together with the woman whom he had placed under my protection. Unfortunately they forgot to deprive me of sight as well as of speech, for I saw two men approach the unfortunate Bussy caught on the iron spikes. I heard the wounded man ask for help, for in these two men he had every right to count on two friends. Well, sire, this is horrible to tell, but it was far more horrible to see and hear. One ordered that he should be shot, and the other obeyed."

Crillon clinched his fist and frowned.

"And you know the assassin?" asked the king, moved in spite of himself.

"Yes," said Saint-Luc, and turning towards the prince he said, with all his pent-up hatred bursting forth in his words and gestures, —

"It is Monseigneur! The assassin is the prince! The assassin is the friend!"

The king was expecting the blow; the duke received it without emotion.

"Yes," he said calmly, — "yes, M. de Saint-Luc saw and heard rightly. I had M. de Bussy killed, and your Majesty will appreciate this action, for M. de Bussy was my servant; but this morning, in spite of my expostulations, he was to fight against your Majesty."

"You lie, assassin," cried Saint-Luc. "Bussy, covered with wounds, with his hand cut to pieces, with a bullet through his shoulder, — Bussy hanging suspended from the iron spikes could only inspire pity in his most cruel enemies, and they would have helped him. But you, the assassin of La Mole and Coconnas, you killed Bussy as you have killed all your friends one after the other! You killed Bussy, not because he was your brother's enemy, but because he was the confidant of your secrets. Ah, Monsoreau knew well your reason for this crime."

"*Cordieu!*" murmured Crillon, "why am I not the king!"

"I am insulted in your presence, brother," said the duke, pale with terror; for between Crillon's clinched hand and Saint-Luc's bloodthirsty look he did not feel safe.

"Leave us, Crillon," said the king.

Crillon obeyed.

"Justice, sire, justice!" repeated Saint-Luc.

"Sire," said the duke, "will you punish me for having saved your Majesty's friends, and for having done justice to your cause which is also mine?"

"And I," replied Saint-Luc, who could no longer contain himself, " I say that the cause you uphold is accursed, and that the anger of God will follow your footsteps. Sire, your brother has protected our friends, woe to them ! "

The king shuddered in terror. At this moment they heard rapid footsteps and a hasty interchange of words, followed by a deep silence. And then, as if a voice from Heaven came to confirm Saint-Luc's words, three blows were struck slowly and solemnly on the door by Crillon's vigorous arm.

Henri grew ghastly pale, and his features contracted.

"Vanquished!" he cried, "my poor friends."

"What did I tell you, sire ? " cried Saint-Luc.

The duke clasped his hands in terror.

"See, coward!" cried the young man with superb contempt. "It is thus that assassinations save the honor of princes! Come and kill me, too. I have no sword." And he flung his silk glove into the duke's face. François uttered a cry of rage and became livid; but the king saw and heard nothing; he had buried his face in his hands.

"Oh!" he said, "my poor friends are vanquished, wounded! Oh! who will give me certain news of them ? "

"I, sire," said Chicot.

The king recognized this friendly voice, and held out his arms.

"Well ? " he asked.

"Two are already dead and the third is breathing his last."

"Who is the third who is not yet dead ? "

"Quélus, sire."

"Where is he ? "

"At the Hôtel de Boissy."

The king waited to hear no more, and rushed from the room uttering lamentable cries.

Saint-Luc had conducted Diane home to his wife ; hence his delay in reaching the Louvre.

Jeanne spent three days and nights watching her through the most frightful delirium. On the fourth day, Jeanne, overcome by fatigue, went to take a little rest. When she returned two hours later, Diane had disappeared.

Quélus, the only one of the king's champions who had survived with nineteen wounds, died in the arms of the king, after an agony of thirty days, at the same Hôtel de Boissy whither Chicot had him carried.

Henri was inconsolable. He raised three magnificent tombs for his friends, and had their effigies carved in marble on the top. He had innumerable masses said for them, recommended them to the prayers of the priests, and added to his daily orisons this distich which he repeated every morning and evening to the end of his life, —

> "Que Dieu reçoive en son giron,
> Quélus, Schomberg, et Maugiron."

For nearly three months, Crillon kept guard over the Duc d'Anjou, against whom the king conceived a profound hatred and whom he never forgave.

It was now the month of September ; and Chicot who did not leave his master, and who would have consoled Henri had he been consolable, received the following letter, dated from the priory of Beaume. It was written in a clerical hand, —

DEAR MONSIEUR CHICOT, — The air is soft in our country, and the vintage of Burgundy promises to be good this year. They say that the king whose life I seem to have saved still grieves very much. Bring him to the priory, dear Monsieur Chicot, and we shall make him drink some wine of 1550, which I discovered in my cellar, and which could make one forget the greatest sorrows. This will please him, I am sure ; for I find in the Holy Scriptures these words, " Good wine rejoices the heart of man." This is very fine in Latin, and I shall make you read it. Come, then, dear Monsieur Chicot, come with the king, with M. d'Epernon, with M. de Saint-Luc, and we will fatten them all.

The reverend prior,
DOM GORENFLOT,
Your humble servant and friend.

P. S. — You will tell the king that I have not yet had time to pray for the souls of his friends, as he requested, on account of the occupations attendant on my arrival here ; but as soon as the vintage is over, I shall surely see to them.

"Amen," said Chicot; "here are poor devils well-recommended to God!"

THE END.